HOPE

ALWAYS RISES

A NOVEL BY

KATHIE GIORGIO

Black Rose Writing | Texas

First printing

ISBN: 978-1-68513-242-2
PUBLISHED BY BLACK ROSE WRITING
www.blackrosewriting.com

Printed in the United States of America
Suggested Retail Price (SRP) $21.95

Hope Always Rises is printed in Garamond Premier Pro

*As a planet-friendly publisher, Black Rose Writing does its best to eliminate unnecessary waste to reduce paper usage and energy costs, while never compromising the reading experience. As a result, the final word count vs. page count may not meet common expectations.

Cover art by Julie Boglisch.
Author photo by Ron Wimmer of Wimmer Photography.

For those who backed away from the edge.
For those who embraced it.
And for those who were left behind.
My heart goes out to all of you.

ACKNOWLEDGEMENTS

Some of the chapters in this book appeared previously in different form as short stories in magazines and anthologies. Thank you so much to the editors who read and believed and encouraged.

"To The Woman Who Died On The Train Tracks", appeared in Al-Khemia Poetica for National Women's History Month, March 2021.

"Poof!", appeared in the Bryant Literary Review, Volume 23, April 2022.

"Found", Oyster River Pages, August 2022.

"Even The Air", appeared in the *Corona Chronicles* anthology, published by Cutthroat Literary Press, Summer 2021.

"The Fat Girl Takes The Long Way", appeared in the St. Petersburg Review, Issue SPR4/5. It also appeared in *Enlarged Hearts*, a short story collection by Kathie Giorgio, published by the Main Street Rag Publishing Company, April 2012.

HOPE

ALWAYS RISES

"There is another world
There is a better world
Well, there must be
Well, there must be
Oh, there must be."

The Smiths
Asleep

CHAPTER ONE

Hope

As I drifted under the whims and grips of Zinfandel and Zoloft, I felt my body slow, organ by organ, but my mind sped through my brainwaves as if they were a freeway. I found myself again at my sixth birthday party. It was a day of pink balloons and a rented pony, children dressed in ruffles and pleated pants, and it was the day I hid in my closet and pulled out my own hair for the first time. I remembered the surprise of red-gold strands clutched between my knuckles. I likened it to the pony's mane, when I gripped it just ten minutes earlier to stay in the saddle.

I don't remember ever not being sad, and by the time I turned six years old, I knew "sad" was the word to identify it. At my sixth birthday party, I blew out my candles and thought, Well, it's all over now. I couldn't have said what "it" was, or why "it" was over, but there was this Gulf inside of me, getting bigger every day. Lapping at me. Eroding my shore. And I couldn't do anything but watch it all happen and feel every bit of me wash away over a grand total of forty-three years.

On that birthday, after eating pink-frosted cake, a bakery cake, not even a box mix cake, and after I had the first ride on the pony because I was the birthday girl, I went in the house, climbed under the clothes hanging in my closet, shut the door, and cried until I fell asleep. My mother found me, my terrified mother, terrified that I'd been kidnapped from my own birthday party and she hadn't been observant enough to witness it. The kids were getting ready to go home when my mother realized I was missing and everyone, the kids, their parents, my parents, the guy who owned the pony, began to search. They scattered around the whole block. The police were called and they considered dragging the little pond in the park across the street. But my mother found me first, thank goodness.

I quickly dropped my handful of hair and then I cried some more while forming my first big lie about the Gulf. I told my mother that I slipped away after the pony ride because the bouncing in the saddle upset my stomach, which was full of bakery cake, and I didn't feel well and I didn't want to spoil it for anyone else. My mother became immediately sympathetic. I was a good sweet girl, she said. I put others first, I made them a priority, even at my own birthday party. It was okay, no harm done, once everyone's frayed nerves were calmed, once I said thank you and hugged every single one of my six friends. Even the boys. I patted the pony and gave him a carrot.

That night, after it was dark, after it was silent, I returned to my closet. I wanted to find my hair. With a little pink flashlight, I searched for the strands and gathered them up. I held them, admired the color (I always thought my hair was my best feature), and then tried to find the spot in my head where I tugged the clump out. I couldn't find it, which was a relief, as my mother thought my hair was my finest feature too. Then I found a small pink rubber band, wrapped it tightly around the strands, and put it into my jewelry box, a brightly flowered thing with a twirling ballerina that popped up whenever I opened it and danced to the tune of "Once Upon A Dream". I held her down so the music wouldn't wake my mother.

Now forty-three years old and in my car, I continued to sink, slipping down through layers of golden wine and light yellow tablets. I knew where I was, but I also knew I wasn't, that I was on my way impossibly out. Putting my fingers in my short hair, I tugged. Over the years, I moved that little hunk of hair from jewelry box to jewelry box. I never got rid of it. This morning, before I drove away, I took the clump out of its latest jewelry box on my bedside table and I tucked it into my jeans pocket. It was coming with me, wherever I was going. I knew it was the sign of something. The erosion. Whatever "it" was. The Gulf.

Thirty-seven years after that birthday party, I gave in to the tug of the Gulf. I gave in to the tug of my hair. The gold and yellow of Zin and Zoloft spun around me in widening circles and I felt like I was watching fireworks. A celebration. For me.

Because I finally put myself first. I made myself and my life a priority. And as I did, I worried that I was no longer a good sweet girl.

• • •

Opening your eyes after you've killed yourself is like no other awakening, on Earth or in Heaven, in life or in death. When I opened my eyes, I found I was no longer in my car, the last place I remembered being. At first, I fell into a panic because I thought I failed and I was in some sort of hospital or psych ward. But I wasn't in a bed. I wasn't tied down. I wasn't even in a straitjacket.

I wasn't in my car either, unbuckled, seat reclined, an empty bottle of pills beside me, an almost empty wine bottle on the floor. I was sitting on the grass and leaning against a tree, a weeping willow very like the one that used to be in my childhood back yard, and the branches draped me behind a great green curtain. I could hear the sound of water, and when I leaned down to look below the sweep of the branches, I saw a river flowing a short distance away. The sound of water always calmed me and I took deep breaths and decided, for the moment, not to question. I didn't know where I was, but I was apparently safe, even though I didn't seem to be dead.

But then, directly in front of me, the curtain of branches even behaved like one, a theatre curtain, separating in the middle and pulling away to the sides. I could see the river now, performing as if it was a show in itself. When the sunshine spilled in, changing the air to a richer golden that the gold of Zin, the yellow of Zoloft, I realized I wasn't alone. On my right was an older-looking man. He had that look of being a grandfather, but not one who was ready for the grave. Silver hair. Blue eyes. And a smile like every fairy tale I ever read.

"Hi, Hope," he said. "I'm God. And welcome to Heaven. I'm going to sit with you for a while, until you're ready to see where you're living now."

He used the word "living," even though it was apparent I was dead. I seemed to be in Heaven, not Hell, the place some believed you would end up if you ever gave in to the Gulf and sank.

"You can just call me God," he said. "People get freaked out talking to me at first. They seem to want to genuflect."

"Hi, God," I said, very aware of how odd those words felt. "I'm happy to meet you." The use of that word, happy, startled me. It wasn't a word I used often. That was, after all, why I did this. The most profound relief swept over my body, my body which I still had. No wings. I was the age I was this morning, not a younger version of myself. I didn't want to return to a younger version of myself. I was still wearing my favorite jeans and a white v-neck t-shirt, white sneakers, my short hair gelled and spiked on my head. I was still just me. And I was dead.

"It's nice to meet you too," God said, "though I've known you for a very long time." He gave me that smile again. "I have a gift for you." He handed me something small and brown and fuzzy and soft.

A teddy bear.

Not a teddy bear. THE teddy bear. I burst into tears and clutched him to my chest.

On that eventful sixth birthday, after the party was all over, my parents brought me to a toy store and told me I could pick out whatever I wanted, though my father added the words "within reason". I wandered the aisles for a while, pausing at board games, dollhouses, a working race track, and bicycles. But I slowed to a stop in the stuffed animal aisle.

I already had many stuffed animals. But in the middle of a display of classic brown teddy bears, one stuck out to me. He even had one paw raised, as if he was waiting for me. Unlike the others, who bore broad smiles or at least neutral expressions, this bear's mouth turned down. He looked sad. And I so recognized that expression. I stood on the tips of my toes and lifted him down with as much gentleness as I could muster. After I hugged him, I turned him around to show my parents.

"This," I said. "I want him."

My mother looked closer. "Are you sure, hon?" she asked. "I think this one has a mistake on it. I think the person sewing it made his mouth wrong."

I turned him quickly and hugged him again. "That's why he's perfect."

And so he came home. I gave him the very unimaginative name of Teddy, but really, there was no other name. He sat on my bed through my childhood and college and then my first apartment as an adult. Somewhere in the rush of time, adding a husband and then children, apartments and houses, I lost track of him. During my darkest times, I thought of Teddy, and I even took myself, alone, to a toy store the day I turned forty. But there was no other bear like him. His was the only expression I ever saw, beyond what was in my mirror, of what I felt.

And now, he was in my arms again.

"We'll sit with you for as long as you like," God said. "Just you, me, and Teddy."

Mostly, when I was six years old, and sixteen years old, and twenty-six years old, and so on, I sat by myself.

That morning, in my car, I sat by myself.

"So here we are," God said.

I drew up my legs, pressed my face into the familiar and worn denim, my skin and bones beneath the material the same that had been with me for forty-three years, and I gave in to tears.

• • •

When the sobs and shudders died away, God escorted me to my new home. It was a condo on the fourth floor of a building in a massive gated community. I couldn't even count how many buildings this complex contained. But each building was somehow a different color and there were large numbers above the door, so I realized right away that I would never get lost. My number was 10032025. I puzzled at the long number for a while. I was used to the simpler addresses of Earth. But then I realized it was today's date. It was my death day.

God nodded, as if he understood my understanding. "Buildings go up every single day, in different sections of Heaven. There's never a day that someone new doesn't join us, and that someone doesn't have neighbors that are just as new as he or she is. So everyone you meet here in your building will share this important day with you. And in this particular section of Heaven, everyone chose to leave their lives, just like you did. So you will be surrounded with familiar stories and stories that are very different, but all of you will have something in common." He opened the door and swept his arm in a grand Vanna White gesture, telling me to go on ahead.

On the fourth floor, I had an end unit. I could hear some vague bumps and bangs. God said, "That's the next floors being added on. The condos are filling as we speak. By tomorrow, everything will be done and it will be very quiet. There will be a new building going up next to you, but we provide profound sound-proofing. You won't hear the construction."

I stepped in and was immediately stunned. There were floor to ceiling windows; I've always loved sunshine and open windows. The views were beautiful, the buildings of this day and previous days in a huge circle around a bright blue lake. The furniture was exactly to my taste. A big, comfy microsuede couch and loveseat, deep red. Maple end tables. The artwork was the artwork from my own house, at least the pieces that I chose or made myself over the years. One over the fireplace mantel was from when I was in high school, a favorite of mine that earned me an A and that I entered to win a scholarship, which took me to college.

For the longest time, I was an artist. It was all I ever wanted to be. But somehow, like Teddy, that identity disappeared. I noticed, but felt helpless to stop it.

The living room was wide open to the kitchen, white cabinets, gray and white granite countertops, barstool seating. It was like God watched all of my favorite HGTV shows.

"That's my favorite channel," God said behind me.

I wandered through the condo, unable to say a word. A bedroom with a special reading nook in bowed-out floor-to-ceiling windows. Another bedroom, but set up with a desk and what looked like a huge cabinet in one wall. I realized it was a Murphy bed, something I always wanted, and that would be here, should I ever have visitors. Could you have visitors in Heaven? Dead or alive? Built-in bookshelves on the other three walls. Books! I wondered if they were all mine, if they'd somehow traveled with me. There was an easel set up in the corner, a canvas already set on it, and I stared at that the longest of all. Then I saw a bathroom with a walk-in shower and so many body jets, I would never have a speck of dirt on me again. Jacuzzi tub. Tucked in a closet was a state of the art washer and dryer.

I looked at God. "We have to do laundry in Heaven?"

He smiled. "You can't have everything. And two of the things you must have in order to feel happy are responsibility and purpose." He shrugged. "But the washer and dryer not only clean your clothes, they restore them to new. Nothing will ever fade or wear out."

I looked at my jeans. My favorites. Now no longer destined to one day be in the garbage.

Returning to the bedroom, I carefully nestled Teddy against the pillows. He was where he belonged. I wasn't so sure I was, but it all sure seemed to be real.

I couldn't go any further. I sank into my reading chair, the perfect reading chair, a hunter green with burgundy trim, and it was a recliner. Draped over one arm was the softest and warmest of blankets.

God laid a hand on my arm and his skin was a blanket too. "I'll leave you to get acclimated. Everything you need is here – there's no need to run to a grocery store. Yet. You will eventually...responsibility and purpose, remember. Sometime tomorrow, you'll have a visitor, who will fill you in on how things work. You'll have lots of questions by then."

I nodded. There were still no words. But as God left the room and I heard soft footfalls toward my front door, I suddenly found my voice and called out. "God?" I said. "Why am I here? Didn't I do something wrong? Didn't I go against you?"

There was silence and I waited to the point where I thought he'd left without answering. But then his voice drifted back, like a breeze, but impossibly more gentle. "You know the answer to that, Hope," he said. "It's what allowed you to do what you did. It isn't in you to do something bad. You're here because this is where you deserve to be."

And then there was the click of my door.

I thought about how I felt that morning, driving away from my house after my husband left for work, my kids for school. I didn't have to call in sick to my own job, because I no longer worked, and hadn't, for almost a year. I was asked to leave my job, because I called in sick so many times. And I *was* sick, and I had been sick for a long, long time. I was sick at heart. But as I left my house and my life behind, that all fell away. I felt strong. Confident. I felt I was doing the right thing, for myself. For me.

Even as I felt so sad. And alone. But I also felt the way you feel when your life suddenly falls into place.

That's so rare. Now imagine feeling that your life has suddenly fallen into place in the exact moment that you've decided to stop living.

I *sang* in the car this morning.

Sitting back in my chair, I was just raising the footrest when I saw something on one of the bedside tables. A sound came out of my throat then, a sound caught between a scream, a shout of joy, and a sob. I shot out of my chair.

It was a book I'd had since the third grade. It was called *Daddles* and it was written by a woman named Ruth Sawyer. My third grade teacher, Mrs. Campbell, read us from a chapter book every day after recess. When she finished a book, we could ask to take it home and read it ourselves. Despite my hand shooting up right away, I had to wait for five other students to bring it home, read it, and bring it back, before I had the chance to do so. When I finally did, I read and reread that book. It was the first time, the very first time, that I read a book that had an unhappy ending. It resonated with me more than anything I'd ever read.

And so I sort of forgot, repeatedly, to bring it back. Over and over and over. Finally, my mother brought me along to a PTA meeting, and she insisted I bring *Daddles.* After the meeting, she marched me over to Mrs. Campbell. I held out the book to her. "I'm sorry I kept forgetting to bring this back," I said. "I really love this book."

Mrs. Campbell smiled. And she told me to keep it. And I did. For the rest of my life.

This book here, in Heaven, wasn't a new copy, but my own. My own. My bent pages. My broken spine. The wrinkled page where I spilled my apple juice on it when I was ten years old and reading the book, again, again, again, beneath the shade of the weeping willow tree in my back yard. Just like the tree I sat under today. I sat on the bed, put one hand on Teddy and the other on my book, and God help me, I felt happy.

There was that word again. *Happy.*

With the most care, the most reverence I'd shown in years, I opened the front cover. I read the first chapter, and while the words were in front of me, I read it out of pure memory.

Like Teddy that morning, I hugged the book to my chest. And just like that, the bedside table transformed to a small bookshelf. I set the book where it belonged, where it always belonged, on the top shelf, where I knew it would always be. While Teddy disappeared from my life, the book never did. It always sat at my bedside, on top of a small bookshelf.

On top of the bookshelf, in the exact center, was my jewelry box from when I was a kid. That special box where a ballerina danced and where I hid my treasures. It was back, returned to me like my lost teddy bear. Reaching into my back pocket, I pulled out the stash of hair I stuffed there before leaving the house that morning. It was the hair I'd pulled out of my own head at my sixth birthday party, pulled it out in frustration and sadness that I just couldn't express any other way, and then kept hidden for the rest of my life.

The rest of my life. I could say that now, with finality.

Opening the jewelry box, I put the hair back in its place. The ballerina twirled and danced, the tinkly music filling my new bedroom with the sound of my childhood. Then I carefully closed it and restored the silence. I glanced over at the other bedside table. The one on the left side, where my husband usually slept.

And I saw a framed photograph of my children.

I didn't kill myself by slitting my wrists. But I sure felt stabbed now.

• • •

When I woke up on the morning that I ended my life, I never expected to be climbing into bed that night. And I certainly didn't expect to be in the best bed of my life in Heaven. I didn't expect to be anywhere.

But, as God would say, and so, here we are.

I sat in my recliner for the balance of the day. I wandered briefly into the kitchen for lunch and found all the makings for my favorite sandwich – grilled ham and cheese with tomato and bacon – set out and warm on the counter, complete with a pile of sour cream and onion potato chips and a dill pickle spear. The fridge was also fully stocked and I didn't see a single thing in there that I disliked. The cupboards too were full of my favorite cereals and snacks and the ingredients for a variety of favorite meals. I cried again when I found the cupboard for dinnerware. The plates and bowls were those Melmac ones from my childhood, hardy dishes that never broke if you dropped them, in vibrant rainbow colors. I didn't think they made these dishes in these bright colors, but I remembered wishing for them. And here they were.

Next to a bright red Cadillac of a coffeemaker, I found my favorite mug from home. It was from my kids. "Best Mom Ever," it said, and there was a photo of them on the other side.

For now, I put it back into the cupboard. I didn't know if my kids still felt that way. From what I'd read and heard and learned on Earth, suicide was a guarantee of your kids hating you forever. *Forever.*

But I figured they were already well on their way to hating me before I got up this morning.

I ate my sandwich in my reading chair, far away from the kitchen. Then I just stayed there, sometimes aware of looking out the window at the changing colors of the sky as night came, and sometimes not. The darkness surprised me when I realized it was there. There were no curtains on the windows, just as I would have designed it. Let the light in. Let it always in, even if it's only from the stars and the moon.

I made another sandwich for dinner, something I never minded. I was a big fan of the sandwich. And then I poured a glass of wine, topped it with some white cranberry/peach juice and white soda, and sat down on the couch. It was a recliner too, so apparently, I would be spending a lot of my afterlife with my feet up. I picked up the remote for the television and noticed a laminated card of instructions beneath it. It told me to just type in the name of the show or movie I wanted to see. If I wanted something new and current, I could just say, "Something new," or I could describe what I would like. I could also type in a network, so my HGTV favorites were available at the tap of my finger. This was like Netflix and Hulu and all the other streaming networks all combined and on steroids.

The remote reminded me of something else. I pulled my cell phone out of my jeans pocket. I swiped the screen and it only showed me my wallpaper. Another photo of my kids. But the phone, like me, was dead. I wondered aloud how people around here communicated with each other. I thought about throwing my cell phone away, but instead, I laid it carefully on my coffee table. I looked at it until the screen faded, taking the photo of my kids with it.

Then I asked the remote to show me the television show, *The Waltons*, from the first episode of Season 1. It was my all-time favorite program. But I only made it through two episodes before I decided I was ready for bed. I was exhausted. I didn't know you could be exhausted in Heaven. But then, I didn't know for sure there was a Heaven either until I got here.

According to the alarm clock by my bed (you needed alarm clocks in Heaven? Purpose and responsibility, I guessed), it was only 10:00. Not an unusual time for me to turn in. Toward the end, it was a good day if I managed to stay awake and out of my bedroom until the kids went to bed for the night. But now, it was just me. I had no one else to stay awake for. I had nothing to prove.

I wondered what my kids were doing. What my husband was doing. Even my mother; I was sure she'd been told by now.

But my kids.

I stared at this new ceiling, utterly devoid of popcorn, as I would have chosen. Outside my uncurtained windows, stars winked at their reflections in the lake. The bumping and banging stopped a while ago, and everything was so quiet. I pictured everyone in this building, laying in their beds, staring at whatever ceiling they always wanted, and wondering how in the world this all happened.

And thinking about their kids, if there were kids.

I was more confident that morning when I drove away in my car than I was now. Now, it was just so permanent. And I never planned for being conscious afterwards. Conscious and wondering just what was happening at home. I wasn't prepared for having to deal with the aftermath, even if the aftermath was very far away from me. I didn't know there would be an aftermath.

I tucked Teddy under one arm. Then I closed my eyes and wondered if insomnia was possible in Heaven.

It was.

CHAPTER TWO

Hope

But I did sleep eventually, and the sleep I had was restorative and dreamless. When I opened my eyes, I didn't feel disoriented, which really surprised me. I knew right away where I was. I set Teddy aside and went down the hall to the bathroom to take my shower. It occurred to me that the bathroom wasn't part of my bedroom, which would have made it an en suite, which I'd always wanted, and for that moment, a frown puckered my forehead. Then there was a blur and a zap and I found myself in that same bathroom, with the soaker tub and the million-jet shower, but there was an arch, covered with the most gorgeous sliding gray barn door, connecting me to my bedroom. Startled, I did a U-turn, ran down the hallway to where I was just seconds before, and found a powder room in the full bathroom's original spot. My new home now had a bath and a half. And no speck of construction dust.

"Wow," I said out loud, and then returned to my bedroom. Last night, I'd slept in an old familiar t-shirt and a pair of my own panties from my dresser drawer. I normally slept in the nude, but I wasn't sure if that was appropriate in Heaven. Now, with a burst that almost felt like joy, I stripped, not caring that there were floor to ceiling windows, and walked back into the now connected bathroom for the best shower of my life, or my death, for that matter. I felt like every bit of my past was pummeled away with the body jets, and the newness of today fell on me from the dual rainshower heads. When I got out, the towels were softer than I ever imagined, and I remembered God saying the washer and dryer would always restore everything to new. Back in my bedroom, I glanced at my windows as I dressed and I wondered if anyone in the buildings on the other side of the lake had a much-coveted telescope. But God, I figured, would protect me and everyone else against such things. Heaven didn't feel like it would allow an unwanted invasion of privacy.

In my closet, I found all of my clothes, except for the things I hated, and a selection of new items as well. It seemed to be sunny outside and the temperature yesterday on my arrival was lovely, so I selected a new, but soft, pair of light blue jeans, a bright pink v-neck t-shirt and the white sneakers I'd arrived in. In the top drawer of my dresser, there were pull-out trays of all my jewelry. I was very picky about my jewelry, and I was delighted to see all of my pieces here.

I ate breakfast at the island, perched on a very comfortable barstool. My favorite muffin, butter rum, slathered with butter that would no longer clog my arteries, and a really good cup of coffee in a turquoise Melmac mug. I wasn't rushed. No one pulled at me. As far as I knew, I wasn't expected to be anywhere. As I loaded my dishes into the dishwasher and poured a second cup of coffee, I thought how it would be nice to have an outdoor space. I was never a garden girl and lawns were neither here nor there for me. But a place to sit outside in the sun, in the air, and look around, read a book, drink coffee or wine, hear birds, even the hum of traffic would be...well, Heaven. I was four stories up. A large balcony would be wonderful. I had a corner unit, so it could wrap around to my bedroom as well.

When I turned away from the coffeepot, I looked across my living room to find new French doors which opened wide to a balcony. There was no blur or zap this time, I figured because I wasn't actually standing in the place to be changed. Delighted, I stepped out onto it and paced its length. I found myself looking into my bedroom through another new set of French doors. I opened these too, to allow in a breeze. I never liked air conditioning when I was at home. The more I could have the windows open, the better. Now, these doors and the ones in the living room created a relaxing cross-ventilating airiness, not to mention a lovely place to pace in a broad circle, inside, outside, inside, outside. Pacing was important to me, crucial in times of high anxiety, but I wondered if now, it might not seem so important. I returned to the living room side and sat in a bright red wooden rocking chair. I sipped my coffee and looked around.

Some of the other units had balconies, some didn't. Many people were sitting outside, raising coffee mugs or juice glasses. We were close enough to be aware of each other, but not close enough to invade. I waved and several people waved back. One woman called hello, and her voice floated to me like a musical note, and I called back. The building to my right was filled with people who died the day before me. To my left, a new building was going up; today's arrivals. This calendar of buildings spread away from me as far as I could see.

As I sat and rocked slowly, I wondered if it was a bad thing that I was enjoying myself. That I felt sun-soaked and comfortable. My shoulders were released, I didn't have a headache, and I didn't have an overwhelming urge to crawl back into bed.

Was I awful? For a moment, my shoulders drew up and I felt a wave of deep sadness wash through me. A wave that I would never have expected in Heaven.

I considered going to get Teddy, but before I could, God stepped out on my deck with my coffeepot and refilled my mug. He also handed me another muffin, warm to the touch and slathered with butter. "You're not awful," he said. "Why should you feel awful for finally getting what you wanted? For going after what you felt was truly right for you? The only thing you felt would give you some peace?" He sat down in the rocker next to me, this one a bright blue, and he hoisted a second Melmac mug, pink, to his lips. I was inordinately pleased that God was into coffee, and even more pleased that he would pick a pink cup. He also had a muffin and he bit into it, chewing and licking the butter from his lips before he spoke again. "What people have the hardest time accepting," he said, "is that those who commit suicide are doing the one thing that will make them happy, at least in their opinion. Were there other options? Maybe. Should you have tried them? You did. I know, I watched you. But what matters most in the end is that you did what you thought was right. So it's not awful, Hope. In many ways, you're brave."

I gasped. Bravery was certainly never associated with suicide where I came from. I'd heard people who killed themselves called cowards.

God patted my hand. "Hope, keep thinking of how you felt yesterday morning when you drove off in your car. That solid feeling of absolute determination and rightness doesn't mean you won't have moments of regret or sadness or fear. You're still going to worry about your children and about those you left behind. Know why?"

I shook my head.

"Because you're a good person." God drained his mug. "Geez, your version of coffee is wonderful. I may have to stop by often for a cuppa at breakfast time, or at three in the afternoon." He winked and his wink surprised me. "I tend to start to drag about then. Anyway, your guide will be here as soon as you've finished your morning ablutions."

I was still puzzling over God dragging at three o'clock in the afternoon. I expected him to be an eternal font of energy. "My what?"

God smiled. "Get your teeth brushed and anything else you typically do in the morning, beyond showering and getting dressed, which you've already done. What do you do to get ready for your day? I know you don't like an unmade bed, so go ahead and make it. For some, the idea of never having to make a bed again is worthy of Heaven. For others, that need for neatness, but also artistry and a feeling of completeness in your home, is important. You have time before your guide shows up. We don't ever have people appear at bad times here. So when you're ready, she'll be here. Talk to you soon, Hope. Oh, and I love the en suite. You can change the design of your condo however you want, except for adding a second floor or a basement. That would be architecturally difficult, even for me." He left his mug on the table between us (I couldn't help but notice he left it for me to clean up) and walked away.

I loaded our mugs and dishes into the dishwasher and then went to make my bed and do my "ablutions". When I returned to my living room, there wasn't even time to sit down before my doorbell rang. It was the first that I knew I had a doorbell. When I opened the door, I found a woman who looked to be about my own age standing there.

"Hi, Hope," she said. "My name is Faith." She laughed. "God thought we'd be a good match because of our names. But also because of our ages and situations. I chose to leave my life, just like you did, though I did it ten years ago. I was also married, and I have a child."

"It's nice to meet you, Faith," I said, and it was. "Would you like to come in?"

"Oh, no, not right now," she said. "Why don't we go on a tour of this place? I'm sure you're wondering where everything is." She looked me over. "Yep, you're dressed just right. We do have seasons here; it seems to make people the most comfortable. We're transitioning from summer into fall now, so it's warm, but never ever uncomfortably hot or cold." She shrugged. "It's Heaven. Just wait til you experience full-on winter, complete with snow for skiing and sledding and playing and ice for skating, but without the bitter cold. You can go out in just long sleeves. And you won't get soaked to the skin."

Amazing. I'd always hated winter. Maybe here, I wouldn't.

Outside, the breeze was fresher than I ever smelled it. The sun was unsifted and the clouds seemed to move to a melody. Faith led me to a hot pink golf cart with her name painted in gold along the side. "Cool," I said, settling onto the padded leather seat.

"You have your own cart too. I'll show you where the garage is when we get back. As we ride along, imagine what you'd like your golf cart to be like. Color, features...whatever you can think of." She smiled and touched a button. The cart began to purr. "It'll be waiting for you when we're done."

As we moved away from my building, I looked at it again to try to remember the color. I knew the number. But the color was a sort of sky blue mixed with yellow. It was pleasant and I liked it. I turned to Faith. "So there are no cars here?"

"Oh, there are cars for those who want them." She waved at a passing cart. "God knows that some people like to drive by the ocean, or in the mountains, or out in the countryside. So you can do that, if you wish."

"I *do* wish," I said to Faith. "I'm one of those people."

I loved to drive. And I knew what car I would want, if I had my choice. A 1995 hunter green Chrysler LeBaron convertible. I owned one, until my kids came along, and then I had to trade it in for a minivan. I cried through the entire process and the car salesman was just stumped that I wasn't excited over owning a new vehicle. But that car...that car was my life for a while. I could go out in it and the sadness would lift. I drove it with the top down even in the winter sometimes, with the heat blasting and my body wrapped in a heavy winter jacket, scarf, and hat, the thickest of mittens on my hands. I remember telling my doctor I didn't need antidepressants, because I had my LeBaron. His name was LeB, pronounced Luh-BEE. I wondered if LeB, like Teddy, would be beside me in Heaven.

Faith patted my knee. "Then your car will be in the stall next door to your golf cart."

Sometimes, Heaven felt like Christmas.

We putt-putted around the lake and Faith pointed out the beach. There was a boardwalk, just like you would find in tourist areas, and even though it wasn't the ocean, there were places that sold salt water taffy. She showed me the grocery store, where I could pick out anything I wanted and not pay for it. There were recreational areas, golf courses, tennis courts, baseball and football fields, basketball courts. Bowling lanes and bocce ball courts. There were restaurants and bars and coffee shops. There were bookstores! And a mall that made the Mall of America look like a solo K-Mart. There was...everything. And it all looked new.

"It always will," Faith said when I remarked on it. "No urban blight in Heaven."

"So who works in these places?" I asked.

"People who want to." She pulled over by a coffee shop and turned to me. "There are people who love to work. Perpetual vacation just isn't for them. And so they'll find jobs in Heaven too and they work for the sheer joy of it, not the money. God isn't about taking joy away. You find it, He gives it." She looked at me. "If someone's job was only about the money, then he or she won't find a job here. It has to be about the joy. The passion."

I thought of the easel set up in the second bedroom in my apartment. The bookshelves. The desk. I remembered my cell phone, now useless. "So how do people communicate here?"

Faith hit a button and the little golf cart shut down. "By the time we get back, you'll find a laptop and a cellphone waiting for you. They'll be pretty much the way you remember them, but I'll teach you how to use the directory to find anyone that you might be looking for." She nodded toward the coffee shop. The sign over the door read Caffeine Heaven. "Come on, let's go inside. God told me how much you like coffee."

Faith led the way. I had the impression of battered bookshelves with scattered books, scarred and comfortable tables, with chairs that could be interchanged throughout, and the coffee shop comfy chairs that I always loved, placed next to a roaring fireplace, even though the temperature outside was warm. There was a fireplace on every wall, flanked by two of the comfy chairs, so it seemed there wouldn't ever be an argument over who got to sit there. We kept going through the shop and went out the back, into a sun-dappled courtyard. Finding a cozy two-seater table, we settled in. When the barista came, I ordered an iced toffee nut latte, topped with whipped cream, and a club sandwich, extra mayo. Faith ordered something, but I'm not sure what, as I was too busy looking around.

This could have been a coffee shop, an ideal coffee shop, anywhere. Anywhere. Except for one thing.

Everyone, even those who were sitting by themselves in tucked-away shady corners, looked happy. Coffee shops always had a few people who looked glum, who looked intense, who looked like they were maybe ready to walk off the edge of the earth. In the coffee shops where I used to go, it was always me. But here, well, not here. No one was glum. I wasn't glum.

While we waited for our meal, Faith began filling me in on some of the rules and regulations, facts and freedoms. We could move about at will – we didn't have to stay in our little gated community of Heaven. But we could if we wanted to. We could visit with people, both those we knew in life and those who were complete strangers, as long as the interaction was welcomed. If there was someone we absolutely didn't want to see, we wouldn't have to see them, and there would be no possible way they could reach out to us, though they would know we were here. If we did want to see someone, and that person wanted to see us, they could come into this area.

"This is the only place in Heaven where people chose to die." Faith said. "We also have one thing in our special area that is required. And sometimes, it's not so fun."

I watched as our plates were dealt out efficiently, our drinks set on coasters. I smiled my thanks at the barista, who smiled back. Then I looked back at Faith. "What is it?" I couldn't help but think that even Heaven came with a catch.

"We all have to go to group therapy. Once a week. Forever."

"What?" I set my sandwich down.

"Usually, the groups can have up to twenty people in them. The facilitator is someone who has been dead for at least ten years, and who died by his or her own hand. You change your group every twelve weeks, starting from your first meeting, and facilitators are required to be in groups too, participating, not just leading their own."

I decided to eat for a bit, to keep my mouth too busy to talk. It seemed like I spent my entire life in therapy; now I'd have to go in death too? "Why?" I finally said. "If therapy didn't work in my life, why would it work now?"

Faith looked at me steadily. "It worked sometimes, didn't it? At least in some ways?"

I'd had some good therapists. But there were some who left me feeling worse than when I went in for the first time. "Faith," I said. "I'm here. And for the same reason you are. I think that means therapy didn't work. Neither did medications. Psychiatrists. Tests. Behavior modifications." I waved my fingers in the air, jazz hand style. "Woowoo stuff. Potions and eagle feathers and the laying on of hands." I picked my sandwich back up. It was the best club sandwich I'd ever had. "It didn't work, Faith. None of it."

She laughed at my sarcasm. "Actually, Hope," she said, "I think we're here because our therapy worked. Our therapy was supposed to encourage us to choose happiness. And to be ourselves. And so we chose to be here." She looked around. "Everyone here is free to be themselves. They don't have to hide anymore. They don't have to mask their feelings."

I looked around and again felt the contentment, even from those sitting in shadow.

"And the therapy here is all about communication. Not just learning how to. But being able to. Being free to." When I put down my drink, Faith grabbed both my hands and tugged me in, so we leaned close over the table.

"Hope, in group therapy, we don't have to be silent anymore. We don't have to censor ourselves in fear of what will happen if we tell the truth. We can say what it was like, how we felt, we can talk about who we are, and you know what? It'll be okay. We won't be locked up against our will anymore, just for admitting what we really feel. We won't be talked out of what we want to do, because we've already done it. We won't be shamed, and we won't experience the one person we trusted with our deepest secrets – our therapists – suddenly branding us selfish or cowards or whatever other awful thing they might say."

I sat back. And all I could think of to say was, "Really?"

She nodded. "Hope, we can tell the truth here. And honestly, there is no getting real help unless we can do that. And we can."

I thought of how hard it had been. My life. My internal life, my secret life. Wanting to talk, to tell, but knowing I couldn't because the result would be disastrous. The result could put me in a prison made to look like a hospital, and I would have to be there until I began to pretend that I felt better, that I felt the way everyone thought was the right way to feel. Not being able to talk about it, having to hide who I was even as I tried to get help, became years and years and years of hard.

And right now, I wanted to go back to my condo. I didn't want to hear any more.

But I also wanted to finish my sandwich. It was so good!

"Faith," I said, "I'm feeling kind of overwhelmed." I was being polite, but then I thought about what she just told me. I didn't have to be polite. I didn't have to be silent. I could say what I wanted. The truth. "Can we just finish lunch and go back? I think that's what I need. I can't take in any more today."

She reached for her sandwich. "Of course. I get it. It's an adjustment. Let's finish up, then I'll take you back, after I show you where your cart and your car are. Do you need anything from the grocery store?"

I shook my head. "Everything seems well-stocked."

She laughed. "It is, but it won't stay that way. You will have to replenish your supplies. But not for a while. God gives you some time to settle in before you have to start doing things for yourself."

Purpose and responsibility, I thought. Laundry. Dishwasher. Alarm clock. Grocery store. And group therapy.

On the ride back, we were silent, but it didn't feel oppressive. It wasn't an uncomfortable silence, but a silence that was understood. I kept my eyes straight ahead, and even closed them for a bit. I just couldn't take much more in. But I didn't feel any pressure to do so. I didn't feel like I was disappointing anyone. Not even myself.

When we approached my building, Faith scooted down a side drive that I hadn't noticed before. It curved around and then down to a garage door that was below the ground's surface. Underground parking! It went down as many floors as the building went up.

"Your stalls are on the fourth floor, going down, just like your condo is on the fourth floor going up," Faith said. "It makes it easy to remember. And you're in the fourth aisle of the fourth floor as well. The end space, because your unit is a corner unit." We zipped around easy curves and went down and down. In the fourth aisle of the fourth floor, we were almost to the end when I saw it.

Not it. He.

LeB.

My overwhelm for the moment shot away and I shrieked. As soon as Faith brought the cart to a stop, I tumbled out and ran to the car. There he was! There wasn't a scratch on him, he was as pristine as I ever kept him. His top was already down. I opened the driver's side door and slid in to the seat that always made my spirits lift.

The tan leather interior was the same. On the floor in front of the passenger seat were four long slim plastic boxes. Inside were cassette tapes; LeB didn't have a CD player and he didn't have Bluetooth. All my tapes! I grabbed one of the boxes and hugged it to my chest.

Faith leaned on my door and laughed. "Do you even want to see the golf cart?"

I smiled at her. "Oh, Faith. Oh, this car!" I put the case down, tucking it, as it should be, in an even line with the others. Inside, the tapes were all alphabetized. In my younger, more risk-filled days, I could lean over while driving, flip a lid on the exact case that I wanted, and find a tape while watching the road with my gaze skimming the dashboard.

Faith walked to the passenger side, leaned over the window and touched my cassette boxes. "I know this is how you loved it," she said, "but you know how our TV remotes work? If you'd like, all you have to do is talk to your car and it will play whatever song you want, whenever you want." She nodded toward the key in my ignition. "Try it."

With a grin that felt like it would extend past the boundaries of my face, I turned the car on. Then, automatically looking toward where the cassette player was, I said out loud, "LeB, please play Heart And Soul by T'Pau."

And the song played. I rocked in my seat and, beside the car, Faith swayed.

"Can I still keep the tapes though?" I asked when the song ended.

"Of course." Faith came back around and opened my door. "Come on, let's go see your cart."

I laughed when I saw it. I hadn't really pictured the cart like Faith suggested, not after I learned that I'd have a car, *the* car that I wanted. But the cart matched the car. The same hunter green, the same tan leather seats. The roof was a cream color, which LeB had, though I rarely drove him with the top up, and here in Heaven, I figured I never would. The dashboard of the cart looked like LeB's. My name, like Faith's, was painted on the side of the cart, though mine was in silver. I always preferred silver over gold. Under it were two more words. *Always Rises. Hope Always Rises.*

It was a phrase said to me years ago, by my favorite art teacher in high school. One day after class, she asked me to stay a minute, promising me a pass to my next class so I wouldn't get in trouble. We stood in front of a painting I was working on, surrealistic, a blur of colors, both bright and dark. There was a general feel of chaos about it. I intended that. It was the painting that hung over my mantel in my condo now, the one that won me a scholarship for college.

After praising the painting, she said, "Hope, I couldn't help but notice that your work is usually on the...Dark? Intense?...side. I don't know what word to use. Your work is beautiful, but I have stopped expecting ever to see a vase full of daisies on your canvas, or a deer standing in a field of sunflowers while bluebirds land on its antlers."

I laughed and reached out to touch a streak of burgundy. "I guess not," I said. "I don't think I'm a deer and flowers type of artist, if I'm an artist at all."

"Oh, you're an artist, Hope," she said. "Oh my god. You're an artist."

We stood there together, looking at the painting. Student work was displayed throughout the large classroom and, now that she mentioned it, I could see how mine were different. Not just the colors or even the subject. It was the feel. It was how I felt.

"Hope," my teacher said, "I just wanted to take a moment to make sure you're okay."

It was the first time anyone, outside of my parents or therapists, asked me that, asked me in that way. Not "are you okay?" after having mono or getting smacked in the nose with a volleyball or getting a bad grade. But *are you okay*, as in if I was, as a person, as me, okay. I felt so appreciative. Someone saw me, beyond the face I showed to the world. But how to answer?

"I get sad a lot," I finally said. I hesitated, and then said again, "A *lot*."

These cries for help people like me supposedly give – sometimes they're just two words.

She nodded. And then suddenly, she hugged me. "I get it," she said. And when she held me at arm's length, I saw that she did. I saw it in her eyes. The deep, deep blue that went beyond just the genetics that gave her her eye color. She looked out of her eyes, and I saw beyond her face too.

My eyes filled with tears and, as if a reflection, so did hers.

"I want you to remember something, Hope," she said. "Always paint. It helps. Whether you end up with a show in the Guggenheim or only in your living room, always paint. It's you. It's who you are. And it's what makes you, or will make you, okay." My teacher smiled. "And remember this too. Your name."

I blinked. "What?"

"Hope. Hope always rises."

And now, here it was on my golf cart in Heaven. And I always did rise. I kept trying. I tried so hard. And the day I made my final decision, I rose then too.

But my art was a different story. It disappeared, just like Teddy. And like my teacher told me, if I was my art, then it felt like I disappeared too. I thought of the easel in my new spare room. It shouldn't be in a spare room, I decided. It should be in a studio. Just like I'd always wanted, but gave up on when my second child was born, a different gender than the first. He needed his own room, more than I needed my own space to do art. That's what my husband said, when the ultrasound showed a boy. And I was so in love with the baby riding inside me, I agreed, without thinking through how I would feel a year later. Five years later. Ten.

I patted the top of the golf cart, and then, just to be fair, I patted LeB's rear end. "Thanks for showing me around, Faith. I appreciate it."

She pointed out the elevator that would take me back up to my condo and then she got behind her wheel. "Is it okay if I come pick you up again tomorrow? So we can continue our tour and we can talk? And I need to show you how the laptop and cellphone work, though I bet you'll be able to figure it out on your own."

I looked at my car. My car! "Why don't you pick me up around one and we'll go out in the convertible? Can it take me to the ocean?"

Faith beamed. "Oh, that sounds like fun! We can talk on the beach! We can pretend we're in a television commercial! Do you need to know about feminine freshness?" She laughed and then said, "That's another good thing about Heaven, Hope. We're always fresh here." She started her cart and waved. "I'll see you then!"

I'd be ready by then, I thought. I hoped. But right now, I needed to take my spinning head upstairs and think about this group therapy thing.

• • •

Back in my condo, I poured myself a glass of water, fresh from a pitcher that appeared in my fridge, complete with floating cucumbers. I walked back to check out the spare bedroom again, to see what I could do to make it into an art studio. Instead, I found the room transformed and made larger, all walls between it and the end of my condo opening up into what appeared to be the art studio of my dreams, the dreams I didn't speak to anyone about, because I was afraid of looking selfish. I walked slowly into this new space. It must have shown up in just the last few minutes, when I was thinking about how I could change that spare room into more of an art studio. Change it, but keep the Murphy bed. Change it, but keep the bookshelves and all the books. Change it...but now, I had both. There was a new room, a smaller room, directly across from my bedroom, and it held the Murphy bed, the bookshelves, a desk that held the promised laptop and cellphone and a comfy office chair. The art studio was only and unbelievably for art. For me. For me to make art.

I wanted an art room that was a commitment, a commitment that I never made to myself when I was alive. This room was broad and light, the sun coming in through two walls of floor to ceiling windows that wrapped round the corner of the building. There was a long battered library table, with an equally battered stool tucked beneath, perfect for working on pieces when I didn't want to be at the easel. Stacked against the back wall were many canvases of various sizes, and also pads of paper for different mediums. There were racks and shelves for drying pieces of artwork, and I found a large closet behind a door, perfect for storing my filled sketchbooks and canvases. A large piece of furniture, that looked like a wardrobe, caught my attention, and I went to investigate. Opened up, the doors folded out even further, exposing shelf after shelf of acrylic and oil paints, charcoal, graphite, colored pencils and pens, brushes, palettes, and every possible implement that I would ever expect to use. It was all here, and whenever I was done working, I could close the doors and restore my room to instant neatness. It was creativity, organized. My paintings were often chaotic, as my canvas was in that high school art room, but it helped me so to have my space, my room, neat and organized. Instead of organization coming from chaos, my chaos came from organization. It gave me a steady ground to stand on as I delved into the things I saw when I stared into the air and no longer saw what was in front of me, when I shut my eyes and phosphenes gathered and I saw things that no one else could, until I put them on canvas.

Since my son's birth, twelve years ago, when I turned my little art room into a nursery, and then into a young boy's bedroom, I'd had no grounding for my chaos. I'd had no expression for it either. The only place it could go was in.

The walls of windows looked to be one solid sheet of glass, but when I looked closer, I realized they were a set of lanai doors, that slid away and allowed the entire room to join with the deck outside. I did just that, then sank onto a couch that suddenly appeared. It was older, but still in great shape, its comfort stemming from years of relaxation, even though I didn't recognize it. When I stretched out, my face toward the open outdoors, the couch molded around me as if we'd been partners forever. I thought about everything that Faith told me, and I thought about the group therapy.

At home, I didn't tell my current therapist about my decision. I was a veteran of therapy, the parade of therapists beginning with a guidance counselor in middle school, then my parents brought me to my first official therapist while I was a freshman in high school, and then on and on through PhD's and MSW's and life coaches and preachers and faith healers, a veritable army in my battle with trying to break through the bleakness that sat on me like an invisible layer of skin. I knew better than to say anything to my therapist a few days ago. And that was the silence that Faith talked about. The silence I no longer needed to keep, apparently.

Which made sense. What could I do here? I couldn't kill myself again. I was already dead.

I closed my eyes and breathed in the fresh air. "That silence is the ultimate conundrum in therapy," I said out loud.

It was true. Whenever I left therapy, swearing I'd never go back, and then eventually chose a new therapist out of desperation, out of a desire to find that desire to live despite the darkness, I'd walk in with the hope that, this time, I could talk about what I felt, really dig into that darkness and peel it off to find the skin that the rest of the world wore, and not be faced with an immediate expression of alarm. Every therapist seemed to assume that if you said you were feeling like you wanted to kill yourself, you must already have a plan of action in place. I'd never met a therapist who saw my words for what they were: a plea for a legitimate way to reverse that feeling. I never had a plan in place until a few days ago. And when that plan came, when that final decision went down, I felt like not only was it the right thing to do, it was the only option I had left. Maybe, if there was a Heaven, I'd have the possibility of feeling okay there. And if there wasn't a Heaven, then I would no longer feel anything at all.

Even harder than a therapist's look of alarm when he or she caught the scent of suicide was the instant rebuke. "How can you even think that?" and "What about your children?", instantly punishing me for the way I felt. Instead of offering help, I was smacked down. I was made to feel awful, mean, the worst kind of person ever. A monster. One therapist called me selfish. Another called me a coward. And once, in high school, I was sent to a hospital for treatment.

Several weeks of doing arts and crafts. You want to drive an artist crazy? Tell her to ignore her talent and just paint her feelings. I was actually told my artwork was too good, that I was avoiding my feelings, when my feelings were all over the canvas. Chaos. I didn't know what they expected me to do, so I resorted to drawing little stick figures like a first grader. Then there was the individual therapy with a shrink who only knew me for the time I was there, and the waiting in line for meds that I didn't want. Feeling sicker than when I went in. Being asked constantly how I was feeling, though by my second day in the hospital, I knew to answer, "Oh, much better, thank you!" so I could get out sooner.

And the group therapy. All of us sitting there, looking at each other, and knowing that none of us were telling the truth. We were just saying whatever we had to in order to be released.

My hospitalization occurred when I was fifteen years old, when I didn't know yet about keeping the silence. When I still thought of therapists as safe to tell everything to. But I learned. I watched my words so carefully. The only option out there seemed to be therapy, so I took my careful words and I tried every kind. CBT, ACT, IPT, EMDR, MBCT, M-O-U-S-E. I tried alternative medicine too. Reiki. Drumming. Cranio-sacral massage. I dripped liquids under my tongue, swallowed pills, rubbed in tinctures, and bathed myself in the forest. But I never spoke of suicide. I kept hoping that I could figure out how to say what I needed to say without really saying it, because if I did, I would be punished. Or shamed. Called names. Judged. Jailed under the guise of hospitalization.

I hoped and hoped and hoped some more. Hope always rises.

But with each passing year, it grew harder for me to stand back up.

The last time I saw my therapist, it was a couple days before I drove off in my car. I'd already made my plan. Everything was in place. It was the one time that, if I told a therapist I felt suicidal, and he asked, "Do you have a plan in place?", I could have answered, "Yes, I'm going to wash down my newly filled prescription of Zoloft with a big ol' bottle of Zin." The *only* time. But thanks to all the times I couldn't answer yes because I knew better than to say anything at all, I knew not to say a word then too.

So instead, I told my therapist that I had a good week. Several good days in a row. I said that I felt better than I had in a long time, and I thought maybe I was turning a corner.

"That's wonderful!" he said.

When we said goodbye, after making an appointment I wouldn't keep, I turned quickly away so he wouldn't see the tears that were rising. My hope rose with my decision, but so did my tears at saying goodbye. I so wanted to tell him. Just like I'd wanted to tell him for over a year, so that he could help me figure out how to fix me, how to make me feel otherwise. But I never could, because as soon as I confessed those words, I knew the door to possible healing would slam in my face and the only way the door would open again was if I lied and said I was now feeling better, I wanted to live, let me at it, my eyes were on a bright tomorrow.

For years, I searched for a group of suicide survivors, those who tried it, failed, and were still here, struggling through. I never found one. There were plenty of support groups for people who lost someone to suicide. But none for those of us who kept trying to live through that dark desire.

And now Faith said I had the opportunity to tell the truth and the door would remain wide open. I'd be surrounded by those who understood because they'd been there, were there now, right next to me. The facilitator, as Faith called it, would also understand, having experienced it him or herself.

Maybe this would be the group.

"The ultimate conundrum," I repeated as I closed my eyes for a nap.

But I could feel my hope rising.

CHAPTER THREE

Hope

By the time Faith showed up at my door the next day, I was practically jogging in a circle, from my living room to the balcony to my bedroom to the living room and again and again, in anticipation. I was going to put my key into the ignition of the car I thought was lost to me forever. I was going to drive. And the dream I held onto even after the car was gone, of driving that car alongside the ocean, was about to become real. This was Heaven, metaphorically, literally, in every way possible, up and down.

When my doorbell rang, I opened the door and pushed past Faith, grabbing her hand along the way. I didn't even give her a chance to say hello. "Come on!" I said. "Let's go!"

Faith laughed the whole way down the hallway, down the elevator, and to my car. We buckled up. I looked over at her. "We need to get some iced lattes," I said. "We have to, to make it perfect."

She nodded and guided me again to Caffeine Heaven. I waited in the car, because I couldn't stand to get out, and Faith ran in to get the drinks. She said there weren't any drive-thrus in Heaven, because one of the points of Heaven was to slow down and savor. I was more than willing, even as my foot jiggled on the accelerator, ready to put the pedal to the metal.

As we pulled away, I glanced at the new cell phone I brought with me, settling it into the perfect holder on my dashboard. "Do I need to turn on the GPS?" I asked.

Faith hooted. "Just go straight here," she said. "You'll see what I mean in a moment." We stopped at some massive gates, the very gates that truly made us a gated community. Faith waved at a man in a booth and he waved back before turning a huge wheel. I watched as the gates opened like something out of an old movie. "He has to hand-crank these?" I asked. "God's not all caught up on technology?"

Faith laughed. "Whoever is in charge of the booth gets whatever means he most wants to operate the gates. Ed is old school. He loves to crank."

We followed the road through the gates, then turned onto another and followed it as it seemed to lead us out of town. It went up a hill, and then split into what looked like four exit ramps. Each had a sign over it. One said Mountains, another said Countryside, the third said Forest, and the fourth blessedly said Ocean. I tore down it.

"By the way," Faith said, "there aren't any speed limits here. Though God does like us to be reasonable. There isn't a way to get into an accident. The car will correct itself, as will any oncoming cars. But focus on how you've always liked to drive. And then drive."

I pressed down on the accelerator, bringing LeB up to a glorious 80 mph and whooped as the wind zipped through my spiked hair. We went up and over another hill and there was the bluest, biggest, widest, white-capped beautiful vista I ever saw. The road ran alongside rich coffee-with-cream colored beaches. People laid out in the sun and didn't have to worry about skin cancer, or even getting burned. They ate food from stands and didn't have to worry about getting fat and they drank without getting any more than pleasantly tipsy. Faith explained it all. "You can even get high here," she said, nodding as we passed a stand with the familiar five-leafed cannabis plant on its sign. "But again, within reason. No hard drugs. Pot is fine. Even God uses, from time to time. But he truly prefers to just sip some sangria."

God. High. Drinking sangria. The wind whipped my laughter behind me.

"You can stop anywhere," Faith said, slurping her latte through a straw. "We'll talk when you do. For now, just enjoy. Savor."

I did.

The car was everything I remembered. I asked it to play a compilation album of the Moody Blues, my all-time favorite band. Suddenly, I was driving by the ocean, the salty wind in my hair, my left arm propped on my door, holding my latte, my right arm steering, and I was singing at the top of my lungs. Singing words that I fell in love with in high school and never let go of with age. Faith joined in. I have no idea how long we drove. The ocean was endless. All I knew was my latte was gone, my voice was hoarse, and my ribs ached from laughing.

I pulled into a beach that looked deserted. I noticed that, every now and then, one of these showed up, and when I mentioned it to Faith, she said, "God knows that sometimes you need to be alone with the ocean, or the mountains, in the woods, in a meadow. So he makes certain that there are places for a lone communal."

We got out of the car and pulled off our shoes and socks. I wore shorts for this trip today, with a swimsuit underneath, fully intending to immerse myself into the ocean. We walked out to a picnic bench and sat down. It was the first I noticed that Faith carried a basket.

She set it on the worn wooden table. "I picked us up some lunch too," she said. "You can't visit the ocean without a picnic lunch." She handed me a duplicate of yesterday's sandwich and a bottle of water which somehow had cucumbers floating in it, and another latte. We set out our meal between us.

"I've never been," I said quietly. "I've never been to the ocean, and it's more than I ever imagined."

Faith looked surprised. "Never?"

I shook my head. "I always wanted to. I saw Lake Michigan, of course. Those of us in the Midwest tend to think of it as our ocean. And it is beautiful. But..." I looked out over the water. "It's not this. This feels...holy."

Faith laughed. "Well, this is Heaven's ocean. But I promise you, it's exactly like the oceans on earth. It contains aspects of all of them, so that no matter where people come from, they will feel at home."

"Or feel at home even if they never saw one, but just dreamed of it. Oh, Faith, this is beautiful." I ate my sandwich, which, in the salty air, tasted even better than yesterday.

"So have you given any more thought to the group therapy?" Faith asked. "Not that you have a choice, mind you, it's a requirement. But I want to make sure you're comfortable with the concept. I'll be with you in your first group for three weeks, so that you'll know at least one person already.

God picks out someone in their ninth week of a session to be a mentor to someone new, so they can be together for the newbie's first three weeks, then they're on their own. "

That was a comfort. It was even considerate. "When do I have to go?"

"Groups meet once a week, on Wednesdays, from one to four in the afternoon. Everything comes to a standstill then, because everyone goes. You start on the first Wednesday after you arrive. Today is Sunday. So it's in three days."

Three days. I shuddered, though I tried not to. "Do I have to start right away, or can it wait til next week, since I just got here? I won't have even been here a week on Wednesday. I need time to acclimate."

Faith patted my shoulder. "No, God will want you to start right away. You'll have been here five days by then. Other new people will be joining with you on Wednesday, and others will have been around for a while. Each week, there are new ins and new outs. It's a little bit confusing, but it makes for a really dynamic situation." She patted my knee. "I'll move on in three weeks and you'll stay there until you've reached a total of twelve weeks."

I watched the waves. All I really wanted to do was pull off my shorts and top and go run in. Taste the ocean's salt for the first time and see if it reminded me of French fries. See if the water was warm or cold and revel in either. Maybe see a fish. Maybe see a whale!

But group therapy. I'd been in group therapy, and it was nothing like seeing the ocean in Heaven. It was nothing like French fries.

But Faith said this was different. It was group therapy where I could tell the truth.

I tore my eyes away from the ocean and looked at Faith. "Why are you here?" I asked. "I mean, I know why you're here. But what caused you to come here?"

It was her turn to stare at the ocean. "Like I told you, I've been here for ten years. I'm from South Thomaston, Maine, but I hung myself in the middle of a forest in Wyoming. I stepped off the Jenny Lake Trailhead, near Jackson Hole. I was thirty-two years old. When I drove out there, I saw your Lake Michigan." She turned to smile at me for just a second before looking back at the ocean. "You're right, it is ocean-like, but it's not like the ocean I grew up with." She shook her head. "I just couldn't face another day. And I knew I had to end it far away from home. Thirty-two years and it felt like a long life. A long, long life."

Two days ago, I drove three miles away from my house for the last drink of my life. I drove to a park and faced the Fox River. I toasted it, and then drank straight from the bottle. Anyone would think I was an alcoholic, parked in a deserted parking lot in the middle of a Friday morning. But I wasn't. I only had a drink on Saturdays when we went out for dinner. "You said you had a child."

She nodded. "My daughter was five. I took her to my parents' house in Florida, told them I needed to get away and to keep Elizabeth from going back to her father. My husband was..." she stopped and shook her head. "He was horrible. But not in a conventional way. I didn't have any bruises I could show, nothing that was physical to prove the damage. But I had to keep Elizabeth safe, and to keep her safe, I had to make sure she was no longer with me."

I frowned. "I don't understand."

Faith smiled a smile that wasn't a smile at all. "Neither do I. I never did. But I couldn't keep Elizabeth with me because wherever I went, he would find me. He wouldn't care where she was. I was his target." Tears slipped down her cheeks and I was startled. Tears were more possible in Heaven than I ever imagined.

The things that happened didn't disappear because we died. But we were no longer tethered to them.

So maybe that was why the group therapy. Where we could tell the truth. We could tell it, deal with it, push it away, and it couldn't follow us. It couldn't lead us into our next days. At least, that's what I hoped.

"What happened?" I asked.

"I had to make sure that he would never find me," she said. "I had to become invisible. Poof!" She flared her fingers like a magician's assistant. "And so I came here." And then she sobbed.

I grabbed her, held her, and we rocked together to the rhythm of the waves. It felt like Heaven rocked with us.

Eventually, we sat back. Faith wiped her eyes. "Despite current appearances," she said and laughed, "I really am better. It was ten years ago. Elizabeth is fifteen now. She's still with my parents and she's doing fine. I just cry when I think of that day. Leaving my daughter behind with my parents while I drove to Wyoming was so hard. Leaving her forever was even harder. But it was the best decision I ever made. It got her out of danger."

I gawked. "You know how she's doing?"

She nodded. "God will be talking to you about that, Hope. Yes, you will be seeing what your family is up to. It's kind of like group therapy. You don't have a choice. We all have to see the consequences of our actions."

This wasn't something I considered. And I didn't know if I would want to see or not. I just couldn't handle any more blame.

But it seemed that, in the end, I would have to handle it.

I let out a breath. "Okay," I said. "Okay. I know I don't have a choice. But okay to group therapy. I'm glad you'll be there."

We pitched the garbage into a nearby recycling bin (they recycle in Heaven!). And then I yanked off my shirt and shorts. "I'm going in!" I shouted.

Faith shrieked and then she stripped down to her bra and panties. "I didn't come prepared, but I'm going in too!"

The water was amazing. It was warm with an edge of cold to it that was exhilarating and thoroughly enjoyable. It was like falling into Mexican fried ice cream. I dove under and the world turned blue. When I shot up through the waves, my head breaching, I pretended I was a great blue whale and raised my hands to the sky. When I licked my lips, I tasted salt, and it was better than French fries.

Imagine being better than French fries!

"Look!" Faith called. "It's God answering your wish!" She pointed.

A whale split the water, its body blue and big and startling. It seemed to hang in the air for a moment, before crashing down with an enormous upraising of water. Then it flipped its tail in a goodbye.

As the water reverberated and shook around me, an oceanic earthquake caused by the miracle of a whale, I found myself overcome.

Sometimes, getting just what you've always wanted is overwhelming.

Particularly with what I did to get here.

• • •

That night, after the sun went down and after a satisfying summer picnic of a dinner (cold fried chicken, a cold pasta salad, fresh dinner rolls, strawberry shortcake), I sat on my balcony, looking out at the brightest of stars. I didn't know if it was Heaven's geographic location that made the stars look so close, but they seemed to hang over me like Christmas ornaments used to, when I was little and would crawl under the tree, lay on my back, and look up. The stars even seemed to sway with the breeze. I didn't know where my dinner came from; it was in my refrigerator when I returned from my trip with Faith. I wondered when I'd have to start cooking, instead of having surprises show up in my kitchen. Not that I minded. I felt a bit like I was being treated by Heaven's version of the Welcome Wagon.

Even though it was Sunday, not a Saturday, the day I typically went out to dinner with my family and had my once-a-week cocktail, I'd made myself an Irish coffee, topped with whipped cream, and I sat quietly, sipping it. It didn't seem to cool off, even though I drank slowly. Another miracle, I supposed. I sipped, looked at the stars, considered trying to touch one, breathed deeply, and...

Thought about my family. I felt the sudden pressure of tears.

I heard the front door open and wasn't surprised when God joined me, sitting in the blue rocker next to me, the one I now thought of as his. No one else sat on it yet, and I liked the idea of having a special chair just for visits from God.

Imagine having God as a guest on your balcony. Imagine having a chair that was only for him.

Just like Faith said, God carried an icy frosted glass filled with what looked like sangria. It was a pinky-yellow, with pieces of watermelon, grapes, and a slice of lemon floating in it.

For a time, we sat in silence. I didn't feel the pressure to provide conversation. It felt perfectly fine to sit in silence with God. Just like it felt perfectly fine to sit in silence with the ocean. A lone communal, Faith called it. I knew I'd be going back there tomorrow, and maybe for several days in a row, if not weeks.

Eventually, God said, "Your family is fine. They're sad, but they're fine."

I considered the word sad. Were they? "Are they angry?" I asked.

He nodded. "I don't think you could expect anything different, Hope. Though your daughter..." He hesitated. Then he said, "Your daughter's first words, when she was told what happened, were, 'Well, of course.'"

My daughter. Fourteen years old. For the last two years, she made her own breakfast and lunch and her brother's too on those mornings when I couldn't get out of bed. If I was still there when she came home from school, she would bring me a cup of coffee and some cookies and she'd find the book I was currently reading. She sat on the floor, leaning against the side of the bed, close enough so I could reach out from time to time to stroke her hair, and she'd read to me. Sometimes, my son would come in too and lay across the foot of the bed. Usually, by the end of a couple chapters, my daughter's sardonic running commentary of the book, inserted in between paragraphs, would have me laughing and I'd get out of bed to dress and make dinner. On days that didn't happen, my daughter would kiss my forehead, put the book within reach, and take away my untouched snack, saying, "It's okay, Mom. I'll put in a frozen pizza."

It's okay, Mom.

I wondered if she would say that now. I thought of her simple, *Well, of course.* She was only fourteen years old, but I knew I'd made her much older than that.

I wrapped both my hands around my mug. The outdoor temperature hadn't dropped that much since coming out here, but my fingers were suddenly cold. "Faith said something about my being able to see my family," I said. "Observe them? I'm pretty sure that's what she meant."

God nodded. "There will be a portal in your en suite bathroom here. It will look like a mirror, but through it, you can see your family, or others that I feel you need to see." He patted my knee. "It will show up sometime between your first group therapy meeting and your second."

I felt the slow flush of anger pass through me and it surprised me as much as Faith's tears did earlier that day. "What if I'm ready to see it now?"

God kept right on patting. "You're not."

I thought about arguing. But arguing with God didn't really seem like a wise thing to do. Plus...he was right. Of course he was right. I slumped in my chair.

"They'll be okay, Hope," God said. "You'll be okay too."

I noticed the future tense in both those sentences. And I remembered countless therapists saying to me, "It'll be okay. You'll be okay." A little bit of fear began to catch fire in my stomach. What if even here, in Heaven, I still wasn't okay? What if the Gulf was in me here too?

God reached over and took my mug, setting it down on the table. Then he turned sideways in his chair, enfolding my hands in his, pulling me to the side too, so I faced him. His skin was even warmer than my Irish coffee. "Hope," he said, "I know all of this is hard to understand. But it *is* going to be okay. It actually already is. It's just going to take a little while for you to realize that. It's hard to shake off the old feelings right away. And it's hard to just walk away from the enormity of what you just did." He stood up and kissed me on the top of my head the way a father would. "It's like buyer's remorse, in a way. You made a decision, and for you, it was the right decision. It doesn't mean that it was right for everyone, and it doesn't mean there won't be fallout, but it was the right decision. For you. You are already okay. You just have to catch up with yourself." He gave me another kiss and then left.

His glass remained on the table for me to take care of again. And it wasn't even my glass.

Even God wasn't perfect. And that felt exactly right.

I took a sip of his remaining sangria. And I marveled at the possibility of drinking what God left behind. I drank what he literally drank. My lips touched where his did. The top of my head held his kiss.

This was all so amazing. And so weird. I wondered for a moment if I was actually in a coma and this was all drug-induced dreaming. I hoped not.

When I went to bed that night, I noticed a new painting on one of the walls in my bedroom. As soon as I drew near, I recognized it. It was the one I worked on after my son was born, the only painting I completed after my art room became his bedroom. I started others from time to time, trying to paint at my kitchen table or the dining room table or even outside on our deck. But I never finished any others.

I stood before it and looked at all the colors, slashed and curled and roiling over the canvas. The brightness contrasted with the shadows. Chaos.

It was the chaos that was within me then. The chaos that was within me for my entire life.

And the chaos that was within me now too, after my death. It came with me to Heaven. It was along for the ride that morning two days ago as I drove to the river, and along for the ride that afternoon with Faith, as I drove to the ocean for the first time. And yet, even with it there, I was able to whoop, to glory, to jump in the water and savor an experience I never had, to watch a whale breach and know it was there just for me and to gasp at the gladness in my heart.

I climbed into bed. I knew I would sleep. That knowledge made me feel guilty; I could never sleep at home, or when I did sleep, it wasn't restful. But that knowledge also filled me with relief.

• • •

On Wednesday, I sat beside Faith in the first row of six rows. I was surrounded by the twenty people Faith predicted. I did a doubletake when the facilitator introduced herself as Virginia Woolf. I knew that Faith said that all the facilitators were living here as well, so they'd also committed suicide, and Virginia Woolf committed suicide, but surely there was more than one person named Virginia Woolf. Was this really her? The author?

I leaned forward and studied her face. She certainly could be Virginia Woolf, from the photos I remembered of her. I knew from my literature classes in college that Virginia killed herself in 1941, when she was fifty-nine years old, and the woman sitting at the front, facing the group, could have been fifty-nine. She had a slender, long, delicate face and dark brown hair pulled back into what was now called a messy bun, though I didn't know what Ms. Woolf would have called it. But this Virginia Woolf certainly wasn't dressed in the clothing of her time. She wore a simple burgundy polo shirt and blue jeans, the knees ripped out, and sneakers.

There was another difference too. In all the photos I ever saw of Virginia, there was an air of melancholy around her. The first time I saw her was in my freshman level women's literature class, when we read *To The Lighthouse.* Her photo was on the back cover. But the woman at the front of the room wasn't melancholy; she felt light. I realized she looked the way I wanted to feel, and the way I caught myself feeling from time to time in Heaven since my death. If this was the real Virginia Woolf, she'd been dead for eighty-four years. She looked darn good. Maybe eighty-four years in Heaven could make you glow.

She must have noticed me staring, because she leaned forward too and smiled directly at me. "Yes, dear," she said. "The real Virginia Woolf."

This released the whole group into laughter and I wondered if it was at me or with me. Faith told me that the groups were mixed, so there were new people, like me, and then there were others who could have been here since the very first suicide, and anywhere in between that and now. I supposed most of them knew that Virginia Woolf was a resident.

I wondered for a moment who the first person was to commit suicide. Who came up with the word? Who tied it with "committed"?

Virginia sat back and laughed too and said, "Welcome to the group, and to Heaven, Hope." Then she went on to talk about how the group was run and so on, which has always been my cue to tune out. I was much better at learning in action.

So instead, I sat back and considered how Virginia Woolf, the real Virginia Woolf, knew my name, and we hadn't even done introductions yet. It was a lot like having a special chair for God, and God himself, on my deck. From there, I began to think about all the famous suicides that I knew of, and I wondered if they were all here too. Sylvia Plath, for sure. John Berryman. Chester Bennington, the lead singer of Linkin Park, one of my favorite groups. Robin Williams. Eva Braun, Hitler's wife, and Hitler too. Hitler in Heaven? Ernest Hemingway. Kurt Cobain. Hunter S. Thompson. Maybe I would run into Amy Winehouse and find out for sure if her death was accidental or intentional.

Noting how heavy my list was with artsy-type people, this list that just came from the top of my head, I began to wonder if this section of Heaven was filled with creativity to the beyond sky-high roof. Even Eva Braun dabbled in photography, and Hitler painted. What was the percentage of artists, writers, musicians and other creatives here in this gated community, as opposed to the rest of Heaven?

And what of me? I was a creative once. I dreamed of being an artist, and I tried so hard to be one, until I was gobsmacked off my rails by motherhood. And then later, by the sheer distance of time between where I was and when I last thought of myself as an artist. I certainly hadn't been one for a while.

But now I had the studio of my dreams. Could I be an artist now? Could I be an artist in Heaven?

Faith nudged me. "Pay attention," she whispered. "She's going to have us share our stories soon. The ones who are brand new always have to tell theirs first. And then we'll get into topics and people share what they want to."

I sat back and sighed. How would I tell my story? How could I say that I finally decided that I could no longer handle trying to stay afloat in the Gulf that constantly threatened to sweep me away? And how could I say that I had no real answer, no diagnosis, no identification, no string of abusive attacks or relationships or one huge horrific transformative tragedy, for how I felt? Despite all the years of this therapy and that therapy, I never had an answer.

There was only my life.

I listened as three other people went before me, and I worried about my own choice of words. Somewhere in the middle of the second person's story, Faith reached out and held my hand. I think I had waves of anxiety wafting off of me in all directions.

And then Virginia looked at me and smiled. "So here you are, the real Hope Sanders." I was startled that she used my maiden name; I hadn't been Hope Sanders in so long. "So tell us how you came to be here, Hope. You arrived here on Friday, right? This is your fifth day?"

I nodded, but then asked, "Why are you using my maiden name?"

Virginia glanced at the list in her lap, but then said, "We use those names here, unless the woman wants us to use her married name. We figure that your name is what you were given at birth, not the name you took on when you were married. It's the way you first identified yourself, so it's who you are. Men don't change their names when they get married, and they're known here by the names they had at birth and held onto for their entire lives. So why shouldn't women?" She looked around at the others. "I was a bit of a rebel for my time, I guess. I didn't use my husband's name. I always remained myself." She looked at me expectantly.

Faith squeezed my hand.

"I don't think much about my last name anymore," I said. "I just think of myself as Hope." I smiled. "But I did like Hope Sanders. Somehow, my married name always seemed like an add-on, which I suppose it was." I nodded. "Okay, I'm in. I like Hope Sanders. That's who I'll be again."

Everyone applauded and I was surprised at my own pleasure.

"Your name is lovely," Virginia said. "So tell us how you got here."

I sat back and crossed my arms, despite so many of my therapists telling me that this was a defensive, lock-out gesture. My left hand was tucked under my right elbow so I could continue holding onto Faith. "This past Friday, I waited until my kids and husband were off to school and work. My kids are twelve and fourteen. A boy and a girl. And then I got into my car, along with a full bottle of Zoloft and a full bottle of Zinfandel." I shook my head. "I've never done anything halfway; those bottles had to be full to the brim. And I liked that their names began with Z's, like what you see in comic strips when someone is sleeping. That's what I was going to do – go to the big sleep. We live by the Fox River in Wisconsin and I drove to my favorite spot, which was deserted, since it was a Friday morning. And then I had a little party. Some might call it a pity party." I saw the frowns wash over all the faces around me like the wave at a football stadium. I quickly added, "I wouldn't call it a pity party. I call it a facing reality party. Or facing what reality would never be." There were small smiles and nods and I clenched Faith's fingers. I wondered if her fingertips were turning white with my shame.

But not shame. I wasn't ashamed of what I did. But I squeezed her fingers with all the intensity that I felt that Friday morning. "I looked at the river and I washed down each pill with a swallow of wine. I remember that, by the last few, I was having trouble finding my mouth. But I think I did it. I think I took them all, and only left a little of the wine." I swallowed now and wished I had that wine. But in this case, Heaven didn't provide my wish. "I remember closing my eyes. And the world spinning. And then I opened my eyes, and I was here. God welcomed me, and he gave me my favorite teddy bear from my childhood."

No one laughed.

We sat in silence and I could feel everyone's held breath. I knew that the other new people kept talking after telling about their methods. They talked about what made them want to commit suicide. They were all able to pinpoint it. One woman was gang-raped as a teenager and she couldn't tolerate the memory any longer. A man lost his job and could no longer support his family. He hoped his life insurance would still be honored, if he could make his death look like an accident. He was looking forward to receiving his portal, so he could find out if he succeeded. Another woman had miscarriage after miscarriage, and she thought she might find her babies here.

And then there was me. And the Gulf.

Virginia said quietly, "And what led you to do this, Hope?"

"Do I have to answer that?" I whispered.

They all nodded and Virginia didn't take her eyes off me.

"Then I have to say that I don't know. I've just always been sad. Always. I don't remember a time when I wasn't. I call it the Gulf. It's always dragging at me. And sad isn't even the right word, it's so much bigger than sad, bigger than a downturned mouth, than a few tears, than an emoji." I laughed a little. "This just overtakes me. Drowns me. I can't function. And before you ask, I tried everything. I tried meds and therapies galore, reiki, shamanic journeys, all of it." I shrugged. "In the end, the Gulf was always right there. I was asked to leave my job because of so many days that I missed, and I didn't start looking for another one because there was just nothing I wanted to do. I was making my whole family miserable. And I just couldn't handle it anymore. So I chose to leave." I looked around the circle. "I wish I could say why. I really do."

Virginia stretched out her arms to me, as if she wished she could embrace me from the front of the room. I didn't know if I was supposed to move, so I stayed in place and her hands dropped back into her lap. I hoped she didn't think I rejected her. "You're not alone, Hope," she said. "A lot of us have Gulfs. I do. And what a great word for it."

Three other voices called out that they had Gulfs too. One person said, "I have a specific reason I did what I did, so I know where the sadness comes from. But it feels like a Gulf in me too. It's just a Gulf I can name. My Gulf is my daughter. Her name is Allison."

The others agreed.

That made me feel better. But I noted the present tense. Virginia said, "I do," not "I did." "Did it go away?" I asked. "After you were here? Virginia, you've been here eighty-four years. Is your Gulf still there?"

She looked startled that I knew how long she'd been dead, but then she gave me a look of appreciation. "It is, but it's not the same. It's not a sad thing anymore. It's very different...very quiet, very..." The writer seemed to struggle for words. "It's like it went from a surging ocean undertow to a still glassy pond."

I tried to picture that. "Not even a ripple?"

She shook her head. "No. And there's a reason for the Gulf now. A purpose." Her smile this time wasn't beaming, wasn't bright, but it was soft. Peaceful. "You'll see, Hope, I promise."

I took a deep breath and then we moved on from me.

When group ended, Faith followed my cart to my building. She walked me to my door and hugged me tightly. "It'll be all right," she said, and I thought of God's saying the same thing the night before. The future tense, *You will be okay,* and then he said I already was, *You just have to catch up with yourself.* I thought of those moments since Friday when I felt the way Virginia Woolf looked.

When Faith left, I started toward the bathroom, to see if the portal arrived the way God said it might. But then I stopped and decided, like God said yesterday, that I just wasn't ready for it yet. Maybe it was here, and maybe I was supposed to go right in and look at it, rip off the bandage and look into the faces of my family, but my feet just wouldn't go in that direction. Instead, I grabbed my car keys and LeB and I drove out to the ocean, stopping at the third isolated beach we found. I walked out so I was just about two feet away from where the water reached before it drew back. I sank into the sand, and then I sank into the blank stares. Sometimes I saw the ocean. Sometimes the sky. And sometimes I only saw air. They were all blue.

And here's the thing.

While I was silent, while I was still, and while I felt things churning through me, puzzlement, frustration, worry, I wasn't sad.

I wasn't sad at all. The sadness might have been reaching for me, like the waves of Heaven's ocean, but it drew back before it could touch me. I stayed out of its reach.

I took in the rhythm of the waves and I breathed with them. And after a while, I stretched my bare feet out in front of me, so I could feel the ocean cover my heels. I reminded myself that while it made for a good metaphor, the ocean was not my enemy, it wasn't sadness, and I only just touched it for the first time ever a few days ago. It gave me such joy. I leaned back on my elbows.

And then suddenly, there was a bright blue blanket under me, the blue in descending and ascending waves of shade and luminosity, just like the waves of the ocean. And sitting next to me, his legs stretched out too, and the length of his legs allowing his feet to enter the water up to his ankles, was God. I noticed his toes, sticking out of the water, sprouted light hair.

God had hairy toes.

Just try to sit next to God and notice this sort of thing and not laugh. I tried to cover it, but I snorted and I was afraid my lungs would blow up and so I roared, the sound carrying over the waves and my special whale leaped with the joy of it. God joined in.

"For heaven's sake, Hope, what would you expect?" he finally asked. "I made man in my image, remember?" He handed me a beautiful tall glass of iced tea.

I ran my fingers over the sharply cut diamond shapes in the crystal. The glass was heavy and cold, and when I took a sip, the tea was perfectly balanced to my liking, sweetened, and slices of lemon gently knocked against the side. I'd only been here for five days, but by now, I should have started accepting that things in Heaven, from the furnishings in my home to what I ate and drank and even what I drove, were perfect. "Thank you," I said.

God nodded and then he clinked his matching glass against mine. He also had lemon slices in his, and I wondered how closely our iced tea tastes jived. "Very close," he answered without my asking out loud. "I tried yours and loved it, so I kept it and had a new one made for you."

Even God was careful with hygiene. Though what in the world could I have caught from God? What could I catch from anybody here?

I thought of Virginia's glow.

We watched the whale for a while, who cavorted and breached and then gave me a classic whale tail wave before he disappeared. I heaved a great sigh.

God patted my knee. "You did just fine in your first group therapy session," he said.

I shrugged. "It was okay. I really like Virginia. It was amazing to have her as a leader. Are other celebrities who killed themselves here?"

"Yep." God slurped the end of his drink, then waited a second while it refilled. New lemons appeared too. "Everyone who ever killed themselves is here, Hope. Everyone. Those who are celebrities, as you call them, sometimes keep to themselves, tired of the notoriety they had on earth. Others are out and about. But really, it's just the same with everyone. Some people just need more quiet when they get here. And for some, that changes over time."

I thought of my first morning on my deck, my building occupants all dying on the same day I did, the woman who sang hello to me, the others who didn't.

"I know you talked about your Gulf, Hope. And you know now that you're not alone in that. Many here feel that same way, though you're the first one to give it that word." He smiled at me. "Others have talked about an emptiness or a shadow or a cave within themselves. But I like Gulf. It's more than empty. It's a force that pulls you. Like an undertow."

I swallowed and watched the ocean, reminding myself of the whale, the metaphor, the joy of the blue. "It's like being drowned, but in a different way. With drowning, it's eventually over. You die. But with the Gulf, you just keep getting pulled deeper and deeper. Just when you think it can't get any darker, it does."

My glass refilled too and between us on the blanket, a plate of lemon bars appeared. I immediately brightened. Lemon bars were my favorite.

"I know," God said. "Take a couple bites, and then tell me what color the Gulf is."

Is it wrong to call a lemon bar heaven when you're in Heaven? I wondered, but then I didn't care. The taste was amazing. While I chewed, I pondered what God asked. The obvious answer, the cliché answer, was blue. How many country songs have been written about feeling blue?

But the Gulf wasn't blue. Blue was joy, like the ocean in front of me. All that undulation. The sky too, with its cobalt of evening, or the light shining through at noon. Robin's egg.

I tried to think of how the Gulf felt. And I tried to picture all of the acrylic paint tubes back in my special artist closet in my new home.

"Purple," I finally said. "A deep, deep purple, that you can only see when you stare at it long enough. It's laced with black. There are times when it lightens, almost sheer, like lavender, and you think you might be able to break through, to breathe, but then it goes dark again." Involuntarily, I shivered. "It's thick, like oil."

God considered that for a minute. Then he said, "Like this?" and nodded toward our blanket.

I looked down and found myself in a quagmire of purple. It swirled in a broad circle, a sucking tunnel, and the color roiled like a bruise. I shot off the blanket and ran a few feet away.

"Hope!" God called. "It's gone, I have the blue back! I'm sorry." He patted the blanket. "But I take it I got it right?"

I nodded, unable to find words, and wondered if it was possible for God to get it wrong. I went back to the blanket, sank down into the returned blue, and wrapped my arms around my knees.

"I'm sorry, Hope," God said again. "I should have warned you. That was quite the color."

"I never painted it," I said, just as much to myself as to God. "I was afraid to make it that vivid."

"Maybe you need to. In your new room. You can create a new color. And call it Gulf."

Eventually, my heart slowed down. With only knowing it a few days, I fully appreciated the ocean and I wondered what my life might have been like if I had it by my side throughout all my years. My real life, my breathing life.

"Hope, I do need to tell you something else, since it came up in group therapy today."

I groaned. I really thought I'd had enough for one day. And I thought Heaven was about never reaching that level.

"No, it's important."

I looked at the blue, breathed with the waves. My whale did a tail flip in slow motion.

"There is a reason for the Gulf. There is a reason you feel it. The purple started somewhere."

I never thought of that. With all the pulling down, the swirling, I never thought of it as having a start. I supposed it was like a Slinky. Near the bottom of the spiral was a beginning.

God laughed and handed me a coppery-colored Slinky. "Yes, like this."

I slinked it from my left hand to my right, the metal coils making that special slinky sound. *It's Slinky, it's Slinky, that wonderful magical toy!* There was no fear in a Slinky. It didn't threaten me. *It's Slinky, it's Slinky, it's fun for a girl and a boy!* The rhythm, like the ocean, settled me down. "So where did the purple start?" I asked.

God hesitated, then said, "We'll talk about that, in time. When you're ready. And when I'm ready too."

When I was ready. There it was again. And what in the world could God have to be ready for? Wasn't he always ready, because he was God? I concentrated on the Slinky. Left, right, left, right. Then I asked, "So you know? You know where it started, why it started?"

"Of course," God said. "But the thing to get used to now, the thing you need to accept, is that you're safe. The Gulf isn't a danger anymore. Not even when you realize what it is, where it is, what caused it to be."

I stopped the Slinky. "*When*?"

God nodded. "Heaven is all about truth, Hope, remember? You can tell the truth? You can know it too. And you will, when you're ready." Then he added softly and again, "And when I'm ready too."

Just like the portal to see my family.

God stood up. "Like you were thinking just a few minutes ago, that's enough for today."

God gave me that fatherly kiss on the top of my head and then he was gone. He left our glasses and the blanket behind. I knew I would find room for the glasses in my kitchen. I found an empty shelf in my cupboards and I designated it God space. I thought the blanket would look lovely in my art studio, draped over the forever comfortable couch.

I sighed and leaned back on my elbows again. In my mind, as I blank-stared at the blue, I ran just once through the events of the day, just once, and then I shoved all of it aside.

I thought instead of another woman who was at my meeting. She was the one who said she had a specific reason for killing herself, that she had a Gulf too, a Gulf whose name she knew.

And then she said the most curious thing. She said the Gulf's name was Allison. And Allison was this woman's daughter.

CHAPTER FOUR

The Gulf Named Allison

Beth's Story

When her daughter was young, a toddler, a child, Beth dreaded silence. It meant that Allison got into something, and Allison was always getting into something. Silences led to that little girl body being covered with permanent marker, and Beth giving in to laughter when she saw the red circles like bullseyes around her daughter's pink nipples. Silence led to scissors being used wherever they shouldn't be, on Allison's hair, her bedspread, the special flower girl dress for her aunt's wedding. Some silences led to serious things, like a softly crying girl under a backyard maple tree, a broken arm the result of her fall, but her fear of being in trouble – again – keeping her from calling out. Later, silence meant sneaking in after curfew, or trying to hide a hickey or a new dent in the car door. Sometimes it meant smoking cigarettes under that same tree in the backyard, or an open bedroom window in the middle of the night, an empty bed.

But as Allison left her teens and entered her twenties, when the little girl was long ago, and even the exasperating teenager was in the distance, silence began to mean the exact opposite of chaos. It meant the house was peaceful. Allison was asleep.

She wasn't howling in pain from her latest involuntary attempt at withdrawal.

She wasn't screaming through a hallucination caused by drugs, the names of which Beth didn't even recognize. Chiva, Aunt Nora, Stardust,

Speedball, Apple Jacks, White Horse, Dancing Shoes, Glass, God's Drug. God's Drug!

Beth thought Stardust sounded kind of pretty. But what was happening wasn't pretty. Allison's cheeks were sunken in. Her skin was blotchy, her eyes a raccoon's. She was so skinny that the few times she allowed Beth to hug her, all Beth felt was bones. Like the names of the drugs, Beth didn't recognize her daughter's skeleton. She only knew the chubbiness of the toddler, the child, and the smooth curves of the teenager, Allison's unique softness. She didn't know who this skeleton was, and she didn't recognize the banshee voice that came from her daughter's room.

Allison was all about screams now. Screams of agony when she was detoxing. Screams of rage when she reached for stashes and came up empty-handed after a raid on her room. Even when she spoke at a normal level, which was rare, her voice was raspy, the way Beth imagined a witch's voice would sound. Her daughter was a skeleton, a banshee, a witch. She was someone Beth didn't know. Some*thing*.

But when rare silence settled like a fragile white flag over the house, Beth would creep to her daughter's door and open it. Allison would be asleep, the way she slept since she was a little girl, on her side, both hands pressed together under her cheek, her eyelashes glorious against her skin, her breath even. Beth pulled up the covers and tucked her daughter in. She buried the skeleton body under a mound of blankets because Allison was always cold. The banshee shriek and witch voice silenced, Beth could remember who her daughter used to be and who she hoped she would be again.

Those moments were so short. Allison rarely slept for more than an hour.

On this day, in this hour, Beth carefully closed her daughter's door behind her. She reveled in the silence, but braced herself for what she knew was coming. Allison was newly home after spending the night in lockup at the police station, after being pulled over. Again. Beth received the phone call, mercifully early at ten o'clock last night. The officer, his voice familiar, informed Beth that they would be keeping Allison until morning, to give her time to sober up. Beth thanked him. Then she enjoyed a silent cup of tea and a few cookies before crawling into bed. She slept the whole night through, the first full night's sleep since the last time Allison was in lockup or rehab. This morning, Beth called in sick to work – again – and then took an Uber to the police station, collected her daughter, drove her home in Allison's car, held onto the keys, and watched as Allison stumbled into her bedroom and fell into that blessed silence.

When she woke, she would discover that her mother ransacked her room – again – and all the pills and drug paraphernalia were gone. The silence would be gone soon too.

Beth searched for a new place to hide Allison's car keys. So many hideaways were already used and exposed and found in Allison's desperate searches. Eventually, Beth went down to the basement. Under the stairs, she kept her collection of luggage, all different sizes from all different trips and all different stages of life. Allison's sleepover suitcase, pink with purple bubblegum bubbles. An overnight professional bag, with room for one change of clothes and a laptop. Suitcases they shared, suitcases Allison used for her brief semester in college, suitcases for hospital stays.

How could there be so many suitcases for so many escapes, when they were both so thoroughly trapped here in this house?

Beth considered, then put the keys into an inside pocket of a medium-sized suitcase, tucked under the stairs. She locked the suitcase with the little matching padlock, then put the suitcase into a larger one and locked that one as well. Going outside, she tucked these tiny keys inside her glove box in the car, then locked the glovebox with a key she kept on her keyring. She tucked the keyring into her back jeans pocket, vowing to always keep her keys somewhere on her person. Then she went to the kitchen and made herself some chamomile tea, a rare treat in the mid-morning, and she pulled out some shortbread cookies too. When she settled back in her chair, she felt together, intact, and even a sense of refinement, sophistication, class, sitting there with her tea and her cookies and the blessed, blessed silence. She took a nibble and a sip and pretended that everything would be all right. Looking outside, she thought she might take a walk later and she imagined the sound her sneakers would make in the steadily falling leaves, their oranges and reds looking as crisp as they sounded. She didn't quite dare to imagine her daughter walking calmly beside her. Pretending could only go so far.

The maple tree in the backyard was turning color too, the way it did every year. Beth remembered the tender way she held the child Allison as she carried her to the car for that trip to the emergency room after she'd fallen from a branch. Despite the broken bone, her daughter then was just warmth and gentle tears and the smell of fall and soft, soft skin.

As much trouble as Allison was, then, now, Beth missed her little girl.

• • •

First, there was the sound of shuffling and Beth carefully placed her teacup on the end table. The little plate with her cookies went there too and then Beth lowered the footrest on her chair.

Just in time for the first shriek.

"Where is it! Where is it!"

Beth moved steadily toward her daughter's room.

"It was here! And it was here! Where is my stuff? What did you do with my stuff? Mom! Where is my stuff!"

Beth opened the door. Allison was standing near the foot of the bed. Her elbows were out and locked and her long hair was wrapped around her fingers, held away from her head. Beth watched in familiar horror as her daughter yanked out two fistfuls of long brown strands, threw them on the floor, then drew her fingers through again. "Allison," Beth said, "Allison, it's all gone. I got rid of it all. Again. You were told to never have that here again."

"It was mine! It was my stuff, Mom! This is my room! You can't take my stuff!"

Rather than approach her daughter, Beth approached the bed. She smoothed the sheet, the blankets, and then pulled up the bedspread, tucking it under the pillow, pretending she was neatening her daughter's room before taking her to kindergarten, first grade, second. Beth used to help her daughter get dressed, she used to braid her long hair. Allison would brace her hands on Beth's shoulders as she lifted first one foot, then the other, into the legs of her pants. She chattered the whole time and Beth provided a syncopatic "Uh-huh," to all of it, their voices blending and her daughter's body balanced, steadied, on Beth's own shoulders.

Now, Allison continued to shriek and she paced the room, throwing handfuls of hair into the air. Beth knew her daughter's head would have to be shaved. Again.

"As soon as I'm done here, we're going to the rehab center," Beth said. She looked on the floor and found the armed husband pillow Allison used for reading in bed. Beth got it for her when she finally gave up trying to keep Allison from staying up late when she was twelve years old. Beth figured instead of hunching under the covers with a flashlight, her night owl book-happy daughter should be comfortable, so there was a bright pink reading lamp on the bedside table and this pink corduroy husband pillow. When she picked it out, Beth laughed at the name of it, but it fit with Beth's dreams of her daughter carrying her love of reading into the future, into college, a degree, a great job, a supportive husband, and children.

Beth didn't know when the last time was her daughter used the pillow, and she couldn't remember the last time she saw Allison reading. Beth was glancing over at the bookshelf, seeing all the authors she remembered, Walter Farley, Marguerite Henry, A.A. Milne, Mary Norton, J.K. Rowling, C.S. Lewis, when Allison's fist connected with the side of Beth's head. She fell onto the bed, her ear ringing, but through the ringing, she heard her daughter's declarations that she wouldn't go to rehab, she would *not* go, she would never go there again, and where was her stuff, her stuff, her stuff?

Allison's skeleton bones fell onto Beth's back, arms flailing, landing punches, pulling Beth's own hair. Beth felt it separate from her scalp. She pictured her own gray strands joining Allison's on the floor. The dresser. The desk.

Won't go, my stuff!

Beth threw her arms back and tossed the skeleton banshee witch off her shoulders the way she would an old cloak. Standing, she raised her hands to her burning cheeks, her scalp, her ringing ear. Allison was still screaming, climbing to her feet, her fist already drawn back. Beth threw her own voice between them with enough force to stop Allison's fist. Allison was instantly muted.

"Get out! Get out now! Get *out*!"

Beth never spoke those words before.

This new and sudden silence was different. It wasn't a blessing. It wasn't merciful. It weighed so much more on Beth's shoulders than her daughter's bones. They stared at each other through the heavy, heavy air.

And then Allison turned and left. She didn't shriek. When the front door closed, it was gentle, not even a slam.

Beth measured her movements, carefully controlling her shaking, as she remade the bed and swept up the hair, her daughter's brown and her own gray turning into a bird's nest in the dustpan. Then she returned to her recliner, raised the footrest, and took a sip of her cold tea. She held the cup in both hands and ignored the way it shuddered between her fingers. She pretended that the tea was hot. She pretended that everything would be all right.

But pretending could only go so far.

• • •

This new silence lasted for two hours before it was shattered by her doorbell. The police officer at the door asked if he could come in.

This was also new, but it seemed to be a day for new. The fist against her ear. Beth flinging her own daughter and shrieking like a banshee herself, saying those words she never said before. *Get out.*

And now this police officer, in the chair beside her, sitting forward, his hands clasped around his knee. His words were new too, saying that Allison stepped off a curb into the path of an oncoming SUV. He said that Allison was dead. That Beth needed to come identify the body.

Beth found she had to focus on her lips, raising her hand to her mouth, trying to manipulate and mold the words she wanted to say. "Was she high?" This new silence was only a couple hours old. It wasn't that long ago that Allison quietly closed the front door. Where would she have gotten something so quickly?

"We don't think so, Beth."

With the use of her first name, Beth realized that she'd talked to this officer before. He'd brought Allison home many times. He might even have been the one to call her last night.

"The driver of the SUV said she saw Allison standing on the curb. As she got nearer, Allison looked her right in the eye. And then she stepped off. Allison gave her no time to put on the brakes."

Beth drove an SUV.

She waited for the officer to say the word she was thinking, but couldn't say herself.

Instead, he said, "Beth, could she have left a note?"

A note. It wasn't the word she suspected, but it was essentially saying the same thing. "No," she said out loud. "I told her she was going back to rehab. She hit me. I yelled at her to get out, and she left. That was just a little while ago."

"An impulse then. I'm so sorry, Beth." He offered his hand. "I'll drive you to identify the body. And I'd like to take you to the ER to have your face looked at. You're very bruised. I'll bring you back here after."

Beth touched her fingers to her ringing ear, to her cheek, and she felt pain zing through her like an exposed wire. She wondered if she could consider that flash of pain a note. It said every word the officer didn't.

• • •

The silence in the house stretched now, extending to weeks, a month, three months. Beth thought grief would keep her awake, but every night, she slept for at least eight hours, uninterrupted. She ate entire meals at her kitchen table, while reading the newspaper or watching a whole episode of a television show. If it was a sitcom, she found herself laughing. She sat in her recliner every evening at ten o'clock, had some chamomile tea, some shortbread cookies, and then she washed her few dishes before bed. Her daughter's bedroom door remained open, and the bed was neatly made. One night, as she passed by, Beth turned on a whim and picked up the husband pillow. She carried it into her own room, then relaxed against it as she read a book in bed. She'd stopped at the used bookstore on her way home from work, a store she hadn't visited in over a year, as she always rushed home to check on her daughter. Before. But that day, she picked up a book on display in the window, a book that promised tears and laughter both, and that's what she read while leaning into the husband pillow.

She found herself smiling.

And then she thought, I'm such a terrible mother.

Again.

She thought about throwing the book across the room, pitching the husband pillow from her bed. She thought about screaming, about throwing her voice into her silent room with the force of her daughter's fist. But she didn't.

Instead, she kept on reading, wiping the tears from her eyes when the words blurred.

• • •

The next day, she called in sick to work. Again. Then she went into Allison's room and started cleaning out the closet, the dresser drawers, the bookshelf.

It was on the bookshelf that she found the orange pill bottle, tucked behind a copy of *A Wrinkle In Time.* The prescription was for Oxycontin. The name on the bottle wasn't anyone Beth knew. It was full.

Beth wondered how Allison got this. And she wondered why she didn't find it when she ransacked her daughter's room. She wondered why Allison didn't remember this hiding place when she was looking for *her stuff, her stuff, her stuff.*

Beth sat on Allison's bed. She cradled the bottle. She thought of the sound of her daughter's voice, and then the lack of sound, the crash of it, right after Beth shrieked, *Get out!* She thought of the gently closed front door. She thought of the husband pillow, now in her own room. She thought of her own smile. In this new, stretched-out silence.

She tried to tell herself that she was grieving. But pretending could only go so far.

She was such a terrible mother.

Again.

Beth opened the bottle.

It was an impulse.

CHAPTER FIVE

Hope

I stood in my studio, poised to paint for the first time in years. At first, I felt like I was dancing with my easel more than preparing to work, with the number of times I moved it, trying to find just the right spot. I opened the lanai doors all the way and moved out onto the deck, setting the easel there. I faced forward, then to the left, then the right, then turned so I was facing back into the studio, which didn't make any sense at all. Then I moved all around the room. I set the easel in front of the couch and tried lowering it so I could sit while I was painting. Moving, lifting, turning, shifting, I worked up a sweat before I even placed one brushstroke.

Finally, I set the easel in the exact middle of the opening to the deck. It was the perfect balance of inside/outside, left/right, front/back. I sighed in relief, pulled over a battered paint-spattered table that showed up that morning when I realized I didn't have a place to rest my working brushes, paints, and water, and then balanced a bright white empty canvas on the easel's ledge.

Everything was perfect. Even my clothes. When I dug into my closet after lunch, I came across the droopy gray sweatpants I used to wear when I painted so long ago, and the paint smears were exactly placed on the fabric, just where I remembered them. Excited, I dug through the selection of t-shirts and I found my Kilroy, the white aged to a soft unwashable gray. Kilroy's nose was a piebald black and white from the time I leaned into a canvas because I just couldn't get the impression that I wanted. My t-shirted breasts against the black and white canvas gave me just what I imagined, and that painting hung in my bedroom for years. Glancing over my shoulder as

I pulled on the old clothes, I found the painting now, hung over my dresser. And Heaven's best trick yet – the clothes fit, despite the extra twelve pounds I carried around since the birth of my son. They fit me just like they used to, comfortably loose, and I thanked the miracle that was Heaven and God and the insight into a woman's mind.

And now I stood in front of an easel for the first time in over twelve years. I gave up painting while I was pregnant with my son, and then painted just one more, the one at the kitchen table after he was born. My husband couldn't wait to turn my art room into a little boy's nursery and so I was unmoored even as I was anchored by the baby weight in my belly. I gave up my room gladly, watched my husband paint it blue while I stood in the hallway, just outside of the fumes, guided the placement of a masculine-looking crib and changing table and a hardy rocking chair. I watched artwork that wasn't my own, but mass-produced basketballs and footballs and baseball mitts, go up on the walls. Above the crib, my husband placed a framed football jersey, sporting the number of someone from the Green Bay Packers who he deemed a god and who, to me, was just a green and yellow (my husband called it gold) shirt with a number on it. But it was for my son, and it was my husband's great joy, and it was all right.

Though there were nights, over the twelve years since my son's birth, that I sat at the kitchen table, everyone else asleep. I placed a canvas flat on some newspapers to protect the table's finish, spread out paints and paintbrushes. And then I couldn't do a thing. I tried, but eventually, I packed up my art supplies and tucked them away in the basement. I looked in at my son, sound asleep in what was now most assuredly his room, then at my daughter, and finally crawled into the bed I shared with my husband. He rolled over in his sleep and draped his arm around my waist. I heaved a deep sigh and tried to tell myself it was one of contentment.

It wasn't.

From time to time, especially as my son grew older, I stood in that same hallway and looked into his bedroom. I remembered that art room, just for me, and I missed it. But I also knew I'd never trade one for the other.

And now...here I stood in Heaven. My children were at home, doing whatever it was children do when their mothers die. When their mothers choose to die. Their mother, who would never trade them away for something purely her own.

This new canvas glared back at me.

I told God that I would try to paint the Gulf and so I set to work on my battered table, mixing different paints, trying to come up with the right shade of purple. Then I decided I would paint the canvas black, to get rid of that awful intimidating white, and to have a base to work off of. It was satisfying, using a thick brush to layer on the paint, but it still wasn't going the way I wanted it to go. I told myself to be patient; this was like a bicycle; it was a long time and I would have to recapture what I knew, in my fingers, my arm, my mind.

I gave up on mixing the paint and began to just slather color onto the black, swirling purple and mixing in splotches of red and brown and more black and even lighter colors of pink and gold (yellow?). I remembered the swirling tunnel on God's blanket and I glanced over at the copper Slinky that he gave me. I had it sitting on the table by my couch, and the blanket from yesterday, restored to its original blue, draped over a back cushion. I began to carve in great circles, using the wooden tip of my brush, to get texture and the sense of being sucked down.

The colors were good, the darker-than-purple howling, the other colors an echo, sometimes brighter, sometimes a step darker, even though that didn't feel possible. I felt the creeps, looking at the canvas, and that was what I wanted. The sense of being swallowed was there, the tunnel gripping and dragging. But when I stepped back, something was still missing.

I looked around my studio. I didn't know how to ask for something, a brush, a tool, to create what was missing, because I didn't know what it was.

One of the things about being an artist, or any kind of creative, really, a writer, a musician, a sculptor, is our ability to allow in distraction. At home, when I still painted, I would work a while, then check the mailbox. Paint some more, then throw in a load of laundry. Paint another ten minutes, then grab a cup of coffee. Once my daughter was born, the distractions multiplied. Paint, see if she was breathing, paint, see how cute she was while she took her nap, paint, look at her, look at her, look at her!

And now...well, now it was time to go in search of an art supply store, of course. I needed to find out what I was missing, and with my mind empty, I needed to look at supplies I didn't even know existed. I dropped my brushes into the glass of water, immediately dousing the clear into murk, and considered changing my clothes. But then I decided not to. I was going to an art store, not a boutique. Though a stop at the coffee shop might be warranted.

Distractions, distractions.

In the parking garage, I patted LeB as I passed him and then climbed into the golf cart. It would be our first time together, and so I grasped the steering wheel like I would a hand, introduced myself, and announced that from this day forward, he was to be referred to as LittleB. As we zipped around the curves that led to aboveground, I delighted in the little cart's perkiness. I'd never aspired to a golf cart as I never aspired to be a golfer. But the idea of barreling this vehicle over the rolling hills of a golf course was tempting. Maybe I would go at night, just to let the cart loose in its native land, and not to smack a little white ball.

I knew how to get to the coffee shop, so I went there first, parking in a row of about a dozen other golf carts. I smiled at the bright colors and shapes, thinking of a circus and clown cars. Inside, I approached the barista and asked for the Heavenly equivalent of a Starbucks iced cinnamon dolce latte. He knew exactly what I wanted and how to make it. I commented on that, as this was Caffeine Heaven, and it didn't have any attachment to any earthly coffee chain, as far as I could tell.

"For those of us who choose to work in the coffee shop, we are given an instant memory of any recipe from any coffee shop anywhere," he said, calling over the espresso machine. "Someone could come in here from some remote corner of some remote country I've never heard of and ask for an independently owned coffee shop specialty. I would know, just like that, how to make it. I'm not even conscious of it. I just reach for the ingredients, and the knowledge is there."

"Wow," I said. "The next time I come in, I'll ask for a latte called the Lug Nut, from a little shop in Port Washington, Wisconsin."

"And you'll have it," he said, handing me my drink. "Though it will help if you remember the name of the little shop." He laughed.

I took a sip and thought, trying to place myself back into that lovely little shop, right next to a harbor on Lake Michigan. "Smith Brothers," I said. "Yes! Smith Brothers Coffee House! But they spell Brothers with the abbreviation – B, R, O, S, and a period."

The barista closed his eyes. Then he nodded. "Toffee nut," he said. "Almond, hazelnut and macadamia. Espresso, of course."

"That's amazing." I looked at my cup. I was tempted to order the Lug Nut as well, but then decided that it was sometimes better to hold off gratification, even in Heaven. "That's for next time," I said. Then I asked him if he knew of an art supply store in Heaven, and he directed me down the road a few blocks, a left turn, a right turn, and there it would be. He grinned at me then and said, "Of course there's an art supply store in this section of Heaven."

I thought of the list of creative suicides I came up with at the group therapy session.

I sipped my latte as LittleB and I putted our way through the streets. Most everyone I passed raised their hands in greeting and I toasted them with my cup. And then I pulled up in front of the Color'n'Create art supply store. The logo showed a sculptor chipping an artist holding a brush and a palette out of a human-sized block of stone. The artist was painting the sculptor. I felt a shot of adrenaline I hadn't felt in years. I loved art supply stores. They were dangerous, because I would want to buy at least one of everything. But here, in Heaven, everything was free.

I remembered my fully stocked studio in my condo and tried to remind myself to have some decorum and common sense. But I had to find something to help me show something I didn't know how to show. Because I didn't know what this magical tool was, I didn't know if I owned it already, and besides, inspiration was always in stock at an art supply store.

As soon as I opened the door, I smelled it. The scent of paint. Of clay. Of every art material known to man or woman. Delighted, I stood for a moment, closed my eyes, clasped my hands, and just breathed.

Oh, how I missed this.

Hearing laughter, I opened my eyes and looked over at the counter. A woman looked back at me and she cut back her laughter to an easy grin. "Hi," she said. "You must be Hope."

Apparently, God preceded me again. "That's right," I said, stepping up to her. "How did you know?"

"God let me know that you were new here, and that you were going to be working on something that you likely wouldn't quite know how to do." She held out her hand. "My name is Joy."

Instead of shaking her hand, I smacked both of mine onto the counter, attempting and failing to hide the gales of laughter that instantly hit. "Oh, come on!" I said when I could speak. "It is not!"

She laughed too. "You're right. It's not. God told me that your name is Hope and your mentor is Faith, and I just had to join in. But my name is close, really," she said. "It's Joyce."

Hope, Faith and Joyce. That worked for me. Now I did shake her hand. "Well, God was right. I am working on something that needs a way to make it..." I squirmed, squiggled my hands around, tried to find a way to give a gesture to what I needed.

"Depth? Dimension? Texture?" Joyce guessed.

"Yes. All of the above. It needs to look like a big, sucking tunnel. The paint needs to be thick, almost sculptured, in parts, and smooth in others." I dropped my hands, hating my inability to describe. "I've been away from art for a while. I guess I don't quite know what I'm doing anymore."

Sadness swept over me. Not the Gulf, exactly, but a trickle that could lead to the Gulf. I felt like my intuition, that used to lead me through every painting, through the start when I thought it was *this*, to the end, when it turned out to be *that*, was gone. Swept away by the Gulf, maybe. An undertow, like God said.

"Come on," Joyce said, lifting a part of the counter that served as a gate. "Let's go play. Don't be sad, Hope. This is *fun.* This is what you *do.*" She nodded. "It's you. You just have to get used to being you again."

I followed her, feeling my spirits rise the further I got into the store. We experimented with different brushes with stiff bristles, thick bristles, uneven bristles. We looked at sponges and scrapers and finger paints. I crowed when we came to a section of tools and I saw a putty knife.

"This!" I said. "This is what I need! And some of those sponges! And that brush with bristles so stiff, they hurt!" We loaded a small plastic basket and I added a few more acrylic paint colors that grabbed my attention, even though I knew I probably had them already. I threw in some finger paints too. Suddenly, I wanted to throw my whole self into this canvas, just the way I leaned into the black and white painting so many years ago.

We carried the basket between us back to the counter and Joyce bagged everything for me. There was a stool on the customer side and I sat down, suddenly overwhelmed. "Thank you," I said. "This is amazing. This just felt...so good." I wondered how long it was since I said a sentence like that.

So long.

"You're welcome," Joyce said. "And I get it. When I first got here, I hadn't done anything in years. I sculpt mostly, but I like to paint too." She sighed, and I saw an expression cross her face that reminded me of the sweep of sadness I felt just a bit ago. "Do you know how long I went without saying that? Years. *Years!*" She sat down too. "I don't even know what happened, exactly. I went to college, then to grad school, got an MFA, even had a couple of shows once I graduated. And then...nothing. I had to get a job because you can't make a living as an artist, you know. So I worked in a bank. Nothing important, just a teller, and every day, I stood there and took people's money and handed them their money and life was money and that was all there was. People were happy with their money, or sad, or angry, and when I went home, I found I couldn't do anything. I'd been on my feet all day, talking money, money, money, and so I either collapsed in front of the TV and watched shows about people whose lives were good or bad, depending on money, or I sat on the computer and tried to figure out schemes that would make me rich so I could be happy with money too." She looked at me and I saw her eyes overflow with tears. "Years," she said.

"I'm so sorry," I said. I didn't know what else to say. I got it, I really did. Especially after having the kids, money seemed so important. Not even just for the basics, like food and a roof. But to give your child a life worth living, so much had to be provided. Dance lessons, sports teams, good clothes, the best shoes, technology equipment, entertainment, vacations...

A life worth living. I felt a chill.

"Joyce," I said, "how did you end up here?" I shook my head. "No, not end up. That's too negative for what this place is. How did you come to be here?"

She wiped her eyes. "I got into a Ponzi scheme. I lost everything, which wasn't much, I didn't have much. But for a while, it looked like it was going to work. Like I was going to have everything. Everything I wanted. I was going to be one of those happy people coming into the bank, stuffing their accounts full, pulling piles out when they needed to make a purchase. A boat, a car, a house. I was on my way! And then it was all gone." She raised her palms up, empty. "I was evicted from my apartment. My car was repossessed. I couldn't even live in that." She shrugged. "I had twenty dollars in cash to my name. I went to McDonalds, bought a Big Mac, fries, and a strawberry shake." The smallest smile came on her face. "I ate my meal, then went next door to a hardware store. I bought the sharpest box cutter I could find. Then I ducked behind the store and hid in back of their dumpsters. When it was dark and the middle of the night, I went to one of the trees that were boxed in in the middle of the parking lot. You know how they grow trees in parking lots? With those railroad ties around them, and it looks like the tree is growing right out of the blacktop?"

I nodded.

"I sat there and I slit my wrists and I died. I wanted to make sure someone would find me. I didn't want my body to be abandoned." She shook her head. "I didn't want to be abandoned, and that's how I felt. And then I was here."

We sat there. Our afternoon started by her offering her hand for me to shake. I held that hand now.

"Once I was settled in, I found I was in a condo that had a huge room attached to it where I could sculpt. But I told God I wanted to do more. I wanted to work in a job that really meant something to me." She looked around. "Here I am. This whole store is mine, given to me by God. I even designed the logo." She squeezed my fingers. "I love it here. I can do my art and I work my art and I live my art. It's who I was supposed to be."

"How long have you been here?"

She smiled genuinely this time. "After a while, you lose track of time here. It no longer matters, except for knowing what day Wednesday is, so you get to your group. What year is it now?"

"2025," I said. "October."

She scrunched up her face, drawing figures in the air. Then she laughed and reached for a calculator. After punching in numbers, she said, "I died in 1987. It's 2025. So it's been thirty-eight years. Can you believe it still makes me cry when I talk about it? But really...I am so happy here. Just as happy, if not happier, than those people with their money."

"I think I am too. I haven't been here long, but...I sure feel different." I stood up and gathered my bags. "Your sculptures...where are they?"

"My favorites are in my condo, though they keep changing as I get new favorites. I have a gallery that features my work a few blocks from here and people pick out pieces for their homes. They commission me too. There are also parks all over the place, Heaven has no limit, and God chooses pieces too, to put there. No matter what I make them out of, all my sculptures are instantly protected from weather, which we do get here. Sometimes, I'll be wandering along a trail and I'll suddenly come across myself. It's wonderful. There's room for everyone. You don't have competition. There will always be a place for your work. Someone somewhere will love it. And sometimes, it's God."

I hadn't even started thinking yet about what I would do with my own artwork. At home, before my son was born, it really was a consideration. I began to run out of walls. If you weren't a world famous artist with your work in demand, it just began to stack up. There was a spot down the basement in my house where my canvases lined the wall, several pieces deep, all facing in so I wouldn't see them every time I went down there to get out the Christmas supplies or anything else we kept in storage.

My work was in storage.

I was in storage.

Joyce said she felt abandoned. I felt like I abandoned my artwork when I stuck the canvases down in the basement, for years and years. But I abandoned myself too.

I looked at my bags. Not anymore, I thought. No more abandonment. "Thanks so much, Joyce," I said. "I'm sure I'll be seeing a lot of you."

"Great!" she said. "Maybe we'll end up in the same group sometime. But otherwise, give me a call and we can go out to coffee or dinner." She held up her phone and mine suddenly pinged. I looked; she was automatically added to my contact list.

So was someone named Joe. I clicked on his name and a photo came up. It was the barista from Caffeine Heaven. And his name was Joe! How appropriate.

I drove back home in LittleB and breathed a sigh of relief when I let myself in. I set out my new supplies like a doctor preparing for surgery. Starting with the finger paints, I scooped up handfuls, gobbing them on the canvas. I used my palms, my fingertips, my fingernails. Then I grabbed the putty knife and built heavy paint mountains and hills, and I sponged the areas around them and I jabbed with the bristles of the painful paintbrush. All of it in spirals. All of it in circles. Down and down and down.

Until I felt myself fall on the floor.

It was time to step away from the Gulf. It was sucking at me from the canvas, and I had to step away. I had to remember where I was. I had to remember that while I let the Gulf get me, while I dove down its throat that day by the river, I wasn't in the Gulf now.

I was here. In Heaven.

Without looking back, I staggered to my shower and I stood, clothes and all, under the streaming hot water. The body jets churned me like a washing machine and I eventually stripped and then held my hands to one of the jets, letting it pulse away all the colors. When I stepped out, I was pink again. Pink and tired.

After dressing in comfortable jeans and a t-shirt, I threw my sodden painting clothes into the washing machine. From there, I returned to my studio and cleaned up, washing my brushes, the putty knife, the sponges, all of it, in the utility sink that appeared while I was in the shower. There was a mop too, that magically got all the paint off the floor, dripped there from my fall and then my trip to the bathroom. I scrubbed and my floor returned.

I didn't look at the painting. Lifting the easel from behind, I brought it further into the studio. I closed the lanai doors. Then I went in search of supper.

It seemed tonight would be my first night of cooking.

• • •

I realized, when I stood in the middle of my kitchen, that I had no idea how to cook for one person. For years, it was me and my husband. Then it was me and my husband and our daughter. And for the last twelve years, me, my husband, my daughter, my son. My twelve-year old son, who, in the last year, became an eating machine and made me feel like I was cooking for eight.

And now, just me. I wondered what my family was having for supper. I wondered who cooked. My husband used to cook early on in our marriage, but since the kids, he was more of the pick-up take-out guy. My kids were great at putting frozen pizza into the oven, and in a pinch, my daughter could make spaghetti if there was a box of noodles and jar of sauce in the cupboard. She would likely throw hot dogs in it, in lieu of ground beef or meatballs or sausage. I taught her early on that hot dogs could be added to pretty much everything and make it a better meal. As far as I was concerned, despite being processed food, despite being made of who knows what, hot dogs were the perfect meal. I hoped my family was eating well. Well being relative, of course. I knew there were several packages of hot dogs in the fridge when I left, plus five frozen pizzas in the freezer, and I was relatively sure there was at least one box of spaghetti in the cupboard and several jars of sauce.

As I explored what was in my Heavenly fridge and my cupboards, I realized, once again, that God was a genius. Everything here was something I loved, and everything was magically repackaged into one-person size ingredients or staples.

And then I found it, the most unhealthy beloved meal of all time, something I created in middle school and still ate when I was home alone, the kids in school, my husband away, and I could sit and slurp in peace. And I found yet another reason to celebrate being in Heaven.

No longer was any food unhealthy. There was nothing that could kill us. We were already dead.

And so I pulled down the shiny cellophane package of chili-flavored ramen noodle soup, the type sold for ten dollars for ten packages in the grocery store. When I looked in the deli drawer of the fridge, the hot dogs were there, not one package, but seven, and they weren't single-sized at all, because hot dogs didn't need to be. Tucked beside them was a package of string cheese.

I whooped.

Two cups of water brought to a boil in seconds on Heaven's stovetop. Noodles dropped in, then flavor packet added. While it simmered, I sliced two hot dogs into neat little circles, then threw them into the pot. And then, when it was all heated through, I added it to a lovely soup bowl, just the right size. On top, I stringed the cheese into a latticework fit for an apple pie. And I let it melt.

All alone in my condo, I slurped my soup, sucked and chewed the noodles, the cheese, the hot dogs, and I reveled without giving a damn about cholesterol or heart disease, cancer or even the dial on the scale. It's amazing how much more enjoyable food is without those worries weighing down your tastebuds and your hips. I half-expected God to show up with a bowl of his own, but he stayed away and I was okay with that. I wasn't lonely at all. In my new kitchen, sitting in a banquette that reminded me of all the divey diners in my life, in my new condo, in my new world, I found I wasn't lonely. I missed my family. But I wasn't lonely.

It was weird. But it was true.

I was tired. My muscles ached from painting. The stretch, the reach, the bend, even the tapping fingers while waiting for the next move to arise into my brain, all taxed me and left me limp, body and soul. After dinner, I found a box of drumstick ice cream cones in the freezer and ate two, enjoying especially the hunk of solid chocolate stuffed into the pointy end of the waffle cone, and then I switched my paint clothes to the dryer. They looked restored to the condition I found them in. I deliberately avoided my studio.

I would face the painting, face what I'd done, tomorrow. Instead, I took another shower, then prepared for bed. Looking out my huge floor to ceiling windows, and through my open French doors, I watched the stars until my eyes wouldn't stay open any longer. I remembered how my mother always said the stars were "in the heavens." I wondered how she knew.

It was at 3:00 in the morning that I discovered the mirror when I staggered to the bathroom, half-awake. Apparently, middle-of-the-night bathroom breaks were still around in Heaven too, but I did have plenty of soup for supper, along with several glasses of water, a cup of coffee after dinner, hot chocolate right before bed. Off to the side of my vanity, in a place where I wouldn't expect to find a mirror, was exactly that. It was about two feet tall and oval and gold. When I had the involuntary thought that I was not a fan of gold, it changed to a lovely aged silver.

The portal. It had to be the portal.

I dried my hands, then stepped to it. Keeping one hand on the vanity counter to steady myself, I looked into the mirror. My face appeared there first, looking worried and apprehensive. And then I saw my daughter.

She was sleeping. Curled on her side, facing me, her hair looked unwashed and oily, spread behind her on the pillow. Her sheets and blankets were twisted around her waist and legs and one foot stuck out. I thought it looked cold and I longed to cover it. In the light from the moon, I thought I detected tear tracks going down her cheeks and I hoped it was my imagination.

Next to her on her bedside table was the same book that was on my own. My copy of *Daddles.* That same copy was here with me too and I didn't for a minute question how. Instead, I was so glad she had it. So glad it was next to her. So glad she had something that was so important to me.

My daughter said, "Well, of course," when she learned about my death. Well, of course. What else could she say?

I wanted to sit beside her on the bed. With that thought, it seemed like her face relaxed a little. I watched her fingers unfurl.

Then the view changed to my son's room. It was empty, the bed still made, and I wanted to yank the sides of the mirror apart, until it was big enough for me to climb through it like a porthole. Where was he? I couldn't imagine that he was at a sleepover. Not now, not so soon after...well, me.

My view changed to my bedroom and there was my husband, asleep on his side of the bed. On my side, there was my son. He faced his father, and his father faced him, and in the blank space between their two pillows, or actually, my husband's pillow and my own, their hands were clasped. My twelve-year old son, too old to kiss me goodbye in the morning before school, to kiss me goodnight before bed, who wouldn't even let me go with him to shop for clothes, was holding hands with his father.

But they were sleeping. Oh, thank God, they were all sleeping.

But then I noticed my husband's eyes were open. He was looking directly at my son. He blinked so very slowly. And every time he did, new tears fell.

I gasped, stepped backwards, then ran to my bedroom. Sitting on the edge of the bed, I couldn't work up the energy to lay down, to lift my legs and tuck them under the covers. And then the bed sank and God sat next to me.

He wore pajamas. Blue flannel, and despite the darkness, I could tell they were a beautiful blue. The blue of the ocean, plaided with the sun-shot blue of a spring sky. He was barefoot and his hair was rumpled.

I never knew God slept. I certainly never expected him to wear pajamas or have rumpled hair. But if he looked like the God I always imagined, the God with long white hair and a beard and a mustache and a serious, serious face, I never would have been able to rest my head on his shoulder, like I was able to do now.

I was very glad he wore blue flannel pajamas.

"You knew you couldn't expect them to be happy, right, Hope? You knew that," he said, and wrapped his arm around me. "It was part of your choice to end your life."

I turned my face into his chest and wept.

It had been my choice. I didn't expect them to be happy.

But I never thought I would witness their sadness.

For the first time, I regretted Heaven. I wished for the black void that I thought death might be, that day that I swallowed each pill with a gulp of wine.

"It'll be okay, Hope," God said. Not a booming voice from a burning bush or a dark cloud. A soft voice that soothed me as I cried.

• • •

I didn't remember God leaving. I woke the next morning, and I was under the covers in my bed, Teddy by my side, and the sun streaming in like a cliché. I glanced at my clock and saw it was already eleven. I slept in. I hadn't set an alarm yet in Heaven, but this was the first day that I slept past seven, the time I usually got up to make sure the kids were off to school. Except for the days that I couldn't get up at all, and there was no time, and my room remained dark.

So I rolled over now and fell back asleep for another hour. The exhaustion just pulled at me. This exhaustion was so familiar, but I hadn't felt it since the day I died. That day, I didn't roll over, but forced myself up and out of my dark room and did what I had to do. I found myself thinking that horrible phrase chirped by righteously busy people: "There's time enough to sleep when you're dead."

And now I was. So I could sleep. I wondered if those same busy people were able to sleep here.

On this day, this Heavenly day, when I finally got up, I followed my morning ablutions, as God called them. But I studiously avoided looking toward the wall in my bathroom where the portal hung. One fast glance assured me that I hadn't dreamt it, it was really there, and so then I just looked the other way. Just the way I treated my painting last night, when it was done.

I wondered if, in Heaven, you could look away forever. I thought of what God, and Faith, and Virginia said about the truth. I thought I welcomed truth. Now I wasn't so sure. That portal was full of the truth.

As I dressed, my right arm felt heavy and I bemoaned the loss of my artist muscles, located in my shoulder, my upper arm, even my wrist. But they would come back, with practice. I made my bed, settled Teddy in the center of the pillows, and then walked out to the kitchen. I couldn't stand the thought of lunch, even though it was going on one o'clock. Lunch should never be the first meal of the day. I found hot coffee already made in the coffeepot; I never had to set the timer, this pot just seemed to know when caffeine would be necessary. I poured a cup, buttered another fresh-baked butter rum muffin, which was exactly what I wanted to reach for that morning, warmed it just a bit in the microwave, and then went out to sit on the deck and enjoy my very late breakfast.

The temperature was perfect and I basked, trying to keep the guilt over what I saw in the portal at bay. My husband's eyes, his clasped hand with my son's, my daughter's stringy, dirty hair that she always insisted on washing every single day...they all kept popping up and I kept pushing them away, instead looking at trees, the sun glinting off other windows, listening to birds, tasting, tasting, tasting fine bakery and even better coffee.

But those little pops of homeward glances were still there.

When there was a knock at my door, I just yelled to come in. I didn't remember if I locked the door the night before, and I wondered if it really mattered. Sure enough, I heard the door open and then Faith joined me on the deck. "Oh!" she said, looking at my plate. "That looks good! Is there one for me?"

"Look and see." I waved my hand, though really not energetically enough to call it a wave. "Get some coffee, and could you refill my mug too?"

She came back with a plate filled with muffins and the coffee in a carafe. I didn't even know I had a carafe. She settled in the rocker to my right, a yellow one which suddenly appeared and I supposed it was to keep God's chair, on my left, God's. She said, "So I heard you had kind of a rough night."

I nodded. "The portal showed up. I thought I wanted it. But I don't." I closed my eyes for a minute and put into motion what I thought of now as Heaven magic: I imagined that particular wall in my bathroom as blank. Or not blank, maybe with a nice wall hanging. Years ago, in college, I took a metal sculpture class and I made a bright silver lizard. He could hang on the wall and look like he was crawling up it. I pictured that, opened my eyes, sat back and sighed.

Faith placed another muffin on my plate and she shook her head. "You can't wish the portal away, Hope. Once it's there, it's there for good. They come standard in everyone's homes everywhere, not just in our community. You can't take it down. You can't imagine it away."

"What?" I brought my rocking chair to a halt. I looked at everything around me and thought of everything that wasn't there when I first arrived, the deck that appeared when I thought of it, the French doors, the art studio, my own artwork on the walls, my book on my bedside table, my clothes in the closet, and even hot dogs in my fridge. "But isn't this place supposed to be mine? All mine, all my choice? There hasn't been anything here yet that I haven't wanted, that I haven't appreciated." I stretched both arms out toward the town below. "Even out there, there's an ocean, or a mountain, or a forest if I want to go to them. There's a coffee shop and an art supply store. There is everything I could possibly want! My gosh, my car is here!"

"That's right." Faith held her mug between both of her hands. I noticed her knuckles were white. "But there's also what you have to see. What you have to accept. The truth. The consequences of your actions."

"No!" I ran off the deck and down the hallway to my en suite bathroom. The portal was there and the only face in it was mine. I grabbed it in both hands and yanked. It didn't move. I tried twisting and it was like it was a part of the wall. It didn't even shift an inch. I slammed both of my fists into the glass. It didn't shatter.

Faith stood in the doorway. "Hope, it's permanent. It won't go away."

I stared at the mirror. My reflection blurred, then cleared into my kitchen at home and my daughter standing by the table. The surface was a wreck of breakfast cereal and milk, as if they were having a late breakfast too, and she'd knocked over boxes and bowls. My daughter didn't do things like that. She put things away, especially when I couldn't find the strength to. But here, she shrieked, "I don't want to go to school, Dad! I can't! It's too soon!"

My husband sat in his chair, at the head of the table, directly across from mine which was now and forever empty. His face rested in his hands. He shook his head slowly, almost to the point I thought I was imagining it. I wondered where my son was. Did he create the mess on the table?

"Come on," Faith said and she grabbed my hand. "You painted yesterday, let's go see what you did."

I followed her down the hall to the studio. When we entered, she gasped. "Ohmygosh, Hope. This is stunning." She looked around the room as it glistened in the mid-afternoon light.

My easel was set up just inside the lanai doors, where I left it. Stepping beyond it without looking at the canvas perched there, I opened the doors and once again joined the inside with the outside. "I think it's amazing," I said. "Having my own room, my own art studio, is just the most wonderful thing. I could do without everything else in Heaven, everything, even LeB, or the ocean, if it meant I could have this room." I looked out, admiring the remaining greens of summer, the hints of fall in the trees. Fall was always my favorite time of year. The oranges, the reds. The pumpkins. "This makes me wonder what would have happened if I was just able to keep my own space when my son was born. What if I'd had a studio? There was room. I could even have used the dining room. We never used the dining room." This studio was so amazing. The portal, so awful. The contrast, I thought, was stunning. How could both exist in one place, and that place was called Heaven?

I heard Faith's footsteps, and when they stopped, I knew she was in front of the easel. I heard her gasp again, but this time, it was different. The gasp upon entering the room was fast, a giggle of a breath. Here, she drew her air in slowly. When she let it back out, I swear I felt every last bit of it leave her lungs.

"Hope," she said, her voice soft. "Come look. Come look at what you did."

I didn't want to. I remembered the way it brought me to my knees, the way I had to bring it in from the outside without facing it, sneaking it into the room like it was a secret. But I did create it. I worked hard at it. And so I needed to take ownership of it. I looked at the floor as I walked around. When I was next to Faith, I raised my eyes slowly, taking in the canvas from the bottom up.

And there it was. The Gulf.

The purple. *That* purple. I had no idea how I even created it. It wasn't the purple of a horrendous bruise, but it was. It was and more. The depth it conveyed threatened to come right off the canvas. The swirl was there, the sucking down, I could hear the sound. I saw the flashes of color, phosphenes of future torture and the promise of pain to come. It would come and it would never stop. It was all there. And I felt it reaching for me.

It was my turn to gasp, in a desperate attempt to get my air back.

Faith grabbed me and brought me to the couch. She sat beside me, and then God showed up too. They both wrapped their arms around me, Faith's arm snaking around my waist, God's around my shoulders. I felt squashed, but it was the best ever squash. We all looked at the Gulf, which really seemed to take on a life of its own on the canvas.

"Holy cow, Hope," God said. "It does look like what was on the blanket at the ocean, but it's even more. It's alive. I can just feel the dragging."

"Me too," said Faith. "I can't take my eyes away."

When both Faith and I gasped for air, God got up and crossed to the canvas. He turned it around, so all we could see was the back. The purple was muted from behind, just a shadow, and suddenly, I could breathe again. I could see the sun and the room which was my own. I relaxed, leaning against the cushions.

God sat down again. "It's amazing, Hope. My gosh. Imagine what you could have done, if you'd only just kept painting."

That made me feel so unbearably sad. I covered my face with my hands and sobbed. "I just didn't have any space. There was just...nothing. There was this room for my son. That room for my daughter. This room for my husband and me. His workspace in the basement for him. The other rooms for all of us. There was nothing, nothing of just me. Of who I was." I swallowed. "Of how I kept myself alive." I thought of my high school art teacher.

"Always paint. It helps. Whether you end up with a show in the Guggenheim or only in your living room, always paint."

"I didn't," I said out loud, trusting that they likely heard my thoughts. "I stopped when I had my son. And I never asked to have that part of myself back. It seemed so selfish. Once I was a mother, I knew I was supposed to put my children first. Always. They were to be enough for me, they were to be all of me, and the thing is, they were. They are. But I was still missing. Everything I had around me, my home, my husband, and my kids, especially my kids, that was supposed to be who I was." I looked at the backside of my canvas, the purple leeching through, not looking nearly as dangerous from here, but I knew that danger could lurk in the barely seen and the unseen. "But it wasn't who I was. How could it be that my kids weren't enough to make me happy? How could it be that I wasn't willing to give everything up for them? I was willing, when they were first born. They were my world. But then the rest of my world, what was my world before kids, began spinning in too. Late at night. During lunch, when I was on break at work. Weekends, when the kids were out doing things with their friends and my husband was doing something in the basement. But there was no place to go, no place that was *me*. No place where I could leave my stuff out, leave a canvas half-painted, any place I would try to paint, I had to pack myself up when I was done for the day. It felt so impermanent, like I was an afterthought. If I did something on my own, it was taking away from my family, even taking up space that was theirs. What kind of monster doesn't live for her kids?"

I heard Faith quietly sobbing. I thought of her daughter, left behind with her grandparents, while Faith took her own life to lead her abusive husband down the wrong path forever.

Faith wasn't a monster. But me?

God rubbed my back. "And that's part of the Gulf. You sunk in even deeper, when you had children and gave up yourself."

I leaned back, tilting my head and staring at the ceiling, letting the remainder of the tears roll down my cheeks. "But the Gulf has always been there. I felt it long before I had children. I felt it long before I could paint."

"Yes, it did come from somewhere, much earlier. But look, Hope." God sat me up and he pointed at the easel. "Look where it is. It's all contained there. In one spot. Not in you anymore. You got rid of it."

"I got rid of it when I decided to come here. When I drove to the river." The calm of that day. The purple roiling, but in an organized fashion, leading me down a clear path, that allowed me to gather what I needed, get in my car, and take one pill, one swallow, one pill, one swallow. Until it was all gone. Until I was all gone.

"Yes, Hope." This was Faith now, and her voice was soft and full of the tears she must have shed over her lifetime. "That was when you stepped away from it. Out of it. And shook your feet free."

I sat up and stared at the back of the canvas. I knew what was on the front. But it was different now. It was separate. I thought of what I felt the night before, when I first stared into the portal. What I felt when I saw my daughter screaming a few minutes ago, when I saw my husband shaking his head impossibly slowly. "But isn't the Gulf still here? Isn't it coming back? The portal—"

"No." God put his hand on my cheek and turned my face toward him. "That's not the Gulf, Hope. That's grief. Actually, Grief, with a capital G."

I ran my mind over that thought, the way my tongue would run over my lips after a bite of that butter rum muffin. Grief. With a capital G. It tasted bitter.

With my face turned toward God, I couldn't see Faith, but I felt her hand rest on my shoulder. "You're grieving the loss of your own life, Hope. And you have to grieve what your family is going through. Because of you. Because of what you did."

"You have to accept it," God said.

What I did. Accept it.

The shock crashed through my body like my God-given whale returning to the water. I had to see what I did. I had to accept my part in what my family was going through. I had to accept my blame.

God shook his head. "No one here is blaming you. There isn't a single person here that wouldn't know and understand what you did. Your family is blaming you, that can't be denied. And you have to accept your responsibility for that. It's not saying that what you did wasn't right. It was, for you. But it wasn't, for others. You have to accept the responsibility for the consequences too."

I groaned with the enormity of it. I thought that maybe Heaven and Hell were the same place.

"There is no Hell, Hope," God said. "There is only here. Heaven. And in time, it really will be okay." He stood and went over to the canvas. "I want to take this and put it on display in one of our art galleries. I'll put it on limited viewing, only for certain times every day, and with a notice that it might hit people kind of hard. But at the same time, they need to see it. Some will call it a trigger. I personally can't stand that word; that certainly wasn't something I created. Facing something that makes a person feel this way helps that person to face it. To become familiar with it as something outside themselves that they can acknowledge and walk away from. You've created on that canvas exactly what brought everyone here. Do you think you can sign it, Hope? And should we call it The Gulf? Almost everyone here knows that you've coined that state of being."

I wondered at the necessity of people seeing the painting. Coming here got them away from the Gulf. Why should they be reminded of it? Familiarized to it?

"Because," God said, "it's easier to realize how far you've come when you can see what was after you to begin with."

I hesitated, and then nodded. This was God, after all. He had to know what was right. As God turned the canvas back around, I walked to my cabinet and got out a slender paintbrush and a tube of black acrylic. As I returned to the canvas, I kept my eyes on the lower right corner. Carefully, I scrolled my name. I remembered what Virginia said, and so I wrote *Hope Sanders.*

"Perfect," God said. He hugged me quickly, then picked up the canvas. "For now, you're required to look in the portal once, at most twice a day. Take it slow."

I chose once. Once a day, and only for a second.

After God left, Faith took me by the hand. "Come on. Let's go get a late lunch at Caffeine Heaven. We'll take my cart."

"Okay," I said. "I just want to grab some ibuprofen first."

I hadn't seen ibuprofen in the medicine cabinet in my bathroom. For that matter, I hadn't seen a medicine cabinet. But I knew it would be there now, because I needed it. I never would have expected it was possible to get a headache in Heaven.

But Faith laughed, and before I reached my bathroom, the headache was gone.

• • •

I covered the portal with a faux silk scarf I found in one of my dresser drawers. I remembered it; it was a birthday gift from my son when he was eight years old. It was a solid blue and he told me it reminded him of the sky. He thought I liked looking at the sky because whenever we stepped outside to drive here, there, and everywhere, I always looked up. And so, he said, I could always see the sky if I wore this scarf, even when I was stuck in the house. Even when it was cloudy outside.

It was a love my son and I shared. He would never close the blinds on his bedroom window, night or day. His desk sat under the window and I often found him there, his chin resting on his two fists, his eyes opened wide to the clouds. At night, he always lay on his left side, so he could see the stars. Just like I admired the stars now, from my new bed in Heaven.

I smiled when I found the scarf and then I draped it over the portal without actually looking into it. Once a day, I thought, I would lift the scarf, glance under, then lower it again. It would keep me from accidentally looking toward it.

The scarf didn't fall and a couple days passed, so I figured this arrangement must be okay with God.

Those glances were the hardest part of my day, and I hadn't yet found a routine time when I was most steeled to face them. I'd hear the edge of a shriek, the end of a sob. My husband staring into air, his face slack, or my daughter's face hidden behind her hands. My son's silence was so loud. I never heard him. I only saw the back of his head. He always seemed to be on the move somewhere. I wondered if he looked up whenever he went outside. I wondered if he still looked out his window. Was he looking for me, in the Heavens?

I'd lift the scarf, glance, then lower it. Every time, I thanked my son for his birthday gift. I really did like to look at the sky.

CHAPTER SIX

Hope

The day before I had to go to group therapy for my second session, I decided to clear my head by taking a walk. I'd been pondering what my next painting was going to be, and now that I had all the time in the world to do it, or all the time in Heaven, which was endless, and the best possible place to do it in, it was like my imagination choked. I made a few false starts, and these sad canvases leaned against a wall in my studio, waiting for inspiration to show me what to do with them. I felt guilty; I'd been given what I most wanted, and now I didn't know what to do with it.

A walk would help, I thought.

The slow wander felt good, and I loved Heaven's mix of clusters of small businesses, followed by a park or playground, then a more citified section. I knew that further out, but still within the gated community, there were even some farms. I decided to follow a cobblestone path through a park, and a few minutes in, I recognized someone from my group therapy group. It was the woman whose Gulf was named Allison. I stopped to watch her for a bit, unsure if I should approach her.

She was sitting at a picnic table under a tree, reading a book. She had a hand wrapped around a Coca Cola bottle, its distinct shape and color and red label visible and bold. I loved that whatever we wanted was here in Heaven, whether it was deemed good or bad for us on earth. If we liked it, it was good. I left the path and strolled, trying to look aimless, until I was in front of her. And at that moment, she took a sip of her Coke, her face uplifted, and she saw me.

"Hi," I said.

She smiled. "Hi. You're Hope, right?"

I nodded. "Yes, but I'm afraid I don't remember your name. I'm sorry; it was just my first time last week, and it was a little overwhelming."

"I get that. It can be overwhelming even now, and I've been here three years." She motioned toward the seat on my side of the picnic table. "I'm Beth."

I sat down. "Thanks."

She closed her book. "I saw your painting. The one you called The Gulf. It's up at the Wings And Things Gallery." She shook her head. "It's amazing, Hope." She looked a little rueful. "It could be a portrait of my daughter."

I startled. The Gulf wasn't supposed to be a person. "Your daughter?"

"Allison."

She told me the story of her daughter, of herself, her daughter's suicide, her own. She spoke of the guilt of being a mother who just simply couldn't find a way to help her daughter, and who had moved on from a passionate motherhood to just putting one foot in front of the other, trying to get through the day every day, and then her involuntary sense of relief after her daughter died in the most awful way possible. The way her body relaxed into the freedom of no longer being braced all the time. The way she found herself able to laugh, to smile, to read. "To breathe," she said. "I found myself able to breathe. And my daughter was dead. Had chosen to die." She shook her head. "I was such a terrible mother."

I shook my head with her. "No," I said. It was the simplest thing to say, the most truthful. And then my mind boggled a bit, at the logistics of the situation. "So Allison...is here?"

She nodded. The tears that fell steadily during her storytelling slowed, then stopped.

"Have you seen her?" I wondered if they would be allowed in group therapy together, if that would even be helpful.

"God doesn't make you interact with anyone if you don't want to, especially if that person is involved in your decision for suicide," Beth said. "Allison and I see each other, from a distance." Beth tilted her head to my left. "If you look in that direction, you'll see a young woman with blonde hair, sitting under a tree, reading a book, just like I'm reading a book. That's her. We get near each other. But not too close." She patted the book's cover. "We both love to read."

I looked, and there she was. Allison lifted her head and looked at me, as if she was aware we were talking about her. She held my gaze for a minute, but then returned to her book.

I knew I was still new here. And so it was normal that Heaven still surprised me, but sometimes, the way it surprised me also surprised me. A mother and a daughter, both in the same unique spot of Heaven, both here for the same reason, and neither one talking to the other.

"Do you miss her?" I asked Beth.

Her eyes misted, but didn't spill over. "I do. But...the quiet. I just need the quiet." She opened her book again. "God says I'm forgiven, and that there really wasn't anything to forgive me for. He says I'm not a terrible mother, just like you just did, but it's still hard to feel that way. And I know that here, in Heaven, my daughter is no longer a drug addict. The drama that was my daughter is different now. Maybe she's even returned to who she used to be. But..." She shook her head again and I got the feeling that she did this a lot. "I'm just not ready. I need the quiet."

I looked over at Allison again, and like before, she lifted her head and looked at me. "Do you know if she wants to talk to you?"

"God knows," Beth said. "But I've asked him not to tell me. Not until I'd be ready to say I want to see her. I just...need the time."

Even from here, I could see the grief that bloomed in Allison's face. It had been three years since their deaths. I wondered if she could hear what her mother was saying.

I looked back at Beth. "When you got here today, to read and enjoy your Coke, was Allison here already?" I thought maybe, even with her resistance, she still sought her daughter out.

But no. Beth shook her head. "She got here about fifteen minutes after I did."

There was such grief in Allison. And in Beth, such need. A need for quiet and a need for healing.

I stood up. "I hope it gets better, for both of you," I said. "I miss my daughter."

I walked away. There was sadness in Heaven. But God was right. It wasn't the Gulf.

It was Grief. Grief with a capital G.

Considering where I was, this wasn't a surprise at all.

• • •

On Wednesday, I climbed into LittleB and drove myself to the group therapy session. I felt sort of proud. I'd been here almost two weeks, and already, I could find my way around. Though it certainly helped that both LeB and LittleB came equipped with a GPS that understood anything I had to say. If I said to either one, "I kinda want to go to a restaurant that serves great chicken wings, but without being too hot, and that also has steak if I change my mind," they would get me there. But still, getting into LittleB and not having to ask for directions to group therapy made me feel remarkably in control. I knew that both the vehicles had the capability to drive me themselves, but I hadn't opted for that yet. Driving was just too much of a joy.

Inside the therapy room, I slid into the chair beside Faith and glanced around. Some people from last week were gone, and a couple were new. I remembered Faith telling me that the group was fluid. People stayed with a group for twelve weeks, and the count started on the day of their arrival. The group would always be changing. Someone who joined the group thirteen weeks ago would be in a new group today. If this was week twelve for someone, they'd be gone next week. And each week, there were new people coming in, whose time ended in another group, or who were newly arrived in Heaven.

Faith patted my knee. "I'm here with you for this week and next," she reminded me, because of course she knew what I was thinking about. "Then I move on." She laughed when she saw my face. "Don't worry, I'm still your mentor, and more than that, I'm your friend. I just will be in another group at that point, and who knows when we'll be in the same group again. Eventually, I hope I'm leading groups too."

I tried to smile. "You'd be a great leader, Faith. How does God pick the mentors and leaders?"

Faith started to answer, but then Virginia came in and sat down and so the group began to settle. "I'll tell you after," she whispered.

I sat quietly as Virginia gave the welcome and the quick explanation to the new folks. I wondered at how I wasn't a "new folk" anymore, and how quickly this became my life. Or whatever it was that I was supposed to call this existence now. I listened as the new people told their stories and relistened as the people I already knew re-introduced themselves. Then I was startled when Virginia turned and looked directly at me.

"Before we start going around the group, I just wanted to say that, Hope, that painting you did, The Gulf, is just incredible. How many of you have had a chance to see it? It's at the Wings and Things Gallery."

I looked around as more than half of the people in the room raised their hands, and some began to call out comments. Beth was still in this group and she nodded at me and smiled.

"It made me cry."

"I loved it, but I could only stand to look at it for about a minute."

"It's so true, Hope. So real. That was exactly how I felt."

A different woman than the one who confessed to tears began to cry now. "I thought it was really good, but I just couldn't...couldn't take it. I felt overpowered all over again."

I flinched. I couldn't help myself. I remembered wondering about the necessity of people seeing the Gulf when it was the Gulf they died to escape from.

Virginia leaned forward, addressing the sobbing woman. "It's okay, Annie. Just take a deep breath. And it's all right that you feel that way. I'm sure Hope understands that, and I know God does too, since that's why he put it up with such limited viewing times. But remember last week, when we said that Hope came up with just the best ever word for it? For the thing that had its hold on us when we were still alive? Now she's taken it beyond words. She's made it a tangible thing, something we can stare at, and even more importantly, stare *down* and then walk away. We can walk away from it."

A man named Bill folded his arms and said, "I thought I did that when I came here. I walked away."

Faith nodded. "We all did. But Hope's painting shows us just what we walked away from. It makes it real and separate. Not a part of us. Not forever inside of us."

Everyone fell silent for a few breaths. Then one of the newbies said in the softest, saddest voice, "I'd like to see it, I think. Yes, I would. But I don't know how to find it."

Her mentor, sitting beside her, like Faith sat beside me, promised her that they'd go to see it the next day. I wondered if the GPS in her golf cart would take her if she asked it, "Can you take me to see The Gulf please?" Was my painting a location now?

It felt good, actually, having it tucked inside of four walls, outside of my own home. It wasn't in me anymore either. And it wasn't just on the canvas. It was someplace else. I could walk in. I could walk out. Just like all of these people could.

Maybe I would go see it too.

It was then I noticed the boy sitting three chairs away from me. It was movement that caught my eye. He was swinging his legs, because his feet didn't meet the ground. He was a *boy*. He couldn't have been more than ten years old. Of its own accord, I felt my jaw drop. He didn't introduce himself with the newly arrived to Heaven, so he wasn't brand new, but I didn't remember seeing him last week. Maybe this was his week to switch, and he was only new to this group.

As if he felt me staring at him, he turned to look at me. "It wasn't the right color," he said. "My Gulf was red."

His voice piped. It was a shock in that room of mature tones, gravelly and deep and sometimes soft, other times loud. His voice was young. Just young.

I remembered my son sounding like that. Now he was twelve, and his voice was a conundrum of old and young and somewhere in between. There were cracks and squeaks and the sounds of his father and sometimes I heard the toddler he used to be.

What was this boy doing here?

Virginia pulled the attention back away from my painting, after giving me one more smile. Then she started around the group, asking if we had any moments of difficulty this week. I listened as people talked about impromptu memories, brought up by a scent or a glimpse or a taste. There were birthdays and missed birthdays, anniversaries and missed anniversaries, and a new word for me, deathaversaries. "It's my thirtieth deathaversary," a woman said. "I took my life thirty years ago today."

I watched as she smiled. I wondered how long it would be before I would smile at my deathaversary. Before I saw it as a day to celebrate.

When it was my turn, I talked about receiving my portal. "I thought I wanted it," I said. "I thought I wanted to see my family, make sure they're all okay. But what I saw, and what I've seen since..." I stopped, cleared my throat. "I don't want to see anymore. But God says I have to."

Virginia nodded. "We all have portals, Hope. You haven't even been here for two weeks yet. Your family is in full grief, I expect."

"Yes. My husband. And my daughter and son. They're fourteen and twelve." I couldn't stop the tears, so I didn't. "I didn't think I would see this. See them. And I can't do anything to help."

"Well, no," another person said. "Because you're the one who did this to them."

I gasped.

"We all are," someone else said quickly. "I left my family six years ago. They're doing pretty okay. My son...well, he still has some issues. He's ten years old now. He's the one who found me. I shot myself in the garage."

Ten minus six. His son was four years old then. Four! I looked at this man and our eyes met. I admit it, the first thought that came to my mind was, *How could you? How could you do that?*

But how could I? My son was twelve. Only eight years older than this man's son when he died. Granted, my son didn't find me.

Did he?

Who found me? Who identified me?

The blame I directed toward this man drifted away like a dandelion wish. It floated toward me.

"Hope," Virginia said, leaning forward. "God told you to take it slow? To just look in the portal once or twice a day?"

I nodded. I wondered what would happen if I didn't. Would the sky scarf disappear? Would I be in the middle of something and suddenly find myself in front of the portal, unable to move? Unable to look away?

"Yes," Faith whispered.

"Just do what God told you," Virginia said. "It will get easier. And the day will come when the portal will let you see something that you would have otherwise missed, and you'll be happy it's there."

Right then, I couldn't believe that this would ever be. Showing me what I would have missed? More like showing me what I didn't deserve to see.

We moved on and I listened to others. I didn't join in much; I didn't feel qualified. I hadn't been there that long. I might know how to use the GPS, but I still didn't know the lay of the land. Certainly not the lay of Heaven's land, and definitely not the lay of the paths into people's minds and reasons for doing what they did. I couldn't even say why I did it, other than to get away from the Gulf.

Then one woman, who introduced herself as Madeline, said, "I was watching my daughter in the portal a few days ago." She sighed and smiled and shook her head. "It's hard to believe she's thirty now. She was fifteen when I left. But she was reading something off a computer screen to her husband. It was an article on how treatment for breast cancer has improved so much in the last ten years. How more women are surviving, and while it's still hard, women are suffering less. Treatment is taking less time. There are less drastic surgeries, more targeted radiation, and chemo...well, chemo is still bad. But my daughter said, 'I wish Mom was here for this.'" Madeline took a deep breath and I could hear the tears in her inhale. "I found myself wishing I was too."

After the session, LittleB and I putted behind Faith and her cart to Caffeine Heaven. I was sure there were other coffee shops around, but I was always one for routine and continuity, so I stuck with Caffeine Heaven. Joe was amazing at producing every single latte I'd ever enjoyed, as long as I could remember the name and the place. After I saw Beth in the park, I went to the coffee shop for a latte. I really wanted a specific one, but couldn't remember the location of the coffee shop. We dug through my memories until I found enough of a road map that Joe was able to search through his vast God-given Google mind and find what I was looking for. Another day, I felt adventurous and just said, "Give me the house latte from a coffee shop in a town in the dead center of Maryland." Joe found one. It was amazing. I was able to be more adventurous than I'd been in life, but surround myself with familiarity too.

Today, we got there just as Joe reopened after the therapy sessions. I needed an extra boost of the familiar, so I ordered a grande Starbucks toffee nut latte, with just two pumps of toffee nut syrup and whip. I decided to have it extra hot and in a for-here mug, so I could clasp the warm ceramic between my palms.

He smiled at me. "Tough session?"

I shrugged. "It was only my second. I don't really have anything to compare it to yet."

"Your second? Then yes. Tough session. It will be that way for a while." He increased the size of my drink and threw in a cheese danish. "On the house," he said.

I laughed. Everything was on the house in Heaven.

Faith and I sat out back, in what was quickly becoming "our" table, or "my" table when I was alone. I already had a corner by one of the fireplaces, a cozy spot with two comfy chairs and a table between them, pegged for when it grew colder. For a second, we were quiet, listening to the soft drone of after-session chatter and the songs of birds. A breeze ruffled the leaves on the trees and the few that were on the ground. In session, Faith had talked about seeing my painting in person for the first time, how it affected her, and how she went back to her own home and watched her daughter for a few hours. She worried sometimes, she said, that her daughter had a Gulf of her own.

I hadn't worried about that, when I was alive. But now...I worried. Faith's Gulf was created by an abusive man. But mine had been with me for my whole life. What if it was something within me, something genetic? What if my children inherited it, and my suicide triggered it? God hated that word, but what if I'd set my children off?

"That woman who talked about breast cancer," I said. "Why is she here? Didn't the cancer kill her? That's not suicide. Or did she decide to end it before the cancer got that bad?"

Faith sat back. "She's an interesting case. She did die of breast cancer. But she died by choice – she refused treatment. She let herself die, even though there was the possibility of survival."

I considered that. "But is that really suicide? If she wanted to die, why didn't she just end it right then and there? Why wait? Suicide isn't a gradual thing."

Faith looked at me. "How long did you think about it before you did it?"

I took a deep breath, then nodded. This truth thing stung sometimes.

"Well, like I said, Madeline is an interesting case. It was her third bout with breast cancer. She went from a lumpectomy to a double mastectomy, and then it showed up in her bones." Faith shook her head. "Madeline was in massive pain and treatment would have added more pain to what was already intolerable. She wanted it to be over, but she didn't want her family to bear the brunt of her suicide, or to blame her. So she decided, against medical advice, to do nothing. She let the cancer kill her, so she could die, but without doing something outward. She didn't tell her family there were options. She didn't know the doctor would tell them later, after her death."

I sat back, incredulous. "And God considered that a suicide?"

Faith nodded. "Madeline herself calls it a suicide. She chose not to live, and she chose cancer as her weapon. That guy in group today shot himself in his garage. You chose pills and alcohol. I hung myself from a tree in the middle of a forest in Wyoming. There's really no difference, except her suicide came from the inside out."

"Wow."

The coffee shop was packed. Apparently, caffeine was the drug of choice after therapy.

"So tell me about how God picks mentors and leaders," I said. "You told me you'd fill me in."

Faith laughed. "That's easy. I don't know. Nobody knows!"

"What?" I gaped at her.

"It's the old 'God works in mysterious ways' thing. We don't know. If you lined up a group of 20 mentors all in a row and interviewed them, there wouldn't be enough in common for you to say, 'That's it! That's how he chooses!' He just does."

I thought of Virginia. "So when do the leaders go to group therapy? You said we have to be in it forever. How can they be, if they're leading groups?"

Faith took a sip. "They lead for thirty-six weeks, then they're back in a group for twelve weeks. So they're in therapy less than the rest of us, but I'm sure leading it feels like being in therapy too."

What a complex system. But God figured it out, so it must work.

Shortly after, we went our separate ways. It wasn't until I was at home, contemplating what to have for dinner, that I realized I didn't ask about the boy who saw his Gulf as red.

What was a boy that age doing in the suicide section of Heaven?

CHAPTER SEVEN

Found

Madeline's Story

Madeline set her cell phone on her desk. Years ago, when her first breast cancer diagnosis came over the phone, she'd dropped the receiver and the cord caught it before it hit the floor. It dangled there, strung up like an animal in a rope trap, and her doctor's disembodied voice called out, "Maddie? Are you there? Maddie? Did you hear me?"

She did. A month later, she had what was called a partial mastectomy, and she lost an ice cream scoop-size portion of her right breast.

The next time the bad news came, Madeline was on a cordless phone. She slammed it into the cradle, and then, for good measure, she picked it up again and threw it against a wall. There was no cord to rescue it and it fell to the floor, its battery case cracking open and batteries rolled across the floor like severed organs.

Like her breasts. She lost the rest of her right and all of her left that time, and many of her lymph nodes as well.

And now, the cell phone.

Her doctor said the cancer spread to Madeline's bones. *Breast* cancer in her *bones*. She talked about treatment options. More surgery. Radiation. Chemo, lots of chemo. And then she said, "I'm so, so sorry, Maddie."

Madeline didn't answer, but she hit the red spot on her phone's screen that allowed her to hang it up. It was remarkably unsatisfactory. She thought about throwing the phone like she had the last one, but this was an expensive device and financial respect caused her to set it gently down.

How in the world did breast cancer get into bones? It belonged in breasts. She didn't have breasts anymore. She hadn't had them in years. So how could it be in her bones?

Her doctor said that a single cancer cell could have drifted during the double mastectomy or even the first partial mastectomy, wandered down her body, and settled at the base of her spine. And then sat there, dormant, sleeping, all this time. All this time that she felt good. That she felt she was cured. That she thought cancer was gone out of her life forever and she'd never again see a surgeon smiling at her before she was put under, she'd never again lie strapped and still under the radiation machine as everyone else ran from the room to avoid what was being done to her, she'd never again be hitched up to IVs and watch as poison flowed into her veins through a special port that stayed in her chest for months and flooded her body and nobody stopped it. That's what she thought.

But the cancer was sleeping. Peacefully tucked way down deep at the base of her spine. She carried it with her all these years. Her doctor said it woke up and it began to run, producing more cells behind it like the dust behind sneakers pounding on a gravel road.

Madeline thought she just had a backache. Arthritis, maybe. Caused by her getting older, which she was able to do because she'd beaten breast cancer. Twice.

What was that phrase? That cliché? *Third time's the charm.*

She looked at her phone, the screen black, as it slept, just like the cancer did, waiting to be awakened.

Financial respect be damned. She picked up the phone and threw it against the wall. It shattered.

• • •

When her husband walked in that night, home from work, he immediately looked at her face, wet with steam and tears she thought were hidden, as she stirred a pot boiling with spaghetti. He set down his briefcase. "You heard, didn't you," he said, not asking a question. "And you didn't call me."

She kept her eyes on the rolling noodles. "I thought it was better if we were all together when we talked about it. Emma will be home from practice in about fifteen minutes. We'll eat, then we'll talk. Okay? Please?"

Her husband took off his coat and carefully hung it on the row of hooks by the garage door. Then he came behind her, wrapped his arms around her waist as he had for twenty years of marriage and four years of dating, and two cancer treatments and the removal of her breasts and innumerable cancer scares, and he rested his head on her shoulder. Then he sobbed.

Madeline allowed her tears to mix more obviously with the steam. She thought about telling her husband that there was still a treatment option, this third time, this charmed time, this time when it wasn't in her breasts, but her bones.

But she didn't say a word. She just kept stirring the noodles. Eventually, he went to change into everyday clothes and she prepared the sauce. By the time their daughter came home, Madeline's face was dry. She told Emma to wash up and then she put dinner on the table.

As they ate, Madeline avoided looking at her husband. She kept the conversation light, talking about Emma's day at school, her classes, what her friends were up to, how basketball practice went. She marveled with her husband over their daughter's height, her leanness, the mean strength of her body. She had next to no breasts, due to her athleticism. And her bones were strong.

Madeline took a couple bites to hide the fact that she was praying for the continued health of her daughter's tiny breasts and solid bones. *Please, God, please. Don't let her be like me.*

They were finishing up their dessert, a surprise treat of ice cream with chocolate syrup, when Madeline set down her spoon. "So, we do have something we need to talk about."

Her husband and daughter put down their spoons too. Emma, sounding eerily like her father, said, "You heard, didn't you."

Madeline nodded. "It's back. And this time, it's in my bones. It started at the base of my spine, apparently, and then spread up and out. That's why I've been having the backaches. But it's likely other places too. The MRI showed that it's pretty widespread."

"So what exactly did the doctor say?" her husband asked. He'd reached out and held their daughter's hand. Emma's free hand was fisted.

Madeline looked at them both. "She said she's so, so sorry."

Emma pulled herself free from her father and wrapped herself around Madeline's shoulders. Madeline felt the shudders she'd known for fifteen years, her daughter's body growing in mass and strength, the shudders that used to only shake Madelyn's arms, where she cradled her baby, and now they made her whole body tremble in sync. Her husband put his face in his hands.

Madeline stared straight ahead. It's not lying, she thought. I'm not lying. That *is* what my doctor said. It's just not all that she said.

She didn't want to say anything more just then. Not yet. She needed time to think.

• • •

After the sound of pacing from her daughter's room faded away, and when her husband finally fell asleep after sad and careful lovemaking, Madeline slid out of bed. There was a bay window seat in their living room, and Madeline loved it and often sat there on nights when chemo left her too sick to sleep or the surgeries left her in too much pain or if she was simply too scared or worried to shut her eyes. She sat there on good nights too, admiring the moon, the new snow, the budding daffodils, the every-now-and-then deer. On the bad nights, she would look at all this and whisper, "Please, please, please," over and over. On the good nights, she whispered, "Thank you."

Tonight, she said nothing. She looked and she considered.

She wasn't sure if she could take any more of this. The pain of illness followed by the pain of treatment followed by the pain of recovery followed by the pain of failure when cancer just came back again, like her whispers of gratitude and her whispers for mercy. She didn't know if she could do this again.

She thought about her options. It seemed like there were only two.

Treatment. Again. At the hands of surgeons and radiation oncologists and medical oncologists.

Or end it now. On her own. Under her own terms and under her own hands.

And she wondered, if she chose that second option, would God even listen to her anymore? Would He listen to her "Please, please, please," or her "Thank you"?

Did God put the cancer in her? Again? Did He send it on its way quietly down her body, allow it to nestle in peace in its cradle, rocking for years on the curve of her hips? Did He wake it, put it in motion? Is that how breast cancer ended up in bones, of all places?

Getting up, she first went to the medicine cabinet and cataloged the many bottles. She wandered to the kitchen and studied the knife block. Glancing at her wrists, she doubted that it would take much. The garage was her next stop and she sat in her car, wondering how air-tight the windows were, wondering if air escaped where the automatic garage door touched the driveway, and she thought about turning the key in the ignition.

And then she thought about who would find her. How they would find her. Her fifteen-year old daughter whose shudders vibrated Madeline's whole body, whose pacing shuffled through the shared wall of their bedrooms. Her husband, who put his face on Madeline's shoulder and cried.

Emma was four when cancer struck the first time and removed part of Madeline's breast. She and her husband decided then that there would be no more children. Madeline was disconcerted by the fact that she'd fed her daughter for the first year of her life from a place in her body which would become so, so sick. She couldn't knowingly feed another child from a breast that held disease. And quietly, she whispered to her husband, "What if I'm pregnant and it comes back?" So no more children.

For that matter, six years later, there were no more breasts.

Six years later, Madeline saw the way ten-year old Emma snuck sideways glances at her mother's newly flat chest, as flat as Emma's own. She never cried in front of Madeline, but Madeline heard the sobs through their shared wall in the bedrooms. One night, Madeline went in to her daughter's room and she held Emma on her lap, despite her ten years, and they rocked for an hour or more. Emma was already tall; in her mother's lap, her bare feet touched the floor.

She thought of Emma finding her now, if she chose to dig into the medicine cabinet or climb in the bathtub with a knife from the kitchen or turn the ignition on her car. And she thought of Emma watching her again, if she chose to go through treatment. What would Madeline lose this time? Her hair again, for sure. But what else? How could bones be carved out of her body? If random cells wandered then, where would they go now? How long would they sleep? Would they travel to her brain? To her heart? Could you get cancer in your heart?

She returned to the bay window and watched the moonshine slide across her yard. She would buy a new cell phone tomorrow and she would call her doctor back. She would make an appointment and they could talk.

Then she would consider her options again. She needed to know more, even if she didn't want to hear it.

• • •

The first number Madeline called as she stepped out of the cell phone store was her doctor's office. When she asked for the next available appointment, the receptionist said, "Actually, we have an opening in an hour. Dr. Franklin was hoping you'd call back today and she saved a spot for you, in case you did."

Madeline was both flattered and worried by this. She loved that her doctor thought enough of her and cared enough for her that she saved an appointment. She also worried that the doctor thought it was so necessary for her to come in right away. But then, on the phone yesterday, Dr. Franklin said she was so, so sorry. Just what did Madeline expect?

Madeline stopped for lunch even though she wasn't hungry and then she went in to the clinic. The nurse patted Madeline's shoulder and skipped all of the preliminaries, the weight, the blood pressure, the questions, instead leading her into an office. Madeline settled in a chair and only had to wait a few minutes before Dr. Franklin walked in.

"I'm so glad you're here," she said. "I tried calling you back yesterday, but –"

Madeline held up her new phone. "I threw my phone across the room. It broke. I'm sorry." She tried to smile, at least just a bit. "This little side effect of the new diagnosis cost me a bundle."

Dr. Franklin stretched across her desk, offering her hands. Madeline took them. "Maddie, this is bad. I won't sugarcoat it. But it's not hopeless. We can treat this."

Madeline nodded and then sat and listened as, first, Dr. Franklin talked about surgery, more than one, actually, surgeries. The cancer weakened several places in her spine, and already, there were fractures that needed to be repaired or Madeline would soon be unable to walk. Dr. Franklin talked about something called spinal cement and suddenly, Madeline pictured her back looking like a concrete driveway. More surgeries than expected could occur, depending on if more weakened spots showed up. Second, there was round after round of radiation, of course, that would be pinpointed to all of the spots where the cancer was already known to be. They would have to map a route over her body, as the spots were too widespread to cover all at once. And third, there was extensive chemo, using a variety of drugs. Madeline would be sick, yes, she would lose her hair, yes, she would get burned, yes, she would be in pain, yes, and ultimately, it might not work, yes, but –

"How long?" Madeline interrupted.

Dr. Franklin sat back. "How long for what?"

"How long would the treatment last?"

"Well..." Dr. Franklin looked on her computer and jotted notes on a notepad. "Probably at least a year," she said, sounding unsure. "Maybe a little over. A lot depends on how it goes, how quickly you recover from the surgeries, how you handle the chemo. We have to balance when each treatment should come in."

A year.

"And if I don't have treatment, how long will I live, with the rate that this cancer is growing?" Madeline wanted to feel calm, she wanted to feel stoic. Logical. Reasonable. She sat still, trying to paint herself as that picture, even as everything in her wanted to run away. Maybe in front of a bus. Over a cliff. Somewhere that wasn't a year. Maybe backwards in time, before she had her first backache that didn't seem to go away.

Dr. Franklin took her hands again. "Two, maybe three months? It's been growing for a while, Maddie."

Madeline thought of the massages, the chiropractor, the ibuprofen, the heating pad. All things she reached for to treat a backache, refusing to think the unthinkable. But how could she think it? Why would breast cancer be in her back? She had no breasts!

And now she wondered how she couldn't have known. The pain was already pervasive. She just didn't feel well.

"All right," she said, knowing the veneer of reasonable was fast wearing thin and she needed to get out of there. "I have to think about this." She stood up and wondered for how long she'd be able to. "And...you can't talk to my family about this, right? Because of confidentiality?"

"That's right," Dr. Franklin said. "But Maddie –"

"It's okay. I just need to think. I'll call you next week with my decision." And Madeline left.

At home, Emma noticed her new phone. "It's really cool, Mom," she said, sliding out the mini-keyboard and sending her fingers flying over the buttons, finding things to do that Madeline would never do. "Why'd you get it? What happened to your old one?"

"I dropped it." Madeline wondered if Emma saw longevity in that phone. New phone, long life.

One year.

Two to three months.

Madeline wanted to throw the phone all over again. Even though this one was more expensive than the last.

• • •

Madeline returned to the bay window that night. She looked out and considered. Then she held her hands out in front of her, palms up, and she lifted one, then the other, as if they were scales and she was trying to decide which was heavier. But in this case, heavier wasn't necessarily the better thing.

One year.

Two to three months.

Or immediately, if she decided to take her life right now. The pills. The knife. The car.

And then she rested her hands on her knees. There was no movement outside. There was no movement inside of her. She thought, *I am so done. I am just so done. I know this. I know this in my bones.*

She allowed herself to smile, just a little bit, just like in the doctor's office. Of course she knew this in her bones. That's where the cancer was, wasn't it.

But her daughter. But her husband. Who would find her?

How would she do it? How could she do it that would bring the least bit of trauma to them?

And that's when she realized it. She already held her weapon. Her body held her weapon. The knowledge slid into her veins like the poison she'd already taken in, suffered through, and survived. Cancer had her. She would grasp it in her own hands, under her own skin, deep within her own bones, and she would use it to kill herself. It was her decision, not cancer's.

It wouldn't be easy. It wouldn't be fast. Two to three months. Her husband and daughter would witness it, but they would witness what they were expecting and not see it as their wife and mother giving up and taking her own life. They would think that cancer took her life.

They wouldn't know that she swallowed cancer, sliced her wrists with cancer, breathed it in as deep as she could in lungs that were likely already affected.

Madeline felt cancer's ache, starting at the top of her hips and branching upwards. She rested her hands in that hollow at the base of her spine, before her body swelled out into the cradle that once carried her daughter. She pressed down, felt the ache spread.

Then she went upstairs and finally fell asleep.

• • •

Two months later, Madeline was bedridden and her husband was calling in hospice. A hospital bed was in the living room, next to the bay window so that Madeline could look outside when she was capable of turning her head.

Emma sat down next to her mother and held her hand. Madeline treasured the warmth. She breathed shallowly; every movement, even the raising and lowering of her chest, hurt. There would be no ventilator, no oxygen, nothing but morphine. Madeline signed the Do Not Resuscitate order; her husband witnessed it. Dr. Franklin watched, her lips in such a tight line, Madeline wondered how the doctor could breathe herself.

Madeline didn't wonder much anymore. She just waited.

"Mom," Emma said. "In school today, I was doing some research for a paper for my social studies unit on social justice. Mom, in Oregon, if you move there, they allow assisted suicide."

Madeline searched, found capability, and turned her head, not to see outside, but to see her daughter. She widened her eyes. It hurt.

"Mom," Emma whispered, leaning forward, resting her head beside Madeline's on the pillow. "Do you want to go there? Do you want me to take you? Dad and I could take you."

Tears rose, rolled down Madeline's cheeks, soaking her daughter's hair. "You'd be okay," she said and then drew breath, let it out, "with that?"

"I just want you to not be in pain anymore!" Emma cried and wept.

Madeline breathed in her daughter's scent, the feel of her skin against her cheek, the shudders, the so familiar shudders, that rocked her own frail, fractured body. Then she closed her eyes and breathed out, letting her daughter be the one to find her.

CHAPTER EIGHT

Hope

Painting the second canvas after painting the first after years of not painting at all continued to be a challenge. At home, years ago, after I moved my art supplies to a shelf in the back corner of the basement, I would see something, either right in front of me or inside my head, and think, Oh! I'd like to paint that! And then on the way down the basement stairs to collect my things out of hiding, out of jail, out of retirement, whatever it was they were doing down there, I'd see the baskets of laundry waiting to be done, or I'd be called back upstairs to help with homework or answer the doorbell or bandage a skinned knee or hurt feelings. By the time I would start down the stairs again, by the time I even remembered that I started down the stairs at all, it was two in the morning, and I could no longer remember what it was that I saw and that I wanted to paint. And I was tired. So I'd turn around and go to bed instead.

And to be fair, there were months that would go by, or even more, that I wouldn't even remember that I had art supplies and dreams hidden, jailed, retired in the basement. I was too busy, I was too depressed, I was too in love and angry with motherhood, I was too depressed, I was too afraid that I'd miss a wonderful moment, miss the chance to see who my kids were now, who they would be, who would be gone someday, I was too depressed, and I wouldn't be able to remember every minute of their lives. And I wouldn't remember a single minute of my own life. I was too depressed.

On rare and miraculous days, usually a Saturday, when my husband was off and golfing, my son playing video games with friends down the street, my daughter at the mall, I would stand at the top of the basement stairs and look down. My hand would stop before I even touched the light switch. Between me at the top of the stairs and my hidden things in the back of the basement, there was a solid wall that I couldn't see. That I couldn't walk through. It pulled at my energy when I had a little bit of energy to give, and it pulled it into the mortar that held together its invisible bricks. I simply couldn't walk past it, through it, around it. It was invisible, but it was palpable. Busyness and my responsibilities often could put this depression, my Gulf, in a corner of the basement with my art supplies. But when it was just me, all by myself, the Gulf reared up and took everything from me.

I would turn, go upstairs instead of down, and take a nap.

I fell asleep crying. I woke up crying. And in between, there was a sleep so deep and motionless and still that I thought it felt like death. When I climbed off my bed, hearing the sounds of my children downstairs, my husband calling my name, sleep pulled at me to come back. I would look at my pillow, my head's impression still there, and think, That is where I want to be. Asleep. Still. Dead.

I didn't know death would be like this.

I felt that same fatigue now, the pull for sleep, in my art room. I was dead. There was nothing stopping me, interrupting me. My time was my own. I'd set up a new blank canvas, actually out on the lanai this time. Before I returned to face it, armed with my paints and my brushes, I sat on my comfy couch, closed my eyes, and looked at all the colors dancing behind my eyelids. Phosphenes, they were called, a wonderful word I discovered one day about a year ago, and that I thought of frequently. Those thoughts were often accompanied by that, *Oh, I want to paint that!* moment. But on this day, this day in Heaven where my time was now my own, when I approached the canvas, the phosphenes blew away. I just saw nothing.

I turned and looked back inside my art studio. What if I was a fraud? What if all this was for someone else, for someone I could have been, maybe, but really wasn't, at heart, because if I was, wouldn't I have found the time and the energy while I was alive, no matter what? Wouldn't I have faced down that wall at the bottom of my basement stairs, wouldn't I have pulled a fist back and, like Superwoman, plunged a hole in the bricks, pushed the Gulf away, and taken what I so wanted?

So much of my energy was spent pulling away from the Gulf, and then being drawn back into it. Sinking. But the Gulf was gone now. It was contained on a canvas, where I put it, at some gallery called Wings and Things, somewhere in Heaven. I reminded myself that I wanted to go see it.

I set down the paints and the brushes, went to my kitchen and had a cup of coffee.

Returned to the canvas. Nothing.

I ate a sandwich and some chips.

Returned to the canvas, and nothing.

Drank some water. Water is good for you.

Nothing.

Sighing, I walked away. I decided that after the coffee and the water, I had to go to the bathroom. I didn't, but that was always a great excuse when I was living and still painting, before my son was born.

As I washed my hands, I glanced over at the sky scarf covering the portal. It wavered, as if a breeze came from somewhere to move it. There wasn't a window in the bathroom, so there couldn't be an organic breeze. It must be Heaven-sent, a Heavenly reminder. I dried my hands for far longer than was necessary, working the towel over every segment and knuckle of each finger, and then I glanced at the scarf again. It swayed.

I stood in front of it. I hadn't done one of my twice-a-day looks yet, and it was another way of avoiding the blank canvas, I supposed. Carefully, I lifted the scarf up, ready to look, blink, then drop it.

Instead, I ripped it off, letting it fall to the floor.

There was my son. He was by himself, sitting on his bed. It was dark, but I knew it wasn't night. His curtains were drawn.

My son's window was never covered, even though there were always curtains. They transitioned from the sport ball café curtains from his nursery – a white background covered with footballs, baseballs, basketballs, soccer balls, tennis balls, you name it, they were there – to the royal blue and electric green ones now, that coordinated with his bedspread, covered with a giant globe. The earth, it seemed, was covered with green and tan lands, and the vast ocean and rolling hills were represented over and over in his curtains. But they were never closed. I always knew I could find my son there, at his desk by the window, his chin propped on his palms, looking out at the sun and the blue sky, blue, like this scarf, or lying on his bed, looking at the moon and the glitter of stars.

He told me once, "I can see the sky from my bed. Whenever I wake up, I look out. Even when there's no moon, I can see the clouds moving across the sky. In the middle of the night, they're magical."

He was nine years old then. Magical.

Now, the curtains were closed. His back was to his window. His palms didn't support his chin, but covered his face, and his shoulders shook. He didn't make a sound, but his misery was as loud as any shout or scream could be.

And so I shouted. "Sweetheart!" I grabbed the sides of the mirror, tried to shake it, drew my face as close to the glass as I could. "Sweetheart!"

And he looked up.

His face was flushed, the way his cheeks reddened with baby bellows, toddler tantrums, and the hidden sobs of a middle school boy. I knew that red. I thought of the boy in my group therapy session, the way he turned to me and said, "My Gulf was red."

"Mom?" my son said. His voice cracked, but not from his maturing vocal cords. He looked toward his ceiling, around his room. "Mom?"

"Sweetheart," I whispered. I placed my thumbs on the glass, pushing where his shoulders were, pressing down and massaging, just as I used to soothe his sadness by rubbing his back. "Sweetheart, open your curtains."

He closed his eyes and let out the most shuddering sigh. I swear I felt the heave of his breath under my thumbs. Then he stood up and opened his curtains before sinking into his desk chair. He propped his chin on his hands and looked out the window to the sky. "Mom," he said, and he still cried, but the sobs were softer. These tears just fell without effort.

"Sweetheart," I said. I watched as his elbows loosened and his arms flattened, and when his head rested in the cradle made by his own body, his body which I made, cradled within my own, I felt his breathing lengthen as he fell into sleep.

The portal returned to a mirror. My thumbprints smudged it.

I staggered back to the toilet, lowered the lid and sat down. I held the sky scarf to my face. I could smell him. I could smell my son.

I made his body. And I made his misery now.

"Yes, you did," God said, standing in the door jamb. "But you had to in order to take your own misery away. What a horrible choice you had to make, Hope." He shook his head. "What a horrible, unthinkable choice."

"Selfish," I whispered.

"No," God said. "You chose yourself for once. How many times did you choose your family over your own deepest need?"

I couldn't even begin to count. Those times when the Gulf had me up to my neck and then I would catch a glimpse of my son or my daughter, or my husband would come home and wrap himself around me in that way he knew I loved, and I would take a deep breath and stow away the pain again. I would store it next to my paints in the basement. I would store it behind that wall.

Until I didn't.

"Yes, you did this," God said again, motioning toward the portal. He took the sky scarf from my lap and draped it over the mirror again. "But you also saved yourself." He took my arm and we walked to the deck off my living room, where his designated chair was, and mine too. There were already two glasses of iced tea on the table between us and a plate of lemon bars.

I sank in the chair and sighed and heard my son's sigh again as well. I hoped he would sleep for a while. He must be exhausted. "Did he hear my voice?" I asked God.

God shrugged. "Probably. It happens sometimes. Sometimes that love just overcomes the barrier." He picked up his iced tea in one hand, a lemon bar in the other. "When a parent kills him or herself, people say that he or she must not have loved their children." God shook his head. "If you ever overhear that, even from your children themselves as they work toward recovery, Hope, don't listen. You did love them. You still do." He motioned toward the table. "Breathe deep. Have a snack." He bit into the lemon bar and powdered sugar ringed his lips like a halo. "As for your empty canvas today, you don't have to paint every day to be an artist, you know," he said.

I watched as sugar sprinkled onto his shirt. I found myself charmed by a God that could be sloppy.

"Nobody does what they most love to do every day," he continued. "On the days that you don't love it, you don't do it." He nodded toward the town. "Especially here."

I sat back and ate a lemon bar. And then two. I saw the sugar sprinkle my own painting clothes. I decided I would change when we were done eating. For now, painting was finished. For now, lemon was enough. Lemon bars and lemon in my iced tea. I sat back, let the sugar fly, and tried not to think of my son in the portal. Which only made me think of him more. Of his face. Of his voice when he called, "Mom?"

And the miracle when I was able to answer, a limited answer from a distance, but my son opened his curtains and slept.

God and I went for a while without talking, but then I decided to break the silence. "There's one thing I still don't understand," I said.

"One thing?" God said. "Still?" His shirt was no longer covered with sugar.

I looked down at mine. It still was. Figures. "Okay, so there are a boatload of things I don't understand," I said. "And I suppose 'still' doesn't work either, since I haven't been here long. But I don't understand why the people in my therapy group all seem to know exactly why they killed themselves and exactly what was making them sad. Even though they call it their Gulf, it's nothing like mine." I thought of some of the people I heard speak in the sessions. "My Gulf isn't made up of cancer or unpaid bills or the death of someone else or the abuse by a spouse. My Gulf is just my Gulf. It's been around as long as I can remember. I don't know what it's made of."

God drained his glass, then turned in his chair so he could look at me directly. "I told you there is a reason, right? A reason for the Gulf and a reason for why you ended up here," he said. "I sometimes forget who I've told what to."

I added forgetful to the list of surprises. I nodded. "You did."

"Okay. This is moving fast, given that you haven't been here that long, but maybe I can answer one of your questions."

I was struck by his "maybe". I never expected God to be unsure. "One? I have more than one question?"

He stood up and held out his hand. "One question is where the Gulf came from. One is why you ended up here. So yes, two questions. Go get changed. You're a mess. And then we'll go."

I trotted off to my room, wondering what I should wear to talk about something that I had no concept of with God. Or two somethings. I never thought of these as individual issues. I came here because of the Gulf. But I didn't know where the Gulf came from. Somehow, God thought of this as two questions, and by now, I knew that God had his own way of figuring and it usually made sense. Once it sunk in.

I reached into my closet, pulling out a nice button-down blouse, since I didn't know where we were going, and a pair of jeans. When God tells you that you're a mess, you have no choice but to believe him. And when he says to go, you go.

• • •

God let me drive and we chose to take the golf cart. I drove slowly, still taken in by the sights of the streets of Heaven. So many nice little businesses!

God must have seen my head swiveling. He smiled. "Many of these are the small businesses these folks owned and ran when they were alive. The shops are labors of love, all of them. Here, the people can just enjoy the business itself, doing what they set out to do, without having to worry about being in the black, being in the red, being in business at all. There is no way a business can fail up here. There are no bills. There is no money. If one day, you have twenty customers, and then the next day, you have none, it's okay. You just keep doing what you love."

I took a couple business classes when I was in college, thinking I might want to open up a teaching studio someday, or maybe even a gallery. I never did; parenting came along and the need to supply money to hungry mouths meant that starting a business just wasn't practical. I hadn't thought about this in years, but now, I figured there was yet another spot in the corner of my basement where this dream dwelled. "But some of these are new businesses, right? Like Joyce's? She never had an art store when she was alive."

"Sure." He waved his hand, taking in the whole colorful block. "That's what some of these are. Dreams. We do get some people who simply want to retire and enjoy themselves when they get here, and that's fine. But others either want to experience what they were already experiencing, without the stress, or they want to live the dream of what they never had."

We stopped in front of the same large ornate gates that I drove through on the way to the ocean. God waved to the same man in a little booth. "Let us out please, Ed," he said.

The man spun the majestic-looking steering wheel and the gates slowly opened.

I waved at Ed as we went by. Since the gatehouse was inside my community, I assumed he was one of us. I thought of what God just said, about how some chose to live out their dreams here. "Why would someone want to spend all day every day in Heaven, opening and shutting a gate?" I asked.

God laughed. "Ed likes to talk and to have a purpose. Believe it or not, he was an elevator operator in a really fancy hotel back in the 1940's and he loved it. He enjoys this – he's opening and shutting something, and he gets to talk to people as they leave and come back. It's also not day in and day out. He has his days off, and he says they mean more to him because of his work days. It gives him a schedule and a routine to follow."

I thought of my attachment to Caffeine Heaven and understood.

Up ahead, I saw a young boy and an older woman walking along the sidewalk toward us. As they grew close, I recognized the boy from my therapy group. He was lugging a backpack. He smiled at me as we passed. "Hi, Hope," he called. The older woman smiled too.

"Hi!" I said, and then waited until they were out of earshot. "What's he doing out here? And who is she? I saw them both in my group therapy session, but I haven't had a chance to meet them."

God pointed ahead to a large brick building. There were kids walking away in all directions. "He was at school. That's his grandmother; she died before he did. She was here to greet him when he arrived and I gave permission for her to live with him here. He's too young to live on his own, even in Heaven. I pair up young children who pass away with someone from their family who got here before them." He glanced over his shoulder. "Owen is an anomaly, though his demographic is growing and I'm afraid he won't be an anomaly much longer. I don't typically see young children taking their own lives. But the incidence isn't so rare anymore."

I slowed the cart as kids ran by, squealing. I was nervous they might dash out in the road. "You have a school for kids who died? And did the grandmother commit suicide too?"

"No, just him. He needs to live in your community, and so his grandmother joined him there, and will stay with him indefinitely. If he chooses to stay this age, she'll be with him forever. If he decides to age as he would have on earth and eventually live on his own, she'll move back to her own condo when he reaches eighteen years. And yes, to school. Babies and children who die, and even adults who died before they finished earning the education they wanted, are able to go to school here."

Talk about higher education. "How old is he? How is it possible for someone that young to kill himself?"

God had me turn down another street. "He's ten. He killed himself last year, when he was nine. He's been here nine months. Long enough to have a birthday. He wanted his birthday, especially the one where he turned double digits. We had a real nice party. You can probably imagine what our Chuck E. Cheese's are like here. Every child's dream." God began to look around and I wondered what he was looking for. "And of course, it's possible for a child to kill himself. Once you're old enough to know what death is, you're also old enough to find a way to cause it."

I thought of myself at nine years old. I was already sad, already aware of my Gulf. I tried to remember if I ever thought of killing myself at that age. I thought of dying, for sure. Every night, when I went to bed, I prayed that I wouldn't wake up. I even remade the goodnight prayer to more accurately reflect how I felt:

Now I lay me down to sleep,
I don't want my soul to keep,
Please let me die before I wake,
I pray the Lord, my soul please take.

Every morning that I opened my eyes to my life was a disappointment.

"I remember that," God said softly. "And I chose not to grant that prayer."

That was one of the reasons why I didn't think I'd end up in Heaven. I didn't think there was one. If there was a God, he sure didn't listen to me.

Next to me, God sighed. I silenced my thoughts.

I was in middle school before I realized I could end my own life. I was at least twelve years old. "What did Owen do?" I asked, using the boy's name. I didn't know if God meant to let it slip. HIPPA laws might or might not be in effect in Heaven. Though he must have used his name when he introduced himself, so I suppose it was already public knowledge, and the victim of my own blippy memory. "And why?"

God shook his head. "I'll let him tell it. It's his story, and he should be the one to do so." He suddenly smiled. "Oh, there we go." He pointed.

It was another coffee shop. This one was called Grounds to Glory. I wondered why we were going to this particular shop, when Caffeine Heaven was so much closer, but I was impressed with the sidewalk café feel of it. Caffeine Heaven's outdoor space was in the back, hidden from view from the street, providing privacy in sun and shade. But this one had a seating area, a little stone patio, between the shop and the sidewalk. The tidy white chairs and tables were lovely, decked out with pastel-colored umbrellas. The aroma coming from the shop was lovely too. I found a parking spot easily and slid in between two other golf carts.

"Pick a seat, Hope," God said, and I chose one at the corner, but near the sidewalk, so I could watch people as they walked and scooted by in their golf carts, and hear them too. After I was settled, God asked what I wanted, and I told him to get me the specialty of the house. Then I sat there alone while he went inside.

The people who passed smiled at me and I smiled back. I couldn't tell by looking who was from my community and who wasn't. I didn't know much about Heaven outside of my area. I didn't know if there were other gated communities, or if everyone just lived in a mix of causes of death. Accidents with diseases, old age with murders.

God came out with our lattes. His was hot and the steam carried peppermint. He sat down and breathed deep over his mug. "Peppermint is my favorite," he said.

I sipped, discovering the taste of gingerbread and cinnamon. "A gingerbread latte?" I asked and God nodded.

"They specialize in Christmas flavors here," he said. "Christmas through the whole year." He sat back, nudged one of the empty chairs out from under the table and crossed his feet on it. "So let's talk a little bit about the Gulf.

Before now, were there ever times when it seemed like the Gulf went away for a bit? Or almost disappeared?"

I considered that. "Sometimes, I guess, when I was really busy, immersed in family life and work. And when I slept, of course. Everything was very quiet when I slept. I rarely had dreams. I loved sleeping." An image of the art classroom in high school appeared in my head. And a few of the art studios in college. After I graduated, I remembered going to various parks with paper and pens or paints and sitting somewhere comfortable, under a tree, at a picnic bench, and drawing and painting and sketching and just getting lost in it. "And when I worked too. I mean, at art. Sometimes, that feels like conscious sleeping. I step away from myself, just like I do when I sleep." I took a sip, thought that maybe what I was about to say was silly, but then said it anyway. "When I draw or paint, it's like I'm creating the dreams I don't see when I'm sleeping. But it's still as peaceful as sleep is. Even when what I'm drawing is chaotic."

God laughed, but not like he was making fun of me. He laughed in appreciation, and I laughed with him. Then he went on, "So when you felt the Gulf, Hope, it was wherever you were. No matter who you were with, no matter what you were doing. Unless you were sleeping or drawing or just really busy with life."

"Right."

"So...what's the common denominator there?"

Denominator. The bottom number in a fraction, if I remembered my math correctly. I hated math. I groaned.

"All right, throw out the math term. In all the times you felt the Gulf, what was the one thing that was always there?"

I frowned and shuffled through as many different instances as I could. Childhood, adolescence, adulthood. And then I froze. And I thought, *No.* There was only one constant.

"Me?" I whispered.

God's gaze remained steady.

No.

"And what made it almost disappear?"

"Sleep." I still whispered. My voice was gone, sunk somewhere far into me, and I wondered if I would ever speak aloud again. Maybe the Gulf wasn't captured on that canvas. "Being busy. And painting or drawing."

God put his feet down and leaned forward. "Hope, what did your high school art teacher tell you?"

The image of her appeared again. I saw her. And as she said the words she told me that day, standing in front of my canvas, that day when she asked me if I was okay, I repeated those words out loud to God. "I want you to remember something, Hope. Always paint. It helps. Whether you end up with a show in the Guggenheim or only in your living room, always paint. It's you. It's who you are. And it's what makes you, or will make you, okay. "

When I finished speaking, when she finished speaking through me, I could see God again. He nodded. "And what did you do, Hope?"

The basement. My paints, my pens, my canvases, my sketchpaper, all of it, in the back corner of the basement. Even the dreams I no longer dreamed about were there.

"I stopped," I said.

God stayed quiet.

On the café table in front of me, I suddenly saw my home's floorplan. The dining room, which was never used. The reading nook in the living room, where no one ever read. The basement, that very corner of the basement, which had a casement window allowing in a small stream of sun and where my easel sat, empty, but could have had a canvas on it and I could have stood in the sun stream and looked at what lit my own mind, behind my eyelids, and painted. If only I'd pushed through that wall. The Gulf.

But I didn't. I stopped. I sat at my kitchen table and cried. Or I looked in at my son while he slept, in his room with the curtains opened, in the room that used to be my studio, and I loved my son, and I resented him too. I resented my entire family. And I loved them so hard, it hurt.

I sat back.

God took one of my hands. "You wanted to know why you were here, Hope. You wanted to know why you got to the point of suicide. This is why. You had a way to keep the Gulf at bay. To quiet it, to make it almost disappear. And you had a way that fed who you are, who you wanted to be.

It wasn't busyness. It wasn't your family. You had a way to be you. And then...you stopped."

I didn't know what to say.

"Hope, do you know the helicopter story?"

That jarred my voice out. "What?"

God chuckled. "It's a classic. So there's this house, set next to a river. And a big rainstorm comes. The authorities show up and tell the man who owns the house that he has to evacuate. 'No,' he says. 'My God will save me.' The water gets higher and he's stuck on his second floor. The authorities come with a rowboat and tell him to climb out a window so they can get him to safety. 'No," he says. 'My God will save me.' Eventually, he's forced onto his roof and the authorities come again with a helicopter and drop a ladder to him. 'No!" he shouts. 'My God will save me!' And then he drowns. When he gets to the Pearly Gates," God's mouth quirked here and I smiled. There were no pearly gates. "He asks God, 'Why didn't you save me?' And God says, or I said, actually, 'What do you mean? I sent an early warning and a rowboat and a helicopter.'"

God smacked the table and sat back and roared. People passing by laughed with him, even though they hadn't heard his story. God's laughter was contagious, but I wasn't laughing. I wasn't sure what the story had to do with me.

"Did that really happen?" I asked.

God wiped his eyes. "All stories come from the truth somewhere, Hope," he said. And then he leaned forward again. "Just like here. Just like you. I sent you crayons and paints and colored pencils and pens. I sent classes. I sent your teacher. I sent a scholarship and a way to go to college. And what did you do?"

My eyes filled. "I drowned."

"And that's why you're here. That's why you chose to die." He shrugged. "It's probably the hardest thing for people to accept, who are in your community. You all chose to die. But you also all chose to not see the help you were offered. There was always help, Hope. There were always alternatives. But after a while, you couldn't see them. It was like there was a wall between you and your own ability, your own answer."

There *was* a wall.

My shoulders suddenly weighed tons.

"No, Hope." God squeezed my hands so hard, my knuckles popped. "It's not about blame. It's about the truth. No one is blaming you, especially not me. But the truth is always the most important thing. We learn from it."

As he squeezed, the weight on my shoulders lifted, like he was popping balloons filled with sand. Eventually, I took a deep breath. "Okay. That's why I'm here. But...where did the Gulf come from? I don't know where it started, who started it, how it started."

God stood up. "That's for another day. This is a lot to take in. Let's get you home."

I stood up, swayed, and brought both my hands to rest on the table. It was white again, no longer a blueprint. God offered his arm.

The drive back was silent. God held one of my hands the whole way.

At my door, he hugged me. "Hope, remember what else your teacher said."

I couldn't remember a thing. I wondered if I was going to drown again.

"She said to remember your name. Because hope always rises." He shook me a little. "Even here. You rose here. You're going to be just fine."

I nodded and then went inside and crossed immediately to my deck. Sitting in my red rocker, the chairs to the left and right of me empty, I watched as it grew dark. And then I stayed there even longer.

• • •

Another sleepless night in Heaven. And not by choice. I really wanted to go to sleep. To forget everything. To sink into that deep stillness that I knew and loved so well, the sleep I now knew was a gift. I wanted to forget my own role in what brought me here, to forget the visions I'd had of my kids in the portal, to forget it all. But I knew if I went to bed, there would be no sleep. Not even here.

At least on my deck, with the brightest of stars shining down on me, I felt in good company.

At around two in the morning, I went in to my bedroom and studied the doorway to my bathroom. And then I went inside.

I stood in front of the portal for fifteen minutes before I lifted the sky scarf. I hadn't looked at my family the second time that day. Actually, it was now the next day, and so this was again my first time. But I wasn't counting...I just wanted to know my family was all asleep. All fine. Despite what I did. Despite the way I ignored the helicopter.

They were. My daughter was breathing evenly, her covers smooth, not twisted. My husband was alone in our bed, his hand resting on my pillow. And my son was no longer with his father or asleep at his desk, but in his own bed, his curtains still open, his face toward the window. I took a deep breath, covered the mirror with the scarf, and returned to my bedroom.

Where I found God sitting in my recliner. Again.

"Geez!" I said, startled. "Why aren't you asleep?"

God raised the footrest. "You think I sleep?"

"You're in pajamas. And you were in pajamas the last time you were here in the middle of the night."

"I was just resting my eyes."

I rolled mine and got into bed. I plumped the pillows and put them behind me so that I could sit comfortably.

"I came back because I knew you weren't sleeping," God said. "And because I realized you probably misunderstood something I said, when we were talking on your deck earlier."

This day's conversations were all jumbled up in my head. I couldn't sort through God's words in the bathroom, on my deck, or at the coffee shop. "What did I misunderstand?"

"When I asked you, 'How many times did you choose your family over your own deepest need?', what did you think I was referring to?"

I opened my arms to the room. "My decision to come here. All the times before this that I decided to stay alive, stay with my family, even when I really just wanted to die."

God shook his head. "That's what I thought. But really, it's about more than that. It's about that and about the helicopter story. All those times you had an idea for something to paint and you started to move toward it, but then stopped to do something for the family. You were reaching for what you needed to do, and then you did what they needed you for."

The times I reached for the light switch to the basement. The times I started down, then had to go back up to take care of something. Of someone.

"Your deepest need," God said. "To create. To do your art. To keep the Gulf at bay."

I thought of the blueprint I saw earlier. "I could have found a way. I could have made a space. I could have said, 'Hey, I need to do this.' Hell, I could have done it at the kitchen table. People have. Instead, all I did was cry." I heard the derision in my voice. Since arriving in Heaven, I'd found the new sensation of liking myself. But now, all of that began to fade away. I was here because of my own fault, of course. But now it seemed like my whole life was my fault.

"You put your family first. You didn't accept that putting yourself first *was* putting your family first. Art was your lifeline, your helicopter, and you kept turning back. And you got sadder and sadder. The Gulf got bigger and bigger. And you thought and thought about killing yourself. But you didn't. You put your family first again. Time after time after time. Until now."

I suddenly pictured a whole battalion of helicopters. Zooming over where my house was under a roaring river, the only thing reaching through the water was my hand. And my hand was closed.

I couldn't breathe. There. And I couldn't breathe now. In Heaven. I gasped.

"Hope!" God shoved the footrest in and leaped to the bed, pulling me out of it. The French doors to my deck blew open and he led me out there. He rubbed my back and I felt my lungs ease. I inhaled, then exhaled, and felt thankful for breath. "Hope, remember, this is just about the truth. That's all. No blame. No regrets."

How could that be? If I'd just known the impact of what I was doing, or not doing, I might still be with my family today. If I only knew that what I missed in my life, more than anything else, was actually my life preserver. Not selfishness. I looked out at Heaven in the darkness. Here and there, small spots of light still glowed from condo windows. Even at this hour, I wasn't the only one sleepless in Heaven.

God looked out too. "No, you're not the only one. Ever. There is always someone here who understands." He looked back at me. "There is no blame,

Hope," he repeated. "There are no regrets. You're here. It's done. You're fine. Your family will be too."

My shoulders slumped. "If I'd only just kept painting. If I'd only said something—"

"There are no if onlys either, I'm afraid. You turned away from what you most wanted to do for a good reason. You love your kids and wanted to do your best by them. Even if it meant denying yourself. Until the Gulf took you over. Until you had to choose yourself. Save yourself. Which you did." He sighed. "You needed to breathe. So you came here." He wrapped an arm around my shoulders. "It's complicated, Hope."

Complicated. For God.

Tiredness hit me so hard then. It felt like my body was dragging itself to the floor. Instead, God tugged me back to my bed.

Imagine having God tuck you in. And kiss you on the forehead.

But I was just too tired to marvel.

CHAPTER NINE

The One Less Traveled By

Owen's Story

Twice a day, nine-year old Owen stood on the sidewalk at the proverbial fork in the road. His third grade class had to read Robert Frost's poem, *The Road Not Taken,* and he was delighted to learn that a fork was more than a piece of silverware. The class read and memorized the poem for English. In Art, they had to draw a picture of what they thought Frost meant. Owen drew a picture of one sidewalk meeting another, like a big T. Although his perspective was impressive for his age, he hadn't gotten a good grade.

"Owen," his art and classroom teachers both said, "the first line says, 'Two roads diverged in a yellow wood.' There are no sidewalks in the woods."

Owen didn't argue, but he kept the drawing and thumbtacked it to the bulletin board above his desk at home. To fulfill his homework assignment in English, he had to recite the poem to his parents. Standing in front of their recliners in the living room, he folded his hands and spoke the words carefully, making sure each one was pronounced separately.

Partway through, his father said, "Can you hurry it up, Owen? My show's coming on in a minute."

Owen hurried, but he still made sure there was a little space between the words. Words were important. He knew this.

His mother nodded when he was done and told him to go do the rest of his homework.

Upstairs, Owen stood in front of the mirror behind his door and recited the poem again, slowly, the way he wanted to do it for his parents. He tasted the words. He loved them. At least, *these* words. He knew other words weren't as nice. But these...

"I shall be telling this with a sigh," he recited, and then he sighed.

Twice a day, he stood at the fork he drew in Art, that T where the sidewalk from his front steps met the sidewalk that ran parallel with his street. He thought of Frost, standing by two roads in a yellow wood.

Two roads diverged in a yellow wood,
And sorry I could not travel both
And be one traveler, long I stood

Owen stood long too, in the morning and in the afternoon. He was but one traveler. But he knew he was different than Frost in the forest. Frost wanted both choices. Owen wanted neither. He wished for a third. A road, or a sidewalk, to softer words, nicer words, like the words he tasted when he recited the poem.

Every morning, he stood at the fork and considered. To turn right meant to go to school, to face whatever words would come out of the kids' mouths that day. If he turned around to go back into the house, he would face his parents, and their mouths worked in much the same way. They always left for work shortly after he set off for school, and so he could sneak back and hide in the house, the wonderfully quiet house. But his teacher would call out attendance in his classroom and he wouldn't be there to say, "Here!" Then there would be a phone call to his mother's cell, tattling his unreported absence. He got away with this once, when he fibbed that his teacher must have not heard his "Here!", and so his mother shrugged it off. But when it happened a second time, he was caught. And then there were not-nice words. Words from his teacher and words from his parents. He knew he would be caught again. So while he considered, it wasn't really a choice.

In the afternoon, Owen stood at the same fork and considered again. To turn left was to go into his house, where he would have a couple hours before his parents came home from work, his mother first, his father second, and then whatever happened would happen. Or he could turn around and go back to school, where he could conceivably slip inside, if the janitors were still there and hadn't locked the outer doors yet. He could find a place to hide. The media center, maybe, in a far back corner, though he could slip out after dark and pull as many books as he wanted from the shelves to read. Or in the last stall of the boys' restroom in the gym. It was so quiet in the school at night, without any classes going on. But he'd likely be found, possibly even by the police in the middle of the night, and then the school would be angry and his parents even angrier. There would be not-nice words from the police. From the principal. From the school counselor and his teacher. And words and words and words from his parents. Again, this choice worked once. It would likely never work again.

But he still stopped and considered every morning and every afternoon, even though it was hopeless, a word he knew well, and then he went to school in the morning and came home in the afternoon. He wished for his third option, but at nine years old, there just wasn't much he could do. He and the other kids at school laughed over the classic joke about the little boy who ran away from home, but who only went to the end of his driveway because he wasn't allowed to cross the street. It wasn't all that different for Owen, but he joined in the laughter anyway.

This morning, Owen stopped, considered and turned right. He left the house unnoticed, which was fine, because he'd been noticed enough the night before. It was report card time. There was no spanking, no being grounded. Owen heard on the news about kids found locked in cages, in dark closets in basements, in car trunks. Owen was never locked anywhere.

But there were the not-nice words that fell from his parents' mouths. They rang still in his ears. They kept him awake all night and he hadn't needed his alarm to get up this morning. He remembered the name-calling. And he remembered his father shaking his head and saying, "You're hopeless, Owen."

Hopeless, that familiar word, was not a nice word. It was not like yellow wood. But hopeless, and the names, repeated in his ears like an echo off a cliff.

At school, Owen barely stepped onto the playground before two boys took his backpack and began ransacking it. Owen walked to a bench by the basketball net and sat down, waiting for them to finish so he could get his backpack back. His homework was crumpled and tossed aside. He watched it blow off the blacktop and down the street. The boys ate his lunch and his brown bag tumbled after his homework. They didn't know that he carried a few extra dollars in his shoe, so he could still get hot lunch. And in the pouch of his hoodie was a neatly folded extra copy of his homework. He always made a copy. The lunch and homework in his backpack kept the kids, sometimes these two boys, sometimes others, satisfied and they didn't search any further. During class and at lunch, no one paid him enough attention to see that he still handed in his work and he still ate.

Owen just waited. When the bell rang, the boys threw down his backpack and ran. Owen picked it up and went inside with his classmates. The day went on as usual.

The words from those boys combined with the echo from his parents. They rang and rang. Owen struggled to hear the teacher. It made him angry when the words he didn't want to hear blocked out the words he did. There were more words added on at recess and Owen's ears rang some more. Rang always.

Hopeless.

At the end of the day, Owen waited in the quiet last stall of the boys' restroom in the gym until he was sure that everyone was on their way home, either walking, being picked up, or taking a bus. Afternoons were different than mornings, because he hadn't yet made copies of the worksheets his teacher handed out, and so they were precious. He couldn't take a chance on his backpack being taken again. That night, he would do the worksheets, then carefully copy everything, the questions, the answers, on a new sheet of paper to hand in. His teacher no longer asked him what happened to his original worksheets. She knew his answer was always, "I spilled milk on it," and his previous teachers knew this too. His first grade teacher said, "Clumsy." His second grade teacher said, "Careless!" His third grade teacher just shook her head like his father did and expected his copies.

Hopeless. Careless. Clumsy. So many echoes.

Owen left through a side door, walked through some back yards, and then eventually moved down his own street. Whenever he heard a kid shout or laugh, he flinched, but no one approached him.

At his house, he stood again at the fork and considered. He turned left and went inside. He had two hours on his own, so he poured a glass of milk, found some cookies and he watched television. Twenty minutes before his parents were due home, he turned off the tv, brought his glass to the dishwasher, and then he disappeared into his room. He never did homework with a glass of milk close by. He heard the garage door open and close, and then fifteen minutes later, open and close again. Nobody called out, but he knew they were home.

He was having trouble with his math, but he knew better than to ask for help.

The not-nice words could even be about numbers.

Hopeless.

He just did his best.

At dinner, his parents talked while he ate. Those words flew over his head and he didn't mind them, unless the voices rose. He gave monosyllabic responses to the few questions directed at him. His father shook his head a lot. He said some words.

They rang.

Before bed, Owen read a book he checked out from the school library. He found a whole collection of Frost's poetry. The librarian said it would be too hard for him, but he checked it out anyway. He read out loud, whispering the words, covering himself in softness and rhythm and joy. The ringing quieted in his ears, replaced with the poetry and the gentle of his own voice. And then he went to sleep.

Day after day after day. Everything was the same, really. Owen knew what to do. He knew how to sit and wait. He knew not to ask for help. He even figured out how to return Frost's book to the library, wait a few days, then go back to the library and surreptitiously slide the book from the shelves into his backpack. It was his now. He read from the book every night. He tucked it into the pocket of his hoodie on the way to school.

But those words, the not-nice words of his parents, the kids, even his teachers, always felt new. Even when they weren't. They never became routine. They never became soft. They never grew unheard. Owen always flinched.

And then one day, a boy reached into Owen's hoodie pocket. Owen wasn't expecting it; he was sitting on his bench, watching his worksheets and his brown lunch bag blow down the street. He pretended they were fall leaves in the yellow wood. And then the boy's hand pulled out his copies.

"Look!" the boy shouted, the K sharp as a bullet. Owen barely had time to grab his library book, holding it with both hands and refusing with all his might to give it up.

They pushed Owen. They turned him upside down. They jumped on him. His copies disappeared down the street, down the yellow wood. His shoe fell off and the boys grabbed his money.

The bell rang. Owen put his shoe back on, tucked his book back into his hoodie, and he picked up his backpack. He went inside with the others.

His teacher shook her head when he said he didn't have his homework. She shook her head again when he didn't have his homework for the next two days. He sat without eating in the cafeteria. His teacher placed a phone call to his mother's cell.

The words that night. They rang and rang. "Hopeless!" his father yelled. He shook his head.

Owen didn't do his homework that night. He didn't read his library book before bed. He just clasped it to his chest and stared at the ceiling.

The next morning, he faced the fork again. The fork that was nothing like the one next to his dinner plate, and nothing like the one in Frost's poem, the fork that his teachers failed to see in his drawing. Frost stood in the yellow wood. His choices were both good. Owen didn't and his choices weren't. He knew his drawing was very accurate.

Standing straight, Owen folded his hands over his library book and he recited the poem in a whisper. A whisper, he knew, would break through the ringing in his ears.

Yet knowing how way leads on to way,
I doubted if I should ever come back.

Owen stopped. Then he repeated those lines again.

He glanced over his shoulder. His parents would be pulling their cars out of the garage soon and he needed to be gone. He could hide behind a tree across the street until they left, then return to the house. He could stay downstairs. He could eat lunch when he was hungry. He could wander from room to room without any fear. He could even sit on his parents' bed. He could read his library book there and pretend it was his parents reading to him.

But he didn't.

Owen looked to the right. He could go to school. He could surrender his backpack, sit on the bench, and then go inside with the others. He could shrug when his teacher asked for his homework, and he could sit without eating at lunch, and then return to his bench at recess. And he could hide in the restroom after school. Then walk home.

But he didn't.

Two roads diverged in a wood, and I—
I took the one less traveled by

Owen took the path he never chose, the one less traveled by, the one never traveled by, and turned left, away from his home and away from his school. He didn't have permission to go that way, just like the little boy who couldn't cross the street. But Owen chose to do what that little boy didn't. He followed the sidewalk, wondering where it would go. It wound through his neighborhood and then into the little downtown. Owen walked past a diner where he and his parents ate sometimes on a Saturday night, a barbershop where his mother took him for haircuts, and a used bookstore where he never went before, but he looked in the window now. He wondered if they had any books by Robert Frost. And then he kept on going, to where the sidewalk ended. Across the street was a park, with a cobblestone path running alongside a river.

Owen followed the riverwalk. The river didn't talk, but it made sounds like words, like the softness in Owen's library book. Owen listened to the whisper as it broke through the ringing in his ears and then he listened some more.

There was a boat landing. And a little dock. Owen walked out to the end of it.

He could turn around and go to school. Or he could turn around and go home.

But he didn't.

Owen set his backpack onto the dock. He held his library book to his chest, and then, he walked straight ahead.

Owen couldn't swim.

Underwater, Owen held onto his book with both hands with all his might and refused to give it up. He listened as the river sang soft words. He heard the poetry. There was no ringing at all.

And that has made all the difference.

CHAPTER TEN

Hope

I woke up the next morning, feeling just as I had every morning in Heaven; rested, relaxed, and intact. The ache, the regret, the sadness of yesterday was still there, but the overwhelm that would have hit me during my life remained at bay. When the Gulf was a part of my every moment, anything that happened that was negative just seemed to heap more hurt upon a hurt that I could never rid myself of. My reactions were always extreme; everything was always the end of the world. Not being able to find the last necessary ingredient for a recipe I was shopping for would send me home to my bed. An unexpected bill led me to expect complete financial ruin. An angry child turned me into someone who should never have been allowed to have children.

But here in Heaven, the Gulf was gone. And I could see the things that made me sad or angry for what they were. I could focus on the way my son looked as he sat on his bed, his back to the window, his face covered, his room dark. Or I could focus on the way his shoulders felt under my thumbs, I could hear his voice as he called my name, and I could see him lift his face to the sky. I could see him grieving, and I could grieve too. But I also knew the grief wasn't forever.

It was becoming a routine now to smile on my way to the bathroom as the word ablutions seemed to float to the forefront of my mind. It was a God word and it made me laugh. I did my ablutions on this morning, and then I tugged down the sky scarf. As the portal panned through my house, I saw that each room was empty. I was surprised. The kids must have gone to school, my husband to work. I waited to see if the portal would show me their whereabouts, and it did, though from a distance. My son was in gym and they were on the volleyball unit. I watched as he stepped from foot to foot on the court, not actually doing anything with the ball, but he was there and ready if the team needed him. Then the scene switched and I saw my daughter in a classroom. I recognized the teacher and so I knew that the open book on my daughter's desk must represent contemporary American literature. I wondered who she was reading, because then I could read it too. Obligingly, the portal scanned in and I saw the title and the author: *The Hotel New Hampshire* by John Irving. I had that book already. The portal showed me her marker was at page 52, so she wasn't too far in and I could catch up quickly.

I wouldn't be able to discuss the book with her. But I could read it at the same time, maybe see the paper she would write as a result, maybe hear her answer discussion questions in class.

I worried for a moment about what my daughter would do when she came to my favorite line in that book. *Keep passing the open windows.* It was when I read that line for the first time that I knew that novel would be one of my favorites, one of those that never left my bookshelves. I was twenty years old when I first read it, six years older than my daughter now, and I read it at least once a year since then. I repeated that line to myself so many times, to get me through a week, a day, a moment.

I didn't repeat it on the day I drove to the river.

I would read that book now, here in Heaven. And I would read it with my daughter, to see what it would mean to her.

Then the portal switched to my husband at work. His hands hovered over his keyboard, but his fingers weren't moving, His head was turned away from the screen. I tried to follow his line of gaze and the portal changed the perspective for me so I was now looking out of my husband's eyes.

He was looking at a photograph of me. It was one I gave him for our anniversary a few years ago. I'd thought about doing one of those Glamor Shots, where they dolled you up in make-up and fancy clothes and spotlights shone upon you as you stood in exotic or erotic settings, but in the end, I decided that really wasn't me. There was a second person who knew this as well as I did, and that was my husband. I didn't even put on make-up if we went out someplace fancy. So the photographer I hired followed me out to my favorite spot by the river. The photo showed me leaning against the weeping willow tree, the branches like a curtain behind me, glints of light sparkling between the green leaves. The river could be seen too, and I was smiling and relaxed.

The perspective changed again and I saw my husband's eyes as he sat at his desk this morning, his always level gaze still level, as he teared up. This photo, this anniversary present, showed the spot where I killed myself. In the photo, I was smiling.

I was pretty sure I was smiling as I drank my wine and swallowed my pills too. I wasn't standing under the tree, but I was parked where I could see it. The tree and the river were the last things I remembered seeing with any clarity, before they smeared as I went under.

My husband reached out and turned the photo so the back of the frame was facing him. Then he returned to his work, his fingers moving again, as tears rolled down his cheeks.

I didn't have that option of turning the portal so its back was to me. So I covered it with the scarf instead. And then I continued to follow my Heavenly routine, showering, getting dressed, making my bed, tucking Teddy between the pillows. Then breakfast out on the deck. Another butter rum muffin. Excellent coffee. I did my best to let this new familiar block my vision from what I just saw in the portal. I knew it wouldn't work, but I tried anyway.

I didn't linger long over breakfast. God's words yesterday and the realization that I might have been able to keep the Gulf at bay if I'd just kept painting rolled through my mind, parallel streams with my husband's tears, my son turning from his window, my daughter shrieking in the kitchen. I stood up, intending to go put paint on the canvas I set up yesterday. I felt a new sense of adrenaline and purpose...even if I didn't know what I was going to paint next. I felt driven by trying to make this right. The Gulf was already gone, held captive elsewhere. Now, I had to do what I would have done, if I hadn't allowed the Gulf to completely take me over.

Before changing into my painting clothes, I went back to my studio. The easel was still outside on the lanai, the canvas already on its ledge. I'd brought out paints and brushes too. They still sat there, and I felt like they'd been waiting for me. But my mind was still blank of images, even as it rolled with words and visions of my family. Even as my fingers twitched with this new adrenaline.

And then my fingers stilled and straightened and I knew exactly where I wanted to start. But it would require a much larger canvas.

Going back inside, I looked at the wall where several blank canvases were lined up, according to size. But none of them were large enough. I thought about what I wanted, and then waited to see if one appeared, in Heaven's magical way. But it didn't. I puzzled over that for a minute, but then squealed in delight.

There was no sudden canvas appearance because Heaven knew what I wanted even more than the canvas; the trip to the art store to get the canvas! To look at all of them first, to touch them, run my fingertips over them, and then grab that special one. The one where my still-not-fully-imagined painting hid, just waiting for me to bring it out.

I grabbed my car keys. The canvas that I needed would not fit in a golf cart, and I even wondered how I would keep it in the convertible. God told me that things would transition slowly to where I was running out myself and getting what I needed, doing what I needed to do. The magic of the objects I desired just popping into my hands would gradually fade as I grew used to Heaven. While I wasn't too thrilled at the idea of doing grocery shopping, being able to go to the art store was a different thing entirely. I was glad this was one of the chores that became mine to do so soon after my arrival.

When I went inside the Color'n'Create, I was delighted to see Joyce behind the counter. She was busy with a canvas herself. She didn't seem to hear me as I drew close, and so I was able to watch for a few minutes as she worked with oil pastels. She put down some solid lines here and there, but then, with the heel of her palm, she smeared some of them together. The blended colors became magical clouds that glittered and moved one color into the next as if it was all a natural progression. It was very surreal, and I loved it. The picture seemed to come from her to the canvas, and then it reached back again, as streaks of the pastels appeared on Joyce's hands and arms. Streaks were on her shirt too, and, as I watched her place her hands on her hips, the back pockets of her jeans.

When she looked up at me, I saw she had more pastel across her cheeks and nose. "Oh!" she said. "Hope! I didn't hear you come in!"

"Sorry, I didn't want to disturb you." I joined her behind the counter and leaned over the canvas. "I like this! I haven't worked with oil pastels much. I didn't realize you could smush them together this way."

She laughed. "I think smush is the technical term for it! But thanks. I don't like it yet, but I think I will soon. This started as a sketch for something I was thinking about sculpting, but then it morphed into this, and I don't know what *this* is yet." She grabbed a paper towel and wiped off her hands. "Can I help you with something?"

I shook my head. "No, I'm just here for a canvas. I'll go back and look myself. I'll shout if I need any help." Before I even stepped away, she tossed the paper towel over her shoulder and was bent over again, smudging and sketching. I knew her enthusiasm and sense of exploration. I felt it. She made me even more eager to get back home and to work.

Home. I wondered at that for a moment. I was already calling Heaven home. But my home was on Earth too.

The canvases were in the back of the store and I took my time, pulling some off the shelves, leaning them against the wall and stepping back to observe. It didn't seem like any of them were big enough and I wondered if I was going to have to change my vision. But then I went down a new row, and there they were. I should have realized. These were too big to be on a shelf. So they were hung from hooks on the wall. I looked at them all, walked down the row and touched each gently with my pointer finger. And then I lifted one off the hook and leaned it against the wall so I could measure myself against it. It was taller than I was. Which was just what I wanted. I turned sideways, as if I was in front of a mirror, and checked the width. My body could fit within the canvas' edges, leaving about six inches framed around me. I hauled it to the front.

"This is the one I want," I said, stopping in front of Joyce's counter.

She looked up. "Wow. I think that's the biggest size we carry. Are you feeling ambitious?"

"I'm feeling *something*. What do I owe you?" And I froze, realizing I didn't even have a purse or a wallet with me.

Joyce rolled her eyes. "How quickly newbies forget. Or regress. There's no money here, remember?"

"Oh, geez." The familiarity I was feeling lost a bit of its shine as I was reminded how new to all this I still was. I started to pick up the canvas, but then stopped. "Joyce, I know you're in the middle of smushing, but would you be able to help me with something? It won't take long, I promise."

Joyce straightened up, groaning, and reached for another paper towel. "Sure. It's probably a good thing for me to unbend this spine anyway. Ow. Wouldn't you think we could have spines like rubber bands in Heaven?" Her hands went onto her back pockets again and she arched. I knew if she turned, I'd see rainbow-colored pastel handprints. "So what do you need?"

I laid the canvas on the floor. "Be right back." Heading to the aisle with pens, pencils and markers, I found a carpenter's pencil, flat and rectangular. Returning to the front of the store, I handed the pencil over to Joyce. She stood by the canvas now and we both looked down on it.

"So I know this sounds weird," I said, "but would it be okay if I stripped down to my bra and panties?"

Joyce snorted so hard, her hair blew straight up. "Hope, you're wearing a bra? In Heaven? We don't have to!" She stretched her arms out. "Look! We have all the support we need! You don't ever have to wear one again! Please tell me you're not wearing an underwire."

So I stared at her chest, even though it seemed really inappropriate. She looked good. I mean, like twenty-something good. And her t-shirt was smooth as could be. "Well, it's what I found in my drawer in my condo. It's what I wore on earth. More like a sports bra."

"Take it off. No binding here."

I laughed, in both horror and self-consciousness. "I will, but right now, I'd like to keep it on. I'm about to strip down in your store."

"Oh, that's right. So exactly what are we doing here?" Joyce knelt down.

I glanced outside. "Do you think we're okay right here? There's a lot of windows." But I knew from wandering the store that this was where there was the most open floorspace, and I needed Joyce to have enough room to crawl all around me.

"I think so. You're going to be down here anyway, so you'll be out of view."

I pulled my shirt over my head. "I'm going to lay on the canvas and then you're going to trace around my body." I nodded at the carpenter's pencil. "With that."

"Oh!" Joyce brightened. "I did something like this when I was in grade school!"

I yanked off my jeans. "I think we all did. But I hope this ends up being more than a grade school project." Carefully, I sat at the base of the canvas and then scrooched myself slowly up until my whole body fit. Then I rolled about three quarters of the way on my side and worked at arranging my arms and legs the way I wanted them. If I changed my mind later, I could always paint over it and switch the pose, but for now, this was what I saw in my head. "Okay," I said and took a deep breath as I tried to settle into stillness. "Start tracing."

I wasn't expecting the pencil to tickle. While I remembered giggling during this project in second grade, I thought that was just from general little girliness. But no. Anyplace that pencil touched sent a shudder through me and I laughed.

"Stop laughing!" Joyce said, laughing herself. Eventually, we both just dissolved and she had to sit back until she regained some control. I rolled onto my back and felt myself vibrate and contort as the laughter worked its way through my body.

It was so long since I laughed like that. It happened so infrequently in my life, even as a child. Of course, the second grade tracing elicited giggling from tickling – I really couldn't remember many other times of helpless laughter that actually came from joy. This laughter started with tickling, but then grew into so much more.

I let myself go. It was just the most wonderful thing.

When I began to catch my breath and my laughter slid down my throat to my stomach, I felt all noodley. It was like being limp in a good way; my body had to pull itself back into control again, but it was with the glow of recent happiness. Joyce and I both took deep breaths and I curved almost onto my side again. Prepared for the tickle now, I was able to hold still with only a few shudders and stifled snorts when the pencil hit particularly sensitive spots. Then Joyce helped me up.

I didn't look until I was dressed. But when I did, I could easily see where my body was on the canvas. It was like looking at a map. "Thank you, Joyce."

"Not a problem. Did you need anything else?"

I didn't think so, since I wasn't entirely sure what I was going to do yet. So I gave her a hug, asked if she would show me her pastel picture when she was done (she said yes and we agreed to meet for coffee in a few days), and then I carried the canvas to my car. I slid it sideways into the back seat and then drove slowly back, worried that it would blow out. It didn't.

At home, I lowered the ledge on the easel as far as it could go so that I could easily reach every part of the canvas. I grabbed even more handfuls of paints and brushes and scattered them on the beat-up table. And then I practically ran to my bedroom and changed into my painting clothes, of which I seemed to have an endless supply. A glass of iced tea and I was ready.

Standing in the sunny spot, I took a deep breath. It was easy enough to outline my body in black, as Joyce saw it, as she drew it, as my body told her to.

And then I began to fill myself in.

• • •

I worked until I couldn't see anymore and I realized it had grown dark. Lifting the canvas and easel together, I awkwardly carried them inside, moving in a waddle, and then followed with the table and paints and paintbrushes. The movement allowed me to break away from the vision I'd been seeing and let me examine the canvas itself. Instead of starting with my silhouette, I began with the background. I decided on a neutral beige and I did the steady work of filling in the canvas behind my figure. Finished with that, I moved to inside my body, that shape that was so familiar to me. What started as random incoherent tattoos on the arms and legs became streams and strings of color, in wild psychedelic flashes. Unlike Joyce, I didn't want to bring my palm to it and smush the colors together. I wanted them separate, lined up one after the other like a demented rainbow on an unpredictable path. And so far, that's what they were.

The evening had a chill to it, and after washing my hands and the brushes out in the sink and rinsing out the water glass, I slid the lanai doors closed. The brushes lined up like soldiers on the counter, drying on paper towels. There were a couple lamps in this room and I turned them on, leaving the overhead lights off. This bathed the room in softness and the new canvas was in shadow. I was fine with that. I needed it to reside there for a bit, as I considered my next day's work. I felt like I needed to reside, to rest, in shadow too, in quiet, but outside of this room. If I was away from here, not so close to the canvas, my brain could burn at a lower pitch.

I simply moved through the evening, making my dinner, sitting on the couch, reading. I found my old copy of *The Hotel New Hampshire,* but then left it on my bedside table for before-sleep reading. I pulled Virginia's *To The Lighthouse* from my shelves. My college copy was filled with my yellow highlighter, pointing out what I thought were the most important parts, which apparently was almost everything. It tickled me – and here I laughed out loud, remembering the literal tickling with Joyce earlier in the day – that my group therapy leader was the writer of this classic book that I'd read so long ago and discussed so passionately with my classmates.

I thought about calling someone, maybe Faith, maybe Joyce, maybe even Joe, or sending out a silent call for God, to sit and talk about these things and anything else that came to mind. I thought about lifting the scarf off the portal and seeing how my family fared that day as they continued to try to re-enter what most would call a "normal life". But in the end, I didn't do any of these things. I sat in a quiet circle of light, under the only lamp I turned on in the living room, and I read. If I raised my eyes from the page and glanced outside, I saw all the windows of lights from the buildings around me. It was enough to know I wasn't alone, even as I was.

I was fine.

I came across some lines in the book that I'd highlighted and I'd also written exclamation point after exclamation point in the margins. I wasn't sure if I was thinking they were important to me, to Virginia, or to the paper

I planned on writing for the class. But when I read the lines, and then read them again, I wondered how I, at nineteen years old, could have known they'd be so important to me now.

"For now she need not think of anybody. She could be herself, by herself. And that was what now she often felt the need of - to think; well, not even to think. To be silent; to be alone."

I'd felt alone when I was alive too. But not like this. Then, I was alone because I felt something – the Gulf – that no one else seemed to feel. It didn't matter what I was doing – if I was at a birthday party or at the library or shopping or walking the halls of school or college or speaking to people in classes or at home or at work, if I was making love to my high school boyfriend in the back of his pick-up truck or with my husband in the bed we shared, if I was giving birth or gazing at a sleeping child or buttoning the back of my daughter's special dress for a dance at school – something was constantly going on inside of me that didn't seem to happen to anyone else, and I knew I couldn't say a word about it. Partly because I didn't know what to say. And people didn't know how to hear. Even when they really wanted to. My parents tried so hard to understand.

I remembered trying to talk to my mother about the Gulf. I was sixteen and she tapped on my bedroom door. When I told her she could come in, she found me laying in the dark, tears streaming down my face. I wasn't listening to music, I wasn't reading, I wasn't doing homework. I was just lying there and trying so hard to make myself look forward to something. To anything. Going to sleep and having a good dream. Going to school the next day, seeing friends, laughing at the commons table during lunch. Maybe seeing a boy glance my way, wink, and then know he was following me with his eyes when I got up to go to class.

But there was nothing. All there was was my ceiling above me and the tears running from the corners of my eyes to my hairline. I knew that most girls my age daydreamed. I cried and didn't think of anything to dream at all.

"Honey, what's wrong?" my mother asked, sitting on my bed. She laid her hand on my knee, and while I loved the warmth of her palm reaching through my jeans to me, just to me, it didn't make the Gulf recede.

"I'm sad," I said.

She then went through a whole litany of what could make me feel that way. Was there a boy, was a girl mean to me, did I have a bad grade, did I feel fat? No and no and no, I said.

I didn't know how to tell her that saying, "I am sad," felt to me like I was saying, "I'm five foot two," or "I'm a redhead," or "I'm your daughter."

I just was. And I didn't know how to change. If I wanted to, I could make myself taller by wearing heels. I could dye my hair. I knew there would be roles in my life beyond being a daughter. But there didn't seem to be anything I could do to the Gulf. It was a part of me that was beyond change.

I could feel my mother's pain building, her anxiety over not being able to soothe me the way a mother should. So I struggled to suck up my tears. Reaching over to my bedside table, I turned on the light and said, "I'm okay, Mom. I think I'm going to draw a bit. That always makes me feel better."

Remembering myself saying that now made me shudder. I'd said the answer out loud, all those years ago, and didn't recognize it as such. Didn't recognize it when my teacher told me not to stop painting.

A doorbell, a rowboat, a helicopter.

If only, I thought. If only, if only. Would I still be with my family? Would I have kept on breathing? Would I have wanted to?

But God said there were no regrets. I didn't know if I believed that, I certainly felt like I was full of regrets, despite feeling like ending my life was inevitable and had been inevitable for my entire existence. But there really was no turning back now. I'd done it and I'd arrived surprisingly in Heaven. Even if I changed up here, which I felt I already was, it wouldn't do the people I left behind any good. I had to live with that. Or exist. I still didn't know what to call whatever this was that I was doing.

I turned the page on my book. I looked outside at the lights, fewer now that we were moving well into the night.

I was alone. And I was fine. Maybe the sadness I felt now was the type my mother searched for in me. Was there a boy, was a girl mean to me, did I have a bad grade, did I feel fat?

Was there a husband and a daughter and a son, left behind?

Yes. And I was sad. This was a new sad, a sad that was real and a sad that was caused by me and a sad that would lessen, naturally, with time. Not like my height or my hair color or my role in life. Not the Gulf.

I turned out the light and went to bed. I would cry, but I also held the knowledge and the reassurance that I wouldn't cry forever. In Heaven, forever went on an impossibly long time.

• • •

I slept well and long and had my breakfast while standing in front of my easel. Eating was always one of those things that would make me ambidextrous; I had no trouble painting with my right hand while stuffing my face full of muffin with my left. Coffee followed right along.

I did take a break for lunch, but then I was back at it. I was still there when someone rang my doorbell and I yelled loudly that it was open. I figured it was probably God or Faith, but the voice that called out, "Hope, where are you?" wasn't theirs, though it was familiar to me.

"Follow the hallway," I called. "I'm in the studio. Come all the way back." I carefully dipped my narrow brush in bright blue and then traced it beside a line of red down the thigh of my canvas-self, until it stopped at the edge of my knee. Then I turned to see who was here. I was out on the lanai again and my eyes were sun-dazzled, so it took a minute to recognize the silhouette. Virginia! "Well, hi!" I said.

"Hey, Hope," she said and stepped outside, her eyes never leaving my canvas. "I'm sorry to disturb you. You should have told me you were working."

I felt myself blush. Virginia Woolf, *the* Virginia Woolf, was in my studio. She was looking at my painting. A painting that was nowhere near done yet. "Oh, it's fine," I said. "I'm about to take a break anyway. I've been at it since breakfast and my wrist is shrieking." I put my brush into the glass of water on the beat-up table and then clasped my fingers together. I turned my hands so my palms faced outward and then I stretched my arms out in front of me. I hoped that Virginia couldn't hear all the little pings and pops that came from my fingers, my wrist, and my elbow. Even the arm I wasn't using for painting groaned.

Virginia came to my side. "Wow," she said.

I didn't care if she said anything else. Earning a wow from her was enough. "It's not done," I said. "I just started it yesterday. I don't know quite what I'm doing yet."

"It sure looks like you do." I could see her eyes tracing my scrolling lines, my rainbow colors, the way they twisted over my canvas body. "Is there a word in there? Am I seeing a word?"

I swallowed and nodded. That just happened about an hour before. Suddenly, as one of my colored paths wandered up to the belly, I had the urge to make an S. And then two more letters. "Can you see what it says?" I whispered. It felt abruptly important. The word was meant to be hidden, but seen all the same. Seen as a surprise, as a realization.

Virginia frowned and cocked her head sideways. "Sad!" she said suddenly.

"Yes!"

We both stepped back and looked at the word painted deep into my canvas body's belly. It curved in an inverted arc under where the belly button would be and was surrounded by many streams of color.

"Will there be more words?" Virginia asked. "More of the same word? Maybe others?"

I shrugged. "I don't know yet."

She turned to me and smiled. "When I work, I never know what word is going to come next either, until I write it."

I wanted to ask her what she was doing here, but that seemed rude. So I offered a drink instead. "Can I get you something? An iced tea? Coffee? A soda? I have diet Sprite." The soda in my fridge at home mostly reflected my kids' tastes; I just didn't drink it often. But I always kept a little diet Sprite tucked in the back and out of their eye-span. Kids never looked beyond what was right in front of them. I often had upset stomachs and the Sprite helped.

I was surprised when I found it in my refrigerator here. I didn't think I would get an upset stomach in Heaven. I still hadn't opened the 2-litre bottle, though there were nights when I was close.

"Oh, thank you," Virginia said. "This may sound strange, but could I have some iced tea mixed with a little of that Sprite?" She blushed a little herself. "I've always had tea in my life. I was already here when diet Sprite was created, and I love it, but more as an addition. Soda always seems a little too sweet to me, even the diet versions. But mixing a little with my iced tea...it gives it the lemon I love, and just a bit of bubbles." She wrinkled her nose. "I had to get used to the way it makes me belch."

I laughed and assured her that of course I could make her an iced tea mixed with Sprite. I pointed the way to the deck and then went to the kitchen to fix us our refreshments. I wondered if she would notice if I took the time to change out of my painting clothes into something a little nicer. There were almost as many colors on my shirt and pants as on my canvas. But she'd already seen me, I reasoned, and so I let it go.

I brought out our drinks – mine was just my usual iced tea with lemon, I could do without the bubbles – and a snack of Oreo cookies, my favorite, on a tray. Virginia was sitting in the correct chair, the Not-God Visitors Chair. I was relieved; I hadn't told her which one was God's, and really, it would have felt odd to specify it for her. She had *To The Lighthouse* on her lap and was paging through it, looking at all my yellow highlights.

It had been embarrassing to see Virginia looking at my painting, but somehow, it was even more so to see her looking at a copy of her own book that I'd marked up with wild abandon when I was nineteen years old. "I read that when I was a sophomore in college," I said. "I kept it because I loved it. I was so happy when it followed me here."

She smiled and set it on the table between us. "I'm glad you liked it," she said, reaching for her tea. "So I just wanted to stop by and see how you're doing. This can be a difficult place to adjust to. Are you settling in okay?"

My mind stuttered a bit at Heaven being called difficult, but then I nodded. It could be difficult. Not so much for the external stuff, except for the portal. It was the internal that was hard. "I seem to be," I said. "It really depends on the day. Some are so glorious, I can't even believe that I'm here. And others…well, on others, I'm shown exactly why I'm here."

We talked for a while and I relaxed. Eventually, I found myself telling her about my visit with God at the coffee shop outside of our community a few days ago. "I didn't know," I said, and then stopped. I never liked feeling ignorant, and now, admitting to someone like Virginia Woolf that I didn't realize what some people likely would have considered obvious was hard. "I didn't know," I said again, "that I could have helped myself. Just by doing what I love. Painting. Art." I took another Oreo and munched, looking out over this still-new world around me. "I knew it made me feel better, but…"

Virginia shook her head. "Well, you don't know for sure that continually doing your artwork would have made any difference," she said. "Writing, for me, is like painting for you. I love it. It makes me feel happy. Worthwhile. Like…" She stopped for a moment to consider her words, which impressed me. Even though she was a writer, words didn't always come easily. She had to work at it. "Like I'm doing the right thing. Like it's real. The most real thing I can do, and that makes me real." She nodded. "But I never stopped writing. The afternoon I walked into the river, I wrote in the morning." She shrugged just a bit. "In the articles about me, they say my last piece of writing was my suicide note, and technically, they're right, though I certainly don't put letters in the same category as my novels and short stories. But I worked on my new novel that morning. And then I decided I would never finish it." She nabbed an Oreo too. "I never stopped writing, Hope. It did give me some measure of relief. But in the end, it just wasn't enough."

I found it hard to swallow. What Virginia was saying was in direct opposition with what God told me in the coffee shop. God! "The novel you were working on when you died…I know you didn't finish it, but it was published anyway. Are you still writing here? Is there more, after that book?"

She laughed. "Oh, yes. And it's so wonderful. When I write here, it's like the pressure is off. The pressure to perform, the pressure to not only get it right, but to do it better than the last book. To constantly improve. I just *write* here. And when I'm done, God puts it in a bookstore, which automatically generates enough books for everyone. It's like the best print on demand ever!" She laughed. "I'll bring you a copy on Wednesday."

She was so enthusiastic about her work. Yet she was here, in this part of Heaven. That enthusiasm didn't seem to make a bit of difference to being able to maintain her life on earth. "So," I said, "writing wasn't like a life preserver for you? Like a rescue?"

Virginia frowned, but then her face cleared. "Oh, lord. Is God still telling that horrible helicopter story?" She began to laugh. "The doorbell, the rowboat, the helicopter?"

I laughed too, uncertainly at first, because it felt like I was laughing at God, but then sincerely, because it was so nice to see Virginia laugh. "He did. He said sending me my ability to paint, and the people who helped me learn about it, was like sending rescuers to that guy in the flood, along with a rowboat and a helicopter."

Virginia's mouth twisted a little sideways. "Okay," she said thoughtfully and sat back, folding her hands. "Let's work this through."

I had the impression she thought about this a lot. God must have given her the same helicopter speech too. What would he have sent to her? Pen and paper? A typewriter? Mentors? I remembered she was part of a pretty prestigious group of writers called the Bloomsbury Group.

"So the guy in the flood," she said. "His problem was all external, wasn't it? The water was rising. It wouldn't stop raining. And he could have been saved by external forces too, if he'd just left with the rescuers at his door or climbed in the rowboat or the helicopter." She nodded and I nodded with her. I was following so far. "But what we felt, you and me, and everyone in this place, what you call the Gulf...that wasn't external. It was internal, wasn't it." She looked at me.

I thought of the Gulf, the way it felt, the way it was always there. Under my skin. In my mind. Just behind my eyelids. "It was," I said slowly. "Though I was always looking for what caused it. Like something outside of me caused it, an event or something being done to me..."

"I get that," Virginia said. "But the Gulf itself...inside. An interior thing. And God brings you art? The ability to create? Maybe that was in response *to* the Gulf...your painting that's on display in the art gallery certainly is a response. But as a solution? Did it solve your Gulf?"

I thought about all the years that I did paint, I did create. And I felt the Gulf lapping at me the whole while. I thought of my high school teacher asking me if I was okay, which meant that it was really clear that I wasn't. Painting didn't cure it, and it didn't mask it. "Well, no. But I didn't continue with it. I quit, when my second child was born. I think that's God's point."

"Well, I didn't quit. I continued with writing. I never stopped." Virginia tapped her book. "When I died, my husband knew I wanted to be cremated, so he followed through with my wishes. And then he sprinkled my ashes on the ground between two trees we had in our backyard." She smiled, small at first, but then her face erupted in a grin. This sudden playfulness abruptly changed Virginia's whole presence. She lit up, and not from the sunshine. "We were so silly. We named the trees after ourselves. Virginia and Leonard." She beamed. "Virginia had more leaves. And she was greener. Leonard was a little...stodgy." She laughed.

I was delighted. Everything I knew about Virginia Woolf was serious, from the portraits of her to her work to even how she led the group therapy group. Yet here, she burst out into giggles over the trees she and her husband named. I wondered if they tied a hammock between them. If they lay in the hammock and read, she a novel, he a newspaper, or if they napped in the afternoon breeze.

I'd always wanted a hammock.

"Anyway," she said. "He put up a stone, like a headstone, between the trees and on it was engraved the final words from a novel I wrote, called *The Waves.*" She sat up and folded her hands and I could imagine her standing behind a podium at a grand reading somewhere, her back straight, her voice strong. She cleared her throat. "'Against you I fling myself, unvanquished and unyielding, O Death! The waves broke on the shore.'" She looked at me.

"The Gulf," I whispered.

"Yes, the Gulf. That book was published in 1931. I killed myself in 1941, ten years later." She kept her gaze steady. "Writing it and everything that came after didn't keep me from killing myself, did it. Not even that morning.

The Gulf stayed with me, and on that day, I agreed to let the water close over my head."

She literally walked into a river, but first, she loaded her pockets down with rocks so that she would sink. There was no question of her intention.

"Do you know when your Gulf started?" I asked.

Her mouth downturned. "Yes, I know exactly when," she said. "I was six years old. I had two older half-brothers and they began to molest me. That was the start. The molesting didn't end until I moved out when I was twenty-three."

I sat back. At six years old, I already knew that what I felt was sad. I knew the word for it. But I felt it long before I recognized it, named it. By six, it was well underway. "I'm so sorry, Virginia," I said.

When she spoke again, her voice was low and gravelly. "If I was sent a helicopter, it should have been more than a pen and paper and an ability to put words together. It should have been a castrating tool." The words were bitten off. "Writing," she said, "was not my helicopter. I was not saved."

I heard the anger. And I knew who it was directed toward. I knew it was possible to be angry at God on earth, but here? In Heaven? I felt a surge of anger in myself, but then quietly tamped it down. "I don't know when my Gulf started. I can't say when it began. I wish I could."

We sat in silence. After a bit, I turned my head, unsure if she was still there. In Heaven, appearances and disappearances didn't always announce themselves. She was rocking in the rocking chair, her eyes closed, and both hands wrapped around her own book. In that moment, with her fingers on her words, her face uplifted and bathed in sunshine, and her expression so peaceful, writing sure looked like a lifesaver to me.

But she was here, in Heaven, where she was already dead. She'd been dead for over eighty years, dead longer than she'd been alive.

And she wrote that morning, the morning of her death, and then walked into the river.

"In this book," Virginia said, sitting forward and paging through *To The Lighthouse*, "the character Lily is an artist. Remember?"

I nodded. It was why I loved the book so.

She paged and paged. And then she handed the book to me. "Read that," she said, pointing a finger, "out loud."

I cleared my throat.

"...she took her hand and raised her brush. For a moment it stayed trembling in a painful but exciting ecstasy in the air. Where to begin?--that was the question at what point to make the first mark? One line placed on the canvas committed her to innumerable risks, to frequent and irrevocable decisions. All that in idea seemed simple became in practice immediately complex; as the waves shape themselves symmetrically from the cliff top, but to the swimmer among them are divided by steep gulfs and foaming crests. Still the risk must run; the mark made."

I sat back and sighed, clasping the book to my own chest now. I wondered if my face was as peaceful as Virginia's.

Virginia quoted, out loud and by memory, "As the waves shape themselves symmetrically from the cliff top, but to the swimmer among them are divided by steep gulfs and foaming crests. Still the risk must run; the mark made." She laid her hand on my arm. "Steep gulfs, Hope. And you're the swimmer. Even if you made the mark, you might still have drowned, just like I did." She stood up and pressed that same hand to my shoulder. "Maybe you needed a different helicopter, Hope. Or maybe a helicopter just never would have worked. See you Wednesday. I need to get home to Leonard."

I looked up. "Leonard?"

She smiled. "He's here. He lives with me, as he should, and as we should have on Earth, until our natural deaths." Her face clouded for just a minute. "My brothers are here too. But God is good...I don't have to see them. Nor do I have to forgive them. Ever."

And she left.

I sat for a few more minutes, trying to unravel all the words I just twisted with a writer. Then I cleaned up from our snack and decided to go back and take one more look at what I'd accomplished that day. The risks I took. The marks I made. The letters S, A and D, hidden for all to see.

But I wouldn't paint. I was done for the day. After gazing at my partially done painting, which, like Joyce, I didn't like yet, but thought I would eventually, I changed out of my painting clothes and threw them into the washing machine. Then I headed out for Caffeine Heaven, bringing along Virginia's book. I would walk there, I decided. I wanted to sit in the shade in the back of the cafe, drink the remembered iced latte of today's desire, and read *To The Lighthouse.* I didn't want to think about helicopters anymore.

• • •

When I sat down at the next group therapy session, I found myself wishing I could lash my ankle to Faith's. This would be our last session together; she was at the end of her twelve weeks and would be moving on to her next group. I was only in my third week, and while I was relieved to not be losing Virginia, I was horrified at losing Faith. She reassured me she'd still be my friend, still be around, but there were enough instances in my life of people moving to other towns, other states, and never hearing from them again that it made me nervous. I'm sure everyone in the room knew the lack of truth behind, "Stay in touch!" Your hand might have been firmly entwined with someone else's for years, but when that hand tore out of yours, then reached for another in a new situation, there was just no one left for you to hold onto.

But in Heaven, we were supposed to be speaking and hearing the truth. So I reassured myself it must be different here.

As if she knew what I was thinking, which was more than likely, Faith draped her arm around my shoulders. "I'm not going anywhere," she said. "You'll see. I'll just be in a different group in a different room. And we can still go out for coffee afterwards."

Virginia came in then, and I sat back, ready to get this over with. Therapy in Heaven paralleled therapy on earth. I dreaded it before each session, then found myself pulled in to other people's stories and my own emotions as the three hours went on, and finally, found myself leaving, feeling intrigued, relaxed, and soothed. But always with a lot to consider, which would lead me to dread the next time.

Before sitting down in her chair, Virginia dropped a book in my lap. It was a lovely hardcover, bright blue background, two silhouettes facing each other. The title was *Breathing Between Acts.* I looked up at Virginia, my eyebrows and the novel raised. Virginia's final novel, published posthumously, was called *Between The Acts.* I'd read that book in the same English class in college. I remembered that the back of it explained that the book was published the way she left it on her desk that day she walked into the river. I hadn't kept it when the class was over. I didn't like it.

Virginia bent down and whispered in my ear. "I was still revising; I was so unhappy with the book. I never dreamed they would publish it when I clearly left it undone. But when I arrived here, after I settled down, it was like every question and concern I had over the novel suddenly cleared up. I no longer had the real world bearing down on me, confusing me with all of its news and crises and crazy transformations. I knew what to do, along with changing the title." She tapped a finger on the cover. "This book holds what I meant to say. I wish there was a way to swap this one out with the version on earth. It pains me to think that that's what people consider my final work. But..." she straightened and looked around, "one by one, I can be correcting readers, as they arrive up here. And," she smiled, "it's not my final work. There've been more since. And I'm writing now too." She headed to the front of the room.

I folded my hands on the book's cover and then watched as people filed in. Owen was still here, and I saw several others I recognized, like Beth and Madeline. There were some I'd never seen before, and it was hard to tell, looking at them, if they were brand new to Heaven, or just switching groups.

Faith nudged me. "Oh, I know him." She nodded toward a man who was standing undecided between two chairs. "I was his mentor when he arrived here."

I watched as he stepped in front of one chair, the first in the row, and then the other, the second. Finally, he sat on the first, and when someone came along and sat in the second, he moved his chair away in slow scrooches that he probably thought were unnoticeable. "How long has he been here? He still seems new." I remembered my own jitters at the first therapy session, just a couple weeks ago.

She shook her head. "It's been about four years. He arrived during the first year of the COVID-19 pandemic."

I frowned. I wondered if this was another instance, like Madeline's, where she just didn't cure what ailed her and used that as a suicide. Did he go out of his way to catch COVID so he could die? COVID was an awful death; there certainly were a lot of other easier ways to go. "Did he catch COVID on purpose?"

Faith frowned back at me, like what I suggested was preposterous. No more preposterous than Madeline, I didn't think. "No. He crumbled under the pressure, under the fear. He decided to take his life before COVID took it from him."

COVID was difficult, without a doubt. My husband and I found ourselves at home, our jobs transitioned to remote, and my kids' schools followed suit. Our lives revolved around our computer screens. For a while, it was like a family stay-cation. Then it became a family nightmare. We couldn't get away from each other.

But it wasn't any better in our rare forays into the outside world. Every sneeze became the possibility of something else, something worse. If my kids so much as sniffled, I charged at them with a thermometer. My husband too, until he began throwing his hands up over his ears any time he saw me coming.

I was so scared during that time. A time of masks and dire news breaks, eyeballing your distance from the person next to you, picking up your groceries, your medications, your Christmas shopping at the curb after ordering it online without even holding it and considering its weight in the hands of the receiver, and at times, hiding in your house for days on end, to make sure you didn't come in contact with the virus. At first, I didn't know anyone who got sick. Then I knew a few. And then more. A neighbor's mother died, then someone from work died, and then a teacher at the kids' school died.

There was this sense of presence, of something lurking right outside my door that might or might not choose to sweep down on me or someone I loved that day. Or any day. The air became dangerous. If anyone breathed near you, you could be caught. Snared.

It was horrible. I worried every day that I would lose someone. My kids. My husband.

We never got sick, beyond the usual sniffles and coughs. When the vaccine came, we took our turns and gladly bared our arms two times over, and then again for booster shots as different variants still managed to evolve. We celebrated our return to real life, though our re-entry was a path of caution and care and anxiety. Nothing ever really returned to the normal we had pre-COVID.

My family survived. But now, they'd lost me. I didn't catch anything. I just gave in to what I always had.

As Virginia talked, doing the brief intro I now knew well, I kept glancing at the COVID man. He twitched a bit in his seat. I noticed he kept his hands in his lap. There was always a perfect number of chairs for the people attending, and so despite his indecision and care in choosing a seat, he would always have someone next to him. Choosing the aisle seat meant there would only be one, but even with his careful scrooching, that person was not six feet away. I wouldn't have been surprised if he pulled out a mask or squirted hand sanitizer into his palms.

He had to introduce himself, because while he wasn't new to Heaven, he was new to this group. "Hi," he said. "My name is Russell. I died just over four years ago. I shot myself." He stopped, looked at his hands, wrung them, then wiped them on his jeans. "I never considered suicide before COVID. And I didn't consider it for long. But then I saw my neighbor taken away in a body bag. It was a neighbor who delivered a crockpot of chili to my doorstep just ten days before. She made cornbread too." He stopped, inhaled deeply, laying one of his hands on his chest.

I knew he was measuring the depth of his breath. I knew that sigh, remembered watching my kids breathe.

"And then I began to cough. So I left before it got worse. I couldn't stand the idea of being put on a ventilator. So it was really COVID that killed me. I would never have done it, if it wasn't for COVID."

"No," Virginia said gently. "Those are the circumstances that led to your death. But you killed yourself. Only you made the choice."

Russell held her gaze for a bit and she didn't waver, not an inch. Finally, he looked down and I realized he was crying. "I don't really think I belong here," he said. "Even now. I was just so scared."

I was too, I thought. But oddly, during COVID, my life became about survival, my own and my family's. The Gulf was there, but at bay, with the fear of COVID washing up on shore instead. But then it was over and the Gulf returned full force. It wasn't fear that sent me over the edge. It was sadness. It was the Gulf.

But then, like Russell, maybe the Gulf was just my circumstance too. I killed myself. The Gulf didn't. It was my choice.

Russell had been here for four years. I wondered how long it would be before he accepted that his suicide was his own.

CHAPTER ELEVEN

Even The Air

Russell's Story

From the time you are sent home to work remotely, with no definite date for your return or the return of any of your co-workers, you think of COVID as the shark from the movie *Jaws.* The movie is based on the novel by Peter Benchley, and that novel sits on your bookshelf, but it just doesn't bring the impact of the movie's mechanical shark to mind, or the ever-building background music.

Baaaa…dum. Baaaa…dum. Ba-dum ba-dum ba-dum ba-dum!

At the beginning of your lock-down, you mostly hear the music when you watch the news. Or read the headlines on your computer in the morning, on work breaks, and before signing off at bedtime.

Then you stop signing off. When you wake in the middle of the night, you have only to tap your computer and it lights with the current news. Before you even get out of bed in the morning, you check the COVID numbers. The numbers in your town. Your county. Your state. The country. The world. The number of cases, the number of hospitalizations, the number of deaths.

At first, you work only in your home office, coming out for a lunch break in your kitchen, or sit down on the couch in your living room for timed coffee breaks. When you go out, it's usually to the grocery store and you mask up. Your mask is an N95, a letter and numbers that didn't used to mean anything, but mean everything now. The black mask covers your nose and mouth, tucks under your chin. You soak your hands with sanitizer as you walk in, you wipe down the handle of your shopping cart with the disinfecting wipes you carry in your coat pocket, and you apply more sanitizer to your hands every fifteen minutes.

But then it becomes every ten minutes. Then five. Then you wear disposable rubber gloves. Then you sanitize the gloves every fifteen minutes. Ten minutes. Five minutes.

Baaaa...dum. Baaaa...dum. Ba-dum ba-dum ba-dum ba-dum!

You start doing curbside pick-up.

The person who brings your groceries to your car lifts your hatchback, piles the bags inside, then calls for you to have a good day. You wonder, even with his mask, if the air he spouts with his well-intentioned wish flows over your back seat into your front seat. To you. Even with your mask. N95.

You find a service that provides contactless delivery to your door, leaving your groceries on your front step. You watch the delivery person drive away, wait ten minutes for what you believe would be enough time for the fresh air to blow away any contagion, and then you bring in your groceries. You wear your disposable rubber gloves, soaked in hand sanitizer, as you unpack the packages and cans and wipe them down.

As the numbers rise, you stop going out at all. If you crave a meal from a favorite restaurant, you have it delivered and follow the same protocol as your grocery service. Your food grows cold during the ten minutes waiting time, but you warm it in the microwave. You find it hard to believe any virus could survive in a microwave.

You also no longer go to the movie theater. You watch Netflix, Hulu, Amazon Prime, and you laugh by yourself in your living room. You make your own popcorn, you drink your own soda, delivered by the contactless service. Wiped down by you, after ten minutes on your front step.

Then somebody at work gets sick. Then somebody at work dies. There will be no funeral, because there can be no gatherings. The email from work says there will be a "Celebration of Life" at a later time. No one knows when. The pandemic has no duration, no end, predicted. Like lock-down, it is indefinite.

You wonder where the body waits.

You'd received an email from that body a month ago. You wonder, briefly, ridiculously, if the virus can be spread through wifi. Then you acknowledge your ridiculousness, laugh it off, but at night, when you go to bed, you stare at the ceiling.

How did he get it? He was working remotely too. Wasn't he staying home? Wasn't he wearing a mask? N95?

Baaaa...dum. Baaaa...dum. Ba-dum ba-dum ba-dum ba-dum!

You begin to move around the house with your laptop, doing your work in different places, breathing in, you think, different air. Fresh air. You crack open your windows, even as the temperature outside stays cold. You wait for spring. You sit by a space heater. The taps your fingers create on your keyboard become muted as you choose to wear disposable rubber gloves while at work. On coffee breaks and lunch breaks, you take the gloves off, but you sanitize your hands before and after. You begin ordering paper plates and hot-drink cups and cold-drink cups and plastic silverware from the grocery store, so you can dispose of everything you touch. You stop using your garbage cans for trash day, just placing the bags at the curb and putting your recyclables in clear plastic, so that you don't have to touch the bins after the garbage men empty them. They complain and leave a note on your door, which you pluck off with your gloved hand and put directly into a plastic baggie, seal it, and stuff it into a larger bag. They still take your garbage, but they stare at your front window and shake their heads. You wave and call thank you, but you doubt that they can hear you through the glass and your mask. N95.

When your mail arrives every day, you wait the allotted ten minutes, then retrieve it from its box right next to your door, just opening it enough to slide your arm out. You wave at your mailman through the front window. He waves back and from the way his eyes crinkle, you think he smiles at you from behind his mask. You crinkle too.

The only person you talk to is your neighbor, through Zoom. You and she used to share a beer on your deck, or wine on her deck, after work sometimes. On weekends, pre-COVID, she might call over that she made a large salad, come to dinner, or you would holler that you were grilling out, did she want a hamburger. Now, you both work remotely. Sometimes you wave at each other from your decks, when you step outside for a breath of fresh cold air. One evening, you call out and ask for her email, saying you will invite her to a Zoom meeting for a beer. She agrees and smiles. She drinks wine. You start meeting online each evening and talk about the news, talk about the numbers. She shares that someone at her job died. You share that someone at yours died. You both fall silent.

She broaches that since you are both working remotely and not seeing anyone and not going anywhere, maybe you could still meet for dinner on your decks, even though it is cold. You could create your own bubble, a new word being used by the media to reflect personal safety. You say no, it is safer to keep your bubble to only yourself. You can meet for dinner via Zoom. She sighs, but agrees.

You watch movies and series together, Hulu or Netflix on your television screens, Zoom on your computer screens, each of you on your respective couches.

When you talk to her, sometimes the *Jaws* music dies down. Sometimes it gets louder.

Baaaa...dum. Baaaa...dum. Ba-dum ba-dum ba-dum ba-dum!

During a work coffee break, you think you hear a bump come from your kitchen. You get up and look, but nothing is out of place. Then you see a crockpot on your deck, just outside your slider door. It's steaming.

You wait ten minutes, then pull on your disposable rubber gloves and bring it in. The aroma is wonderful; it smells like chili. You know your neighbor makes great chili. Along with the crockpot is a disposable aluminum loaf pan, filled with warm cornbread. You wipe both containers down with your disinfecting wipes and you plug the crockpot in.

For a moment, you smile. For a moment, you consider asking her to dinner. You could even eat in the dining room, where you have a large eight-foot dining table that has never been used. You could sit at either side. You could risk it. You could leave the windows open. It would be so nice to see someone without a screen between you.

You consider. For a moment.

Baaaa...dum. Baaaa...dum. Ba-dum ba-dum ba-dum ba-dum!

Because you don't have a Zoom meeting set up, you call her on Facetime. She laughs at your pleasure. "I just wanted you to have a nice warm meal," she says. "I know you love my chili. I know you love cornbread."

You smile, thank her, then set up a Zoom meeting so you can eat together. She's made a pot of chili for herself too, and her own cornbread.

While you eat, she asks if she made the chili too bland. I can hardly taste it, she says. But the chili is fine; it makes you sweat. You laugh with her, deciding she's become immune to her own cooking. You notice she sniffles. "It's nothing," she says. "Just allergies. I need to dust."

So do you. You wipe everything down with your disinfecting wipes.

A few days later, she is running a fever.

A few days after that, she is coughing.

"A cold," she says.

But from where? Where could she have caught it? She hasn't been anywhere, just like you haven't been anywhere. Where could she have caught a cold?

Where could she have caught COVID? Could it be COVID?

You eat the chili for dinner for four days straight. After the second day, you make your own cornbread to accompany the rest of the chili. You use a box mix you buy from the grocery store. It is delivered to your front step. You let it sit for ten minutes. You wipe it down.

The chili remains in the crockpot. You wipe it every day.

Baaaa...dum. Baaaa...dum. Ba-dum ba-dum ba-dum ba-dum!

On the eighth day, your neighbor doesn't come to your Zoom meeting. You call via Facetime and she doesn't answer. On the ninth day, you watch when the mail is delivered; the mailman waves at you and smiles. You wave back. But your neighbor's door never opens. Her mailbox is starting to overflow.

Where could she have gotten it?

On the tenth day, you call the police. You explain what has happened and that there's been no communication for days. She was sick, you say. She was sick. She had a fever. She had a cough. A cold? She lives alone.

The police come. An ambulance comes. They break down her front door.

You see faces appear at other houses, in other windows, across the street. The mailman pauses, waits on the sidewalk.

When the stretcher appears, you can't see your neighbor's face. She is zipped up tight inside a bag. They load her into the ambulance and they leave. There is no siren.

You stagger to your couch. Where could she have gotten it? A cold? COVID.

You leave her crockpot in a trashbag on the curb.

You stare at your ceiling all night, the next night, the night after night after night.

Baaaa...dum. Baaaa...dum. Ba-dum ba-dum ba-dum ba-dum!

Where could she have gotten it? Through the wifi?

The air. The air that flows through your house, that goes into each room, and you go to each room, looking for different air. You open your windows, even though it's cold. The air comes from outside. Outside is where the people are. People who don't wear masks. Who keep going to work. Who go to the grocery stores and touch things and then put them back. Who go to the bars. Who go to parties. Who laugh and talk and breathe and breathe and breathe and spread particles into the air. The air which floats. Which travels into houses. Which gets into vents. Which spreads through her house. The houses across the street.

Your house.

Baaaa...dum. Baaaa...dum. Ba-dum ba-dum ba-dum ba-dum!

It's coming. It's coming and it can't be stopped. Not by rubber gloves or by hand sanitizer or masks or remote work or deliveries or Zoom or Facetime or Netflix or Hulu or six feet apart or crockpots left in the cold for ten minutes and then wiped down and heated up. Not by cornbread baked in disposable pans. Not by microwaves.

It's coming.

You cough!

Baaaa...dum. Baaaa...dum. Ba-dum ba-dum ba-dum ba-dum!

Someone else at work dies. Someone else's sister gets sick. In the news, seventy-five people at a wedding test positive. A choir at a church tests positive. A newborn baby tests positive. Body after body comes out from a nursing home where no one is allowed in and no one is allowed out.

You can't let COVID get you. It means feeling worse than death. It means being placed on a ventilator. It means having long-lasting effects that go on and on and no one knows for how long. Indefinitely. Like the pandemic. Like the lock-up.

And then the virus starts morphing into something else. Into several something elses.

There's a vaccine being developed, but will it treat something else?

Baaaa...dum. Baaaa...dum. Ba-dum ba-dum ba-dum ba-dum!

You go online and find a local sporting goods store that delivers. You order a pistol. You order ammo. Just one box. You put a rush on the delivery. When it is dropped at your door, you wait ten minutes. Then you pick it up with your gloved hands and you wipe down the package. You open it, wipe down the gun. Wipe the ammo. Load it.

Baaaa...dum. Baaaa...dum. Ba-dum ba-dum ba-dum ba-dum!

You stare at the ceiling that night. In the morning, you check the numbers, then sign off of the computer. You don't work. You stand at the window and wait for the mailman. When he arrives, you wave. He waves back, but you notice his eyes don't crinkle. Neither do yours.

There is no smile. Not even for a moment.

You bring in your mail, find nothing important, toss it on the counter.

Baaaa...dum. Baaaa...dum. Ba-dum ba-dum ba-dum ba-dum!

The music is so loud. You can feel the shark around you. It is swimming around your house. It is swimming through your vents.

You strip off your gloves, throw them away. You take off your mask. N95. Then you call the police and tell them to come to your house. Your door is unlocked. You don't hang up, but set the phone down next to you on the couch. You don't want to be alone and your neighbor is gone. The mailman is gone. There is no one in the windows across the street. Lifting the pistol, you press the muzzle against your forehead.

Breathe in. Breathe out. The air is suspect. Then promise yourself that the air won't get you. Hope that your air won't get anyone else.

You shoot.

The music stops.

Your last breath is a sigh of relief. Of freedom.

CHAPTER TWELVE

Hope

When the group therapy meeting finished up, I told Faith that I'd meet her outside and then I walked over to COVID Man. Russell, I reminded myself. He stood up slowly and stepped away, but made no move to leave, as if he wanted everyone else to go out before him. I walked into the aisle that was two rows in front of him and stood respectfully at least six feet away. I was surprised at how that felt so familiar several years after the "six feet apart" rule was eased, except during outbreaks. "Hi, Russell," I said. "I'm Hope."

He glanced at me, and then backed up as much as he could, the backs of his knees bumping into his chair. He folded his hands in front of him, wringing them a bit. "Hi, Hope," he said, his voice soft.

"I just wanted to tell you...Well, I'm relatively new here. Just three weeks. But I remember COVID. I remember what it was like." I shook my head. "What a horrible time."

He leaned forward just a bit. "Did it ever get better?" He shrugged. "I don't pay much attention to the news from earth. And the portal...well, I only had a few distant relatives, so there's no one to really watch, though I do keep an eye on the people I used to work with. They don't say much about COVID, though I noticed when they returned to the office, they weren't wearing masks anymore." He visibly shuddered.

I turned a chair around and sat on it, facing him, but carefully maintaining our distance. Virginia was still there, I noticed, in the background, pulling together some papers. She had one ear cocked toward us. "It was chaotic for a while. But it got better. When Biden took office, well, things got more organized. COVID became a priority. There were several vaccines and boosters. It's still around, and some outbreaks are harder than others, but now it's much more like the flu that so many originally compared it to."

He took a deep breath, then sat down too. "So...you're all right? You got through it okay?"

I nodded. "I never caught it. No one in my family did. But I can tell you I was so relieved when we were all vaccinated."

He looked at his hands. "I don't know if I even had it. I just couldn't handle waiting around anymore. It felt inevitable. When I died, they were saying the vaccine was still a couple years away."

It did feel inevitable. I finally had to turn the news off during that time. I focused on keeping my home a safe place, and that was where my attention needed to be. "They managed to rush it through, so it came out much sooner than we all expected. That caused its own problems, though, as some were afraid to trust it." I leaned forward just a bit, not wanting to get too close. "I wanted to talk to you, just for a second, because I know what you mean when you say you don't feel like you belong here."

This caused him to look up. "You feel that way too? But...you killed yourself, right?" Which seemed like a nonsensical question for where we were. Who didn't? "And you said you thought about it for a long time."

"Of course I killed myself. That's why we're all here, even you." I heard a small snort and I knew Virginia just couldn't help herself. She tamped pages together to cover for it and she coughed a little. Russell stiffened. "But I feel different from everyone else because I don't know what it was that made me so sad. It wasn't just when I actually did it; I was sad for as long as I can remember. Everyone here seems to have a moment that they remember, they can pinpoint why they did it. Reasons. Scenes. Events. All I have is a feeling." I sighed, stood up and turned my chair back around. Russell stood too and I sensed the conversation coming to a close. "Even you can say, 'I killed myself because I was so scared of COVID.' The virus was your event, and so was seeing your neighbor taken away. All I can say is, 'I killed myself because I was always sad,'." I neatened the aisle. "So I just wanted to tell you that I understand, feeling different from the others, feeling like you don't belong here. I get it."

Russell offered me a smile, a small one, but a smile. "Thanks for telling me. It helps to know that I'm not alone here. Especially when it feels like I should be surrounded by people just like me. People who understand why I did what I did, but who also understand who I was too, not just what I did with my last moments."

I thought about that. "Your neighbor, the one who died from COVID...she's here, you know. Have you tried to get a hold of her? She knew you."

I actually saw his knees wobble and I thought he was going to have to sit down again. Then he said, "I haven't." He leaned forward and whispered, "What if she still has it?" His look of horror was so complete that I wondered if he'd learned a thing in the four years he'd been here. He walked out ahead of me. How could someone in Heaven not feel like he's in Heaven?

Virginia came alongside me. "You do have a reason, you know," she said.

I looked at her, surprised. "I do? What is it?"

"You killed yourself because you were sad, and you couldn't stop being sad."

I laughed. "Well, I know that. But why was I sad?"

Virginia shrugged. "Does it matter?" Then she walked out.

I looked around at the empty room. Just minutes before, it was filled with people who talked about their experiences that led them here, and their experiences since. When they each told their stories, they offered reasons for what they did. I didn't. I just offered the how.

Did it matter?

It sure felt like it did. At least, to me.

I went downstairs to find Faith.

• • •

We were just starting our second lattes when Joyce came barreling into Caffeine Heaven's outdoor area. She looked around and I raised my hand to wave a hello to her. But instead of just smiling and then moving to her own table, she came directly to me, striding with that sense of purpose that let me know I was the reason behind her stopping in. She was carrying a canvas.

I immediately glanced at my cell phone, bringing up my calendar. Was today the day I was supposed to meet Joyce to see the oil pastel canvas she'd been working on the last time I was in the store? No, that wasn't until Friday. I breathed a sigh of relief. Even in Heaven, I could be disorganized.

"Hi!" Joyce said and she pulled up a third chair. She held out a hand to Faith. "You must be Faith," she said. "I'm Joyce. God told me you were Hope's mentor."

"Nice to meet you. Won't you –"

But before she could finish, Joyce plunked down on the extra chair, turned toward me, and lifted the canvas onto her lap as if her body was an easel. "Look, Hope!" she said. "I just couldn't wait to show you, and you told me you usually come here after group. So I searched you out!"

Any annoyance I had disappeared when I looked at Joyce's drawing. I saw the rainbow clouds beginning to gather that day in the store, but now, they were a cloud community. Puffy and light, they gathered together to form what still looked like a rainbow, but in bits and pieces of cottonballs. There were glitter-sprinkles and the clouds sparkled. Here and there, there was the brightest hint of blue, the sky peeking through, and a thin wash of gold insinuated over it all, as if the sun was just behind. The more I studied it, the more I could see shapes and I felt like I was lying on a hillside, naming the clouds as they drifted by. Horse. Balloon. Doughnut. Wisconsin.

"Wow," Faith sighed from across the table and I swear the clouds swayed with her breath. "That's beautiful!"

"Joyce," I said, finally reaching out and touching the canvas. It was warm. "This is –" I hesitated, thinking how my painting showed the Gulf and how this was the exact opposite. "This is...You've drawn happiness! You did! That's what this is!"

Joyce laughed out loud. "Yes, I did! You're exactly right! I've been wondering what this is, but all I know is when I see it, I just want to stare...and giggle. It's like the circus, without any scary clowns. And if it's made of cotton candy." She propped her chin on the top of the canvas, becoming her own Kilroy. "Hope...it's for you. I want to give it to you."

You know that involuntary movement you make when you're so happy or surprised or delighted that your hands just automatically slap themselves over your mouth? As if you're afraid that the emotion of that moment will escape, so you plug your mouth with your own clasped fingers? That's exactly what I did. "What?" I said through my knuckles. "What? Oh, no, Joyce. This should go in a gallery somewhere. People should see this." I remembered only doing this motion three other times in my life. Two were for the births of each of my children. I smacked my hands over my mouth as the just-born baby was set onto my chest. My husband had to pry my arms away to wrap them around the naked little warm body that was impossibly my daughter, then my son. Years before they were born, I did the same motion for my husband himself, when he proposed to me. Just like with the babies, he had to pull at my arm, to put the engagement ring on my finger.

"Well, maybe," Joyce said, shrugging. "But I want you to have it. You said you died because you were sad. Well, now you're in Heaven. And here's happy."

Carefully, I took the canvas from her and held it out in front of me, resting it on the table. In this position, I was the only one who could see it; its back was to Faith, and Joyce was off to the side.

If I could have hugged the canvas, I would have. But I was afraid my embrace would ruin it; the clouds could come off on me. "Is there fixer on this?" I asked.

"Yep." Joyce nodded. "You like it?"

"I love it!" I looked around for a safe place to put it. It just didn't belong on the ground. Faith, intercepting my thoughts, pulled over another chair so I could set it there. "Thank you," I said to Faith. "Thank you," I said to Joyce. "Do you want to join us for a coffee?"

"You bet. I'll go get it. But..." she stood and looked down at me, "I'm still open to meeting on Friday, if you'd like." Then she set off for Joe and the coffee bar.

As we all talked and drank our brew, I thought about how normal this all seemed. If I was at home, I might've been in a coffee shop. I likely wouldn't have been with anyone, as friends were no longer a part of my life by that point, but I would have been surrounded with voices and laughter and the aroma of all different sorts of drinks.

Despite the familiarity, there were significant differences here, beyond my being dead. I wasn't alone, I had two friends. Across the way, I could see Virginia. She was sitting at a single-seater table, her coffee's steam rising up into the leaves of the tree above her, and she was typing furiously into a laptop. I almost laughed at the incongruity of someone like Virginia Woolf working on today's technology, but then I didn't. It was perfect, really. Why should you go without the ability to do what you love, and in the best way possible, just because you're dead?

There was a picture next to me, called Happy. Or if it wasn't called that, it would be now.

There was a barista who smiled at me if I looked up at him. There were friends and friendly strangers, all with similarities to me, surrounding me with the rhythm of chatter and conversation.

And there was me. I felt happy. This was happy. I felt like those clouds. I felt this, even after the terrible thing I'd done. Or maybe I felt this *because* of the terrible thing I'd done.

When I got home to my new condo, I would find a spot for this beautiful canvas that wasn't mine, wasn't something I created, but was a gift to me. I would look in the portal, see my family. And then either dinner and painting, or painting and dinner, or painting and eating at the same time, whatever struck me.

My shoulders felt loose, my neck relaxed. I knew there was a smile on my face and I heard the lilt of my own voice, a higher timbre than I was used to, a laugh tucked just behind the words.

This was what happy felt like.

And gratitude too.

• • •

After walking around the condo for a bit, I decided to hang Joyce's canvas in the hallway between my bedroom and my studio. This way, I would see it for inspiration whenever I walked to my studio to paint, and I would see it when I returned, tired, but...happy.

After hanging the canvas, I walked with purpose into the bathroom. I was choosing to look into the portal this time, not doing it because I had to, to fulfill a chore, or because the sky scarf fell down. I walked in there to see my family. Removing the sky blue scarf from the portal, I leaned against the counter and watched. My arms automatically crossed; while I truly wanted to see this vision of my family, I knew these moments usually brought with them no small amount of pain. I had to brace myself each time.

My daughter was sitting on her bed at home, her laptop open on one side of her, textbooks scattered, and her thumbs were flying over her phone. Texting, more than likely. I studied her, this view so familiar to me, and I looked for any difference, like the differences I'd seen in Caffeine Heaven. Changes from the way my everyday used to look. Her hair now looked washed and it was neatly pulled back into a ponytail, one errant strand slipping down her cheek. She was dressed in jeans and her favorite hoodie. For this moment, everything seemed to be as it would be if I was there. I'd likely be in the kitchen, fussing over something for dinner, or if it was a bad day, I'd be in bed. Though if it was a bad day, she wouldn't be in her room this way. She'd be in my room, sitting on the floor, leaning against my bed, or she'd be checking the freezer to see if there was a frozen pizza.

So this wasn't a bad day. It could have been, if I was still there.

And just then, I heard it. Her laughter. It rang through the mirror as clearly as if I was right there and I knew she must be texting with her best friend. It was best friend kind of laughter.

I just started to smile, to maybe laugh with her, when she did just what I did that afternoon in the coffee shop. Both hands clapped over her mouth and the laughter stopped abruptly. Her eyes widened, and then, if eyes could slam, they slammed shut.

When I was with Faith and Joyce, my hands tried to hold my happiness in so it wouldn't leave me, it wouldn't escape. But from the horror I saw on my daughter's face when her eyes reopened, this was about something else that she wanted to keep hidden. I saw her turn her head and my gaze followed hers to the photograph on her dresser. It was the two of us, my arms wrapped around her shoulders, taken when she received an award at school. In the next second, her cell phone was thrown across the room, her textbooks kicked to the floor, and only her laptop carefully set aside before she stuffed her head under her pillow and sobbed. I could hear her friend shouting through the phone, asking what happened, asking if she was okay.

And of course she wasn't. Because she didn't think it was okay to be okay, even for a moment, so soon after my death. She was horrified at her own laughter.

Like her friend, I called her name. I touched the mirror, placing my hand on her back. Her friend's voice disappeared; she must have hung up. Eventually, my daughter's breaths evened out and she slept. I ran my fingers over her back, in that special light touch tickle that she'd loved since she was a baby, and I heard her breaths go deeper.

But there was that moment, just a moment, when she smiled. She laughed.

It was a good day, because I wasn't there. And it was a bad day, because I wasn't there.

Amazing how guilt could hit on so many different levels. Amazing how the air could be taken out of my lungs as I stood in a bathroom, impossibly far away.

I thought of my son and the scene switched to his room. He was at his desk, the curtains opened, but his head canted down, not up toward the sky. His right arm was moving slowly, so whatever homework he was working on wasn't coming easily. The portal allowed me to move behind him to see over his shoulder.

It wasn't homework.

My son was drawing.

My son never drew. As a child, he rejected crayons for legos and building blocks. I ran through his current school schedule in search of any class that might require a drawing, but none came to mind. He was using Sharpies, they were scattered over his desk like the clouds in Joyce's picture. He picked one up, used it, threw it down, picked up another, used it, threw it down. Caps and markers were everywhere and I wanted to chide him, to remind him to put the caps back on; the pens would dry out.

I recognized the pens. They were a complete set that I bought on impulse one day, when I was picking up a prescription for a new antidepressant at the drugstore. I told myself they were beautiful, and that because they were beautiful, I would use them. It wasn't paint; I wouldn't need an easel or a canvas, just a sketchpad. I could do that anywhere. I picked up a new sketchpad too, even though I knew I had some, still completely unused, on the shelf in my corner of the basement. I thought the two new things together would be motivation enough for me to sit down and actually draw, the way my son was drawing now.

I looked closer. My son used that new sketchpad. When the pens and this new sketchpad soon joined the others in the basement, I tucked them together on the same shelf, partners joined in rejection. I never pulled off a single cap or flipped to a single page. And now, here they were, caps loose and flying, sketchpad open. He must have gone down to my corner of the basement and searched through my things, bringing these up to his room. Where he never drew before.

The sketchpad was not turned to the first page, but several pages in. This wasn't his first drawing.

Then I was glad, actually glad, that I wasn't there. That the portal muted me. This wasn't the time for an artist lesson from his mother. He was drawing. He was lost in it. His eyes drifted so close to the paper sometimes that I wondered how I could get across to his father that we should check if he needed glasses.

I tried to understand what it was he was drawing, but from my angle, I couldn't make it out. It didn't matter. He might not even know yet what it was. But I recognized the intensity. I wondered if he'd been drawing for a while, and I just didn't know it. Did he hide it from me?

Or was I just too far gone already? I felt like I lived the last six months of my life with one foot in reality and the other foot already running away. I must have missed so much.

I turned my thoughts to my husband, but the mirror went dark.

I decided to skip dinner for now and headed down the hallway toward my studio. I looked toward Joyce's canvas as I passed, but right now, the colors just didn't really register for me. I only saw my son's Sharpies, the tense movement of his shoulder. I heard my daughter's friend calling her name.

I thought of Joyce handing me the picture and saying, "Well, now you're in Heaven. Here's happy!" It was there, on the canvas. But it wasn't in me, at the moment.

Even in Heaven, happiness wasn't a steady source. It ebbed and flowed, like the ocean I loved so much. Though the ocean never disappeared either, I realized. So happiness must be in me somewhere, just not always as present from one moment to the next.

At home, if it was in me somewhere, I could never find it. It was buried so deeply, I was never aware of it. It may not have existed at all. Until I came here.

Standing before my canvas, I picked up my brush and continued filling in my silhouette.

• • •

It was several hours later when I realized I was starving. The air was cool with nighttime, and my skin, suddenly aware, sprouted goosebumps.

Stepping back from the canvas, I studied it. Painting was sometimes like entering another realm. Things appeared, new lines, new scenes, and in this particular canvas's example, new words. As I moved around inside my canvas body, I would suddenly grab a slim brush and the black paint and slide in another word. *Stuck. Buried. Blank.* On what would have been my spine, I put *Hopeless.* And then I continued flowing around the body with single lines of color, the words becoming subtle, part of the skin, of the body itself. The overall effect was reminding me of something psychedelic.

The room around me darkened with the outside, but the painting somehow stayed bright. I wasn't loving it yet. But it was okay. My arms and shoulders ached. My knees needed to bend into a sit.

I turned on some lights and cleaned everything up. Before I closed the lanai doors, I stood on the deck and looked out over the starry sky, the lit town, the condo units around me a puzzle of specks and squares of white light. The air was definitely cooler. Apparently, Heaven was moving steadily into fall.

I closed up and left the room, planning to change out of my painting clothes, dump them in the washing machine, and then pull on some comfy flannel pajama pants and a big long-sleeved t-shirt before making dinner. But an aroma caught me by surprise. I hadn't set anything to cook while I painted. Was my dinner delivered again? I planned on fending for myself, and fending for myself tonight meant peanut butter and jam spread on a bagel, a glass of wine, and maybe some Oreos for dessert. But whatever this was smelled infinitely better.

I could see the lights were already on in the living room and the kitchen. I came around the corner and found God serving up spaghetti. I could smell garlic and the zest of Italian sausage. On the table was a plate filled with slices of garlic bread, thick with butter and cheese.

"Oh!" I said, stopping dead in my tracks.

God was wearing an apron, one of those that goes up around the neck and ties around the middle, like overalls without legs. It said across the bib, "Feel free to kiss the cook."

I'd never thought about kissing God. And I didn't think I had an apron in my condo. I never owned an apron in my life.

"It's not yours," God said, following my thoughts and smoothing the apron's front. "It's mine. Spaghetti sauce and I have a long history of ruining shirts together. The washer repairs them, of course, but this just keeps the shirts neat to begin with, and it adds just a *soupcon* of good humor." He brought his pinched-together fingers to his lips and kissed them with a flourish.

God spoke French. Of course he did.

"Thank you," I said, and took a deep breath. "It smells wonderful! Do I have time to get changed?"

"Sure, go ahead." He carried two heaping plates to the table. "I'll get the wine poured."

I hurried to my bedroom and rummaged in my closet. I also had a history of ruining shirts with spaghetti sauce, so I chose carefully. I discarded the idea of the pajama pants and t-shirt, choosing instead a lightweight red sweater and some black jeans.

When I returned to the table, God was already seated. He stood up immediately and held my chair for me as I got comfortable. After returning to his chair, he raised his glass, so I raised mine too. "To hard work and new beginnings," he said.

We clinked. God looked tired. I never expected God to look tired, but, I suppose, being God, of course he would be. His job would definitely be more than full time. It was a job that existed as long as the universe, and was always 24/7. "So," I said, twirling my first forkful, "not that I'm unhappy you're here, but why are you?"

He shrugged. "I just wanted to check in. People like you...well, sometimes, the adjustment period is a little harder." He smiled. "Besides, I like you. I enjoy talking to you."

Imagine being liked by God. It was a different kind of warm feeling. But I wondered at his words. "People like me?" I asked. "What do you mean?"

A splat of spaghetti sauce landed squarely in the middle of his apron bib. I was glad he'd kept it on for the meal. He glanced down at it, but then slurped up the next bite without care. "You're here without an event. You're worried because you can't say why you ended your life. People like you tend to fret over that. I think sometimes you worry that maybe you made a mistake. That the other people here are so solid with bad events and situations, you feel like your decision doesn't measure up to theirs."

I swallowed. "I feel like that in a way, sure. But I don't feel like I made a mistake. My relief at being here...my relief at not being there...it all points to this being the right decision. I honestly felt happy this afternoon. And I feel like I'm doing more here than coming up for air, because that implies I'm going to dive back down. I'm not. I'm stepping right out into the air. And I'm going to stay here." God offered the garlic bread and I unabashedly took the largest piece. He took two. "It's hard to explain, really, how it feels. It's like I don't quite belong. I'm different than the others who I've met so far." I thought of Russell. "Well, most everyone. I met Russell this afternoon, the man who killed himself because he wanted to make sure that COVID didn't get him first." I looked at God and he nodded. "He doesn't think he belongs here, because he never thought of suicide until that moment. That's not me, though. I feel like I'm in the right place. But I don't have a moment, while even someone like Russell has one." The bread was crunchy in the crust, but soft everywhere else. Perfect.

God took a bite too and then talked around it. "You do belong here, Hope. Really. You do." He took a long swallow of wine, refilled his glass. "And there is a reason why you felt sad. I am going to show you what that is. But not yet." His mouth, blotched with sauce at the corners, turned down. "It's not that you're not ready. It's me that's not. It's hard to talk about. It's hard for me."

I sat back. What in the world could be difficult for God to talk about? Was it my fault? What did I do? "God?" I asked. My voice sounded like I was nine years old again. I couldn't get the rest of the words out.

He patted my hand. "Really. You did nothing. It's about me. It's about what I did...or didn't do, really."

I was confounded. This was God, giving me the "It's not you, it's me," line. If I was sitting across from someone else, someone...human, I would have demanded an explanation. But were you supposed to make demands of God? "I don't understand," I said. "But at least I know there's a reason."

"There is." The coffeepot began to gurgle and the aroma of rich and strong coffee blended in with what was already a satisfying dinner. "In a moment, we'll have a lovely dessert – peach pie, I know it's your favorite. And then I want to look at this new canvas of yours. And could I see Joyce's too? Faith told me it was amazing."

"You bet," I said. And then I watched in wonder as God, God himself, cleaned up the plates, loaded them into my dishwasher, and then sliced us some peach pie fresh from the oven. After serving us, he took off his apron.

"I don't have as difficult a time with pie," he said and laughed.

By the time I led him to my studio, I felt like I could have rolled, I was so full. "Now, the painting is nowhere close to done," I cautioned God just outside the door.

"Understood," he said.

There were can lights in the ceiling just before the lanai doors and I turned these on so that they shone directly down on the canvas. God and I stood there and his eyes roved all over. I tried to follow his gaze, to see what he was looking at when.

"Wow," he finally said. "And that's your body, right?"

I nodded. "Joyce traced me."

"What are you going to do with the outside of the body?"

"What?"

"The..." he waved his hands, swinging them in an arc around my body's outline, creating an almost cliché hourglass figure. Again, if he was human, I would have expected a wolf whistle. "...background? What would you call it? The part that isn't the inside of the body."

I laughed. "Yes, the background." I studied it. It was still in the soft coffee-beige I'd given it, to keep it neutral. I hadn't really thought about doing anything else. The important thing was on the inside.

The important thing was on the inside.

I repeated that to myself, then tried to focus on what God asked.

"I don't know," I said. "I think I'm going to leave it as it is. Just a background color."

He nodded. "Can I make a suggestion?"

I didn't know God made suggestions, especially on artwork. "Sure."

"What if you did a partner piece with this? Same silhouette, though maybe facing the opposite direction. And the silhouette is colored in, maybe the same color as your background here. And then you paint the outside. What's happening on the outside?"

My head spun. I'd just had the thought that *the important thing was on the inside*. But God was directing my thoughts elsewhere. At first, my spinning seemed to be away from the idea. But then I realized it was searching for more words. Words on the outside.

"Wow," I said quietly. "I'm not even sure where I'd start. But I feel like I'd like to."

God smiled at me. "Finish this one first, though."

"Oh, I always do. I can't do two projects at once. I've always felt too invested in what's in front of me." I looked back at the canvas. "I've never abandoned a painting. I just keep going with it. I don't know if that's right or not, but it works for me." I pointed toward the canvases lining the far wall of my studio. The false starts the first day I tried to paint. "See? I kept all of those. They didn't do anything for me at the time, but they will. Some artists just paint over and make the canvas white again. I don't. I'd feel like I was suffocating someone, burying something alive. There's an idea in each of those somewhere. They just weren't...ripe yet."

God smiled.

I turned the lights off as we left the room. As God walked ahead down my hallway, in search of Joyce's picture, I looked back. The moonlight flowed in and my canvas suddenly glowed with silver.

I started to love it.

• • •

Standing at my condo door that night, saying goodnight to God, I felt the sudden urge to thank him. "You know, this is really quite the deal you have here," I said.

He raised his eyebrows.

"What I mean is..." I searched my brain for what I meant. "I mean, just look at this one building. This one building, intended for those of us who died on this day in history. Just one day. And in the suicide section of Heaven. You must have hundreds of other sections. And every day, people pour in, and you provide them with a place that matches them and situations that match them, and you surround them with just the right people. I mean, just since I got here, there's been, what, twenty-some more days? And I'm sure everyone has been greeted and treated as well as I have."

God gave a self-deprecating shrug. "I'm glad to hear it. I worry about that sometimes; trying to keep Heaven uplifted isn't easy, especially as it's grown larger and larger. But just because it's Heaven doesn't mean we haven't followed along with Earth's technology. We have computers here now, and algorithms that match everyone's needs up with others that will help meet these needs, and vice versa." He sighed. "I don't think I could keep up otherwise. It used to be a lot simpler."

Which made me wonder something. "You know, I haven't been outside this community much. Just with you, when you brought me to that other coffee house, and when I've gone to the ocean. But I haven't seen Jesus. Is he here?"

God laughed. "Well, of course. But he likes to hang out with the dinosaurs."

"Oh, right. Sure. Of course." I rolled my eyes. "There are dinosaurs here?"

"Everything is here, Hope. Everything that ever lived. Right down to the smallest sparrow."

Sometimes, things are just so amazing, you have to accept it and shut down. There's no wondering about it, no analyzing it, no speculating about it. And that's what I did. Jesus with dinosaurs? A dinosaur community in Heaven? Well, that's just fine. "So I just wanted to say thank you. I was so...lonely before. And here, I've met so many wonderful people. Virginia Woolf. And there's an art store with someone like Joyce in it. And Joe at the coffee shop. And Faith. I couldn't do without Faith."

"That's pretty much true of all of us." God laughed and then patted my shoulder before walking down the hall.

I slowly closed the door, then turned my back to it, leaning and looking around at my place. *My* place. A place that didn't exist three weeks ago. And it only existed because I stopped existing.

At least, maybe. What was this, if it wasn't existence?

And what was my reason for ending it there, and being here now? A reason that God himself wasn't ready to tell me?

Once again, I decided that some things were just better left to acceptance, instead of rumination.

And better left to Faith too. I smiled. I'd call her tomorrow and see what she made of God's reticence. And ask her where we could see the dinosaurs.

CHAPTER THIRTEEN

Poof!

Faith's Story

When I was nine years old, a boy socked me on the arm at recess. He hit hard, enough to cause me to cry out, to bring tears to my eyes, though I wouldn't let them escape. It was also hard enough to turn my skin into shades of purple and black with a deep red center. After hitting me, he spun on his heels and ran back across the playground, joining up with a group of boys who stood clustered, grinning at me.

I didn't know what to do. My arm hurt, but it was my voice that was taken. My best girlfriend grabbed my hand and led me to a spot under the trees, just around the corner of the school building. I sat on the ground and finally cried, my hand clasped over the unexpected sore spot on my upper arm. My friend rubbed my back, but said nothing. Her voice seemed taken too.

At home, my mother clucked over the growing lumpy bruise and she pulled an ice pack from the freezer. After securing it to my arm with an ace bandage, she sat me on the couch in front of the television and put on my favorite after-school program, a game show where people won more money than I knew how to count to. My mother brought me a plate of Oreos and some milk. Then she sat on the arm of the couch and said, "That boy…he must really like you, Faith."

I immediately put my hand on the ice pack, my fingers going numb with the cold. "*Like* me? He hit me! For no reason!"

She nodded. "That's what boys do. It means they like you."

That's what boys do.

Years later, boys later, men later, I stared at my bedroom ceiling and felt like I needed my mother and her ice pack and an ace bandage, even though there wasn't a bruise. Every morning, after I opened my eyes and before I rolled out of bed, I wrapped my arms around my own shoulders and hugged myself, the way I knew my mother would hug me. The way she did hug me after that day on the playground. Carefully, to not bring pain where I was wounded, but fully, to let me know she was there and she always would be.

I started hugging myself soon after my first anniversary with my husband. The hugs started as an intermittent thing, then grew into routine.

But there were never any bruises. Just words. Specific words, not spoken in anger or even in surprise. Not spoken at a certain time of day or month or season or event. They could come first thing in the morning, before my husband even greeted me to the new day, or in the middle of the night or dinner or lovemaking. Once, at our daughter's birthday, just after we helped her blow out her three candles, he smiled at me over the cake, and he said those words. Six of them.

"I'm going to kill you someday."

The first time he spoke them, just days after our first anniversary, it was over a sinkful of dishes. I was draining the water, my favorite part, watching the bubbles circle, chasing them with the spray from the faucet, and he was drying the last fork. He dropped it in the drawer, slid it shut with a gentle slam, folded the towel neatly and hung it on the rack he installed himself after we moved into the house just a month before. Then he turned to me, kissed my cheek, smiled, and said, "I'm going to kill you someday." And he left the room.

I laughed. I saw myself laughing in the reflection of the window. My husband just made the most outrageous joke. Maybe it was a line from a TV show he'd just watched. He liked to entertain me with non sequiturs and from-out-of-nowhere statements. So I laughed and then went to join him in the living room. I knew in an hour or so, we would have a glass of wine apiece while we read our respective books until it was time for the news. Then we'd go to bed, and if we weren't too tired, we'd make love, attempting to conceive the baby we both wanted.

Eight years now into our marriage, seven years after our first anniversary, I sometimes heard these words even when he wasn't home. I heard him whisper. In my car. In the shower. When I was asleep. Sometimes, months went by without his saying those six words, and I wondered if I heard him at all, but then there they would be again, in the air between us, in my presence, to my face, always when I didn't expect it.

He never gave me an explanation. And there was something about the way he said them that kept me from asking. Except for once. We were passing each other in the hallway, me with a basket of newly folded laundry, he on his way out to pick up our every-Saturday pizza. We smiled at each other, I said, "Hurry back," and he said, "I'm going to kill you someday."

I stopped dead. Then I turned and called to his retreating back, "Why do you say that? Why do you say that to me?"

He didn't stop, but looked over his shoulder, winked, and said, "Who else would I say that to?" And then he was gone.

I put away the laundry. I ate the pizza. And I puzzled, pondered and worried. At what point do non sequiturs become targeted statements, heading directly for a bullseye, and what do you do if the bullseye seems to be you?

It wasn't like he said the words the same way each time. Sometimes, he was flippant. Other times, the words were so low, the S in someday so sibilant, that I shivered. But there was always an air of warning around them. *Don't ask. You won't like the answer.*

When our daughter was born, he said the words a week after we brought her home. He was holding her, singing a lullaby, while I curled up on the couch, trying to catch a fast nap. Midway through a line of the song, he looked at me, smiled, and sang with the melody, "I'm going to kill you someday," then he returned to the real lyrics. I was so tired; I fell asleep to it. In the morning, after he left for work and I awoke to the sound of a crying baby, I hugged myself.

Our daughter was five years old now. Elizabeth. My husband and I entered the delivery room, not knowing what we would name our child. Not knowing, by choice, if she was a boy or a girl. But the moment this messy, elegant, outspoken baby was laid between my breasts, the moment I cupped my hands over her head and her bottom, her name rose up through my fingertips. "Elizabeth," I whispered and my husband whispered it after me. I wondered how I didn't know who I carried within me all that time. Who I whispered to for months, and who answered me with gentle stretches and head butts. There would be no shortened version of her name; no Beth, no Liz, no Eliza. She was Elizabeth.

But now, on this particular morning, when I opened my eyes and before I rolled out of bed, I hugged myself and found a new chill I couldn't embrace away. Last night, my husband added five more words. New words. Words that started with a "maybe", but that felt as definite, as solid as certainty. We were arguing over whether or not we should put Elizabeth in swimming lessons, something she begged to do. The lessons were expensive and my husband thought we should just take her for Saturday afternoons at the Y during free swim until we knew if she had an aptitude. I knew she had an interest and wanted to encourage it. Elizabeth sat on the floor, pretending to watch television, as our voices rose.

Suddenly, my husband stopped. "I'm going to kill you someday," he said, his voice heavy with softness. But then he looked at our daughter, looked right at the back of her head. "Maybe," he added, "in front of her."

Then he sat back on the couch, propped his feet on the coffee table, and asked Elizabeth what we were watching. I felt the gap of seconds before she answered, animatedly describing the plot of the children's program. That gap let me know that she heard.

So this morning, I hugged myself. And then I hugged myself again. In between, I heard his echo.

I'm going to kill you someday.

I decided to go to my parents. They'd retired several years ago, tired of the long winters on the coast of Maine, where I still lived, and moved to the gulf of Florida, St. Petersburg, to still have the big blue view they loved, but soaked year-round in yellow sunshine. It was a twenty-four hour drive away.

Maybe in front of her.

It was past time to go. I should never have stayed until the second sentence. This wasn't what boys do. He didn't hit me. Maybe he never liked me at all.

• • •

Elizabeth was still in bed, but she was awake. It wasn't yet time to head to kindergarten, but I knew we wouldn't be going there anyway. I also knew she would protest, she loved school, so I led with a trip to her grandparents, who she loved even more. I smoothed her hair from its nighttime rumpleness. "Get on up and get dressed, sweetheart," I said. "We're going to see Grandma and Grandpa. Pack all your favorites in your backpack and your little suitcase."

She whooped, then blinked at me. "Favorites?"

"Favorite clothes, favorite pajamas, favorite toy, favorite book. And don't forget Miriam." Miriam was the cloth ragdoll she'd had since birth. "I'm going to go pack my favorites now too. We'll get breakfast when we're on the road. Sausage McMuffin with Egg? Hashbrown? Orange juice?"

Elizabeth threw back the covers and whooped again.

Before we left, I quizzed her on what she packed. When we got to her favorite toy, she explained that would be her legos, which I already knew. They wouldn't fit in her backpack, but she had them contained in a storage bin. Then she held up her backpack by both straps.

"I know you said favorite book, but is it okay that I packed, like, ten? Maybe more? I couldn't decide. There are *series,* Mama." She dropped the backpack to the floor. "It's sorta full."

I laughed. "That's fine. I should have known. And you have Miriam?"

She held up the doll. And then she pushed forward a second storage bin. It was full of books. There was no way I could say no. I knew we wouldn't be coming back.

He must like you. That's what boys do.

He mustn't like me.

Years after that moment on the playground, I dated that boy who slugged me. I went to prom with him. When I asked him about that day, he blushed and admitted he did hit me because he liked me, that he didn't know what else to do to get my attention.

I dated him for a year and we discovered lots of ways he could get my attention. Then I went to college. I dated many others. Some caught my attention. Some didn't. Some even hit me.

It's what boys do.

I always walked away.

But no one threatened to kill me. Not in any tone of voice. Not as a statement. Not as a non sequitur, not as a joke. Not over and over, for years, couched in declarations of love and the enjoyment of each other's company. And the birth of a wanted child.

Elizabeth and I would go see Grandma and Grandpa. My parents loved their granddaughter with a ferocity that would stand up to any fist and to any string of words. Together, they were formidable. They loved me with an intensity that would never fade.

I hugged myself before getting behind the wheel. I heard his whisper as I pulled out of the driveway.

Maybe in front of her.

• • •

Whenever we visited my parents before, we flew, but this time, I drove. It was rough, but with two nights in hotels with swimming pools and lots of videos on the iPad and Elizabeth's precious books, we made it. I even allowed her to sit in the front seat, which she did with her eyes wide.

My phone buzzed frequently and I finally put it on silent. My husband's voice went from friendly to strident to soft. The last message I heard caused me to stop at a Best Buy in Georgia to buy a disposable phone with a new phone number. Then I turned my old phone off, pulled out the battery, and dropped it to the bottom of my purse.

I called my parents when we were fifteen minutes out. My mother's shock quickly turned over to surprise and pleasure. "I'll explain when I get there," I said. Both of my parents were standing on the front step when we pulled into the driveway.

Elizabeth spilled out of the car and ran into their arms. I walked slowly to them, enjoying the heat and the sunshine of a Florida October that was so unlike Maine's. I tried to look happy. Comfortable. Relaxed.

But my mother breathed, "Honey," and my father clenched his fists.

"We'll talk," I said.

We pulled in our suitcases and Elizabeth's backpack and buckets of legos and books. It was time for Elizabeth's favorite after-school program and my mother set her up as she set me up, on the couch, cookies, milk, though her milk was chocolate, chocolate right from the carton, served in a tall glass with ice cubes, something my mother never let me have, not even white milk with powder. The motion of the car gone, the goal of this trip attained, it only took about ten minutes for Elizabeth to drop into sleep, her head on the arm of the couch, Miriam tucked to her chest. I asked if I could have the contraband chocolate milk and cookies too, including the ice cubes. When my parents and I sat down at the dining room table, the L-shaped floorplan keeping us in view of my sleeping little girl, my mother set a plate of Oreos in front of me. She still kept them at the ready in the kitchen cupboard, even though it was months between visits.

"Honey," my mother said again.

I thought I had the words at the ready. But instead, I lowered my head to my folded arms on the table and wept.

When my voice came back, I sat up and took a sip of the milk. "This is going to sound crazy," I said. "But I don't know who is crazy. Me or him. Maybe I'm overreacting." I told them everything, from my first anniversary until now. "He changed it," I said. "The night before I left. He said," and I nodded toward the couch, "maybe in front of her."

My parents gasped.

"I'm not going back," I said. My mother's hands were pressed over her mouth. Her eyes were wide. My father's cheeks were red. His fists clenched again.

"You'll stay here," my mother said between her fingers.

"You'll get a restraining order," my father said.

I nodded. But I knew a restraining order was impossible. My husband used only words.

Only.

• • •

A few mornings later, my mother and I walked to the elementary school three blocks from their house. I registered Elizabeth, listing my parents as contacts along with my name, and told the school that her father was no longer in our lives for a reason, and that if he should magically appear, he was to have no contact with her. The principal wagged her head in sympathy, and then took Elizabeth's hand and told her she was going to have a wonderful time there. Elizabeth asked about the size of the school library and how often she would be allowed to go. She would start on Monday, joining kids who had been in school since August, over a month earlier than our Maine school system. She would be behind, but I had no doubt she would catch up, if she wasn't ahead of them all already.

Afterward, we visited the playground before going home. Elizabeth investigated the swings, the slide, the monkey bars. It was mid-morning and there wasn't any recess at that time, so my mother and I stood and admired the way Elizabeth scaled the monkey bars until she sat at the top, grinning down at us. She pounded her chest and roared like a great bear. I shushed her, reminding her that school was in session. "You can roar on Monday," I told her. "At recess, you can roar all you like."

She laughed, then hung upside down. The skirt of her favorite pink ruffled dress hung past her head. "Look, Mama!" she called. "I've disappeared! Can you see me?"

"Oh, no!" I called back. "Where did you go?"

Elizabeth stretched her arms toward the ground. Her Littlest Pet Shop underwear glittered in the sun. Puppies and kittens chased each other across her bottom.

When I was Elizabeth's age, I would have been mortified. I would never have hung upside down, unless I was in pants and a shirt that I could tuck in, never exposing my bottom or my bare belly to the air. My girl hung and whooped despite school hours. I wanted nothing more than to press my lips against that brave bare belly and blow. I ran over, did just that, and shouted, "Found you!" to be heard over her giggles.

Instead, I heard my husband.

I'm going to kill you someday.

But he wasn't there.

Elizabeth curled herself up, wrapping her fingers around the bars and slipping her knees free. She dropped to the ground, straightened her dress, and ran over to the swings. My mother and I slowly followed. I picked up Miriam, who'd fallen to the ground when Elizabeth was upside down.

My mother slipped her arm through mine. "Remember George?"

George was a black and white panda bear who was with me so long, I didn't even remember how I got him. I smiled at my mother. "He's in my suitcase."

As we walked back to my parents' house, Elizabeth skipping in front of us and making exaggerated leaps over the cracks in the sidewalk, shouting that she would never ever break my back, I felt that my back was indeed intact. It was strong. I could do this, even though I didn't know yet what "this" was. I could do anything for my daughter.

It was my heart that was breaking.

He mustn't like me.

Or her? We both wanted her. We planned her.

Maybe in front of her.

Maybe he needed an audience.

• • •

That night, as I tucked Elizabeth in, she grabbed the sides of my face and pulled me close. "Mama," she whispered. "I heard Daddy."

I lowered myself to the bed and shifted her on top of me. A five-year old on your chest is a lot different than a newborn, but I welcomed her weight, her length, and her presence. She kept her hands on my face so I couldn't look away.

"Mama," she whispered. "You know how I disappeared on the playground?"

"You mean when your dress was over your face? I could see you, honey. It was just pretend."

She nodded. In that nod was something as old as the earth. Her torso pressed against mine, her hips too, and her legs were echoes on my thighs. In that moment, we were as close as when she was tucked deep inside of me. "I know. But Mama. You have to disappear. Like magic. Like a magic show."

I frowned. "What? What do you mean?"

She sighed, just the way I did when I was trying to explain something right or wrong to her. It was wrong to take cookies, even if they were bought for her. It was right to say thank you for something, even if she didn't want it or ask for it. She spoke to me in a one-sentence-at-a-time explanation. "Mama, he can't see you. Then he can't kill you. Then I won't see." Her eyes teared up. "Mama. Disappear." And then, like the child she was, she let my face go, fluttered her fingers in the air, and said, "Poof!"

"Poof," I repeated. And in my mind, a plan started to take hold. "You want me to disappear?"

She nodded again, and the tears spilled over. "Not forever and for always," she said, using a phrase from one of our favorite books to read together. A book where we declared we would love each other forever and for always. "Just for now." She rested her cheek against my chest. "Just for now. Like a magic show. The magician always brings the disappeared back."

I wrapped my arms around her and we fell asleep.

• • •

I walked my daughter to her first day at the new school. I sat on a bench across the street at recess time too and I watched as she deftly climbed to the top of the monkey bars and roared the way I promised her she could. I met her after school and walked her home.

My new cell phone remained silent. My old phone was dead, battery pulled, resting at the bottom of my purse. My husband installed a GPS locater app in that phone a year ago. He said he always wanted to know where I was. For now, I was already invisible; the phone had no power. But Elizabeth's idea was for me to disappear. Poof! Magic.

I would do anything for my daughter. And she was such a smart girl.

On the second day of school, my parents walked Elizabeth. She looked over her shoulder at me. I'd kissed her. I'd hugged her. And I told her I'd love her forever and for always. I knew she held back tears, the way I held back tears on my own playground years before, when I was punched.

Then I put my suitcase in the trunk of my car. My parents thought I was heading back to Maine, to speak to a lawyer and to the police. I told them I wouldn't go home, but stay at a hotel. And I would, but not in Maine. There was no magic in Maine.

I set George, my panda bear, my version of Miriam, in the passenger seat and buckled him in. My car's GPS was set on a path toward Chicago, a randomly chosen location that would surprise my husband so much, he wouldn't question that I was going there, once I turned my old cell phone back on.

It was an 18-hour drive. I decided to take a day and a half to get there. When I called my daughter on the first night, I told her I was fine, that I hadn't disappeared yet, but I was on my way to the magic show. She told me a little girl came home with her after school. My mother gave them Oreos and chocolate milk. With ice cubes. Before she handed the phone to my mother, I said, "Poof!" Elizabeth echoed, "Poof!" and then added, "I love you, Mama."

My mother asked how I was.

"I'm fine," I answered. And then I said, "I love you, Mama."

She loved me, the way a mother does. With an intensity. In the days to come, she would look at my daughter and understand.

Poof.

• • •

In Chicago, I found a cheap motel room. I called my mother. In the background, I heard my daughter and my father laughing. The sound made me smile.

"So listen, Mom. He left a lot of threatening text messages and voicemails before I shut my old phone down. Tomorrow, I'm going to mail you that phone. I've taken the battery out, and it will be in the envelope too. When you get it, keep it in a safe place. If he comes for Elizabeth, you can put the battery back in and play the messages for the police and show them the texts. It will be proof that he shouldn't have her."

"Okay," my mother said slowly. "Honey," she said, "when will you be back? Why not keep the phone with you? You might need it, for the lawyer."

And so I lied. Magic. "I forwarded everything to my new phone, Mom. I have it. But I want you to have it too, for Elizabeth's protection."

We said goodnight and I shared poofs with Elizabeth. "Mama," she said, "I miss you."

"I miss you too, sweetheart," I said, and then I panicked. "Do you want me to come back? Maybe I'm disappeared enough there, with Grandma and Grandpa."

I heard her breathe. Then she said, "Mama, you have to disappear. He can't see you." Her last word squeaked and shattered and I knew again that I would do anything for my daughter.

"Poof!" I said.

"Poof!" she said, and then hung up.

I heard him then.

Maybe in front of her.

I searched through Google for where I would go next. I found what I was looking for in Wyoming: the Jenny Lake Trailhead, near Jackson Hole. If I wandered off the trail at some point, I'd soon be deep in the woods. Deep.

And there were grizzlies, among other wild creatures. Magicians of the forest, that roared like my daughter did on top of the monkey bars. They could make things disappear.

It would be another 21-hour drive. I hugged George. Then I turned to CraigsList.

• • •

The next morning, I turned on my old cell phone. I was immediately deluged with text messages and voicemails. In some, my husband rambled.

Some of the texts were incoherent, a string of symbols, like when a comic strip character swears. The last dozen, both voicemail and text, were simply his routine statement, and that new phrase he added which caused me to leave, though it was intermittent.

I'm going to kill you someday.
I'm going to kill you someday.
I'm going to kill you someday.
Maybe in front of her.
I'm going to kill you someday.

I checked to make sure the GPS app was turned on. Then I set my phone on the bedside table. My mind became annotated, a list of bullet points. Turn my phone on. Get a different car. Pay for the motel room. Turn my phone off. Leave my car and the motel behind. Go to a post office. Put my old phone and the battery in a padded envelope, mail it to my mother. Get on the road for Wyoming.

Going to the motel office, I booked the room for three more days. Then I took a bus to meet the man I spoke with an hour before. He had an ad on CraigsList for an old car.

I paid cash, then drove the tiny car, a 2004 Toyota Corolla, back to the motel. I had an affection for this type of car; I learned to drive in one, and called it the Toy Car. I transferred everything I brought with me to this new Toy Car, patted my own car goodbye after leaving the keys in the ignition and locking it, grabbed my old phone and turned it off, pulling the battery, and then drove away.

George was in my front seat. After I left the post office and headed out of town, I pretended he was Elizabeth and we chattered about the landscape, the things I saw out the window, our favorite book. I filled my mind with Elizabeth's voice, with what she would say, with what I would answer. We didn't let my husband speak.

But I felt myself growing cold.

I was disappearing. Poof!

Magic.

He mustn't like me.

Or her.

• • •

I checked into yet another small motel, but this time, in Jackson Hole, Wyoming. I was already breathless with the beauty of the place, and even though I knew how tomorrow would end, I still looked forward to heading out on the Jenny Lake Trailhead.

This motel was different from the others, in its emptiness. All I had left were the clothes I wore, my new cell phone, and a length of rope from a local hardware store. And George. Along the way to Jackson Hole, I'd stopped at a variety of Goodwills, Salvation Armys, and St. Vincent de Pauls. I donated a few of my things at every place. I still had a few dollars on me. My wallet, filled with all but one of my credit cards, I dropped through a sewer grate in the middle of nowhere, Iowa. It was a place called What Cheer, and I liked the name. It seemed like the perfect place to leave behind the last vestiges of my identity, though for now, I held on to my driver's license. Just in case, though I drove very carefully.

When I called home, I got my father first. "He called here," he said, before he even said hello. "When I told him you weren't here and we thought you were on your way there, he started to say, 'I'm going to—' and I told him to knock it off." There was that gap of seconds that let him know I heard him. "Honey," he said, his voice soft, "did you ever tell him to just knock it off?"

I hadn't. But it was very hard to imagine that it could ever be that easy. Not when a certain set of words, said in a certain order, strike a fear in you that runs deeper than your heartbeat. Deeper than your child's heartbeat.

I'm going to kill you someday.

Maybe in front of her.

I just couldn't imagine that *Knock it off* could ever wield that much power. There just wasn't that much magic in the world. Poof.

When I talked to Elizabeth, she told me that her school wouldn't let her check out as many books as she wanted from their library, or at the grade level she asked for. "They say I'm only five, Mama," she said, and I could hear her hands on her hips. "I *am* only five, but I can read older!" She said that her grandmother was going to take her to the bookstore to stock up on more reading material. I told her to find books on magic.

Then I said, "Elizabeth, tomorrow, I'll be at the magic show. Okay? You won't hear from me." I nearly added, "for a while," but I couldn't. I used magic to lie to my mother. I wouldn't, to my daughter.

In the gap of seconds, I knew she heard me. I felt that she also heard what I didn't say.

"Poof," she whispered.

"Poof," I answered. Then I hung up the phone, held George, and cried.

I'm going to kill you someday, my husband whispered. *Maybe in front of her.*

I would never give him that chance.

• • •

The morning was beautiful. The air had a snap to it, and I knew my cheeks would redden as soon as I stepped onto the trail. The sky was endless. It felt like a big blue ceiling. There were mountains that actually matched what I thought of, dreamt of, as mountains. I stopped at a McDonalds and ate a breakfast in honor of my daughter.

Sausage McMuffin with Egg. Hash Browns. Orange juice. But I added coffee for myself. I drank it slowly.

There was a parking lot near the trailhead. The man I bought the car from signed the title over to me, but I didn't use my real name when I signed it. I was disappearing. I left the title in the glove compartment of the car, then, again, put the keys in the ignition and locked the doors. I patted its hood. It did a good job.

I tucked George under my arm and followed the signs to the trail. It was a quiet morning, but there were several people starting off, tying their hiking boots, adjusting their backpacks. I hoped I didn't look too strange in my sneakers and hoodie, carrying a stuffed panda bear. But no one seemed to pay me much attention as I started out.

I walked until the sun was fairly high, and I was beginning to feel hungry again. I looked behind me and found the path empty. Taking a deep breath, I stepped off the trail. Fall's leaves immediately crunched loudly under my feet, though I tried to walk quietly. Within a few minutes, I could no longer see the trail. There were only trees and more trees. They surrounded me and I was grateful to not be alone.

I pushed ahead for about an hour. With each step, I could feel myself becoming more invisible. When I stopped and listened, I only heard the calls of birds, the rustle of leaves, the snapping of twigs, and my own whispered, "Poof!" No other voices. Not even my husband's. I began to look for the perfect tree. The magic tree.

It didn't take long, not really, and in some ways, I felt disappointed. It seemed like it should be a special tree, unique, different from all that surrounded it, a magic tree with magic leaves and special colors. But there it was. While it was colored like all the rest, its leaves still intact, ablaze with red and orange and some yellow, it held out its branches like strong, strong arms. Arms that would hold me, like my mother would hold me. Until it was time to let go, as all mothers have to do. There was even a boulder next to it that I could step on, which would boost me high enough to reach a branch and pull myself up.

But first, I took out my phone. I shouldn't have been surprised to see there was no reception, but I was. I teared up; I wanted to send my mother an apology. I wanted to tell her to say to my daughter, "Poof!" I wanted to tell her that my husband mustn't like me.

I told myself my mother loved me. With intensity. She would look at my daughter and understand. All mothers have to let go.

The ground was softer near the boulder, and I found a loose stick and dug a shallow hole. After turning the phone off, I buried it, along with my driver's license and last credit card. Then, I hoisted myself into the tree.

Now, everything was about the annotated list and the bullet points. My body sweated in panic, but my mind ticked off the next thing, and the next thing, and directions on how to accomplish what needed to be done. The steps to the magic act. It was an act that would keep me invisible, keep my husband searching for me, and never ever find me. If he was searching for me, he would leave Elizabeth alone. By the time I tied the rope around a strong and steady branch, a branch that reached out to hug me, a branch that would drop me to the perfect height, the sun seemed to be going down. It was growing dark. The wild sounds were increasing. It wouldn't take long, I thought, before I was found by the forest magicians. The ones who would complete my disappearing act and set my husband on a search that would never end. Grizzlies. Mountain lions. Wolves, maybe. I sat down on the branch and swung my legs. It seemed such a far way down. I decided, like my daughter, to beat my chest and roar. Even though I didn't feel mighty at all.

I'm going to –

"Knock it off," I said out loud. I said it for my father.

George was tucked under my hoodie and I hugged him against my bare skin. I wished he could blow on my belly, the belly that was trying to be brave, and make me giggle. Then I tied the noose and slid it around my neck.

My husband would never ever find me. He mustn't like me. He mustn't like her.

I loved my daughter. With intensity. Forever and for always. I would do anything for her.

Even magic. Poof!

I disappeared.

CHAPTER FOURTEEN

Hope

Over time, in dribs and drabs, Faith filled me in on the rest of her story. As we walked to a yoga class one morning, she finally reached the end of it. As we stretched and downward-dogged our way through the next hour, I thought about her experience, her fear, the years of being low-grade threatened with death, never loud, never action-filled, but insidious and degrading and soul-destroying. I thought of her love for her daughter, and my love for my children, and what it was like to see them through the portal. A joy. An evisceration. A necessity.

As we walked out with our mats under our arms (I found mine, miraculously as usual, in my front closet that morning), I said, "Why did we just do that? I mean, we're able to have whatever body we want here. Whatever age. Whatever size." I patted my stomach, not flat, but mine. "I chose to keep myself as I was, but I know others don't. And maintenance is a thing of the past; I look this way every day, no matter what I eat or if I run a marathon or sit on the couch, watching TV all day." Heaven truly did have the best streaming service.

Faith laughed and stretched out her arms. "I kept my age, but I asked for my pre-pregnancy figure." She held her mat for a moment as if she was cradling a baby. "Though when I was alive, I wouldn't have given up that weight gain for anything. Not if it meant giving up my daughter." She bumped her hip against mine. "But didn't you *feel* that class though? Just *feel* the movement behind it, the stretch, how good it was, admire the way your body was working the way it was supposed to?"

I had. In one stretch in particular, I looked up toward the ceiling and I felt the stretch and pull of every muscle in my body, elongating, shifting, sliding into place in the way I asked them to go. It was like revelry.

"That's why we do it here, if we want to," Faith said. "Just to feel it the way it should be felt, rather than doing it as a chore, as punishment. We can feel our bodies enjoying it."

She was right. My body did feel like it was smiling.

"We also do it for the joy of going out to lunch afterwards," Faith said, nodding toward a fifties-looking diner with a red and white checked awning. "When I did an exercise class while I was still alive, I always ate carrot sticks afterwards. Now...how about a burger and a malt?"

"Ohmygod," I said.

"Yes?" God said, falling into step beside us.

I laughed. "Never gets old," I told him. "Want to join us for lunch?"

God held the diner's door open for us, and I chose a chrome-lined table with a silver top, located near the center of the room. I could watch everyone around me that way. The chairs were bright red vinyl with silver nailheads going around the backrest. Ketchup and mustard in bright red and yellow plastic bottles stood like soldiers next to a silver metal napkin holder. A jukebox squatted in a corner behind us. I knew without looking that if I wanted to hear a song, any song, it would be there. And it wouldn't cost me a quarter.

Faith and I tucked our mats under our chairs. I found myself not caring that I was in yoga pants and a snug-fitting tank top. Self-consciousness was definitely on its way out of my system.

After an aproned waitress with beehive hair took our order (cheeseburgers for Faith and for me, a chili cheese dog and chili fries for God, plain fries for Faith and me, and chocolate malts all around), I asked Faith what the portal was like for her. Faith had been here for ten years, and so I figured the portal had become a routine. She'd told me her daughter was fifteen years old now, and still living with her grandparents.

Faith was quiet for a moment, twirling the ketchup bottle between her hands. God patted her arm. "I see my daughter almost every day," she said and smiled. "But the thing is, she still believes I'm alive. She knows I disappeared for her safety – like a magic act – and she's still waiting for me to come back." She looked at me and her eyes shone with tears. "That belief – I can't shake it. There's no way I can let her know I'm here, no way I can tell her that I'm gone for good."

God said, "It's her faith in Faith. If Faith's remains are discovered one day, then she'll know. If not, why take away that hope?"

I wondered about that. Was it fair to let a girl believe that her mother was alive and would walk through the door someday, when she never ever would? "But it's the truth," I said. "You've said everything here is about the truth."

God nodded. "Everything here, yes. But you've got to know by now that on Earth, the truth can be hard to come by." He shook his head. "Sometimes I think free will might have been my biggest mistake."

I glanced at Faith and she raised her eyebrows. I wondered how often God admitted to mistakes. Did he make a mistake with me, and that was why he wasn't ready to talk about it? Or did I do something out of my own free will?

But it wasn't free will that made me sad. Sad all the time, as far back as I could remember. I didn't choose to be sad. In fact, I chose to be happy, but I could never find the way to feel that choice. I could say it, act it out, smile and laugh until my face was stretched and my throat was raw. But other than short bursts, I didn't feel it. Sadness and I just seemed synonymous. I was the child who chose a sad teddy bear, not because I felt sorry for it, but because I recognized it.

Faith continued, "The portal showed me when a bear found my body, hanging from the tree. It was the first thing I saw, after the portal arrived. I know what's left of me, which isn't much, and I know it's not too likely that my remains will ever be found. In all this time, no human has walked by my tree. The place where I buried the new cell phone and my driver's license is densely overgrown now. Not too likely anyone will find those either." She sat back as our malts were delivered and then she thoughtfully unwrapped her straw. "Not for my husband's lack of trying though. He just kept looking, until he disappeared."

"Disappeared? Why would that happen?" I asked, turning to God. "Why wouldn't the portal show her where he is?"

He opened one end of his straw wrapper, then blew it at me. I laughed as it bounced off my nose. "He disappeared from Earth because he's here. He died."

My head whipped back to Faith. Apparently, she hadn't finished telling me the rest of her story. But as she calmly took her first sip of chocolate malt, I realized she already knew of her husband's presence. "He's here? As in here-here?"

She shook her head. "No, he didn't kill himself. He was in an accident. He found an old journal of mine, and in one entry, I talked about how much I wanted to see the Grand Canyon. It was number one on a bucket list of places I wanted to go. So he was heading out there, in case that was where I was. He probably would have worked his way through the whole list, but he fell asleep at the wheel, drove off the road and into a tree." She gave a smile that wasn't happy at all. "I guess we both died because of trees."

God drummed his fingers.

Faith sighed. "Okay, I'll amend that. The tree didn't kill me. I used the tree to kill myself. But my husband is here, in the regular part of Heaven. He's asked to see me. I refuse. It's my right to say no."

God carefully carved out the whipped cream on top of his malt and then popped it into his mouth. After swallowing and heaving a satisfied sigh, he said, "He arrived here four years ago. The last two, he stopped asking to see Faith. So he's improving."

"Does your daughter know he died?" I asked.

Faith nodded. "Yes, he was identified. He didn't pull a magic show, like I did."

I wondered about that again. A daughter knows her mother disappeared to save her from her father. Then the father dies. Wouldn't she expect the mother to show up? The danger has passed. "But –"

Faith raised her hand, stopping me. "She chooses to believe I'm still alive, Hope."

"Free will," God added.

"It means I have to watch my daughter wait for me. For ten years so far." The tears spilled over then, and I quickly pulled out a napkin and handed it over. She wiped her eyes. "If I hadn't told myself that I had to perform magic – poof! – and make myself disappear for good so that my husband would look for me forever and never go back for Elizabeth…if I'd just kept running and hiding and then one day, he drove off the road and died, I could have gone home. I could have been with her." She crumpled the napkin. "I chose to do what I did. And her hope keeps her going. But it crushes me. Over and over."

Routine, I thought.

"Free will," God said again. "And there are consequences for our actions."

It was interesting how, in Heaven, with God sitting right beside me, I could hate him for a moment. Even with him knowing what I was thinking.

"It's okay," he said. "Sometimes I hate myself."

Whoa.

Then our food arrived and with it, our mood flew right out the door. We were immersed in the joy of great taste, enjoyed without a moment of guilt. Just flavor. I even licked my fingers in public. And all three of us, when we got to the end of our malts, slurped loudly and with abandon. There wasn't a single person in that diner who didn't do the same. What a chorus!

Afterward, God wandered off to do whatever he did with his afternoons, but not before giving each of us a solid kiss on the cheek. Faith and I moved toward the condos. I wanted a shower. I thought I might want to paint, but there was something about the yoga followed by the incredible food that made me think maybe a nap in the sun on my balcony would be good, complete with a book open on my chest as if I actually intended to do something purposeful. Though sleep could be purposeful.

I waved at Faith and turned into my building. Upstairs, the shower felt wonderful, and so did the worn jeans and white t-shirt I changed into. I went into my art studio and glanced for a moment or two at my canvas, so I could at least say I'd done something with it that day. Then I grabbed Virginia's new book, the Heaven-published one, and went out to the deck, just outside my art studio. Again, its proximity made me feel like maybe I was getting something done, even when I wasn't.

I didn't feel guilty at all. Not about my food choices, my full stomach, my decision to not paint on that day.

About my family…well, I still felt guilty about my family. Just like Faith did, ten years later. I wondered if all of us in this gated community did. And yet we were surrounded with forgiveness and acceptance here. Understanding.

I thought of Faith's husband, here in Heaven, but outside of our own community. He'd done an awful thing. For years. And his awful thing drove Faith to do what she did, even though she chose to do it through her own free will. Their daughter was left behind. But Faith's husband was forgiven here too, even though God didn't require that Faith forgive him. I wondered if she did. I wondered if I could ask her.

But he was *here*. In Heaven. Forgiven. There was no such thing as Hell, even for people like Faith's husband.

On the deck, I discovered a hammock, just like the one I always wanted, already set up and swaying in the breeze. I figured it was possible that, in Heaven, hammocks swayed at any time, even when there was no wind at all, simply because that's when hammocks were at their best. I admired the rainbow-colored fabric, white fringe at the edges, and then climbed in. This was exactly the hammock I would have chosen, if I could have. I stared at one just like this every spring, when they came out in the sales ads. I remembered wondering if Virginia shared a hammock with her husband, tied between the two trees they named after themselves. My husband and I didn't have two trees. But this one, with the rainbow, was just the one I wanted. It came with a stand. I remembered showing it to my husband and to my children, before every Mother's Day, before every one of my birthdays. "Look," I said, pointing at it in the sales ads. "You don't even need trees! It comes with its own stand!"

But Mother's Day usually brought flowers and #1 Mom mugs. My birthday, gift cards, but never to the store with the hammocks.

I sighed as I stretched out and the hammock molded around me. The sky was the blue you think of when you picture a sky, there was a cooling breeze, the sun was warm and I knew that, not only would I never get skin cancer, I wouldn't even get burned. I looked at Virginia's photo on the back of her book, smiled, opened it and spread it on my chest. Then I gave in to sleep.

• • •

I started making a habit of looking into the portal first thing after breakfast. It gave me a little bit of prep time, but also got it over with quickly. I never knew what I was going to see. A happy son, a sad daughter, a husband hard at work suddenly taking a look at my photo, which was still turned backwards on his desk. I was relieved to see that the photo didn't disappear; he didn't throw it away or hide it in a drawer. But there was no part of me showing whenever he glanced at it.

My son continued to draw and while I still couldn't tell exactly what his drawings were supposed to be, I admired the ins and outs of color and form. He saw things in a surreal way and I loved that he was moved by color. Some days, he drew for hours. On others, the sketchpad completely disappeared from his desk and I worried he'd thrown it away. But then it would reappear again. There were days he lay still on the bed and stared out of his window. And other days, he played video games in the family room.

My daughter made frozen pizzas for her dad now. Though she didn't have to coax him out of bed like she did with me; he simply walked in the door after a day of work, just like he always had. Some days, he brought food home. And other days, my daughter and her father pored over a new cookbook and they tried new things. When I wondered what their experiments tasted like, that meal often showed up on my table. Often, not always; sometimes they cooked things I would never have wanted to try. Put kale or quinoa in something and I head for McDonalds.

I thought of Faith, looking in her portal. She told me she saw her daughter, and time and time again, her daughter was looking up at the surprise ring of a doorbell or her grandmother's cell phone. And then, the portal zoomed in on her daughter's face when it turned out to be a stranger, a salesman, a friend from school, a crank call. Faith witnessed the death of her daughter's hope every time. There was no turning away. And yet, inevitably, Faith would see the hope return to her daughter's face.

Over and over. Routine. Consequences for our actions. But forgiveness, acceptance, and understanding here in Heaven. And sometimes, Faith said, in the portal as well. I hadn't seen that yet.

So I always had breakfast first, to at least have the power of caffeine and sugar in my veins when I looked at the mirror. My muffins switched from butter rum to cream cheese to banana nut, and I collected them myself now, from the payless bakery down the street. The muffins stayed amazingly fresh, even when I brought home enough for a week at a time. I ate on the deck, waving at the same woman I waved to every morning, and who I had yet to meet. We each held mugs. I couldn't tell what she ate, but bites were alternated with sips, so I figured she had something sweet and her mug was filled with coffee, just like mine.

On this day, I waved to the anonymous woman, took my last bite of a new muffin, caramel drizzle, and drained my coffee mug. On the way to the portal, I refilled the mug and grabbed another muffin. I planned to look in the portal, and then to paint. Later, I was supposed to meet Joyce in a park with a blank canvas and some oil pastels. She was going to teach me more about using them. I wanted to create clouds like hers, but I didn't want to sketch clouds. I would choose something that was totally my own. I just didn't know what that was yet, because I didn't know how to use oil pastels effectively.

In the bathroom, I carefully lowered the sky scarf and looked into the glass. At first, I didn't recognize where I was. I didn't see my home.

But then I did. And it *was* my home. The original. The one I shared with my parents.

The room was in shadow, but I recognized the shapes of the furniture, the mantel forming shoulders around the fireplace. The curtains were closed over the windows. The curtains that always hung just outside the windows, there only for the look, never for the purpose. The curtains were never closed. My mother loved light.

But now it was dark. The never-closed curtains were closed.

As I looked again toward the fireplace, I saw movement. I could see the back of the couch which faced the fireplace, and above the cushion on the left side, there was the curve of my mother's head. I saw her hair, standing up in the bedhead it stood up in every morning of my still-at-home life, the hair I saw as my mother scavenged through the cupboards for my favorite breakfast cereal or as she buttered a freshly made muffin, the hair that bobbed behind the steering wheel on the way to school, my mother singing with the radio, me staring out the passenger window without a word. Staring, if my eyes were open at all. Mostly, they were closed, dreaming of staying asleep longer. Staying asleep forever.

My mother was sitting in the dark. In the living room that was normally filled with morning light, filled with the scent of coffee, and the sound of her turning the pages of whatever book she was reading at the time.

I listened. I didn't hear anything. But then...a shuddering breath.

The portal moved in. I looked over my mother's shoulder. Even though it was dark, I could see, with detail, what she was holding. It wasn't a book.

When I was a sophomore in high school, I made a painting for my mother. Because of her love of light, I painted a huge sun bursting out of the canvas, throwing beams of light like long streamers. The beams were lemon yellow and gold and white, and from time to time, a stream of red or violet snaked through.

But the most amazing thing – or at least, I thought it was the most amazing because I was the one who painted it – was if you looked closely at the sun itself, you would see my face. My face, my fifteen-year old face, subtle in the yellows. My eyes, my nose. And my mouth was smiling. Something my mother rarely saw.

Something I'm sure she didn't picture me doing now.

I placed my hands on the portal, just as I had with my daughter and my son. I touched where my mother's shoulders would be, reaching over the back of the couch. And while I knew it wasn't possible, I swore I felt those shoulders heaving.

I realized I hadn't thought much about my mother since my death. My focus was on my kids, my husband. But there was my mother too. I resisted picturing what I would feel if I lost my daughter, but that feeling slid over me anyway, and I felt the knife pierce my heart and twist. Then I thought of my daughter dying at her own hands, and that knife ripped my heart right out of my chest.

I gasped and stepped back. The portal went dark.

My *mother*.

With my passing, she was the last one left of our original threesome. There were her two grandkids, sure, but of us, of Mom, Dad, and Hope, there was only Mom. My father passed away seven years ago.

My mind flashed to Faith, to her husband. Here, in Heaven.

I brought both hands to my mouth.

My father was here. Not here-here. He hadn't died of suicide, but of a heart attack.

He was *here*. I hadn't thought of that, not even once, because I was just so used to his not being around anymore. But he was *here*. Somewhere.

I ran for my golf cart. I had to get to Faith's. I had no idea how to find my father in Heaven.

• • •

I'd never been to Faith's place before, but she'd pointed the building out to me as we walked or drove by. I texted her on the way and so she was waiting for me in the hallway, her doorway open.

"What's going on?" she asked as she grabbed my hand and led me inside.

For a moment, my thoughts were knocked out of my head as I looked around. Her place was like a jungle. There were plants everywhere. Standing on the floor, sitting on tables, on the island. Through the French doors, I could see more plants on the deck. Even the wallpaper was full of green leaves and brown stems. "Wow," I said. "I guess you like plants."

Faith laughed. "Didn't I ever tell you what I did when I was alive?" she asked. "I worked in a greenhouse, and dreamed of owning my own one day. Now I do. And yes, plants are everything. Go touch the wallpaper."

I did. And a leaf unfurled. It was real. Despite the thoughts roiling through my head, I laughed. "Do you have to water your wallpaper?"

Faith was in the process of getting us each a cup of coffee. "I probably don't have to, but I do. Even though I know God won't let any of my plants die. Come on, let's go sit on the balcony and you can tell me what's going on."

Faith had a pretty white French bistro patio set and we sat there. My coffee was in a fine bone china cup and saucer. On the table was a bowl of sugar cubes and a little pitcher of creamer.

"Wow," I said again. "I never pictured you to be quite so...prissy."

She laughed again. "I'm used to making everything feel like a secret garden. But you don't have to worry. Look!" She pulled the saucer from under her cup and threw it to the floor. It bounced like it was made of rubber. "Fine china that doesn't break," she said, picking it up and putting it back under her cup.

I touched my own. It felt like china.

"So you've never torn over here like a bat out of hell before," she said, and then stopped. "I guess that's an odd phrase to use here. What's going on?"

I usually liked my coffee black, but in this environment, it seemed only right that I add two cubes of sugar and just a bit of creamer, stirring it with a delicate little spoon that I was sure would bounce as well if I dropped it. "I saw my mom in the portal this morning," I said. "It was the first time I saw her."

"Oh!" Faith said and reached out to grasp my hand. "I'm sorry. Seeing someone new who is affected by your death is always a shock, and –"

I shook my head. "That's not it," I said. "Well, it is, it's part of it, but the thing is, it made me remember something." I pulled my hand away to hold my cup with all ten of my fingers. The cup might not break, but my hands were shaky and I didn't want the coffee to slosh everywhere. "Faith, my father died seven years ago. He would be here, like your husband." I watched her eyes widen. "How do I find him? Does he know I'm here? How would I know if he was trying to find me?"

"Ah, okay, I see." Faith turned sideways in her chair so she could look out over the railings. "Yes, he knows you're here. God doesn't let your whole history know when you arrive, he keeps it pretty much to immediate family.

Parents, siblings, children. With everyone else, they can just do a search for your name on Heaven's directory to see if you're here. It's kind of like Facebook. We also have a sort of Heavenly version of Ancestry DNA. You can, if you'd like, look up everybody in the history of the earth that you're related to, and they can look up you. It's neat, if you've always wanted to meet your great-great-great grandmother, or if you want to see who started your family line." She took a sip. "Now, in your case, and in mine, and in everyone's case who lives here in this community, those people are told the circumstances of our deaths and they're made aware that they can only see us if we agree. Would your father have any reason to think you don't want to see him? *Do* you want to see him?"

"Of course I do!" I said. "So since I haven't heard anything, does that mean he doesn't want to see me?"

Faith shook her head, slowly, like she was considering every possibility. "I think it's more likely that he's waiting to see if you want to see him, Hope. Here, let's look him up." Faith retrieved her laptop. She'd shown me how to access the directory shortly after my arrival, but I hadn't really been thinking about who I could look for. In my head, the dead were still dead. It was hard to come to terms with living with the dead, and realizing they were now my neighbors, instead of the living. Realizing I was dead too, even though I was right here, living and breathing.

She put my father's name in the search bar and I told her his birth and death dates. She found him and turned the computer toward me. "There's his phone number, and his address. Do you want to go there? Or do you want to call first?"

My father's listing included his photo. His face made my eyes well up. He still looked just like himself, though younger. He looked the way he did when I was in sixth grade. "I think I want to call first. Maybe he isn't waiting for me. Maybe he doesn't want to see me because of what I did."

Faith stood up. "Let me refill your coffee, and then I'll leave you out here while you call." She nodded inside. "If you follow the hallway, it will open up into a greenhouse. I have some seedlings to transplant today. God lets me create gardens in the parks. He could do it, of course, but those of us who love plants love to do it for him. Come back and find me when you're done." She took my cup, refilled it, gave me a fast hug, then went inside.

I told myself to drink about half, before it got cold. I looked at my dad's number, then looked at it again, to make sure I had it right, that my eyes hadn't transposed the numbers. Then I finally got out my phone.

It took another five minutes before I was able to dial.

"Hello?" That was my dad's voice. "Hope?" He sounded uncertain, and there was a catch in his throat.

That voice. I never thought I would hear it again. And there it was.

"Dad," I said. And I burst into tears.

"Honey!" he said. "Oh, honey, don't cry! I'm so glad you called! I've been wanting to, but I thought...I thought maybe you..." and he dissolved into tears himself.

Ever cry on the phone with someone else who is crying too? It's probably the most unsatisfactory phone experience you can have. Crying should be done in each other's arms. You need to see the other person's face, so you know that if you're ugly-crying, he or she is too. On a phone, all you can do is hear the noises, and the noises, wailing, sniffling, snorting, heaving, are disgusting.

"Dad," I said finally, when I could get my breath and capture my voice.

"Hope," he said.

"Dad, do you want to see me? I'm so sorry, Dad."

"Of course I want to see you. I've wanted to see you ever since I left. I've wanted to see you even more since you arrived here."

We both heaved a sigh.

"Are you on the computer?" Dad asked.

"I have a friend's computer here. She showed me how to find you." I tapped the screen back to life. There was my father's face again.

"If you click on directions, it'll show you on a map where I am and where you are. We're actually pretty far apart. So why don't we meet in the middle."

I clicked on directions and saw the expanse. Heaven was large, and I was only seeing a portion of it. My father was about three hours away from me.

It felt a little like we were back on earth and searching on Google. We found a coffee shop about halfway. I told my father I wanted to run home first, change clothes since I was dressed for drawing in the park with messy oil pastels, and I would meet him late that afternoon. He agreed.

Then I called Joyce. "I have to cancel, I'm so sorry," I said.

"Is everything okay?" Joyce sounded puzzled. Of course it was okay. We were in Heaven.

"Joyce, I realized this morning that my dad is here. He died seven years ago."

"Oh!" Joyce shifted from puzzlement to excitement. "And you're going to see him? That's so cool!"

She and I agreed to meet the next day, oil pastels in hand and the visit with my father ready to share. After hanging up, I finished my coffee and then brought in all the coffee things. Leaving them on the counter, I went in search of Faith.

A greenhouse in a condo. It was stunning. I could smell fresh rain and dirt. Greenhouses were called that for a reason – it just felt green here, smelled green, looked green, was green. I found Faith bent over a work table.

"I'm going to meet my father, Faith," I said. "I'm going home first, changing into whatever it is you wear when you see your father seven years after he died, and a few weeks after you've killed yourself." I shook my head. "We're meeting in a coffee shop. Another coffee shop. Thank God Heaven is filled to the brim with coffee shops."

"You're welcome," God said, walking in. "Are you ready for this, Hope?"

I nodded. "I think so. Why wouldn't I be? I never had a problem with my dad, or with my mom either."

God glanced at Faith who looked away. "Sometimes things feel different, when you meet someone after taking your life."

I'd left my mother. My husband and kids too. But I left my mother, after my father was gone as well. I chose to leave. My father never would have chosen to leave. His body took him away.

"I think it will be okay," I said, then I hesitated. "Would you guys like to come to dinner tonight, maybe? Maybe...maybe I might need that."

They agreed. Just before I left, I asked that they call to invite Joyce and Virginia too.

I never had friends before. But now I did. And I was about to get my dad back.

Imagine.

• • •

When I walked into the little coffee shop, this one called Beans of Glory, I immediately saw my father. He looked like the dad he was in his forties, and I was suddenly twelve years old again. He stood and I ran across the café, dodging around tables and chairs, and launched myself into his arms.

"Dad," I said, and wept.

I have always been amazed by the differences between hugging my mother and hugging my father. My mom employed an immediate sway. My head rested on her shoulder, my face turned away from her neck, we swayed from left to right and back again. My arms clasped her shoulder blades and her arms wrapped around mine. Shoulders are apparently important in a mom hug. My mother told me once she thought the sway was left over from my babyhood, when she stood and swayed with me for hours to get me to sleep and keep me that way. "It was like my body turned into its own rocking chair," she said, "though we rocked left to right, instead of forward and back."

But my father was different. He was taller than me, and so my head pressed into his chest and I could always hear his heart. I listened now for the beat that faltered on the day he died. But it didn't falter here; it was as strong and steady as I remembered it. His arms wrapped fully around me and I buried my nose in the crook of his elbow and for those few minutes, I was hidden from the world. Or from Heaven. Instead of a sway, it was more a gentle twist and we wound back and forth.

"It's okay," I heard him say in my hair. "It's okay. Here we are. Here we go."

When we sat down, he didn't let go of my hands. I was so glad because I didn't want to let go of his. I knew his grip so well, from the time I slipped my own tiny hand into his as I walked alongside him to when he suddenly grabbed my hand three days before he died as he walked me out to the car. I'd stopped by the house for lunch. I didn't know what made him grasp my hand that day, and I didn't know either that he would be gone in 72 hours, suddenly clutching his familiar hands to his chest as he toppled onto the floor in my parents' bedroom. As I sped to the hospital that day to meet my mother, not knowing yet that my father was already gone, I remembered his sudden need to hold my hand. I clenched my hands on the steering wheel as hard as I did his fingers that day and I said, "Don't you let go, Dad." But he already had.

Now, I held his hands again.

I looked over at the barista and called out, "A Starbucks venti caramel macchiato, please, iced, and extra caramel."

He nodded and set to work.

My dad already had a mug of black coffee. It was a real mug, ceramic, just the way he liked it. I knew there was no sugar. I could see there was no milk. I remembered him saying, back when we were alive and in a coffee shop, "No latte. No frappe. No cappuccino or cold brew. Just a plain black coffee. In a ceramic mug. As hot as you can make it." I always said his mouth must be made of asbestos.

In Heaven, he could have his plain black coffee however and whenever he wanted it. And there would always be a ceramic mug. I suddenly knew that a cabinet in his Heaven condo would be filled with tall ceramic mugs, white, with colored rectangular stripes running up and down. Blue. Red. Yellow. They were a staple in my house when I was growing up. My mother and I drank out of plain white mugs. The stripes were always for my father.

We waited until my drink was brought over, and then we both started talking at once. We laughed, but when the laughter died away, I said, "I'm so sorry, Dad."

"For what?" he asked. "That you're here? *I'm* sorry for that. I'm sorry we couldn't find a way to make you feel better, so you wouldn't have come here the way you did. Your mother and I tried so hard. But we just didn't know what to do. We tried to improve everything in your life, but so much of that was just on the surface. Your sadness went so much deeper. We knew you loved us, we knew you loved your home. But we just couldn't touch that sadness." He let go of one of my hands to lift and sip his coffee. He smacked his lips, then said, "I wanted to excavate it. To somehow reach in you and lift your depression out." He shrugged. "But there was nothing I could reach."

"That must have been awful." I was a parent now, and I thought about what it would be like to have a child who was so, so sad. My children spun around me from babyhood to toddlerhood, preschooler, through all the years of school to now, and they smiled and laughed. There were tears too, of course, they had moments of sadness so stark that I gripped my heart in fear that they were going to be like me. But my kids never failed to brighten. My daughter was serious, but her smile was steady. My son was a balloon. You can't help but feel happy when you look at a balloon and he radiated happiness and generated it too.

But not me.

"Well, to be clear," my father said, and I smiled. It was one of his favorite phrases. "*You* weren't awful. You were never awful. It was awful, as your father, to feel so helpless." He sat back in his chair and even though his fingers slid away from mine, his warmth remained on my skin. "Man, the parade of attempts and treatments. Medications. Meditations. Groups, camps." He shook his head. "We even had a psychic come to our house and smudge your room with sage. It stunk for weeks and you ended up sleeping on the couch because it made you sneeze."

"I remember that," I said and laughed.

"Nothing ever worked. But to your credit, you never seemed to blame us either. You never seemed angry."

"Well, of course not." I tapped my to-go cup against his ceramic in a quiet toast. "That sadness always felt like it came from inside of me. Something that was a part of me. Not from something outside. I couldn't have said that when I was little, but I tried when I was older." I remembered endlessly wrapping my tongue around words that never quite fit what I was feeling.

He nodded. "That's when we tried the medications and such. To try to fix what was inside."

We sat. I studied my father's face. I couldn't believe he was here, that I was here, and I was talking to him. "Dad...I saw Mom this morning, in my portal. I should have thought of her before I did what I did. Well, I did think of her. I thought of the kids and my husband too." I flushed with shame, even though I knew what I did was right. For me. "I should have realized that Mom was going to be left alone. I'm sorry."

"There's nothing to be sorry for. Honey, your mother wasn't surprised by how you died. Neither was I. We both worried about it, and even expected it, for years."

I could feel my eyes about pop out of my head. "What?"

He sighed. "Of course we did. How could we know you as well as we did and not worry about suicide? Hope, you didn't hide your sadness, you know. We were grateful for that, but it scared us too. You wore your sadness, we could see it, we could feel it. And we felt it turning to desperation too. But like I said, there was just nothing we could do. We tried it all. It felt like we were on suicide watch for most of your life."

It was like every bone in my body suddenly dissolved. My head fell to the table with a clunk and the tears I cried were new ones. Tears for my parents. And tears from so deep inside of me, I wasn't even sure where they were coming from. How awful to only have one child, and then to have that only child be me. Someone my parents loved and tried to save and thought they were going to lose, and then they did. Well, my mother did.

I thought of my daughter's response when she was told I killed myself: "Well, of course." My parents weren't the only ones to have that expectation. And my daughter lost me too.

My dad didn't try to raise my head, but he stroked my hair, over and over. "In Heaven, outside of your community," he said, "we have portals too. I watched you, and I still watch your mother. On the day you died, she dropped the phone when she got the call. She ran out to the back yard and she looked up at the sky, like she was looking up at me, and she said, 'Oh, no, honey, she did it. She finally did it. Oh, no. Oh, yes!' And she cried and I cried. And I have to tell you...we were deep in grief. But there was also a sense of...relief. Relief that you were finally out of pain. You finally achieved what we couldn't give you. You righted what was wrong."

I sat up so fast, my father's hand slapped the table. Tears were streaming down his face.

"I mean…it's kind of like having a child with a terminal illness. We knew it would take you someday. And when it did…well, look at you now. Look at you!" He raised his hands to the ceiling. "I've never seen you like this. Even when you cry, you look whole."

I hiccupped. "I am. I mean…the sadness has lifted. When I feel sad here, it's mostly grief. And missing my family. It's not that heavy, heavy feeling. So much of every day was walking through mud."

We stared at each other.

"I saw your painting," he said. "The Gulf. It said everything, Hope. Everything." He pulled out a handkerchief that he always insisted on using instead of tissues and wiped his face. My mother used to iron his handkerchiefs when they were fresh out of the dryer. I wondered if he ironed them now, or if in Heaven, you never had to iron unless you wanted to. "I looked at it, and I could see, could feel, how swallowed up you were. And all I could think of, even as I cried with everyone else who was with me, looking at your painting, was how happy I was that you were free." He nodded. "You walk on that water now. There's no more undertow."

He got it. He understood.

"I wish your mother could see it," he said.

"Me too. When I saw her this morning, in the portal, she was looking at the painting I made for her."

"The sunshine?" He smiled. "That's her favorite. It brings her a lot of comfort now, Hope. You're smiling in that sunshine. And she's so hopeful that you're smiling here now."

It was true that I hadn't seen my mother's facial expression that morning. But I heard her sobs. It was possible, I suppose, that she was happy even as she cried. As she missed me. I could believe my father. I always had.

"So…" I said. "You're not mad?"

"No," he said. "I'm happy. Your mom is too, but she's also grieving. I'm sure that she's going over every minute of your life and trying to see if there was anything we missed, anything we could have done that we didn't think of. I did that too." He shrugged. "We both feel guilty, I think. It's like we're not supposed to feel this way about our child dying. But it lifted you out of that mud. Away from the Gulf. And you know how people always say, 'She's in a better place,'?"

I nodded.

"Your mom thinks that now. And I know it. I know you're here." He came around to my side of the table, pulled me out of my chair, and embraced me again. "I feel like I'm meeting you for the first time. Meeting *you*, who you really are. That sadness you wore is gone." In my hair, muffled, he said, "Thank God. Oh, thank God. Just look at you."

I felt so at home. And so relieved that I could finally give him the daughter he wanted.

Me. But happy.

I glanced over my dad's arm to see if God showed up to say, "You're welcome." But he was nowhere to be found.

• • •

When I walked into my condo that evening, I was immediately bowled over with the aromas of grilled hamburgers, corn on the cob, and garlic bread, and even homemade salad dressing. There was fresh-baked pie scent mixed in there too, though I couldn't tell what kind, with all the other scents swirling around. No one was in my kitchen, but I heard voices coming from out on the deck, off my art studio. Before going out there, I stopped in my bedroom and hugged the stuffing out of Teddy. Well, not literally. Then I placed him carefully back between the two pillows.

I sat for a moment, thinking of my dad back then, and how he was today. Thinking of my mom, how she tried to talk me out of buying this sad teddy bear, and then seeing her sitting alone on the couch this morning, holding my painting. Looking at my sunshine smile. And hoping.

This made me sad, even in Heaven. But this sad, like the others I'd felt since arriving here, had a reason. I knew why it was, and I knew it would dissipate. That made all the difference.

I quickly washed my face and combed my hair. I did not reach for the sky scarf. I figured my portal quota was met for the day.

Stepping into my art studio, I looked out at the deck beyond my open lanai doors. A long outdoor dining table was set up, its red wood welcoming and warm. I'd never seen it before. The table was set and several glasses of wine were already poured, and a few beers too. I saw a cooler nearby, filled with the long necks of beer bottles and the bright shiny tops of soda cans. There were two pails of ice on the table, with a couple of wine bottles in each. One red, one white, I guessed. Even this far from my kitchen, even with the lanai doors fully folded back, I could still smell our supper.

My friends all sat around the table. God, Faith, Virginia, Joyce. It made me think of the woman I shared breakfast with every morning, waving and raising our mugs in anonymous toasts. I decided I would try to figure out a way to invite her over when we had our dessert. I hoped she liked pie.

Then it struck me that I just referred to God as one of my friends. Imagine that.

He was the first to look up when I walked out. "Hope," he said and stood. "You're just in time. Supper is ready." He pulled out a chair for me, next to Faith.

"How did it go?" asked Virginia. "Faith filled me in. Are you okay? Is your dad okay?"

I nodded. "It was pretty amazing," I said and reached for the white wine. "Why don't we get our meal dished out, and I'll tell you all about it while we eat. It smells so good, I could eat the air."

After we served ourselves, I started talking in between bites. When I got to the part where my father told me that he and my mother weren't surprised by my suicide, even expected it, found relief in it, Faith and Joyce gasped. Virginia didn't, I noticed, and neither did God. But then, I figured God saw and heard it all before, and Virginia had been around for a long time already as well. I continued the story to that last embrace with my dad. He walked me to my car, just as he did those three days before he died. He held my hand. When he saw LeB, he laughed out loud. "Your car!" he said. "Your favorite car, Hope!"

I grinned and leaned into him. "It wouldn't be Heaven without a convertible," I said, "and especially this convertible. And without you, Dad."

He assured me that we could talk whenever I wanted, every day if I chose, and we could see each other often too. He invited me to a sleepover at his condo that weekend. I agreed.

On my deck, we all sighed when I finished my story. Even God. For a few minutes, everyone's gazes were distant and I wondered if they were thinking of their own fathers. Well, except for God, of course. He was the first, however that happened.

"Hope," Joyce said, "were you ever hospitalized? Did your parents ever bring you in?" She took a bite from her burger and waved the bun in the air. "I was."

I nodded and reached for yet another slice of garlic bread. My fourth. "They did. I was fifteen years old. I didn't fight it. I just went along. At that point, I was pretty much willing to try anything that might help." I smiled at Joyce. "It wasn't bad, really. Lots of talking. I was involved in art therapy, which for me, was frustrating. I'm sure it would be for you too."

She laughed. "I did art therapy too. I think it was supposed to bring out my deep feelings or motivations or something. I just ignored their questions and played with the paint and the clay. It was then I learned how much I enjoyed sculpting. It was good for me!"

I leaned back in my chair and studied the darkening sky. "The hospital wasn't a bad place. I stayed for a few weeks, I think. Talked in group, talked with my therapist, talked with the psychiatrist. And then I came home." I shrugged. "Nothing changed. No one was able to pinpoint what was wrong with me. I couldn't talk about any big issues that happened before the sadness, because there weren't any. The sadness *was* the big issue. There was no why. All my physical tests came back just fine. So I came home." I noticed that God wasn't saying much. He was, however, focused on his corn on the cob, eating it typewriter-style. I asked what was for dessert.

He looked up. "Two different kinds of pie. Peach and apple."

I moaned and sat back. "It's a good thing you can't eat to exploding in Heaven." I pushed my plate away. "I hope you got ice cream to go with the pie."

"I did," Virginia said.

"God," I said, turning to him. I thought he looked a little wary, and I wondered what he was thinking. Which made me realize that, while God was able to hear my thoughts, I couldn't hear his. I wasn't sure this was fair. "There's a woman who I see every morning in the building next door. The one on the right, if you're facing my front door. She always has breakfast at the same time as I do. We raise our mugs to each other. I was thinking it might be nice to invite her over for dessert."

The wariness went away. "That's a good idea," he said. "Show me where she is."

We walked to the other side of my deck. I pointed out the building and counted the floors up. "Right there, two above me. She has a green and white umbrella on her deck."

"I'll be right back," God said.

I returned to my friends. Faith was gathering up the dishes, Joyce was setting out the pie and dessert plates, and Virginia brought out a full pot of coffee and the ice cream. "What is with God, when it comes to me?" I asked.

Faith frowned. "What do you mean?"

"Whenever I talk about the sadness, the Gulf, he looks away and doesn't say much. Not since he told me he has something to do with why I was sad."

"He said that?" Joyce said. "What did he do?"

"I don't know. He said he'll tell me someday. But he's not ready to yet." I shrugged. "What could God do that he's not ready to talk about? He's God."

We sat back down, and in a few minutes, I heard my door open. A woman's voice joined God's, and I was happy when he walked in beside her. I'd only seen her from a distance, but I recognized her hair and her profile. Now that she was here, in my condo, I could see how attractive she was. She glowed. She wore slim-fitting jeans and what looked like a worn-to-comfortable button-down shirt, tucked in, and sneakers so white, they were blinding. Her beauty was effortless, and I wondered if it had been effortless when she was alive, or if she strived for it all the time. Now, she just seemed so comfortable in her skin.

"Hey!" she said. "Thank you so much for inviting me. It's been great having breakfast with you every morning!"

I laughed and stood up to give her a hug. Hugs were in abundance in Heaven. I hadn't shaken many hands. The ones I did usually pulled me into an embrace. "What do you have? Coffee and something?"

"Coffee for sure," she said. "And a muffin. Usually apple cranberry, but sometimes, pumpkin spice. Oh!" she said, her eyes lighting on the pies. "You have apple! My favorite!" She nodded to everyone in the room as they gave their names and then she sat down on my other side. She unabashedly reached for the apple pie, served herself, and passed it to me. The ice cream was next. "You've realized, right, Hope? The best part of Heaven?"

"What's that?" I asked, as I took a slice of the apple and then reached for the peach.

"You can eat anything," she said and sighed. "Absolutely anything. And all it does is nourish you. Physically, emotionally. It does everything you wanted food to do, when you were alive." She asked God to pass the coffee.

I handed off the pies and ice cream to Faith. "So what's your name?"

"Oh, my name," she said, and laughed.

I sat back and grinned at the sky. If stars made a sound, that's what this woman's laughter sounded like.

CHAPTER FIFTEEN

The Fat Girl Takes the Long Way

The Story of The Woman Hope Has Breakfast With

The Fat Girl wasn't a fat girl the first time she tried suicide. She started when she was the Goth Girl, dressed all in black, her hair dyed to match and spiky like a pincushion, eyes charcoaled and lined, lips like night. She was fifteen then, and she tried again at sixteen, twice at seventeen, and then she settled down to just wait. She didn't do well at life, she thought, and she also didn't do well at suicide, obviously, always chickening out or botching up at the last minute. The slashes in the wrists correctly vertical, but not deep enough; the pills swallowed, but only half the bottle before she began retching; the car directed toward a tree, but screamed sideways at the last minute and the passenger door got smashed instead. Walking into Lake Michigan late at night under a full moon, striding until the water closed over her head, opening her mouth and breathing darkness in, passing out...and then washing up on shore, freezing cold, missing a sneaker and a sock, with seaweed stuck to her hair like green extensions. She trudged home, got under her electric blanket, and shivered for hours. Her mother never questioned her missing shoe. Socks, the Fat Girl knew, always disappeared.

The Fat Girl went away to college and followed that lifestyle of late breakfasts and early drinks, junk food lunches, dinners of more, and middle-of-the-night pizza delivery. Coming back home at Thanksgiving with the freshman fifteen and her backpack saddled to her body, she told her older sister what she'd been eating.

"That stuff'll kill you," her sister said, her sister with the nurse's degree, her sister who went to the gym in the morning and again at night, who power-walked at lunch, who ate her way through two pregnancies so far and Jenny Craiged and gymed herself back down to pre-baby weight. The Fat Girl digested the information.

She kept waiting, but gained a purpose. A plan. If sudden didn't work, maybe long-term would.

She switched to jeans with an elastic waistband, loose flowing shirts with draped sleeves. She stopped dying her hair, letting it return to its normal brown. She scrubbed her face clean. And she ate. The clothes skimmed, then strained over her developing curves.

From blooming, she traveled on to bursting. From bursting to burgeoning, and then to beyond. The Fat Girl was eating to kill.

Herself.

That stuff'll kill you.

Long-term.

It was a slow process and though she tried to vocalize her reasons, she never could find the right words. Or she said the right words, but no one around her seemed to understand their significance.

"Why are you sad all the time?" her parents asked. "We give you so much."

And the Fat Girl agreed, through years spent alone in a room filled with toys, then electronics, then clothes, then moving to an expensive private dorm, and finally to her own apartment, where her parents gifted her with the security deposit and first month's rent and the furniture from her childhood room, plus a new sofa and kitchen set besides. But "I don't know," she said, "I just still feel empty," and she did, even standing in the apartment that was now her home, surrounded by the familiar and new.

"Why are you so depressed all the time?" her sister asked, offering to provide her with information on the latest antidepressants and diet pills.

"Because all the happiness around me is exactly that – around me," the Fat Girl said. "Not in me. I can be happy for you, and you can be happy for me, but it doesn't mean that I'm happy myself."

After college, when the Fat Girl got a job at the Large & Luscious large women's clothing boutique in a mall in Milwaukee, the manager coached the sales staff, "Please make sure to smile at the customers." They all nodded and appropriately bared their teeth. The Fat Girl bared hers too. When she took advantage of her discount, she reverted back to Goth black, diluted it with some white, and she returned to make-up, but kept it neutral.

Though sometimes at work, when she wasn't thinking, when she was caught off guard, when she was swept into the giddiness of all girls in a group, the hormones and camaraderie bubbling to the top, the Fat Girl laughed. And sometimes at night, when she lay in bed and her thoughts rolled like a receipt from the cash register, the Fat Girl recalled the events and conversations of the day and she laughed again, the sound foreign in the lights-out of her apartment. At those moments, the Fat Girl felt alien to herself, strange and oddly buoyant, like an inflatable floatie in a pool. It was that unexpected buoyancy, she thought, that floated her right out of Lake Michigan, the last time she tried suicide.

Laughing or not, she still ate. She stuck with her long-term plan.

Whenever her clothes grew tight, the Fat Girl donated her wardrobe to Goodwill and restocked her closet with black and white clothes in the next size up. She tried to choose the same shirts, the same pants, to keep the girls at work and her family from realizing just how much she was growing. And she threw in a new outfit every now and then too, just to keep them guessing. It got to the point where the Fat Girl didn't even try things on, she just picked out the next size, paid for them and put them on. If her sister or her mother ever said anything about her clothes, like "Nice pattern," or "That looks good on you," rare, but good-hearted compliments, the Fat Girl just shrugged and said, "Oh, thanks, but I've worn this before." She wasn't lying.

Through it all, the Fat Girl went to the doctor religiously, tracking her pilgrimage toward Death. Her blood pressure climbed and she faithfully filled the prescriptions, but didn't swallow the pills. Her breathing became ragged and she accepted inhalers to ease her lungs. She stuck those inhalers in a box under her bed. Her joints ached, her back ached, her knees threatened to give out, and the Fat Girl nodded over the directions on how to take anti-inflammatories and pain medications, and then she stored those too. Acid reflux meds, to put out the fire in her throat and her gut, but the Fat Girl hoarded those as well, feeling the burn as a harbinger of the death she was striving for. At one point, her doctor even gave her an anti-depressant, one that her sister never mentioned, a new supersonic psychotropic, guaranteed to bring glee and glory in one little pill. Let's try this, just in case depression was the root of her problem, the doctor said. Which made the Fat Girl laugh. She did take those for a week, just to see, just to experiment with drug-induced joy, but no supersonic miracle happened; happiness still refused to slip through her folds of flesh and flow through her veins. She looked at herself in the mirror and wondered how she could still feel so empty, as full as she was, but she did, and that's all there was to it.

The Fat Girl was a pharmacy of unused medication. The bathroom cabinet was full, and several plastic tubs were overflowing beneath her bed. The shelves in her closets were lined with pill bottles too, and she knew she would soon run out of space. She never threw the meds away...if she ever changed her mind and decided to pick up the pace of her demise, if she ever decided to see if adulthood brought with it a greater ability to do herself in, she wanted to be ready.

Now fifty-three, the Fat Girl was pretty much alone. Her parents had died, the Fat Girl donning the same black dress in two different sizes for each of their funerals. Her sister, who eventually birthed five children, was now the grandmother of ten, and she'd moved to another state and delighted in doubling her maternity as she kept herself firmly in a size zero. There were only the girls at Large & Luscious, and the Fat Girl still bared her teeth with them, even though her teeth were falling apart, in the hopes that a dental infection would spread from her mouth to her brain or to her heart.

While she still found herself engulfed in giggles from time to time, the Fat Girl, for the most part, was a large gray boulder, rolling through the racks of oversized clothes, her own body just one size away from the largest they offered. Most of the sales staff hovered in the size twenties, wearing clothing that were size 20, 22, 24. A few made it to thirty. But only the Fat Girl ever made it to 48. She wondered when she would hit that fifty mark, the big five-oh, the final size in the store. Everything after that had to be special-ordered and shipped, as women that size tended to be bed-ridden.

When an especially large woman rumbled into the store, all of the other clerks stepped back and let the Fat Girl take over. Her size gave her a special talent; the ability to understand what it was like to wear clothes that were more drapery than fashion, clothes that were wider than they were long, clothes that made a half-assed effort to look hip, using the same material as the rest of the styles in the store, but no zippers, no buttons, no snaps, no waistlines, no bustlines, nothing. Just elastic on the waistband of the pants and then yards and yards of fabric. The Fat Girl knew that, with these women, silence was best, just smiles and pointing and nods, stuck in between the heaving breaths of a body overtaxed just by movement. She led them back to the special dressing room, twice the generous size of the others. She stood behind these large women, twitching and futzing with the fabric, pampering and patting shoulders, as if attending to a model. She accepted their money too, and then folded their clothes gently into pink shopping bags. She sent them on their way without a word between them, other than thank you, from both customer and Fat Girl, at the end.

The Fat Girl assumed years ago that she would turn fifty and hit size 50 at the same time, which seemed fitting, and even poetic, but it didn't turn out that way. At fifty, she wore size 42, and it took three years to get to 48, and now, the clothes were finally tightening again. To the Fat Girl, size 50 was It, the moment of reckoning, the moment her body would bend to her will and take itself out of this world and into another. A world she refused to imagine, but secretly believed would be better, would be a place where all people, even the sad, were accepted, no matter what they felt on Earth. A place where the depressed wouldn't feel a need to hide. And if there was no need to hide, then maybe happiness would find her more easily.

Because, the Fat Girl reasoned, if all the black-clad and empty people of the world came together in one place, in a place where they were accepted and not judged, maybe they would spill together into company, with each other and with everyone else, and then they wouldn't be so empty anymore. But even as she dreamed without admitting to it, the dream made the Fat Girl sad, because Heaven might not exist, and this kind of acceptance certainly didn't exist here, while she was alive. And so she descended, as always, into a black sleep. She had to sleep on her back now, because she just couldn't roll on her sides anymore. If she tried, she fell out of the single bed she'd slept in all her life, scaring the people in the apartment below.

For weeks, the Fat Girl courted the size 50. One morning, she would wake up, and her pants would be just a hair short of totally constricting her breathing. Then the next morning, she would swear out loud when a different pair of pants, same size, felt looser, and not yet terribly uncomfortable. It was like the size 50 was courting her too, playing a hard-to-get game with the conclusion of her life, the marriage of the Fat Girl to What She Wanted And Couldn't Quite Accomplish.

The Fat Girl started adding fifteen minutes to her lunchbreaks, piling more food on her tray. At her coffee break in the morning and in the afternoon, she asked for a double helping of whipped cream in her whole milk cappuccinos. She also bought the frosted sugar cookie of the day, or sometimes a slice of pumpkin bread or lemon loaf, both slathered with butter and warmed in the microwave in the backroom of the store.

And then finally came the day, or the work-week, actually, five days in a row, Monday through Friday, because her seniority guaranteed that she never had to work weekends. Five days in a row, all five pairs of her pants, in black, gray, and navy blue, dug into her flesh. The shirts pulled at her underarms and rode up over her stomach.

This was It.

On Friday, the Fat Girl volunteered to close, shooing the others gently out the door, telling them she didn't have plans anyway, she never had plans, did she? The other Fat Girls smiled and laughed, standing on the other side of the glass sliding doors, waving goodbye, until the Fat Girl clicked the lock and dimmed the lights. Only one light created a white gold aura over the two cash registers so that the Fat Girl could balance everything out and prepare the deposit.

But before she did, she slipped quietly through the racks of clothes, determining which size 50 outfit she would buy. She only needed one, she reasoned. She would only have the chance to wear it once.

She moved through the blacks and blacks-and-whites, and then, suddenly giddy, turned to the colors. Maybe she should go out with a splash. Maybe she would go brightly to the other side that she wouldn't admit dreaming of, dressed for the happiness that would come when she was accepted as she was, when she could reflect out what was sent her way, instead of always having to deflect jovial attempts to cheer her up.

In the denim rack, she found a size 50 jeans skirt, voluminous, with colorful stitching on the back pockets and down the seams on each side. Paging through the shirts, she found a red and white floral number. Belled sleeves, whooshy fabric, a fake belt stitched to create the sense of a waistline. Over in the shoe section, in the post-season clearance, there was a bright red pair of flip-flops, and the Fat Girl decided that for the first time in well over twenty years, she would let her feet bare themselves in public. She also picked out new panties, but she turned away from the bras, choosing instead to let her breasts remain loose and rolling after she released them for the final time from underwires and straps and quadruple rows of hooks.

Against her routine, the Fat Girl took all the new clothes into the special fitting room and she stripped. She left her old clothes neatly folded in a pile, topping it with her white and tattered underwire bra, a snow-capped peak to a fabric mountain. Then she pulled on her new things, marveling at how the skirt left her legs remarkably free to move. She snuggled the fake belt under her breasts and wiggled her toes in the flip-flops. She didn't even look in the mirror. She went by how she felt, rather than how she looked. Whether it was the new size, or the flow of the fabric, or the bright of the colors, the Fat Girl felt lighter. No, she didn't feel lighter, she felt light. She was almost floating.

After calculating her discount and paying for her clothes, the Fat Girl settled the store into complete darkness, collected the deposit bag, and stepped out into the mall, making sure the glass doors were locked behind her, the security alarm set. Her flip-flops, away from the carpet and now on the linoleum of the hall, cheerfully smack-smacked as she headed for the parking lot.

She knew exactly where to go. She knew exactly where it would happen. The place was selected years ago, really, on the night of her last suicide attempt when she was seventeen years old. There was a spot on Lake Michigan that she loved, a little cove of sorts between two bluffs, where the sand was soft and usually free of bird droppings and dead fish. At night, and in late January, she knew she'd probably be alone. It was after ten. The temperature was ready to drop below zero, and the wind chill was worse. There wasn't a full moon, like last time, but a quarter, a sideways smile from the sky. Or, she supposed, it could be a sad downturned mouth, depending on which way she tilted her head and looked at it. Maybe, she thought, this is what Heaven would be like. Smile, frown, smile, frown, interchangeable. The same thing. Accepted.

The Fat Girl hadn't been to this spot in years. There was a long rotted wooden stairway leading down to the cove, and on her last visit, when she was seventeen, she didn't have to worry about her weight on the fragile steps. Now, she figured if she fell, it didn't much matter. She was on her way out anyway. Even so, she held on to the banister where it looked stable, and overhanging tree branches where it didn't. In a few places, she double-stepped, avoiding some particularly rotten wood. She laughed at herself for her caution, and her flip-flops laughed with her. She reminded herself that even death row prisoners were swabbed with alcohol before the end-of-life syringes were inserted into their veins.

Finally on the beach, about twenty feet from the water, the scene stretched out, as beautiful as a softly lit painting in a darkened library. It was beautiful when she was seventeen, and it was beautiful now. Amazing how some things stayed the same. The rhythm of Lake Michigan's waves, similar, she was told, to the sound of the ocean, was always a balm, and she remembered, from her early teen years, how all of them kept rolling in to her, soaking her toes when she made it to the water, and surrounded her with never-ending company. Company that touched her and rolled back, touched her and rolled back, and never once asked her, "Why are you this way?"

The Fat Girl kicked off her new red flip-flops and then carefully lowered herself to the sand. It had been forever since she sat anywhere except on a couch, a chair, or a bed, and she worried for a moment about the possibility of getting herself back up. But then she remembered, chided herself, and settled down to wait. To wait for her waiting to end, the culmination of her long-term plan. It was a quiet night except for the waves, and both the air and water were frosty, but the Fat Girl was almost always overheated and she welcomed the chill. This was the perfect place. She closed her eyes and waited for her body to let her go.

• • •

Which it didn't. The Fat Girl must have fallen asleep there, sitting, her chin lowered, her body like a massive egg, bottom-heavy into the ground. When she woke, her limbs felt stiff and solid, and at first, she couldn't move at all. She felt a coating on her skin, and when she opened her eyes, she saw that she sparkled, her body and hair agleam with tiny diamonds, her new clothes transformed to glitter and angelic white. When her neck crackled and she could raise her head, she looked into a sunburst of reds and oranges and yellows, with the faint and delicate lines of silver filigree weaving in and out and up and down. The sound of the waves was still there, low and quiet, steady as a heartbeat, and they were glittering too, through the gauze of Heaven. For a moment, she barely breathed, and she thought, oh, how lovely.

But then, she blinked, and the angel dust upon her face shattered and sprinkled like salt down to her chest.

She realized it had snowed.

And she recognized the great lake and the just-rising sun. She felt the sand beneath her. Around her, the ground was crusted with white. Her flip-flops had floated away. Through the translucence of the snow, her skin glowed blue on her exposed feet and hands.

She was still here. Her heart was thudding, slowly, she thought, but still here. With a shriek, she thrust her hands up so forcefully that she fell over onto her back and then she lay there, a bright lakeside snowdrift, speckled with red and blue.

The Fat Girl didn't really feel the cold. She was still sleepy, fatigue pulling at her as if she'd taken every one of the meds hoarded away in her apartment. Every one. As she closed her eyes again, she wondered how she was ever going to get up. But then, like a death row prisoner, death row the place she so longed to be, she closed her eyes and slid into that final sleep, its comfort and protection like an alcohol swab on her skin.

CHAPTER SIXTEEN

Hope

"So wait," I said, stopping my coffee cup on its trajectory toward my mouth. I was having breakfast in person this morning on my balcony with my neighbor, my new friend. "You didn't know what made you so sad either?"

She nodded. "That's right. I never knew where it came from. I can't even really remember when it started. It was like a winter jacket with the zipper broken, separated, after you were in the jacket. I couldn't zip up. I couldn't zip down. I couldn't get out of it."

I finished my sip. She brought over cranberry orange muffins and I provided the butter rum. We were each eating one of the other's muffins. I didn't like cranberry, but when mixed with orange and made into a muffin, what a difference! Or maybe it was Heaven that was the difference. "Didn't your parents ever try to...you know, fix you? Help you?"

She laughed and I was reminded again of the stars. "Oh, no. They thought I was just being dramatic. They said they provided me with all these material things, my own room, my own stereo, my own tv, so I had no reason to be unhappy. I owed them happiness. Anything less was not being grateful." She reached for the coffee decanter I'd brought out for the two of us. We both watched as she filled the cup and the steam rose upwards to join the clouds in a brilliant blue sky. "At parent/teacher conferences one year, one of my teachers told them I was 'sensitive', that I 'wore my feelings on my sleeve', and from that point on, *sensitive* was the word my parents used, but not in a good way. 'Oh, look out, here come the waterworks. She's being *sensitive* again.' 'Oh, did that hurt your *sensitive* feelings?'" For a moment, she turned away from me. When she came back, her mouth, which seemed until then to be in a permanent smile, was in a straight line. Her cheeks were flushed with more than good health. "Eventually, they blamed it on my weight. I was so unhappy because I was so fat, they decided." She shook her head. "They just couldn't see that I was so fat because I was so unhappy."

I thought of all the work my parents did for me. The legwork. The research. All the appointments with therapists and doctors. And now I knew that they lived in perpetual fear – and expectation – that I would kill myself someday. I ached. But I felt grateful too. They really looked for answers, when they were pretty sure they would never find one. "So what happened when you arrived here?" I tossed her another muffin, which she snatched out of the air as gracefully as any outfielder. "You sure aren't overweight now. And you're not unhappy either."

She laughed and reached for the butter. "Well, you know how when you first get here, God asks you how you want to look? If you want to look like you did when you died, or maybe an earlier version."

I nodded. I was just as I was on my last day. My father chose to be back in his forties. Faith returned to pre-baby weight. I had no idea about Joyce. I'd have to ask her.

"I told him I wanted to look like what I would have looked like, if I didn't go down the path of deliberately eating myself to death." She swept her hand over her body like a game show hostess. "This is me. This is who I am. Before I got derailed. Or who I would have been, if the derailment never happened."

"You are so beautiful!" And she was.

She blushed, the red returning naturally to her cheeks.

"And did you ask God why? Did you ask him about your unhappiness?"

She chewed and I took advantage of that to take a bite myself. The sun beat down on us in the gentlest of ways. Our skin was open to the air, but it felt like we were covered in the lightest, warmest blanket.

"I didn't," she said slowly. "Honestly, Hope, I have no desire to know. All that matters is it's gone. I am so grateful for that. I just let it go, and really, for me, it was easy, once I knew it was possible. It was like throwing out the trash. I have no curiosity about it. I feel like it wasn't something that was a part of me, it was something that took a hold of me. And now it's gone, and

I can relish just having myself back. Me, as I was supposed to be. If I'd only been listened to." She drew up her knees and wrapped her arms around them, and I knew, before she died, her body kept her from being able to do that. Now she did it without thinking. She was truly in her own skin, as it was supposed to be. "My parents are here. They died long before I did. They've asked to see me, but so far, I've said no." She frowned. "I don't think they caused my unhappiness. I don't remember it that way. But they didn't help, and they certainly created a lot of hurt. Instead, they blamed me. And they made fun of me for it. So for now, I don't want to see them." She looked at me. "Sometimes, I think you have to preserve your happiness with boundaries. Not go out of your way to find something that makes you sad. At least, once you have happiness."

I did have happiness now. But since I didn't know what made me sad in the first place, I didn't know what boundaries to create. I couldn't think of anyone I wouldn't want to see.

She sat back and sighed, lacing her fingers over her belly. I echoed her – we were both full and satisfied. "Do you know," she said, closing her eyes and raising her face to the sun, "when God asked me what I wanted to be called, I didn't even know my own name anymore. I knew it, somewhere inside of me, but I'd thought of myself as the Fat Girl for so long, nothing bubbled up when he asked me to confirm my name." She smiled. "I suppose, if I'd died with my store nametag on, the nametag I never looked at, I could have checked there. But I left it in the dressing room with my old clothes." For a moment, sadness washed away the smile. "I was just so lost. So buried."

But then the sun came out again.

I remembered the night before when I asked her name, and she laughed and God joined in. Now I knew why, and I also knew she never answered the question. "What is your name?" I asked. It felt momentous somehow. It felt like it was the key to knowing her as she really was.

She turned her face toward me. "God showed me my birth certificate, on the computer in his office. My name is Sarah." She said her own name like a breath, a sigh. And when she smiled, oh, there she was.

"Sarah," I said. "What a beautiful name."

We told each other we had things to do. But we sat for another hour longer, in silence, just soaking in our company.

• • •

When I met Joyce in the park that afternoon for our postponed drawing date, I asked her to bring another large canvas so I could start on the painting that God suggested, the complement to my body painting. It was almost done, the body on the canvas a swirl of color, the words serpentining around inside of it. Now, I had to think of the outside world, what it said to me, at least when I still lived in the world. I also had to decide if my body was going to be a silhouette or if I was going to give it detail. I thought of Sarah, of how important the body was in her life. Was it important in mine too?

I didn't really think so, at least not outside of being a solid definition of who I was. I was five foot three. I knew I was thin at 110 pounds, only filling out during the pregnancies and just after. I was never very hungry, and so maintaining my weight was never high up in my consciousness. I was amazed at how much I could eat here in Heaven. It was like I'd never really tasted food before. And as everything I did and ate and drank while alive was firmly drenched and spiced with sadness, I supposed that was correct. In Heaven, I was able to experience real. Real outside of Sad. Outside of the Gulf.

Joyce and I sprawled on the grass and she handed me a set of oil pastels. Free, of course. My new large canvas, blank, leaned up against a tree like a sentinel. Joyce also brought me a small canvas board for the oil pastels and I played with the bright colors. Joyce showed me how to use a finger to blend in a descending and slowly changing shifting of color, a change so subtle, it looked like only the light fluctuated. Then she showed me how to use the heel of my fist, rolling it in great swirls, creating raucous and abrupt changes that somehow still all blended and worked and complemented.

I didn't really create anything organized, I just learned spontaneous bits and pieces of color and transition, but it made me laugh anyway. It was a picture that wasn't about anything; and it was just fine with that.

When we were done, we scrubbed off with some wet wipes Joyce brought. Then we put the big canvas down on the ground and Joyce once again drew with a carpenter's pencil around my body. I'd come prepared this time, and stripped down to a one-piece bathing suit. I tried to recreate the pose from the first painting, just facing in the opposite direction, and Joyce helped me try to remember exactly what that looked like. If I saw differences when this canvas was placed alongside the other, I could adjust, if I decided this new canvas was to exactly duplicate the first.

When Joyce helped me up, we both looked down at my canvas, my body like a chalk outline at a crime scene. "Let's stand that up," Joyce said, apparently having the same impression. When it was braced against the tree again, we studied it.

"So God thinks you should have this one be about what's outside of you, like you made those words and colors express what was inside of you," Joyce said. "Any idea what words you're going to use? Or if you'll even use words?"

"I'm not sure," I said. "At first, I thought it might be a lot of words, the exact opposite of what I originally planned for the inside painting. I didn't know that painting was going to have words at all, and then I thought it was going to be just one word, sad, but then other words began to appear, down my spine, and scattered randomly elsewhere. Because of that, I'm thinking there might be several words on the outside. So far, I've just come up with fear and expectation."

Joyce said, "Those are good...but isn't fear about what you were feeling to the outside world? You were afraid; the world wasn't afraid. I can see where you could feel that the world expected something of you though, that works." She frowned, tapping her chin with her finger in a classic example of deep thought. "What about some verbs? Like staring or judging? Like how others were looking at you?"

I nodded. "That makes sense. Words that mean the outside looking at me, but not seeing what's inside."

We stared some more. At the foot of the canvas was my experimentation with oil pastels, this playful explosion of color and texture, and next to that was Joyce's canvas. She didn't make clouds this time, but a glorious fall forest, the leaves making that season look like a time of birth and glory, and not death and the coming of cold.

I lifted my eyes back to my standing canvas, still basically white, just interrupted by the gray of a carpenter pencil's point. My body looked like a barely there island. "Joyce," I said slowly, "what's a word that means when the outside world feels totally foreign? Separate from you? When you are totally Other?"

Joyce opened her mouth, but then closed it again as she frowned.

"And would that be inside of me? Or outside? Was the world completely separate from me?"

We both sank to the ground, sitting with pretzel legs, to think.

• • •

We didn't come up with anything, and eventually, we packed up, had some coffee at Caffeine Heaven, and then went our separate ways. At home, I set up a second easel and placed the new canvas next to the original one. I decided I did want the poses to be as close to exact duplicates as possible, and so I scrubbed with an eraser and made a few corrections. Then I carefully painted in the outline in black.

Now I had to consider the word or words that I wanted to use. And decide how I wanted my body to appear.

But I didn't need to decide it right then. I'd let it soak in. And I'd talk to someone who knew words. I'd see Virginia tomorrow, for group, and I'd ask her then.

I found a place for my oil pastel picture, if that's what it was – leaning up against the backsplash in my kitchen, it looked so cheerful there! – and then moved on to check in with the portal. I'd gone to a home design store and found a comfortable bamboo bench for inside my shower, for times when I wanted to sit and soak in the heat and drumbeat of the water, and now I pulled it out and used it to sit in front of the portal. I was learning that, at least for now, the portal was better as a sit-down experience. The counter was good for leaning on, but it wouldn't keep me up when my knees got shaky.

I pulled off the sky scarf.

I recognized right away that I was still looking inside my parents' house. I twitched for a moment; it had been a couple days since I saw my kids, and I really wanted to make sure they were all right. But for now, the portal was focused on my mother. I followed behind her as she walked down the hallway and moved into the first door on the right.

My old bedroom.

I moved out of the house permanently after I graduated from college, when I was twenty-two years old. After I took with me what I wanted – my paintings and drawings on my walls, all of my art supplies, my desk, the hope chest that used to be my mother's and before that, my grandmother's – my mother gave my room a complete redesign. She swapped my twin-size bed out for a double and found a gorgeous bedspread of rolling blue splashes of color. My walls went from vibrant purple to a sunny day yellow. I was prepared to hate it, but I didn't. My room became about the sun and the ocean, and I loved that. My window was sheathed in blue and white sheers, which brought in clouds in a blue sky. The only thing missing was grass and I solved that when I found an area rug, fluctuating shades of green scattered over it, that was big enough to put under the bed, but still provide a lawn to step out onto upon waking. I bought it with my mother's approval, and she loved it. I loved that there was still something in there that was chosen by me, that was mine.

My mother and I went to a few art fairs and she found some seascapes that I thought were gorgeous and she bought those to hang on the walls. I always wondered why she didn't ask to keep any of my pieces, but I supposed since I took them with me without offering, she thought I didn't want her to have any. I did provide her with a new painting, a sunset to go over the bed, the sun going down over an ocean. It was an expression of bold color, not of reality, and she loved it. She called the room the guest room after I left, but I always knew it was mine, if I needed it. Sometimes, until the kids were teens, I would bring them over to the house on bad days, hand them to my parents, and then collapse on that ocean bed and sleep a dead sleep for hours. My husband always knew where to find us.

Now, my mother walked into my room and the perspective in the portal changed so I could see her standing there, at the foot of the bed, doing a full circle. She still held the painting I'd done for her, of my face on a big golden sun.

After her full circle, she sat down on the bed, and as carefully as she could, she embraced my painting. I could see she was crying and I wished I could sit next to her, put an arm around her shoulders, reassure her that I was all right. I cried with her.

Pulling the painting away from her chest, she looked at my face in the sun and said, "I'm so sorry. I didn't mean what I said."

What? What did she say? When did she say it? My mother was at once one of the gentlest and most ferocious people I knew. Her words to me were always carefully chosen; softly spoken. She never stopped searching for a way to help me. A few days before I died, she emailed me with a link to a new studio in my town, that provided meditation and yoga and massage. "They mention depression specifically in their services," she said in her email. "I know this sort of thing has failed before, but maybe it'll be different this time since it's for depression in particular?" By then, I knew what I was going to do, how I was going to do it, and when it would be, and her email made me smile and weep at the same time.

She was a good mother. So what was she sorry for?

She set my painting on the bed and then moved around the room, finally stopping in front of the dresser that used to be mine, which she refinished into the color of sand. Above it was a beach scene in acrylic, a row of bright umbrellas creating a rainbow in front of the blue of the ocean. It was about the same size as my sun painting, and she pulled it down, leaning it carefully against the dresser. Then she retrieved my sun and hung it. It did look nice there, the yellow walls making the sun's rays seem to go on forever.

That painting hung in her bedroom ever since I gave it to her. On her side of the bed. She said she looked at it every morning and every night. Why was it being put here? Did she not want to see me anymore?

Why was she sorry? What did she say?

In my bathroom in Heaven, I swayed back and forth on my little bench, my movement echoing my mother's as she stood before the painting. I heard a noise from her and I couldn't place it. High and thin and long, it only broke when she would catch her breath. And then I realized.

My mother was keening.

I thought of my own daughter for a moment, but then I became fully a daughter myself, the reason behind my mother's sadness. I put my face in my hands and sobbed.

After a bit, I realized it was quiet and I wiped my eyes and sat up. The bedroom was still in the portal and it was empty, but I could hear my mother's footsteps. She was coming back into the room.

On the dresser, beneath a corner of the painting, she placed a small ceramic box. It was like a streaked stained glass, bright yellow with smears of blue and orange. The portal obligingly gave me a close-up. I saw my name engraved on a brass plate on top, along with my birth and death dates.

"I want you here," my mother said, her voice soft and back in control. "Where I can always find you. Where you were when you were home."

With a start, I realized what the box was. I'd told my husband years before that I wished to be cremated when I died. My mother must have requested some of my ashes.

The portal blurred and then returned to mirror and I thought we were done for the day. But as I began to stand, it opened up again and I was in my kitchen in my own home. My husband and kids sat around the table, each in their places. My place was empty.

My daughter was crying, not even attempting to stop the tears. They rolled down her cheeks and fell onto her hoodie. My son's eyes were closed and he sat with his hands folded in front of him. All three, my husband, my kids, had ceramic boxes on their placemats. My husband's little box was the deep blue of the ocean, my daughter's the blue of the summer sky, my son's the yellow of the sun. On top of each was a brass nameplate. I didn't need to read them this time to know what they said.

In the center was a simple wooden box. No nameplate.

"So," my husband said, his voice shaky, "your mother wanted her ashes sprinkled under her favorite tree by the river. Where she, you know..."

"Died," my son said, flat, even.

My mother may have keened, but my daughter wailed, tipping her head back, hands over her eyes, her mouth opened in a great chasm of grief. My husband and son held still, my son wrapping his fingers around the ceramic box. I wondered if he was preparing to throw it across the room. My husband carefully rested one hand over his. I thought of how he used to rest that same hand on my shoulder.

When my daughter calmed, she ducked her head and took deep breaths. Then she wrapped her hands around her box too. My son's knuckles were white. My daughter's weren't. Her touch was gentle. I thought of the way she used to smooth my hair when she brought me coffee and cookies after school, on those days when I was still in bed. Her touch was like a mother's. But I was supposed to be the mother.

The little wooden box sat alone in the center.

"I thought this weekend," my husband said, "we'll go out there. Take care of it. Take care of her. Grandma wants to go too."

My kids nodded, picked up their boxes and left the kitchen. I heard the closing of their bedroom doors, quiet, restrained. My husband sat a little longer, then he took the ocean box and he left too. I didn't hear a door shut, but I knew he was heading to our bedroom. The portal didn't follow any of them.

Instead, it focused on that little box in the middle. And then it faded out, leaving the mirror behind, and I saw myself sitting there, my face stark.

Imagine leaving your kids and your husband and your mother to scatter your ashes. Imagine not fighting to stay with them, but leaving by choice.

My mother was ferocious.

I guess I wasn't.

I didn't trust myself to stand.

• • •

The next day, I arrived at group a little early and so I had my pick of empty seats. I sat near the middle and looked around. It felt very odd not having Faith right next to me. I thought what it would be like to move on to another group. I couldn't imagine not having Virginia as my group leader. But even though we wouldn't be in group together, it didn't seem like Virginia would be out of my life, which was a relief. I considered her a friend.

Only in Heaven could I say something like that. Imagine having Virginia Woolf as your friend when she died forty-one years before you were born.

I was only alone for about ten minutes before the others began trickling in. I watched as people chose seats, some sitting together, others starting as islands, but with no hope of staying that way. A woman, maybe around sixty, made a beeline for me. I didn't know who she was.

"Hi!" she said. "Do you mind if I sit by you?"

"Of course not," I said and waved at both seats on either side of me. "Take your pick."

She settled to my right. "I always like to sit next to somebody I don't know," she said, "especially when it's my first day in a new group. I've met so many people that way. It's one of the best things about Heaven."

I thought of Sarah saying that the best thing about Heaven was getting to eat whatever she wanted and her body stayed exactly the same. "What is?" I asked.

"Meeting people! Always having someone to talk to." Her face shadowed for just a moment, and then she added, "Never being alone."

I nodded and she patted my knee, giving me a smile that warmed me to my toes. She made me feel like I was somehow important, just because I was here, right next to her. But all I did was agree to have her sit with me.

Virginia came in and we were off and running. We gave our introductions first. After my turn, I looked to the woman next to me and she took a deep breath.

"My name is Betty," she said. "I've been here about a year. I killed myself by lying down on some train tracks when I knew a train was on its way and wouldn't be able to stop. I was sixty years old when I died. I've chosen to stay sixty years old here."

I couldn't help it. I gasped. This was, thus far, the most violent suicide I'd heard of. I immediately felt for Betty; but I also felt for the train's engineer.

Betty stopped talking, as if she felt the room's reaction. She looked down. I thought of how happy she was to meet so many people, and I wondered how many people stuck around after she told her story. We were supposed to be accepting here, and understanding, and encouraging.

But a train. Involving someone else, someone innocent, in your death.

Virginia said softly, "Can you tell us any more? What led up to that, Betty?"

Betty looked up and stared straight ahead. But even from her profile, I could see she wasn't focused on anything. I didn't think she even saw Virginia. "I was so alone."

The best thing about Heaven was never being alone.

"There was no one left," she said. "My parents were dead. I hadn't talked to my brother or sisters in years. Well, really, they hadn't talked to me. I was always willing." She blinked, and I knew pictures were passing in front of her eyes. "They didn't talk to me," she repeated. "They were ashamed of me, I guess. Or scared. I didn't see my nieces or nephews either. Or my kids. My husband left me and took our kids with him, back when I was around thirty-five years old. Everyone left when I was around thirty-five years old. All of them. My entire family. Friends too. I didn't know where they were, my kids, my brother, my sisters. My husband. There was no one. I was on disability; I didn't work. There were no co-workers. There was just me. Just me. All those people, and there was just me."

I took her hand. She came back into her eyes, turned to me and gave me that big smile again. Like I'd just done something important.

"I was diagnosed with schizoaffective disorder when I was in my late twenties. My behavior was erratic; I suppose some thought of it as odd. I thought of it as odd too, sometimes. The day my husband left, he came home from work to find my son and daughter sitting on the front steps, waiting for him. They were five and six, and they were still in their pajamas. They told my husband that they hadn't eaten all day, except for what they could reach. They said I was stuck in a mirror." She shook her head. "I remember it. I got up that morning and started to brush my teeth. But it felt like my reflection wasn't me. It was someone else. And I couldn't walk away. I had to find out who it was. So I spent the whole day there, making different moves and motions, trying to catch that stranger in the mirror." She shook her head. "The whole day. I thought it was just minutes."

I gripped her hand more tightly.

"When I finally left the bathroom that day, having convinced myself that it was just me in there, everyone was gone. My husband packed up and left with the kids. Their clothes and toys were gone. His entire closet was empty. And I never even knew it was happening. I never saw them again. The divorce papers showed up in the mail. So did a notice that I had to vacate the house. My husband left me a voicemail, saying that I was to sign everything and let him and the kids go, or he would have me committed. He called me a danger to my children." Tears slid down her face. "I was never a danger to my children. And I guess it's not totally true that I never saw them again. I never saw them there. I see them here, in the portal. I know for many of you, the portal is difficult, but for me, it's a blessing. Before I died, I was just alone. For years. Twenty-five years. No one anywhere. I couldn't take pills to kill myself; I didn't have much money and what I spent was on food and rent for my little room. I lived in a *room*, not even an apartment. Sometimes I had enough for my medications, but mostly not. Or I'd just forget to get them. My knives were all dull. I didn't own a gun. I could have stepped in front of a car or a bus, but I thought if I lay down on the tracks, in between the rails, the engineer might not even see me. He might not know. And I'd be gone in a second. I *was* gone in a second."

We all sat quietly. I thought how long a second could feel.

"And you know what?" she whispered and I was amazed I could hear, that we could all hear. "I'm fine here. I'm not schizo-anything anymore. And I see my kids. I see them, all grown up. I see my grandkids, who I never did meet. I see my brother and my sisters. And they're sad at what I did. They're shocked. But I also see..." She swayed a little and I wrapped my free arm around her shoulders. "I also see that they blame themselves. At least a little. And I see the engineer of the train too. I am so sorry. I tell him that every day in the mirror. The mirror where I thought a stranger was once. And now, I see him. He's so sad." She stopped and I thought she was done, but then she added, "He's sadder than my husband, who isn't sad at all. He's remarried. He doesn't talk about me to the kids, and when they talk about me, he's not there. The engineer...he talks about me. He didn't cause my death, but he blames himself. He's so sad. I'm so sorry. I hope I get to meet him someday and tell him that myself." She smiled at me. "His name is Carl."

"It's okay," Virginia said, and the rest of us murmured that too. I didn't know if we were speaking to Betty or reassuring ourselves.

"I'm never alone here," Betty said. "And no one walks away. There's always that moment of cringe when they learn what I did, but I've even found other people who have done something similar. A group of us get together on Friday nights. We talk. We listen." She turned to me. "I'm never alone. That's the best thing about Heaven. It's even better than not being schizo-affective anymore."

We moved forward to the next person. I didn't let go of Betty's hand until the meeting was over. "It was nice meeting you," I said.

"Nice to meet you, Hope. I saw your painting of the Gulf. It was exactly right." She gave me her address and phone number and we promised to meet for dinner or the inevitable coffee, though she preferred tea.

I sat back down and waited for the room to empty out so I could speak to Virginia. As she packed her things away, I told her about the new painting, about what God wanted me to try. "Joyce and I were trying to come up with a word for when the world, or society, totally ostracizes someone. Isolates them. Makes them feel so alone." I raised my eyebrows, thought of the meeting we'd just sat through. "Like Betty, I guess. Kind of." I considered. "Well, not really. I didn't feel like Betty. I always had people around. I just felt like they couldn't see me." I thought of my parents. My art teacher. My kids, my husband. "They tried. But it was like I was an outline. I was invisible, in a way. They saw me, but not me. I couldn't make them understand."

Virginia sat down. "So you're looking for a word that means people look right through you. Never quite seeing you fully."

"Kind of." I sunk my chin onto my palm. "But you know what? I've always known that it wasn't people who made me feel this way. No one specific, no one in general. It wasn't the world. It came from somewhere inside me. No one caused it. No one understood it. And no one knew what to do about it."

"So what will you put on the canvas then?" Virginia stood. "Let's go get coffee. I bet Faith is already there."

"Joyce too. And I also told Sarah to come find us."

"Sarah?" she asked.

"The woman who came for dessert the other night. That's her name." We started to head outside and then I stopped. "I know. I know what I'll put." I stared into space, which to me, looked like my canvas.

Virginia yanked my arm to get me going again. "Okay, what?"

"Question marks. Exclamation points. Maybe even ellipses. And some hearts too."

Virginia smiled. "A painting of punctuation. I think that just might work. You don't need words at all. Because there weren't any."

As we left the building, we saw Betty sitting on a bench across the street. She had her head tilted back and her eyes closed. The sun seemed to pool all around her.

"Go on ahead," I said to Virginia. "I'll be there in a minute." I crossed the street and called out to Betty when I was a few feet away, so I wouldn't startle her.

Her head tilted forward and she opened her eyes. Her cheeks were pinked from the sun. "Hi, Hope," she said. "I always need a few minutes to decompress after these meetings."

I nodded. "I get that," I said. "Would you like to come have coffee – or tea – now? I'm meeting with a few friends, and I'd love for you to join us."

Betty looked delighted. "Of course!"

I took her arm and we headed toward Caffeine Heaven. I knew nobody would mind an additional face at the table. I hoped Faith got our favorite spot in the back area, outside.

CHAPTER SEVENTEEN

A Chapter In A Poem
TO THE WOMAN WHO DIED ON THE TRAIN TRACKS

Betty's Story, As The World Saw Betty When She Was Alone

On Sunday night, October 6,
you curl up like a new baby
in a cradle made of train tracks
in Waukesha Wisconsin.
You let a train carry away your life.
You are sixty years old.
The newspaper says you died instantly.
You didn't. You've been dying for a while.
Five days later, on Friday, October 11,
police report they still haven't found anyone
to notify.
No phone calls. No doorbells. No telegrams.
I'm so sorry, but <fill in the blank> has died.
<fill in the blank> killed herself.
<fill in the blank> is gone.
Gone.
Nobody knows you,
but many strangers wonder who you are.
Your silence and the silence around you
screams.
<fill in the blank>
You've been dying for a while.
Nobody knows you.
Such loud silence.
Such silent screams.

CHAPTER EIGHTEEN

Hope

We'd finished our drinks, a regular representation of coffee shop culture (black coffee, a latte, a cappuccino, an iced tea, a hot peppermint tea, and a frappe) and our conversation was winding down when a shadow fell across Caffeine Heaven's courtyard. I glanced upwards to see if the sun ducked behind a cloud before I noticed that everyone else seemed to be looking down at their tables. I felt a chill and I thought it was from the sudden shade, but then I saw a man working his way through the courtyard. He was tall, with broad shoulders, and he carried a for-here mug. The steam rising out of it wafted my way and I caught a scent of almonds. My gaze rose to his face and I immediately thought, That's where the shadow is coming from.

He moved by our table and no one stirred. In Caffeine Heaven, and in every coffee shop I'd been in thus far in Heaven, it was custom to look up, to greet, or at the very least, smile. I looked at my friends and they were all studying their empty cups and glasses. Except for Betty. She looked up, beamed, and said, "Hi, Buddy."

Buddy. A simple name, maybe a nickname, the name of a friend. A pal. He looked at her, twitched his lips in what might have been a smile, and said softly, "Hi, Betty." If voices were solid, his would have been transparent. There was just nothing there.

Betty seemed about to invite him to join us, but then she glanced at the others and she hesitated. She and I watched Buddy as he moved to the furthest away corner of the courtyard. He sat in a table for one there, moving the chair so his back was to everybody else.

Sound came back to the courtyard, but it was muted, careful. Since coming to Heaven, I hadn't experienced much in the way of caution. But now, everyone's bodies were set on tiptoes on eggshells.

My friends raised their heads and we all looked at Betty. She kept her eyes on Buddy. When no one said anything, I broke the silence. "You know him, Betty? Who is he?"

She came back to me and smiled, the same warm smile I saw in the meeting. "His name is Buddy. I don't know if that's his real name or just what he goes by. It's what he told us to call him."

"Us?" asked Joyce. "I didn't think anyone hung out with him."

A lack of friendliness in Heaven? I felt like a crease just folded across my perfect blue sky. "What's the issue?" I asked. "Why is everyone acting so weird?"

Betty explained, "He's part of the group I talked about in our session. We get together on Fridays. We're suicides who affected others with our deaths."

I frowned and thought of my family. Didn't we all affect others?

Virginia, apparently wanting to save Betty the stress of having to explain her story again, told the others how Betty died. There was the momentary cringe, but then everyone settled down again.

"So what do you mean, he affected someone?" I asked.

There was a collective sigh. Apparently, everyone knew this story already.

Faith, next to me like always, placed her hand on mine. "He's kind of a special case, though there are others like him too. They're people that killed themselves, but out of a sense of desperation or escape."

I frowned again. "Isn't that why I killed myself? Didn't we all?"

Faith shook her head. "Not like this. It's like when there's a mass shooting, and the shooters then turn their guns on themselves."

"Oh." I glanced over my shoulder at Buddy. "Who did he shoot?"

Betty leaned forward. "Nobody. That's not his story. Buddy's marriage ended, and he didn't want it to. He wanted full custody of his son, but the judge went with traditional – full time with the mom, dad gets every other weekend." She sighed, looking at her empty tea mug, and like magic, Joe delivered another. "Thank you!" she said.

"So," she continued after taking a sip, "Buddy picked up his son for his first weekend visit and then he decided not to return him. The boy was two years old. When he wasn't home on time, the ex-wife sounded the alarm and it didn't take long before Buddy was being chased by police cars. So he drove into an embankment, killing them both."

I gasped, and we all sat back.

"So here's the thing," Virginia said. "Buddy killed himself. But he also killed his son. In Betty's case, her death really affected the engineer of the train. But in Buddy's case, he committed murder." Joe appeared with a refill of her black coffee. "Sometimes, Joe," she said to him, "I think you're the biggest angel here."

Joe smiled and stood at the end of our table. He folded his hands and listened.

Virginia took a healthy gulp, then said, "So God treats this a little differently. People who kill others while killing themselves have their own section within our community. Their own buildings. Buddy lives there. Betty lives with the rest of us."

I looked around the table. Of the six of us, seven, counting Joe, three had children. Faith, Betty, and me. I whispered, "What about his son?"

Faith squeezed my hand. "He's in Heaven, of course. He lives with his grandmother, Buddy's mother. Buddy visits with his mother, but God won't let him see his son until his son decides that's what he wants to do. The little boy is four now, and growing normally."

Joe suddenly pulled a chair from another table and then God sat in it. Joe went off presumably to get God's drink. "As of now, the boy hasn't asked about his father," God said. "When he does, he will be told the truth. And then the boy will decide."

I heard a chair scrape back, and then Buddy left the courtyard, taking a path that kept him far from our table. Betty looked like she wanted to call out to him, but she didn't. The chill I'd been feeling left with him.

God sat back as Joe returned and placed a peppermint latte in front of him. "Thanks," he said and then he smiled at Betty as she raised her own peppermint tea to his mug. "Great minds," he said, and she laughed. Then God looked at me.

"You wondered a while back if it was possible to be angry at me when you're in Heaven. The answer is yes, of course, as you experienced yourself. And I don't think there's anyone who is angrier with me than Buddy."

And in that moment, I didn't blame Buddy a bit. "I don't understand," I whispered. "Buddy just wanted to be with his son. I know it was wrong to take the boy's life with his. But why can't he see him here?"

God shook his head. "He killed the little boy, Hope. He took another life, an innocent one. Buddy has to face that. And the boy needs to have the choice over seeing him." He took a sip of his latte. "Buddy also has to face what he took from the boy's mother. That's why he sees a lot of his ex-wife in his portal. It's two years later, and she is still deep in grief for her son."

My anger dissipated. And I was suddenly very happy not to be God.

"Most everyone is," he said.

• • •

I began to pack for my sleepover with my father, something I never believed was possible after his death seven years ago. Going into the bathroom to pack my toiletries, I glanced at the sky scarf. The portal. What was I supposed to do about the portal if I was gone for a day? I wouldn't be able to meet the twice-a-day requirement to look into it. Just to be sure, I tugged at the edges of the mirror. It held tight. There was no way to bring it along with me. I wondered if I'd be able to use my father's. Even here in Heaven, I was anxious about getting into trouble by not following the rules.

With this new worry buzzing in my head, I returned to my bedroom. God was sitting in my recliner, his feet up, a glass of iced tea by his side. He had my teddy bear too, perched on his lap. I laughed and said, "Well, hi, God. You know, you really don't have to keep proving this omnipresent stuff. I believe you."

He grinned back and said, "It's okay about the portal, Hope. I know you're heading off to see your father. We're not such sticklers for rules here that we can't make an exception. This is a special circumstance."

"Okay, if you say so. You're the boss." I tucked the last of my things into the backpack. "Maybe I'm not supposed to feel this way, but it will actually be nice to get away from the portal for a couple days. And for a road trip in Heaven! I never thought I'd be driving again, after I died, let alone taking a road trip in my favorite car to see my father."

God stood and gave me a hug. "You have a wonderful time. Your dad is a nice guy." He handed Teddy to me. "Why don't you take your bear with you? That's what he's here for. He means a lot to your father too. But strap him in. He might blow out with your top down." He gave Teddy a pat on the head, then gave me one too, before he left.

After tucking Teddy under my arm and slinging my backpack over my shoulder, I took a quick look around, shut the windows and doors in case of rain and then wondered if I needed to do so, and headed out myself.

After carefully belting Teddy into the front passenger seat and reassuring myself that he was perfectly safe, I stuck my backpack into the back. Then I studied the GPS. I'd only used it a few times, but never for a longer trip. My dad was three hours away. I punched in his address, then laughed when the GPS gave me a choice of Highway or Scenic. Both took exactly the same time. So I chose scenic, of course. There was no need to be in a hurry, and there was also no possible way to be in a hurry.

Top down, music up, Teddy by my side, I quickly found myself on country roads, coastal highways, tree-tunnels into the woods, and driving through verdant pastureland. There were cows and horses and sheep. "It makes sense, I suppose," I said to Teddy, since I had no one else to talk to. "Some farmers would want to continue farming. Imagine farming without the risk, without the pressure, but only the enjoyment of growing things, for providing people with meals." I wondered for a moment about raising animals for meat. Since I got here, there were hamburgers and hot dogs and steak and other meat-laced meals. The meat had to come from somewhere. I couldn't imagine that, in Heaven, an animal could die over and over again. But there had to be food for the multitude that lived here. I puzzled for a moment and then shrugged it off. This was Heaven, this was magic, and undoubtedly the food was miraculously prepared. "Imagine," I said to

Teddy as an afterthought, "raising animals because you love them, and never having to send them to slaughter."

The animals in the pastures did look happy. So did the farms themselves. Whenever I passed someone out in the fields, on a tractor or on foot, or in one case, on horseback, their hands were raised to me. I waved back.

It was a happy ride.

The three hours blew by quickly and I reveled in the air, the sun, the water, the trees. The easy driving, the smooth feel of my favorite car around me, and the amazement at having a long lost teddy bear riding shotgun. The miracle of going to see my father.

The GPS told me where to exit and I called my dad to let him know I was minutes away. He sounded so excited as he told me where the visitors' parking spaces were and said he would meet me there. And that's exactly where he was when I pulled in.

"Dad," I said and stepped into his arms. I just hugged him a few days ago, but this was still rich, still wonderful, still full of the familiar and the extraordinary. I turned to the car, leaving one hand on his arm. "Do you think I should put the top up?"

He shrugged. "Wouldn't be a bad idea. No one ever checks the weather here. It just happens." He tugged my backpack from the back seat. Roof up, I checked to make sure I had everything and pulled Teddy out.

My father stepped away, his eyes wide. "Hope…is that…"

I laughed. "It is! It's Teddy! Remember when I picked him out on my sixth birthday? You and Mom wanted me to pick something else, because you thought he was defective with his different mouth."

My father's eyes filled with tears. "I remember. You hugged him so hard. But your mom and I…we worried he would make you sad." He corrected himself. "Sadder. We already saw it. Even then."

I nodded. "Teddy was the first toy who seemed to be like me. I was sad, he was sad, but it made me so happy to find him." I hugged my father with Teddy squashed between us. "God gave him to me, when I arrived. They were both waiting for me, under a weeping willow tree. He's been with me ever since."

Dad patted Teddy's head, just like God did, and then he hugged me so hard, I lost my breath. We turned to go up to his condo.

My dad lived on the eleventh floor of his building and he held my hand all the way up in the elevator. When he opened the door to his condo, he moved aside and let me go in first. I made it three steps before I stopped dead. Which I supposed was an odd expression, in Heaven.

It was my house. The house where I just saw my mother, through the portal. I stepped into the living room. There was our couch and the fireplace and the curtains shoved off to the side, the way my mother always liked them. The sunlight just poured in. The same pictures were on the walls. The mantel held our photos. There was a new-looking flatscreen in the corner, we never had that, but this was Heaven, after all. I was disoriented, but I also knew exactly where I was. I glanced at my father over my shoulder and then took off running down the hallway. First doorway on the right. My bedroom.

And it was my bedroom, not the guest bedroom that my mother made it into when I moved out after college. It was *mine*. Just as it was when I lived at home full time. My paintings on the walls, which were still purple. My furniture. The hope chest, the desk. My books on the shelves, my art supplies in baskets lined up under the window. I sat down on my bed, placed Teddy against my pillow, which was where he always lived, always belonged, and I burst into tears.

I was home.

My father sat next to me, wrapping his arms around my shoulders and cradling my head against his chest. "It's all I wanted," he said, and his voice sounded broken. "I got here, and the condo looked like the perfect house I always imagined and dreamed about. But I didn't want it. I wanted home. I wanted your mother. I wanted you." I felt his shoulder shrug against me. "And it all changed, just like that. It became our home, just eleven stories up. I've been here alone for seven years, but I could see you and your mother in the portal. I couldn't wish you here, I couldn't wish you dead. So I just asked for our home around me, and I waited."

"Dad," I said and sat up. "This is amazing."

He continued to hold my hand. "There are some improvements. The television in the living room. The kitchen looks like ours, but everything is state of the art. My study has a bookshelf full of every book I ever wanted to own, most of them signed. I've even met the authors. The bathroom...oh my god. Trust me, it's not what we had at home. I was okay with a change there."

I laughed. I understood. But then I thought of my own condo and I sobered. "My condo...it doesn't look like my home at all. It has my artist studio, the one I always wanted. The whole place reflects my taste. It's like...it's like the kids never lived there at all, and they haven't, of course." I looked at my father and I bit my lip. He was surrounded with our home, with everything we were as a family. "Is that bad? Should I want my place to look like home too? Does it mean..." I couldn't say it. Did it mean I hated my family? That I was happy to be away from them?

"Absolutely not." My father spoke with the firmness I recognized whenever I asked a what-if question. What if I was deranged? What if I was a monster, a monster was hiding in my skin, waiting to come out? What if I was brain-damaged or retarded, that word no one was to use anymore, but everyone still did, and when you used it on yourself, it was like the worst insult ever? What if I never got married? What if no one loved me? What if I was a terrible mother? "Absolutely not," he said again. "Hope, you are one of the most giving people I know. And now you're being given to. You're being given what you always wanted, in your deepest heart of hearts." He motioned around him, patted the bed. "And so am I. This may all change when your mother gets here. Who knows? She might even decide to live on her own, in the condo building created on her death day. But I think...I think she'll move in here with me. And then we'll decide together how Heaven should look. But for now, I have home here. And now I have you." His eyes filled with tears again. "Hope, this sounds terrible to say, because your being here means you're dead, and your living where you are, in that part of Heaven, means you killed yourself, but I am so glad you're here."

Even in Heaven, things could be confusing. Nothing was ever straightforward.

But tonight, I would sleep in my own bed, in my own room, with my father down the hall from me. Maybe we would watch my mother in the portal.

And Teddy would be here too.

• • •

At dinner, my father served up my favorite meal in the world: my mother's meat loaf and baked potatoes. We made Bisquick biscuits together, and I laughed when he pulled out the little juice glass we'd used all my life to cut out the circles of dough that would become glorious golden buttered biscuits. It was a small glass, decorated with a purple vine running around and around it. We'd had many discussions as to what the vine could be, and we finally decided on concord grapes, for grape juice, since it was a juice glass. It was only used to cut biscuits and for my dad to have his three glasses of orange juice every day. I only drank from it once in my life, when I was home alone when I was a senior in high school and my parents went away for a rare weekend. I had my juice, and then scrubbed out the glass and returned it to the cupboard, feeling so guilty, I wanted to throw the juice back up.

But it did taste better, in that glass.

"I can't believe you have this," I said to my dad as I pocked out the biscuits, placing them on a baking pan.

"It wouldn't be Heaven without it," he said.

After we ate, we went out on his deck. It had wooden floorboards, like our backyard deck at home, but of course, it was eleven stories up, so there wasn't any yard. We sat down on cushioned redwood chaise chairs, just like we always had. My parents replaced them every five years or so, always getting the same ones, and finding cushions with a similar pattern. My mother always said that once you loved something, why change it?

In the gathering evening, the deep blue ringed with the blackness that would soon be full of stars, I decided it was time to ask my father about what I heard my mother say. "Dad," I said, "I saw Mom in the portal again yesterday. She moved my sun painting from your bedroom to the guest room. She said she was moving it because that's where she wanted me, where she remembered me most, when I was still at home."

Dad nodded. "I know. I saw that too." He reached between our chairs and took my hand. I wondered how long it would be before I accepted his touch as everyday again. "That painting is here, you know. It's right where it's supposed to be, in your mom's and my bedroom."

So much in this house was me.

"So did you see her sit on the bed and look at my painting and apologize to me? She said she was so sorry, that she didn't mean what she said."

My father was silent. I waited a few moments, in case he was searching through his memories. When he didn't offer any, I tried again, asking specifically.

"Dad, what did she mean? What was she sorry for? I don't remember anything that she ever said to me that would need an apology."

He sighed. "Let me get us each a glass of wine for this."

While he was gone, I looked out over the railing. Lights were starting to turn on. I wondered if, down on Earth, this was how the stars were made. We were actually seeing the lights of Heaven all this time.

I knew the reality about stars. I knew about planets.

But I was learning about Heaven every day. And everything was possible now.

My dad came back and handed me a glass of white wine. "It's a Zin, your favorite," he said.

I took a sip, then sat up and swung my legs sideways off the chaise, so I was facing my father. "Okay. Tell me. What is it, that it requires a glass of wine?"

He took a healthy drink, then folded his hands across his belly. "It was when you were twelve years old. Your mom went into your room to put away laundry and she found you crying on your bed."

My mother found me crying on my bed a lot. That wasn't unusual. When I was twelve?

"Your mother had a long day that day. She'd been to work, she cooked dinner, she did the laundry. I wasn't there; I must have been on a business trip. In between doing all that, she was called into school, to talk to a guidance counselor about you. The school was concerned about you, the counselor said. You had an assignment in English, you had to write a short story. While the other kids wrote stories about puppies and kittens and little mysteries that could be figured out in the first paragraph, you wrote a story about a prostitute." My father couldn't help it. He snorted.

I remembered that story. It was about a teenager named Callie who sold her body to help her single mother make ends meet. She hid it from her mother, and one day, her mother found out. It was the morning after Callie allowed herself to be gang-banged, and she was in bad shape. When her mother confronted her, Callie freaked out and ran screaming into the street, where she was –

"A teenage prostitute who threw herself in front of a bus." My father smiled and shook his head at me. "Not the usual thing for a sixth grader to write about. Between that and your artwork, which also tended to be what they called 'dark', they were worried. Your mother had to explain to them that we were aware of your depression issues and we were trying to take care of you as best as we knew how. And then she came into your room, toting a pile of laundry, and there you were, crying."

My head was clicking through the memories, all the times my mother came into my room, asked me what was wrong, stroked my hair, told me it would be okay. All those times. Except –

"Oh, god," I said.

Amazingly, he didn't show up.

My father nodded. "Yep. Your mother was so tired. And so stressed. She felt like the school was telling us that we weren't doing enough, that we weren't taking you seriously, when really, your well-being consumed us. So your mother asked you what was wrong. And it was the first time you said that you wanted to die."

I remembered. I remembered. I remembered how right those words felt coming out of my mouth, and how wrong it was that my mother was hearing them.

"And your mother said –"

"'Why can't you just be normal?'" I whispered. "'Why can't you just be like every other twelve-year old? Why can't you be what I wanted?'"

I remembered the shock of it, like she slapped me. And then she left the room.

"She came in later," I said to my father. "My room was dark and I pretended I was asleep. She sat by me and whispered my name a few times. She stroked my hair. I could hear her breathing; I think she was crying."

He nodded.

"I wanted to say something, but I couldn't. I mean, what could I say? I couldn't say it wasn't true, that I didn't want to die, because I did. And now I'd just found out that she wished I was someone else. So I stayed silent. Then she told me she loved me, she loved me more than anything and anybody, and she always, always wanted me. She wanted me to be happy, but she never ever wanted anyone else. Then she left the room. When I got up the next morning, we acted like nothing happened."

"A lot happened," my father said. "I don't think she ever forgave herself for saying those words. And now you're gone. Not in a way that we didn't entirely expect, but you're *gone*."

I stared out into the night. "I am so sorry," I said. "I am so sorry, Mom."

My father found my hand again. "She knows, Hope. But some hurts last forever, even when they're explained, even when they're smoothed out. Your mom will be fine." He smiled at me. "*You* already are."

We sat. We drank our wine. I wondered what my mother was doing.

"Hope," my father said, "you told me that on the day you arrived in Heaven, God was waiting for you, with Teddy, under a weeping willow tree." He laughed quietly. "Can you tell me about it? God must have known you wanted Teddy there, that he was important to you."

So I told my father about my last day, and my arrival in Heaven. I finished with God's words to me, said right before I gave in to the deepest of tears, words that I knew I would always remember. "So God said to me, 'So here we are. Just you, me, and Teddy. We'll sit with you for as long as you like.' And they did. Even though it should have been the worst day ever, it felt like the best day, with the two of them there, and I could cry." I stopped for a moment. I was always able to cry. But that day was different, and it had been different every day since. "I could cry because it was what I felt, and I didn't have to worry that I was feeling the wrong thing. That I was letting people down with my sadness."

"Hope," my father said, and his voice cracked as big and wide as my own Gulf. "Hope, your mother and I always sat with you too. We never wanted you to be alone. We didn't care if you were sad or if you cried. We didn't care that you weren't what we expected when we set out to have a child. You were *you*, and you were the only child we ever loved, we ever wanted, we ever needed. We were always right beside you."

Just like that, Teddy was suddenly in my lap. My father was on my right, holding my hand. "I never thought of that," I whispered, my voice like sandpaper. "But you were. Of course you were. Thank you."

When I went to bed that night, I slid easily into my twin-size sheets covering my twin-size mattress. Teddy was in my arms. The moon shone in, just like it always did, and silvered the purple on my walls. My father came in and sat at the foot of my bed. Instead of my hand, he held my toes.

"Dad," I asked, my voice heavy, bordering on sleep. "Has God told you that he knows what made me this way?"

"He told me that he knows, yes," Dad said. "But he didn't tell me what it was. He said he needs to tell you directly. But you know…it might not be that hard to figure out."

I stroked one of Teddy's ears, as I did as a child, calming myself. "What do you mean?" I asked.

"Sweetheart…what made you this way? God made you, Hope. God made us all."

My eyes popped open. "Dad?" I asked.

"Get some sleep, Hope. Sleep like you did as a child. You always did sleep well." My father left the room.

I could feel my eyes wanting to stay open. I could feel them wanting that so hard. But I slid into the sleep I relished as a child, a teenager, an adult. Sleep was always a gift.

And this time, sleep gave me a gift. I dreamed of punctuation marks and Valentine's Day hearts, of rainbow clouds and rainbow leaves, of shadows I was aware of and others that I wasn't. I dreamed of left and right, beside me, behind me. Always next to me.

I dreamed. And when I woke up, I knew what my painting would be.

CHAPTER NINETEEN

All Better?

Buddy's Story

The first morning that Buddy woke up without his son under his roof, he felt his life was over. He lay in bed, waiting to hear a noise from the nursery, a happy incoherent song coming across the baby monitor. But the baby monitor was no longer there, and neither was his son. Buddy's ex-wife picked the baby up yesterday afternoon, and she took with her the monitor, his toys, the high chair, his crib, and almost everything else. There was still a car seat in Buddy's car; both he and his ex-wife had their own car seats before the divorce. His son, BJ, for Buddy Junior, lived in this house with his father and his mother, and then just his father, every day of his two years and few months.

And now he wasn't here.

The judge who was overseeing their divorce said that BJ belonged with his mother, that all children belonged with their mothers, particularly at BJ's young age, and that Buddy could see him every other weekend and holiday. He said that as BJ grew older, they could revisit the custody arrangement and maybe then, Buddy could have equal custody, but not now. Not while BJ was a baby. When his ex-wife asked the judge if she was entitled to BJ's belongings, so that her new apartment would be immediately ready for her son, the judge said yes. So Buddy sat in the living room, rocking his sleeping son, while his ex-wife and a "friend" of hers dismantled the nursery and loaded it into her car and his. Eventually, they loaded BJ too. BJ slept through it all. Neither he nor his mother acknowledged Buddy's tears.

Buddy gave only BJ a kiss on his forehead. He turned his back on his ex-wife. And her "friend".

Buddy called in to work and let them know he wouldn't be in for at least a week. He pulled himself out of bed and went to stand in the doorway of what used to be the nursery. His ex-wife at least left the pictures hanging on the walls and the curtains. Everything else was gone. Buddy realized with a start that when he did pick up his son, BJ would never recognize this place. It no longer looked like home.

Today was Friday. He would pick up BJ in exactly one week.

He stopped imagining staying holed up in his apartment until his son's return. Instead, he got dressed and set out to duplicate BJ's room. His home had to be intact. There could be no mistaking where BJ belonged.

• • •

Open eyes.
Crib.
There toys. There diapers. There rocky chair.
But no blue. White. No blue like sky. White like clouds.
Da! Mama!
Mama.

• • •

Buddy remembered shopping with his wife when she was still large with their son, when they didn't even know he was going to be their son yet. They chose to not know the gender, and so every item purchased came with some heavy thought. Would this work with a boy? Would this work with a girl? In the end, Buddy thought they did a wonderful job of pulling the nursery together in a way that would be perfect for any child, regardless of gender. It became his favorite room in the house, and often, while his wife slept deeply through the remainder of her pregnancy, he sat in the rocking chair and just thought about the child who would occupy that crib. Later, after BJ was born, Buddy sat in that chair and watched him sleep.

Now, visiting the same store over two years later, Buddy found that much had changed, and he couldn't get the exact styles that he wanted anymore. The saleswoman listened to his descriptions and shook her head. "Those sound like older pieces," she said.

Older pieces, for a baby who was only two years old. Buddy thanked her and then worked his way around the floor, grateful he could at least choose a similar finish, if not a style. The trip to the toy store was easier; toys seemed to stay in vogue longer. He bought BJ's favorites, and added some brand new for a surprise.

By Saturday evening, two days after the judge allowed his ex-wife to take their son away, the nursery was a nursery again. Buddy hoped that his son's young eyes wouldn't be able to discern the differences.

Then he sat down in the new and similar rocker to wait for Friday. He watched his son's empty crib and thought about the child who would occupy it.

• • •

Chair here.
Couch there.
Bump!
Table there.
Bump!
Box. And box. And box.
Fall!
Owie. Owie. Owie!
Oh, BJ, Mama say. Oh, BJ. Mama kiss.
All better.

• • •

When his ex-wife still lived at home, Buddy had suspicions that bloomed in the middle of the night. They disappeared with the coming of day, replaced with the visions of his wife singing to BJ, laughing as she dressed him, breastfed him, then helped him learn to use a sippy cup and eat solid foods. "Cheerio for Cheerios!" she sang, and "Chee-ohs!" BJ cheered. But at night, while his son and wife slept, Buddy wondered.

What was that bruise on his son's forehead?

On his cheek?

What were those bruises that appeared in random spots on his son's little body?

Buddy, whose job it was to bathe his son in the evening, often called to his wife. "Where did this come from, hon?"

And when she came to look, she had a variety of reasons. "Oh, he was crawling and not looking where he was going. He plowed right into the leg of the coffee table."

"He fell outside on the sidewalk."

"He tried to run and he didn't quite make the corner. Banged into the wall."

"I'm not even sure about that one! He is such a boy."

And she laughed and, in the tub, BJ echoed her, and when she asked, "All better?", BJ crowed, "All better!" So Buddy shrugged it off.

Until the night time.

And now, with BJ gone, with Buddy's ex-wife gone, those suspicions no longer disappeared with the day. With the visions and the cheers. There was only the memory of the bruises and the new vision of his ex-wife taking his son away. Buddy sat in the nursery in the new rocking chair and watched the rising and falling of the sun. He fell asleep from time to time, sometimes getting up to eat or take a shower. He felt like he could somehow watch over his son from this room, from this chair, and so he stayed. He waited for Friday to come. Then it would be all better.

• • •

Mama give bath. No Da.
Where Da?
No boat. No ball. No bubbles.
Smack water! Cry!
Faucet. Bump!
Owie.
Mama kiss. All better?
All better.
Where Da?
Mama.

• • •

When Friday finally came, Buddy went to his ex-wife's new apartment to pick up BJ. They stood at the open door and his ex-wife said, "Hi, Buddy. How are you?"

Before he could answer, Buddy heard, "Da!" and saw his son appear from down the hall. The little boy barreled through the living room, the floor messed up with toys and books and some things Buddy didn't recognize. BJ tripped and skidded over some big lego bricks and fell to his knees. Buddy pushed past his ex-wife and scooped up his son, cradling him, kissing him, hoping to avoid tears when he missed his son so much.

BJ stuck out his leg. "Mama? Owie."

His ex-wife patted BJ and then picked up a little suitcase. "I put some of his clothes in here –"

Buddy shook his head. "Not necessary. I restocked the nursery. He has everything he needs at home. Just his blanket please."

"Binkie!" BJ shouted, and then scrambled down his father like he was in a tree. He took off down the hall. Binkie was a blue baby blanket BJ slept with since day one. Buddy knew there was no duplicating that.

"You don't need anything?" his ex-wife asked. "Are you sure? I can send –"

"Just BJ. And Binkie," Buddy said. He wouldn't look at her. He knew how her eyebrows would pitch downwards in skepticism. But mothers weren't the only ones who could parent. And babies didn't only need their mothers.

BJ returned, waving his blanket like a flag. When he was back in Buddy's arms, Buddy turned to go.

"Bye, honey," his ex-wife called, and Buddy nearly answered.

"Mama?" BJ asked, hitching himself up on Buddy's neck so he could look over his shoulder. "Owie?"

Buddy sighed and turned back.

"Owie," BJ said, and reached over Buddy's elbow to pat his own knee.

Buddy's ex-wife obligingly kissed the denim. "All better!" she crowed, and BJ echoed.

Then they left. As Buddy buckled BJ into the car, BJ asked again, "Mama?"

"You'll see her in a couple days, okay? This weekend is just for us. And Binkie."

BJ turned his head back toward the apartment door. "Mama," he said. Then he looked at Buddy. "Da."

Buddy smiled.

When they got to the house, BJ trotted next to his father as if it was any other day. Inside, he went right to his room and came out with an armful of toys, some of the usual, some of the new. Then he went back for more.

Buddy breathed a sigh of relief as sounds filled the house again. Sounds he knew and relished. He sank to the floor to play with his son. This would be a day like any other. Just the way it should be. The way it always was. For two years and a few months.

• • •

Room. Mine. Mine room. Me.
Toys. Here, there. New toys!
Yay!
Crib.
Rocky chair.
New toys!
Mama?
Da.

• • •

Sticking with their routine, the routine that was only ever interrupted by the divorce, Buddy ran a warm bath for BJ about an hour before bedtime. His ex-wife, who was constantly researching what was good for a child, said that a warm bath before bed supported relaxation and sleep. BJ was a terror in the tub, splashing and pretending to swim, and Buddy couldn't see how it relaxed him at all. The bathtub even sported a cushioned rubber duckie head on the faucet, to protect BJ from bumping his forehead when he lunged forward to "swim". His ex-wife forgot that, and so did Buddy, until he saw it now. He was grateful she didn't take it. Buddy made a note to send BJ back to his mother in the clothes he came in; maybe he would even wash them first. He would keep BJ's clothes, the ones he purchased, here. They belonged in this house. BJ's house. His home.

When Buddy lowered the boy's overalls, he saw bruises scattered on BJ's legs. There were what looked like older bruises on his knees, along with a couple of pock marks that Buddy knew must be from the lego bricks BJ fell on earlier, in his ex-wife's apartment.

But what were the rest?

When he tugged BJ's shirt up and over his head, BJ's hair pulled back and exposed a bruise on his forehead.

He is such a boy, his ex-wife said.

Buddy tried to keep his face impassive, or not impassive, but his usual smiling Daddy face, routine, and he lifted his son into the warm and bubbly water.

"BJ," he said, as he handed the boy his boat, the bathtub toys also forgotten and left behind by his ex-wife, "where did this come from?" He pointed at this bruise, then that.

BJ followed his father's fingers with pats of his own. "Mama," he said quietly, each time. He sat still for a moment, the water not even moving around him. Then he patted his chest. "All better!" he crowed. "Da!" He scooped water into his hands and pitched it at his father. Then, throwing himself tummy first into the water, his forehead ricocheted off the rubber duckie covering the faucet. He shook his head and Buddy waited for tears, but the duckie did its job. BJ began to thrash with his arms and legs. "Swim!" he yelled. "Swim! Da!"

Buddy forced himself to laugh.

• • •

Water!
Duckie face!
Boat!
Swim!
Mama?
Da.

• • •

After putting BJ to bed, in the crib that BJ seemed to find perfectly acceptable, Buddy turned on the new nightlight and the new baby monitor, left the door cracked open, and then went to sit on his own bed. He listened to the monitor, hearing his son croon in his own special voice, a sleepy lullaby with no words, and Buddy waited for him to fall asleep so he could creep back in, sit in the rocking chair, and watch his son breathe.

He considered what to do about the bruises.

If he called the police, showed them the bruises and voiced his suspicions, what would they do? Would BJ get to stay here, at home? He thought of the judge, saying a child BJ's age needed his mother. How Buddy, as the father, seemed to diminish in importance until BJ was older, and even then, he only "might" be given equal custody. Would BJ just be brought back to his mother? Would he be taken away from both of them, put into foster care until this was figured out? Would his ex-wife accuse him, saying he caused the bruises, or he was just angry over the custody agreement?

He *was* angry over the custody agreement. It wasn't fair. BJ needed his father. Children, even babies, needed their fathers.

If he confronted his ex-wife, what would she do? Would she try to keep BJ from ever going back to Buddy, so that he couldn't report what she was doing? Was she doing this to BJ? Or was BJ just a boy?

Just like he, Buddy, was just a father.

Should he send BJ back and act as if nothing was happening? Wait and see? Put his son at risk?

The baby monitor only delivered sounds of steady breathing now, and so Buddy slipped into the nursery and settled into the rocking chair. His son, warm under a soft new blanket, cuddled Binkie to his cheek. BJ held his hand palmed against his cheek, his thumb touching the corner of his lips, but he was never a thumb-sucker. Buddy was proud of this somehow; as if at such a young age, his son was resisting something that would be temporarily comfortable, but over time, a bad habit. BJ was so strong, in personality, in body. He was such a boy.

His son slept. Buddy watched. He watched over.

This was his job. He was the father. Babies needed their fathers.

• • •

Open eyes.
There Da. Rocky chair.
Mama?
Where Mama?
Da.

• • •

Saturday, Buddy alternated his time between playing with BJ and packing them both a suitcase. While BJ napped, Buddy loaded his car. He hated leaving behind the just-purchased furniture, but it couldn't be helped. He and his son needed to go somewhere where BJ would be safe. Buddy packed the clothes. He packed the toys. And that night, after giving BJ his relaxing bath and dressing him in his footie pajamas, he tucked BJ into his car seat instead of his crib.

"Da?" BJ asked.

Buddy handed him Binkie. "Go to sleep, BJ. It's all right."

Then he got behind the wheel and pointed his car in the only direction he knew was safe. Away.

• • •

Car?
Sleep.
There Da.
Binkie.
Mama?
Where Mama?
Da.

• • •

Buddy drove through the night Saturday and most of Sunday. They stopped at a few parks and playgrounds to give BJ a chance to stretch his legs and be such a boy. Buddy drank coffee to stay awake and he played kids music that he and BJ could sing to. Early Sunday evening, when he felt like he couldn't go forward anymore, he pulled into a small motel and got a room.

After following the routine of a warm bath and a snack, Buddy tried to settle his son in for his first night in a real bed. BJ seemed so small in the middle of one of the queen-sized beds. Buddy surrounded him with pillows, keeping only one for himself. BJ thought this was great fun, but he finally fell asleep and Buddy went right with him.

It was three in the morning when Buddy heard the clunk and then the cry. BJ fell out of bed. There would be a new bruise in the morning.

He was such a boy.

But the rest? What about the rest?

A boy needed his father.

• • •

It was the middle of the fourth day on the road when Buddy saw a police car slide smoothly in behind him. Buddy told himself it was okay, but then the rotating lights went off, as did the siren. BJ, taking his nap in the back seat, slammed awake. He covered his ears.

"Da!" he yelled. And then he seemed caught up in following the reflection of the lights inside the car. "Wed," he said. "Boo. Wed."

Buddy glanced in the rearview mirror at the police car, and he caught his son's face, uplifted, rapt, watching the lights. There was a bruise on BJ's face, from when he fell out of the bed during the first night in a motel. BJ hadn't fallen since.

But the other bruises. What about them?

Buddy pressed his foot on the accelerator. The lights receded, but then they began to catch up.

He pushed the pedal to the floor.

"Wheee!" shouted BJ from the back seat.

His son was not going home to that woman. His son was staying with his father. Babies needed their fathers.

Ten minutes later, Buddy was still flying and beginning to question what in the world he was going to do. The one police car had been joined by three others, at least, as far as he could tell. His rearview mirror was filled with rotating red and blue lights and the sirens screamed so loudly, he could no longer hear his son.

• • •

Car fast!
Vroom!
Scared.
Da?
Scared.
Mama?
Where Mama?
All better?
Mama?
Scared.
Da!

• • •

The last time Buddy looked in the rearview mirror, he could no longer see his son's face. It was behind Binkie. BJ was pressing his blanket to his face. Buddy couldn't hear him.

He couldn't see him.

He couldn't let him go.

Not back there. He had to keep BJ safe.

He was the father. He watched over.

As an overpass approached, Buddy made up his mind. He watched it loom larger and larger. It was solid. It was a place he could go where he knew his son would be safe.

Just before his car slid under the overpass, Buddy yanked the wheel sharply to the right. And there was the wall. Like his son with his blanket, Buddy threw his arms up over his face.

The noise.

• • •

Da?
Mama?
Where Mama?
All be--

CHAPTER TWENTY

Hope

I left my father after lunch the next day, his embrace remaining around me like a comfortable sweater as Teddy and I drove away. I'm pretty sure I drove home on the same route that I came, but I honestly didn't pay much attention to the scenery. I only saw my painting. The world-outside-of-me painting. I wanted—no, needed—to get to work.

In my condo, I left my backpack and Teddy on my bed. After swiftly pulling on yoga pants and a paint-spattered t-shirt, I practically ran to my studio. It was odd, but I could smell coffee as I went; I'd passed the kitchen on my way to my bedroom and the coffeemaker there was silent and empty. But now, there was a second coffeemaker in my studio, and the pot was full. A pitcher of iced tea, its glass sides glistening with fresh-made condensation, sat on one of my counters. I poured a cup of each, helped myself to a muffin from a basket, and threw myself into my work.

I couldn't remember the last time I painted like this. I just knew it had been a long, long while. I noted the darkening sky outside enough to put on the lights and then I just kept at it, switching brushes, switching paints, stepping back, then leaning forward.

I worked on the inside of my body's outline first. Deep inside my center, I painted the fetus that was my beginning. Around that, came the little girl. And then the teenage me, holding a paintbrush. I used different shades of a deep musky blue; the color, I felt, of depression. Shadows within myself.

When I finished with that, I gulped down two glasses of iced tea. I was starving and when I went into my kitchen to make a fast sandwich, I found one already waiting for me. A grilled ham, turkey, and Colby jack cheese, still hot, on a plate with a pile of sour cream and onion potato chips. There was even a dill pickle spear on the side. I laughed and took my meal back to the studio. Stepping for a second out onto the lanai, I looked at the slice of Heaven I could see. It was dark, no lights on anywhere. It was like I was the only one up. But the sandwich in the kitchen told me otherwise. "Thank you," I said out loud, and then went back to work, alternating bites with paintstrokes.

Then came the difficult part, the part that I had to pull all of my ability together to accomplish.

On either side of my body, I drew shadows. Shadows to my left and my right. And then trailing back in a line to the end of the canvas, a crowd of people who were always at my side. Who always had my back.

My parents.

My art teacher.

The dozens of therapists and doctors who all tried to help as best they could, who listened, who worked at understanding and used their expertise and compassion to try to fix what seemed too stubborn to be fixed: me.

My husband.

My children.

God himself.

All the new friends I'd made here. In Heaven, of all places.

At my feet, leaning against my calf, was a shadow of Teddy, the first and only toy I ever had that reflected, in the most subtle of ways, how I felt. That mis-stitched pink downturned mouth.

The shadows inside of me, all the variations of me, were done in that deep musky blue, going from a light tint as the fetus, to the dark right before my body became my body now. The shadows outside of me, I put in various shades of the rainbow. All muted, all misty, all still shadows, but positive ones. Shadows that cared.

Then I scattered at random all the punctuation marks I told Virginia I would draw. Question marks, exclamation points, ellipses. I also put hearts, Valentine's Day hearts, in all different and bright colors, all primary.

My body was surrounded by confusion, questions, surprises, but no answers. It was also surrounded by love and support, which I didn't always realize or acknowledge. But it was acknowledged now, on this canvas, with me in the middle and my life all around. My life then, on Earth. My life that continued here, in Heaven. Another surprise with no answers.

The sun was coming up when I finished, and I dropped, exhausted, onto my couch. The clean-up could wait. I looked outside at the birth of daylight coloring the sky, a painting I could never surpass, and then I fell headlong into sleep.

• • •

I didn't know what time it was when I fell asleep, and I still didn't know what time it was when I woke up. My studio was drenched in sunlight, so it was daytime. There was a blanket draped over me, and a pillow under my head. I looked toward my canvases and found that everything was cleaned up. There were only the two easels, the two canvases, tall, taller than I was. All evidence of the struggle to create them was put away. I smiled. I could get used to this.

"Don't," God said, and I found him sitting on the arm of the sofa behind my head. "This was just a special circumstance." He nodded toward the new canvas. "It's beautiful, Hope. They both are."

I sat up and studied my work. The inside-of-me painting was definitely done. The outside one, the one I worked on all night through…was still missing something. "It's not done," I said. "There's still something else." I frowned, my eyes roving over every brush stroke, every image, trying to find what I'd missed.

God nodded. "And I know what it is. It's time that we talked. Go take a shower and then we'll eat. It's late in the day, suppertime already, but for you, we'll have breakfast."

I got up, stretching out muscles that kinked and groaned and I groaned along with them. A hot shower helped restore me and I pondered what God meant, what he might be telling me, and why now was the time. I was surprised there wasn't a shiver of excitement running through my body. There was just steadfastness, and a beyond readiness to know what this was all about. What I was all about.

Who better than God to tell me? I thought back to what my dad said. *Sweetheart...what made you this way? God made you, Hope. God made us all.*

I joined God on my deck for breakfast. He went all out, preparing plates full of scrambled eggs and bacon and fluffy pancakes, fully loaded with butter and maple syrup. I was suddenly starving and tucked in as if I hadn't eaten in days. Around a full mouth, I told God about my visit with my father, and how amazing it was to be in my own parents' house in Heaven.

God swirled a piece of bacon in syrup and I cringed. I loved bacon and I loved maple syrup, but not together, for God's sake. "Your father is a pretty special man. He knows what he likes. And he knows when he's experienced Heaven. He and your mom...amazing."

I thought of the first two shadows I drew to my left and my right, and I agreed.

"So," God said when we were done and I was carrying our dishes into the kitchen. "We're going on a field trip. To Heaven's headquarters. And my office."

I looked at God. "We're going to talk? In your office?"

He nodded and took my hand, just the way my father did. We went down to the parking garage and he led me to LeB. "Let's ride," he said. "It's a bit of a walk."

We left the gated community and God became my GPS, guiding me around corners and up hills and through intersections. He rolled his hand like an ocean wave just beyond the window. "I've always wondered why people like to do this," he said, watching his own hand. "Now I get it. It's fun!"

Finally, we came to a larger than large building, imposing, filling an entire block. It was growing dark and the building seemed to disappear into the night sky. I couldn't tell what was a lit window and what was a star. God directed me to the parking lot and a visitor's parking space.

"Holy cow," I said as I got out. "This place is huge."

"It takes a lot to run Heaven," God said. He took my hand again and we went inside. "So first, I want to show you something." We stepped into an elevator and God hit a button that said Penthouse. In parenthesis underneath it, it said, (God). I was startled that God could ever be parenthetical.

The ride up must have taken ten minutes. My ears kept popping and I swallowed and swallowed.

"I'll get you something to drink when we get up there," God said. "It'll help. It's a long way up."

When we stepped out, we were in one huge room. All four walls were windows. There were dedicated spaces, like a bedroom, a living room, a kitchen and so on. There was only one door and I assumed it led to the bathroom.

God had a bathroom?

"Of course," he said. "I made man in my image, remember? That includes digestive."

He poured some iced tea for me. Then we went impossibly higher on a spiral staircase, which opened onto a rooftop deck.

It was like Heaven itself opened up to me. The view was so big, so broad, so wide, I couldn't find a horizon, no matter which direction I looked. There were lights everywhere. Some places were brighter, some dimmer, as my eyes roved through communities and cities, suburbs and the countryside. I could see the blue of the ocean, the green of the woods, even the brown of the desert.

"It is all of Heaven," God said. "Well, most of it. It's impossible to see everything. And more is added every day." He walked to the railing at the edge of the deck and I joined him. "Earth," God said, "is like a small town living under the metropolis of Heaven. When I created Earth, it was huge, compared to this. But Earth is a finite size. And lives end. Those lives come here and they continue forever. So while Earth can only hold so much, we can hold everyone. Everyone, since time began. The dinosaurs are here. Animals, wild and domestic. Every version of human, from before the creation of fire and the wheel to now. All of the different ways all of life developed, it's here."

"For Heaven's sake," I said and then laughed. I couldn't imagine the math necessary to figure out the number of hearts that still beat here, under

God's direction. "You know, I always thought reincarnation was a good idea. A sort of recycling program for the living population. It's not real?"

God shrugged. "It's real. And going back and living another life is possible for anyone who wants to do so. But the vast majority want to stay. It's paradise, you know." He sighed and rested his elbows on the railing.

Then he turned to me. "As an artist, a creative person, you know what it's like when something you created goes a different way than you intended. You're the creator, but after a while, you run to keep up with your creation. These things take on a life of their own, and you follow."

I nodded. I did know what that was like. I set out to draw one thing, and something else entirely came out. The painting from last night did not start out the way it ended up. But it still was exactly what it should be, but with one missing piece.

"Heaven is like that. Earth too, it's nowhere close to what I originally envisioned. Things went a different route when I decided to give humans free will. I couldn't predict what they would do with it. At first, everyone was perfect. Earth chugged along like the well-oiled planet I intended it to be. But then surprises developed. People did stuff I didn't expect. Diseases were born. Accidents happened. Not all bad...wonderful developments happened too. And the population kept growing, which meant when people died, the population grew here too. And it grew and grew. After a while, I couldn't keep up, and I had to add people to help me, with Earth below and Heaven above. Luckily, there are many scientists and business folks and computer programmers and planners and schemers who were more than happy to come work for me when they arrived here. For those who live here, this remains paradise. But what Heaven became, Hope, is big business. A corporation. And with it came glitches and mistakes, which is what happens in every business, big or small. I could no longer keep my fingers in every little thing."

I frowned. Looking out over this expanse, it was hard to imagine mistakes. "Glitches?" I asked.

God shook his head. "Not here. On Earth. I still create every life there too, you know." He smiled at me, but it was the saddest smile I ever saw. *God makes us all, Hope.* "Glitches. Disease. Disabilities. I never intended humans to suffer, Hope. Never. That wasn't what life was supposed to be about."

And God wept.

I remembered being in Sunday school the first time I heard the verse in the book of John, 11:35. *Jesus wept.* I was shocked then, shocked that someone like Jesus, the son of God, the savior of the world, would cry. But that shock was nothing like I felt now. "God?" I said. I rubbed his back, the way my mother used to rub mine. The way I used to rub my children's. "God?"

"I'm okay, Hope." He stood up straight. Pulling a handkerchief from his back pocket, he wiped his face and then offered me a watery smile. "Come on."

We left the deck and the penthouse and returned to the elevator. We rode down to the twenty-second floor. "My office is here," God said. "It used to be the top floor. Centuries ago. When twenty-two floors were all this building had." We passed room after office after conference room. And then we turned in to an office at the end of the hallway. "This is where my office is. It's quiet down here, so I just haven't moved it."

The room was smaller than I expected. But being surrounded with so much largeness, I imagined God found some comfort in coziness.

"Exactly," he said. He pulled a chair next to his office chair and we sat down. He opened his laptop. "Hang on a sec."

Through an impossible number of clicks and scrolls, I waited. God's fingers flew. Then he pushed the laptop a little bit away, so we both could see the screen. "Okay," he said. "Watch."

On the screen was what looked like a window into the top of a tiny skull. Inside the skull was a small pink blob, reminding me of chewed bubblegum or Silly Putty. God clicked "play" and the picture went into motion. I watched as the blob became a small brain and then pathways developed and grew, twisting in impossible curves and straightaways. The skull began to fill, like ice cream into a cone. Then God clicked again and the image stopped. "Now see here?" He advanced the screen, bit by bit, and I saw a new curve develop.

"I see," I said.

"Hope, that's your brain. It's your brain developing in your mother's womb. And it's where your brain went left when it was supposed to go right." He stopped the screen, rewound a bit and showed it to me again. "Just like what happens when you paint. That's what happened when I was creating you. Your brain went a different direction."

"Okay…" I said.

"Hope, that's where your depression comes from. Your brain's software went in a different direction than it should have. A tiny glitch among many correct movements happening in your development. At the same time all around you, millions more life forms were also developing. And those already born were growing. And other glitches were happening too. They've become a matter of course. They've become something that I simply can't stop because they start with such a small thing, I never even see them, because there's so much down there, and there's so much up here. So much. Infinite."

I stared at the screen. "Play it again."

God did.

"Again," I said.

God did.

"The Gulf," I said slowly, "all from that little left turn?"

"Yes," God said. "A mistake. My mistake. Because I simply can no longer watch every moment of every person's development." He froze the screen and turned to me. "I'm so sorry, Hope. I'm so sorry. The Gulf is all my fault. Many, many things are all my fault."

I thought, then, of that word, *all.* I thought of all the shadows I created on my canvas throughout the night. My parents, my art teacher. The therapists and doctors. My husband. My children. Plus my artwork. My ability to make art, to put on canvas what I felt, the ability to make it look like something that people could be affected by. I thought of Betty saying to me, "I saw your painting of the Gulf, Hope. It was exactly right." Betty was so alone. On my canvas, she saw that aloneness, which was her Gulf. Others saw theirs as well.

"God," I asked, "what would have happened if my brain hadn't turned left there? If it went the way it was supposed to go?"

He shrugged. "It's hard to say. But you would have been a whole different person." He folded his arms across his chest. "You know how you feel now, Hope, here in Heaven. You just met Betty, who is no longer schizo-affective, another twist of the brain. You are no longer depressed, though you are still the person you grew up to be, you experienced yourself into being. And I told you reincarnation is a thing. I could send you back, and we could start all over again. Just like painting over a canvas. You could go back with your brain operating correctly. But I don't know who you'd be. Do you want to do that? You're living life here without the Gulf. I could make sure that you don't have the Gulf in your brain if I return you to the world."

I sat back. On the screen, my brain was frozen, focused on that little left turn.

Last night, my father said, "Hope, you are the most giving person I know."

I saw my mother, hanging my sun painting in my old room, so she would know where to find me.

I saw my son, drawing, lifting his head from time to time to look up at the sky. My daughter, wanting nothing more than to make me feel better. My husband, laying his hand on my shoulder in the middle of the night, when I hadn't even said a word.

If I'd been someone else, where would they all be? Would they even be at all?

Where would I be? Who would I be?

I'd told God that I never give up on a painting. I never paint a canvas over.

"I don't want to go back," I said.

Then I said what I never thought I would say. I never thought it was possible to say such an audacious thing. "God," I said, "It's all right. I forgive you." I put my hand on his arm. Thinking back to those very first moments in Heaven, I wish I had Teddy with me, to place in God's lap. Then I said, "I'll sit with you here, for as long as you like. Right beside you. And so here we are."

God looked right at me. And he smiled. He smiled like Betty, in a way that warmed me to my toes. That made me feel like I'd done something important, just by sitting beside him.

Just by being me. The person whose brain turned left instead of right.

• • •

I left God in his penthouse and headed for home. It was somewhere in the middle of the night, and I had the worst craving for a Starbucks iced cinnamon dolce latte. I doubted that Caffeine Heaven would be open, but I drove down the street anyway. There were lights on in the cafe, not all of them, but a few, and so I pulled in and parked. Smiling at Joe through the glass doorway, I let myself in. "Hey," I said. "I can't believe you're here."

He shrugged. "Sometimes," he said, "I just get the feeling that someone needs some good coffee and a quiet place to sit. Even in the middle of the night."

I didn't tell him what I wanted, but he set to making my drink, and I knew it would be exactly right. "I can't believe you're open just for me," I said as I followed Joe to one of the comfy chairs by the fireplace. Its flickering light cast out a warmth that was just right. He set our drinks on a little table.

"It's not just for you," he said, and he nodded to the opposite corner.

Buddy sat there, about six feet away, his chair turned toward the firelight.

Joe returned to his post and I sat down. I watched Buddy, who didn't say a word, but sat with his hands curved around a mug of something hot, something that remained hot, as the steam never stopped rising. I glanced toward Joe, who shrugged.

Feeling unsure, I took my drink and went to sit on the hearth, near Buddy, but I hoped not too close for his comfort. "Hi, Buddy," I said. "I'm Hope."

His eyes moved to me and he nodded, but then he looked back at the fireplace.

"I know you don't know me," I said. "Betty told me about you. And I guess…" I stumbled over my words before I even said them. I wasn't sure exactly what I wanted to say, but I kept searching. "I wanted you to know that we all make mistakes. We all turn left sometimes, when we're supposed to turn right."

He turned to me again. There were caves in his eyes. They held sorrow. Grief. Remorse. And what I recognized as hopelessness and desperation.

In Heaven. When it was hopelessness and desperation that drove us here to begin with.

I thought of God, saying he made mistakes. That many things were his fault. And I wondered, quietly, to myself, hoping not to broadcast it to God, if maybe God was making a mistake again, with this sad man.

"Buddy," I said. My voice wasn't much more than a whisper. "What you did was wrong. You know that."

He didn't blink, but tears ran down his cheeks.

"Your son is getting bigger. He's getting older, even in Heaven. And he's living with your mother, right?"

He nodded.

"Your mother will tell him the story. God will tell him the story. They'll both tell him the truth. Probably even more than you could, and more than your son's mother could."

Buddy closed his eyes.

"The truth, Buddy. He's going to know how much you love him. How you did what you did because you thought you were protecting him. He's going to know. And I think…" I wondered if what I was going to say was just as audacious as what I said to God. "I think he'll forgive you. I would, if I was your son."

Buddy looked at me again, and he heaved a sigh as big as all of Heaven. I wondered if the gust of it blew through all of this vast universe.

"Don't lose hope, Buddy. That's what Heaven is all about. And hope always rises." I stood up and impulsively wrapped my arms around his shoulders and gave him the same sort of hug I gave my father.

Then I said goodnight to Joe, who smiled at me, and I went home. I so needed to sleep.

• • •

But it wasn't time for sleep just yet. Instead, I went straight back to my studio again. And I painted in what was missing on the canvas.

Tucked inside the outline of my head, I put my brain, and carefully laid out the path to show where my development shifted suddenly to the left, when it was obvious it should have gone to the right. But even with that, even with that anomaly, I made the brain a beautiful thing. It wasn't gray, it wasn't matter, it was a gentle-yet-fierce lavender into blue into pink and back again, coil after coil. I even added some purple, for the Gulf.

It was me.

I left my brush and paints out, knowing that, this time, when I returned in the morning, they would still be there, and I would clean them then. I would enjoy it.

Going into the bathroom, I kept standing while I removed the sky scarf. One by one, the portal showed me my family, all sleeping. My husband was turned toward my side of the bed and his arm rested across my pillow. In my daughter's room, on her bedside table, was my book, *Daddles.* It was open, face-down. Next to it was *The Hotel New Hampshire.* In his room, my son slept facing his window. His curtains were open and the stars, the lights of Heaven, winked down at him. In my parents' house, my mother slept in the guest room. The ceramic box which held my ashes was no longer on the dresser. It was on the nightstand beside her.

I knew that three hours away, in Heaven, my father slept in the house that was exactly like ours. My room was just down the hall.

I sighed and folded the sky scarf, setting it gently on the countertop. I no longer needed to protect myself. I wanted to see.

• • •

A few weeks later, I walked into a new room for group therapy. I made Virginia absolutely promise me that she would meet me and the others at Caffeine Heaven afterwards, so that I would still see her, and would always see her, on a Wednesday. That promise helped me to tolerate the nerves I felt now, entering a new situation, a new place, with new people. Even in Heaven, familiarity was important.

When I looked around, I didn't see anyone who I recognized. It was like being back in my early days in Heaven. But even on that first day in my first group, I knew someone. Faith was there with me. Now, I knew no one.

But I knew I would get to know them. That was one of the best things about Heaven.

This room was set up differently than I was used to. It was a big circle. We were all like the links in a large bracelet. Assuming that the doorway led to the head of the room, I figured the center chair there would be for the leader. I walked across the circle and sat in the chair exactly opposite.

As people came in and seat by seat was taken, that leader chair remained empty. Those of us who were new looked around, and those who were already a part of this group chatted quietly with a sense of anticipation that I hoped would soon be mine too. I told myself to wait. Just wait and breathe. In a few hours, when the group session ended, I would be with my friends. New ones, in this room. Treasured ones, waiting in a coffee shop. In both places, I had people to my left and my right. They were right beside me.

And here we were.

Five minutes after the group was to begin, there were footsteps in the hallway. We all fell silent and our heads turned expectantly toward the open doorway. I heard some stifled laughter.

And then Robin Williams burst in. “Good afternoon, Hea-ea-ven!” he roared.

The room exploded in laughter, surprised laughter from those like me, delighted laughter from others.

“Oh, good lord,” I said.

“Yes?” God asked, suddenly standing behind me, his hands on my shoulders.

I tilted my head back at him and smiled. “Never gets old,” I said.

And it never would. This was Heaven. It was forever.

THE END

OTHER TITLES FROM KATHIE GIORGIO

NOVELS

All Told, Austin Macauley USA, 2022.

If You Tame Me, Black Rose Writing, 2019.

In Grace's Time, Black Rose Writing, 2017.

Rise From The River, The Main Street Rag Publishing Company, 2015.

Learning To Tell (A Life)Time, The Main Street Rag Publishing Company, 2013.

The Home For Wayward Clocks, The Main Street Rag Publishing Company 2011.

SHORT STORY COLLECTIONS

Oddities & Endings; The Collected Stories Of Kathie Giorgio, The Main Street Rag Publishing Company, 2016.

Enlarged Hearts, The Main Street Rag Publishing Company, 2012.

ESSAY COLLECTION

Today's Moment Of Happiness Despite The News; A Collection Of Spontaneous Essays, Black Rose Writing, 2018.

FULL-LENGTH COLLECTION OF POETRY

No Matter Which Way You Look, There Is More To See, Finishing Line Press, 2020.

POETRY CHAPBOOKS

Olivia In Five, Seven, Five; Autism In Haiku, Finishing Line Press, 2022.

When You Finally Said No, Finishing Line Press, 2019.

True Light Falls In Many Forms, The Main Street Rag Publishing Company, 2016.

ABOUT THE AUTHOR

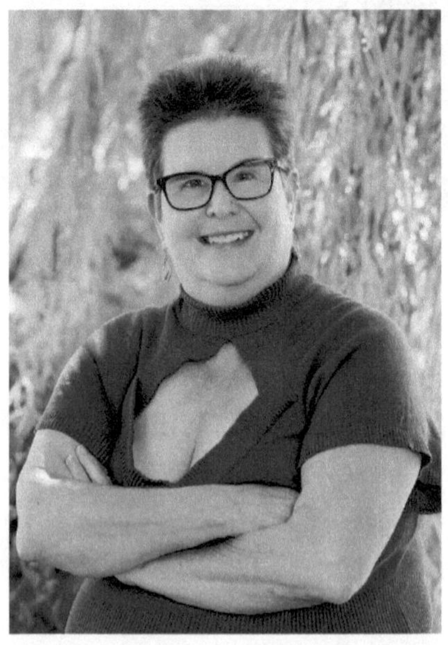

KATHIE GIORGIO is the author of seven novels, two story collections, an essay collection, and four poetry collections. She's been nominated for the Pushcart Prize in fiction and poetry and awarded the Outstanding Achievement Award from the Wisconsin Library Association, the Silver Pen Award for Literary Excellence, the Pencraft Award for Literary Excellence, and the Eric Hoffer Award In Fiction. Giorgio is also the director and founder of AllWriters' Workplace & Workshop LLC, an international creative writing studio. She lives in Waukesha, Wisconsin, with her husband, mystery writer Michael Giorgio, her daughter Olivia, who just finished writing her first novel, an eccentric dog named after Ursula Le Guin, a fat cat named Edgar Allen Paw, and a tiny gray cat named Muse.

NOTE FROM THE AUTHOR

Word-of-mouth is crucial for any author to succeed. If you enjoyed *Hope Always Rises*, please leave a review online—anywhere you are able. Even if it's just a sentence or two. It would make all the difference and would be very much appreciated.

Thanks!
Kathie Giorgio

www.ingramcontent.com/pod-product-compliance
Lightning Source LLC
Chambersburg PA
CBHW050144120726
47903CB00002B/489

* 9 7 8 1 6 8 5 1 3 2 4 2 2 *